The HIGHLAND HEIST

A Freddie & Grace Mystery
(Book 4)

The
HIGHLAND HEIST

PEPPER BASHAM

BARBOUR
PUBLISHING

A Freddie & Grace Mystery

Book 1 - The Mistletoe Countess

Book 2 - The Cairo Curse

Book 3 - The Julet Code

Print ISBN 979-8-89151-141-5
Adobe Digital Edition (.epub) 979-8-89151-142-2

Published by Barbour Publishing, Inc., 1810 Barbour Drive, Uhrichsville, Ohio 44683, www.barbourbooks.com

Our mission is to inspire the world with the life-changing message of the Bible.

Printed in the United States of America.

Dedicated to Jaime Jo Wright

It's amazing how brainstorming with you can end up bringing imaginary people back from the dead. Or. . .un-aliving them. Not sure what sort of influence that makes you, but I do know I'm so grateful for you!

Chapter 1

June 23, 1914

Perfect husbands were rare, except perhaps in fiction, but Grace Percy, Countess of Astley, had married the real-life equivalent, she was certain.

"I still cannot believe this surprise, Frederick!" Grace's shock had continued all the way from the harbor, where her dear husband had announced that they'd arrived in America instead of England. "I thought the terrain looked different than England, but I never suspected we'd go anywhere else except your beloved Havensbrooke."

"*Our* beloved Havensbrooke, I hope?" he corrected, turning from his place in the front seat of the hired touring, next to a rather somber driver.

Her smile immediately responded. At nearly seven months married, Grace still found her thoughts paused on occasion at the idea of his English estate being her home. But how could she help it? They'd only lived in the estate a few months before they'd taken off on their honeymoon tour. But oh, what a delightful introduction to her new home, complete with a murder mystery and a ghost hunt.

She sighed. Married life certainly kept proving to be wonderfully exciting.

She sent him another grin before tipping her head out the window just enough to take in the familiar lane leading to her father's house. "How did you even know where to go? Harrington is such a small place outside of Richmond, and I know I've never given you exact directions."

His low chuckle warmed the already heated June air, skittering a familiar welcome of tickles up her bare neck. "I've written my own letters to your father, darling." His voice, so smooth and English, carried such delicious tenderness that Grace turned to find him shooting a wink to their adopted daughter, Zahra.

Zahra's lips tipped. She rarely showed great affection, but who could blame her? After losing her family and living on the streets of Cairo, the little girl still had plenty of healing to do. So every smile came extra special.

Poor Miss Cox, the young English maid Frederick had hired in Italy to accompany them through the remainder of their trip, blushed at Frederick's wink and smile. After all the overt affection Grace lathered on her darling husband, it was a wonder Miss Cox hadn't gotten used to it yet, but perhaps the trouble lay more in how very handsome her husband was.

Grace thought about that idea for a moment. She supposed if she wasn't married to this wonderful man, she'd find herself a little awestruck too.

Truth be told, he was so handsome, he might fit the description of a dime-novel villain, but she was very glad fiction didn't get it right on that score either.

"Besides, it may be a while before we can travel again." He continued, turning back to face the front of the car. "I know it's a few months earlier than we'd originally planned, but it seemed a waste not to take advantage of being at sea. And I know you'd love to see your family."

Grace would have kissed his cheek if she hadn't been sitting in the back seat of the touring with Zahra between her and Miss Cox. "You are the most wonderful man." She turned to Zahra and Miss Cox. "Don't you think so?"

Miss Cox's eyes widened, and she quickly looked away, but Zahra's grin stretched enough to show off her teeth. The simple white dress she wore brought out the depths of those endless gray-green eyes. Grace still couldn't stop smiling at the very idea that the little girl belonged to her and Frederick now.

"He has all his hair and teeth." Zahra nodded, the tiniest twinkle in her eyes alerted Grace that the little girl might be finding her humor. "That is a help."

Frederick's laugh burst out. "Indeed it is, Zahra. And I'm glad to still possess both of them."

Grace studied his thick dark hair for a second longer, her fingers twitching to push through his locks, but the very idea could send poor Miss Cox through the car window. Grace drew in a deep breath to keep her show of admiration to a more appropriate public display and leaned toward Zahra. "The gardens at Rutledge House are lovely, Zahra. They were my mother's gardens, and I'd often spend time with her there. Hopefully, when we return to *our* dear Havensbrooke"—she emphasized, sending her dear husband a look to ensure her noted her correction—"you and I and, perhaps even Lily, can work to restore those gardens together. Then we can make our own special place too. Gardens are very creative places in stories as well as in real life."

And perhaps she and Frederick could add a few more children to fill the manor house with the laughter those crumbling walls desperately needed. Grace paused a frown at the thought and her palm went to her stomach. Surely they would have an heir—something Frederick hadn't voiced a desire for often but that she knew he wanted, especially for the future of Havensbrooke.

Grace turned her attention back to the window, her focus catching on a change in the familiar landscape of her childhood home as they progressed down the drive. "Father's removed some of the trees in the front." How odd. He hadn't written about any improvements. "Those were lovely trees. Why would he do that?" She leaned forward as the house grew closer, a sudden tightening in her chest she couldn't quite explain. "And it looks as if he's building an addition onto the parlor." Grace turned back to Frederick. "Why didn't he tell me about those in his most recent letters? He always loved sharing news about his improvements with me."

The tiniest of flickers played across Frederick's features. Had that been concern? But. . .but why would he feel concern? Unless his tendency toward clairvoyance—which usually only pertained to her—had spanned the ocean.

"Perhaps he wanted it to be a surprise," he offered, his lighter tone too controlled.

She studied him a moment longer. Frederick had asked about Father over the last few days, but gave nothing to hint at a worry. Could this visit be for more than just her fancy, but because of a real concern? He stared back at her, the intensity in those dark eyes almost attempting to communicate something with her. Clearly her clairvoyance was at a disadvantage to his.

Except on some occasions.

But those were obvious and usually involved kissing.

"How many sisters and brothers did you have, *Sayyida*?"

Grace pulled her attention from Frederick's face and looked down at Zahra as the car slowed to a stop.

She pushed up a smile. "I only have a sister."

The pucker on Zahra's brow deepened. "It is a very big house for such a small family."

Frederick bent ever so slightly, his movement gaining Zahra's attention. "Wait until you've seen your new home at Havensbrooke, Zahra." He nodded toward the home in front of them. "It's been in my family for centuries and is at least three times the size of Rutledge House."

The little girl's eyes widened. "Then I shall lose myself."

"No fear, lamb." Grace's husband cooed out the words, giving her an even sweeter glimpse of the father she knew him to be. "Someone will always find you."

Oh, how she loved him.

The worry coiling in her chest unwound in a wonderful warmth. He did that for her—found her—even if it only meant finding her gaze in a crowd. It was one of her favorite experiences, except when he wore that concerned "what are you doing" expression or the "did you truly say that out loud, darling" expression and maybe the "please don't do what I think you are going to do" expression.

Whatever the concern with her father—if there even was one—she and Frederick would sort it out together. She was certain of it. They'd been sorting through life-threatening situations since their first week of marriage, and the fact they were both still alive gave testament to their compatibilities, God's grace, and excellent timing.

Not to mention a few other people helping them along the way, excellent novel-reading preparation, and the constant availability of ropes.

Frederick sent her a reassuring smile as he opened the car door, likely trying to quiet her worries. Oh, he was simply the very best man she'd ever known. Who but God could have imagined that an unexpected wedding between a second-choice American bride and a reformed roguish British earl could have turned out to be not only a friendship but a love match, as well? And he was positively excellent at distracting her from her concerns.

After giving instructions for Zahra and Miss Cox to wait for them in the car with the driver, Frederick escorted Grace to the door of the three-story, brick mansion.

The familiar gong echoed inside as Frederick rang the bell.

Grace pulled at the edges of her gloves, giving her head a shake at her silliness. There was no need for concern, of course. This was her childhood home. She knew this place. Every nook, every corridor, and even the unexpected hiding spots.

Her smile brimmed. Besides, she'd see her father.

But why did her stomach feel as if the contents wanted to take flight? Her lips tightened. Was this, perhaps, how Lizzie Bennet felt the first time she saw Pemberley?

After a few moments, the door opened to reveal the familiar face of Perkins, her father's longstanding butler. Father had brought him on before Grace could remember.

The man's eyes widened when his attention moved from Frederick to Grace, and his mouth even dropped open. She would have been concerned, but she'd seen that same look on Perkins' face quite often when she'd lived in this house. *Poor man.* He was always finding her in the most unexpected quandaries.

"Miss Grace?" He blinked a few times and cleared his throat, dipping his head with a shake. "Lady Astley, my lady."

The combination of his voice and his immediate confusion with titles had her breaking all protocols of a countess and running directly into the older man's arms. He stayed as straight as a tree, but that didn't stop Grace. His scent of polish and soap had meant home for such a large portion of her life.

Her smile brimmed, and she stepped back, Perkins looking every bit as discombobulated as he always did when she'd hugged him. "It is so wonderful to see you, Perkins. And you look the same as always."

"I should hope so, my lady. It hasn't been a year since we last saw one another."

"No, it has not, though it feels much longer." Grace gestured back to Frederick. "I don't believe you've met my husband, Lord Astley."

The butler dipped his body in an awkward bow, his gaze taking in Frederick, before he dipped his head again. "Your lordship."

"I apologize for not having given you notice of our arrival, Perkins." Frederick smiled. "But I had hoped to surprise my bride with a visit home before we return to England."

"Isn't it the sweetest thing?" Grace sighed back to her darling husband and then tried to peer around Perkins to get a view of the interior of the house. The entry hall really was one of its best features. "The house looks marvelous too." She surveyed the new shrubbery lining the front, pausing on a patch of missing foliage. Had someone removed Mother's rose bushes? Why on earth would Father ever approve of such a thing? "There's new landscaping?"

Her stomach dropped with renewed fervor.

"Within the last three weeks, my lady." Perkins ran a finger beneath his collar and swallowed audibly. "Several new improvements, as you can imagine."

Father had mentioned improvements just before Grace wed Frederick in late November, which was why he'd encouraged Grace and her sister to prepare for the wedding at their friends' home, Whitlock Manor, but Grace had always supposed the improvements involved internal changes. Updates.

Nothing drastic.

Nothing like removing Mother's roses.

"I was sure the improvements would have been finished by now." Grace looked from Perkins to Frederick, whose expression dissolved from welcome into. . .what was it? Concern? Surely there wasn't much to be concerned about regarding house renovations, was there?

Unless one distracted a serious workman with too many

questions and he nearly electrocuted himself.

A twinge of guilt pinched in her chest.

Perkin's brow rose again. "Not—not when the new owners wish for different sorts of improvements, my lady."

And now she doubted her hearing. *New owners?*

"They have more modern views than your father and took to implementing those designs as soon as the purchase was finalized."

It was Grace's turn to blink. Surely, there must be some mistake. "What do you mean? New owners?"

He shifted his attention from Grace to Frederick and back, and with a deep sigh, he lowered his head. "You—you haven't heard?"

A splash of cold branched through Grace's middle and she turned to Frederick to see if he understood. He looked serious. Grace couldn't seem to find her voice, and even if she could, she wasn't certain what to say. None of this made sense.

"Are you saying Rutledge House is under new ownership?" Her husband voiced the slow growing awareness in her mind.

"Yes, sir." Perkins turned his attention to Grace. "I—I thought Mr. Ferguson would have written to you to alert you of the situation."

"The situation?" Her knees weakened the slightest bit, which was the oddest thing, because her knees rarely weakened to anything except Frederick's kisses.

And occasionally while reading an excellently terrifying book.

Her stomach clenched. But this moment fit neither one of those descriptions. So what on earth was wrong with her?

"We've been traveling on our honeymoon trip," Frederick explained, stepping nearer. "So any letter may have missed us."

"But we didn't receive a telegram either." Grace studied Perkins, trying to sort out the reason why her eyes had started to burn a little.

"That explains why a solicitor arrived yesterday in search of you."

A solicitor? *Good heavens, what on earth is going on?*

"I would invite you inside to explain." Perkins glanced behind him. "But the new family. . .well, I stayed on. . ." He cleared his throat. "They are not accepting visitors at this time since they are newly arrived."

Grace's mind stuttered over her thoughts in the most alarming way. Her last letter from Father gave no indication of selling Rutledge House or of any desire to leave.

"What has happened?" Grace stilled herself against the sudden rise in emotions and held Perkins gaze. "Tell me, Perkins."

"My lady, I–I'm not certain—"

"You *must* tell me." A sudden heat rose into her face. "Clearly, you know."

Frederick placed his palm on Grace's back, stepping closer to her side, dousing her sudden anxiety in a sweet blanket of his presence. "I understand you may not wish to break confidences, Perkins, but we are in need of direction, and you have the information to assist us."

"Yes, my lord." Perkins nodded, his shoulders drooping from their stiffened state. She'd seen that look plenty of times too. Usually, when he'd been tasked with finding Grace from some hidden location.

But this reason felt much larger than any of those silly times.

"It is my understanding that Mr. Ferguson has declared bankruptcy and all of his debts have been called in."

The words made sense, but Grace couldn't quite wrap her mind around the meaning. Father hadn't been the most clever with finances, but bankruptcy?

"Six weeks ago, everything seemed to come to a head, so Mr. Ferguson made a quick sale of the house, as well as any of his other properties, to cover those debts."

"But it wasn't a surprise, was it, Perkins?"

Grace shifted her attention to Frederick. What could he mean?

Not a surprise? It completely shocked *her*.

"No, my lord." The butler lowered his gaze again. "It was my understanding that Mr. Ferguson had been struggling with finances for some time, and his last few investments had not been. . .successful."

For some time?

She frowned up at the man. As an amateur sleuth, she'd certainly missed the mark on this one. Not one clue. Not one hint.

Her thoughts paused. Or—or had there been?

Before her marriage, Father had held more closed-door meetings. Whispered conversations with the lawyer. Less frequent visits to town. Cold spread through Grace's body. Had finances been the reason Father had engaged in a desperate search for a groom for Lillias all along? To secure her future?

She turned to Frederick. And wasn't her father supposed to provide a third installment of the dowry at the one-year mark of their wedding? Was that lost too?

Had Frederick been hoodwinked by Grace's own father?

Nausea swelled up through her tightening stomach, and her eyes stung with more ardor. She flipped her attention back to Perkins. "Where is Father now?"

Her voice rasped out the question in the strangest way. Her throat closed. What was wrong with her? Why couldn't she sort out her feelings? An ugly, uncomfortable, and unfamiliar ache bruised deep. Was it hurt? Surprise?

Her breath quivered. Betrayal?

She pressed a fist to her chest. No. Surely not something as devastating as betrayal. Didn't that only happen with strangers and villains? She gave her head a shake as the pain knifed a little deeper. No. In all the stories, betrayal wounded the deepest from those closest and dearest, didn't it? Her fist pushed against the growing ache.

"I'm sorry, my lady." Perkins' words tumbled out. "I know Mr. Ferguson would not wish for you to find out about this situation in this manner. He had me forward mail to your sister's house until two weeks ago, at which time he wrote to alert me that he was going to visit his sister in South Carolina for an extended period of time. It seems that the living situation at Mrs. Dixon's home was not. . .well, your father needed some distance from your sister." Perkins' face reddened all the way from his neck to his forehead. "Or. . .the reverse."

Could this situation get any worse? Her father and sister at odds. Her family home sold. Her father's. . .lies?

Grace leaned back into Frederick's hold. It was one thing to feel betrayed by a crazy archeologist or a wealthy owner of stolen paintings, but quite another by her own father.

"In reference to the solicitor, I do have some mail we received for you that preceded the solicitor's visit, but since it was in the midst of all of Mr. Ferguson's. . .changes, the mail was misplaced. I only recalled it when the solicitor arrived yesterday in search of you and Miss Lilli—" He cleared his throat. "Mrs. Dixon."

"Mail?" Grace's gaze turned back to the man. "From a solicitor?"

"His explicit instructions were that the information be delivered by hand to you or your sister. He seemed quite adamant on me locating either of you." Perkins nodded. "I have it safely placed with the purpose of driving to town to hand deliver it to Mrs. Dixon tomorrow, but if you will permit me, I can give it to you now. Mr. Barclay is staying in town with the hopes of speaking with your sister, since I told him you were no longer in the country. Allow me to retrieve it, my lady."

He turned back into the house, leaving Frederick and Grace standing on the doorstep of her own home.

She tilted her head, studying the familiar door.

No, no longer her home. She straightened a little, allowing

the warmth of Frederick's touch to radiate through her and soothe her untamed emotions. Her home was with Frederick now. At Havensbrooke.

She turned toward her husband, the stinging in her eyes intensifying. "I—I didn't know. . .about the finances. I promise I didn't."

He stared down at her, the tension in his jaw relaxing a little as his palm smoothed her arm. "I know, Grace."

"If I'd known—"

"It doesn't matter." His gaze held hers, deepening his words.

But it did, didn't it?

She looked back at the door as if it was at fault. They'd spent a honeymoon tour enjoying the financial freedom her dowry provided only to be confronted with the very real possibility they'd lost a third of the promised funds.

Havensbrooke was Frederick's ancestral home and the place his heart loved. The place that needed continued repairs her money was supposed to provide as part of the marriage contract.

"Grace." He pulled her attention back to him with a word. "It's not about the money any longer, darling. We will sort through this."

His fingers wrapped around hers, and she squeezed his hand, garnering a bit of courage from his beautifully romantic declaration. The stinging in her eyes produced moisture, but to her wonderful surprise, she kept from sobbing, although she felt a few tears slip down her cheeks.

She'd not doubted Frederick's affection since their first few weeks together, but his legacy and home held amazing power. Could their love prove stronger than all that family history he so often warred against?

She sniffled, took his welcomed handkerchief, and pushed away the doubt. "Why didn't Father tell me about all of this? I should have known." And then her mind replayed Lillias' responses from the week before their wedding. The little comments about Father "being ruined" if the wedding didn't go ahead. Lillias' dismissiveness regarding Grace's ability to understand the financial ramifications of the wedding for their whole family.

Another blow hit her. Lillias had known too.

"They'd known all along, Frederick." The declaration burst from her. "How had I not seen it? The entire marriage contract and the race to find my sister a groom had not been to gain a title at all." She shook her head, another tear cooling her cheek. "It had been to secure Lillias' future so that if his finances crumbled, she'd be cared for."

With all the mysteries she'd read and even solved, how had she been blind to the one closest to her heart?

"Grace," he spoke her name like a caress again and drew her gaze back to his, a grounding to her. "You weren't a part of the initial marriage contract. I can only suppose your father thought it better to keep your mind free of the burden." His lips gentled into a small smile. "And he likely feared, with your forthright nature, you'd confess it all to me and then the marriage would not have happened at all."

Because if she had confessed what she knew, Frederick would have never signed the contract to marry Lillias—and then defaulted to marry her when it was discovered that Lillias was already pregnant with Anthony Dixon's child.

The very idea of never having married her darling Frederick nearly sent tears raining with more passion.

Was this what the Bible meant about God working all things together for good? Her marriage to Frederick had certainly turned out for good, but all the choices leading up to it seemed rather suspect and. . .manipulative. She forced a hard swallow and gathered her wits about her. Surely she could gather her wayward emotions in the knowledge God wasn't worried about this madness.

And—her gaze flitted back to the touring car—she was a mother now. Perhaps not in a conventional way, but in a way that counted nonetheless. So she had to exhibit a bit more motherly control.

"I'm sorry for you, Frederick. How this may change our plans for Havens—"

"Grace." He leaned forward, catching her gaze. "At this very moment, Havensbrooke is not at the foremost of my thoughts. You are, and whatever"—he waved toward the house—"is going on with your father."

She attempted to offer him a smile. Things could be much worse, couldn't they? Surely this was nothing like a betrayal in a Shakespeare tragedy or something like poor Edmund Dantès in *The Count of Monte Cristo*. No. She had Frederick and Havensbrooke and even a lovely new daughter. It was highly unlikely the solicitor meant to send her to an island prison for fourteen years!

She raised her chin, her mind clearing a little with this relief. "Father must have used whatever funds he had left to pay the first two thirds of my dowry. How could I not have known?"

"Well, his actions are interpreted with more clarity in this light," Frederick offered. "His devastation at the possible loss of the contract when Lillias' pregnancy was discovered."

A truth which still stung, especially when voiced aloud.

"Lillias' insistence on the marriage going through, even though she clearly wasn't happy about it." And then another memory popped to mind. "And Father's strange insistence that both his girls would be taken care of." Grace squinted up to him. "He kept saying it, as if to console himself."

The door swung open again, and Perkins approached, a simple envelope in his hands. "Here we are, my lady."

Grace took the mail from him, unfamiliar writing scrawled across the front: "Deliver to Lillias M. and Grace C. Ferguson."

Beneath those instructions, a sharp hand had written the word *urgent.*

She reread the words as if they'd help add some sense to the entire situation.

But no. Everything kept growing more and more unusual.

"Mr. Barclay is staying at the Clarion in town, should you wish to notify him of your arrival."

She looked up at Frederick, whose attention fastened on the envelope before he brought his gaze back to hers, one brow raised. Her look must have alerted him to her own confusion because with a nod, he turned back to Perkins.

"Thank you for your help, Perkins." Frederick gestured back toward their touring car. "I feel certain Lady Astley's sister, Mrs. Dixon, will provide some clarity to this situation for us."

"I hope so sir." The man's expression wreathed with apologies as his attention landed on Grace again. "And I truly am sorry for the way in which you discovered it, my lady."

A kaleidoscope of unanswered questions and wild conjectures swirled through her mind enough to create her own three-volume novel, but she pushed up her most authentic smile—because Perkins really was such a good man—and took a step toward him. "Despite it all, I'm very glad this new family has the benefit of your services, Perkins, for I've experienced the personal goodness of it."

The man's posture fell a little with his softening expression. "If I might say so, my lady, you are very much like your mother. I've always thought so."

The statement sliced through all the chaos in her thoughts to hit a particularly tender place in her heart. She'd always been told she resembled her mother's appearance, but to be compared to her mother in personality meant all the more because, though Grace had vague memories of her mother, time had fogged the edges of what she actually recalled and what others had told her.

"Thank you, Perkins." Grace smiled. "I don't know that you could have said anything else that would have comforted me more."

With that, she turned with Frederick back to the car, carefully slipping open the envelope in hopes of abating at least one piece of her curiosity. Two sheets of paper waited inside—one somewhat yellowed with age and the other crisp and new. The older one drew her attention first, and she tugged it forward, just as they reached the car.

As her gaze trailed to the signature line of the letter, she gasped.

She reread the name three separate times before looking back over her shoulder at the door where Perkins had disappeared.

She'd always known Perkins had incredible foresight, but to see into the future?

"What is it?" Frederick touched her arm.

She dragged her attention from the door, blinking with new fervor, and looked up at her husband. "It's a letter." She drew in a breath, trying to understand, and turned the page toward Frederick. "From my mother."

Chapter 2

Grace had a tremendous imagination.

This was no news.

But to bring someone back from the dead seemed a little extreme, even for her.

So Frederick stared a full five seconds, trying to understand what she'd just declared.

Of course, the two of them had been through a great many unexpected things in the span of their short marriage, and he'd hoped a simple visit to see her family would prove a respite among their many adventures. But he should have known. Whether trouble followed him or her, it always seemed to find them.

Besides, Mr. Ferguson's last letter in relation to the funds associated with the marriage contract to Grace, had induced an unexpected wariness. The man's responses had remained vague regarding the third installment, inspiring a hint of concern. Paired with some of his own recollections surrounding Mr. Ferguson's behavior upon first meeting him, the current situation made sense.

While painful for his dear bride and Frederick's pocketbook, in hindsight, these memories provided clarity.

In all honesty and much more by heavenly hand than his

own, however, Frederick's greatest prize from the contract had been wholly unexpected.

Grace. In more ways than one.

So he'd dismissed the concern at Mr. Ferguson's ambiguity.

But the moment Grace mentioned unexpected improvements to Rutledge's grounds, his suspicion had spiked.

The temptation to fume for the injustice done to his wife stung through his chest, but now was not the time for fury. Grace didn't need that reaction from him. Not with the upheaval this news caused her.

Yet the fact that Mr. Ferguson had lied about the full dowry, whether intentionally or by conveniently leaving out the information, lured Frederick back toward two age-old weaknesses.

Mistrust.

And fear of bringing shame upon his family name.

Fortunately, he had grown enough during the last seven months of marriage to recognize the ghosts before they haunted him for too long. Grace's presence in his life, her love, had brought him to an awareness of better priorities and the power of faith, no matter the unexpected or difficult. And she'd proven her love, strength, and devotion to him and their marriage, taking on all the demands—and at times, life threatening moments—with a passion and assurance that baffled him.

And built up his own confidence.

And to be honest, increased his prayer life.

Despite the many adventures and misadventures they'd already experienced, he couldn't recall a time when Grace looked helpless. She'd faced death on several occasions, from his own estate of Havensbrooke, to the desert of Egypt, and then an island off the coast of Venice. Though he'd seen fear, confusion, or frustration on her face, none of those moments had inspired such a look of lostness as he'd witnessed when she confronted the face of her father's subterfuge.

And now a letter from Grace's dead mother? Surely he'd heard incorrectly.

"Your—your mother is alive?"

She frowned. "What?"

"You said the letter was from your mother." Frederick cleared his throat trying to sort out how to come to terms with a resurrected parent. "Recently?"

"Recently?" Grace's brow creased as she looked from him back to the paper. "Oh, no, no. . ." She shook her head and raised that lovely gaze back to him, tears still resident in those eyes. "It was written the year she died." Grace turned the page toward him, noting the date at the top. "She—she must have composed it when expecting my baby brother. How very strange." She turned her attention back to him, searching his face. "Do you think she knew?"

It was his turn to frown. "Knew?"

"That she was going to die." Her frown deepened as she resumed her study of the letter. "I've read of people having a sense of foreboding about their impending deaths which led them to making certain decisions. Final letters are at the top of the list."

Frederick wasn't keen on continuing a discussion on such a subject—with his wife's veracious love for reading, she'd read a great many sensible and nonsensical things, all of which had somehow come back to either help them or increase the tension when solving various mysteries.

Instead, he attempted to skim the letter over her shoulder, noting bits and pieces as they stood near the car. Out of the corner of his eyes, he caught Zahra leaning toward the window, her sober gaze watching him with the slightest pucker of concern on her brow. He offered her a smile to help douse any anxiety their hesitance may cause the little one, a light squeeze constricting his chest. What sort of past wounds inspired untold fears in that brave little heart of hers?

"She's—she's left us some sort of family property in Scotland," Grace whispered, still reading, and Frederick attempted to follow along. Property in Scotland?

"She knew about Father and was trying to help us." A sad little laugh purred from his wife, and he placed a palm to her back, leaning closer to read the lines she gestured toward:

> *Knowing your dear father's disposition toward rash business decisions, it had been my hope to leave both of you something of substance on which to build a future in the instance finances became uncertain, but since most of my funds went to your father upon marriage, this inheritance along with a small allowance is all I have to give. It is a lovely estate of my great-grandfather's, and at the current owner's death, I am the next lone blood relative left to receive it. Should something happen to me, as this letter would suggest, the two of you represent me as my coheiresses, so I have left it to both of you.*
>
> *The difficulty with this arrangement is that you must both be present to sign for the inheritance in Scotland, or else the estate will be available for purchase. As a long-adored place from my family, I hope you will see the value in it. If after you have accepted the inheritance, you should find yourselves in financial need, however, you may also sell the estate.*

"Isn't that odd? To claim an inheritance together?" She looked up at Frederick.

"It's not common, no, but not unheard of."

She nodded and went back to the letter, reading it aloud:

> *Barclay, my solicitor and friend, will explain more about the situation. However, my darling girls, due to the nature of the longstanding agreement with the family, the inheritance must be claimed within three months of the previous owner's death or it will be forfeit and the property sold. I hope this small token of my love for you will carry over even if I am unable to be with you and you will know my love through this gift.'*

Grace sighed and ran a finger over the signature at the bottom of the paper. "How beautiful to have something from Mother after all this time. Even the letter feels special."

Frederick increased the pressure on Grace's back as an acknowledgement of her words. "Is the other letter from this Mr. Barclay?"

"Yes."

Grace drew it forward, and Frederick's attention fell on the date it was sent. "Grace, the letter was posted at the beginning of May."

"Yes?" She looked up at him, her complacency a clear indicator that she'd not made the same connection as him.

"If you and Lillias must claim the inheritance within three months, from this date it appears the previous owner must have died almost two months ago. Whether by rerouting or difficulty locating you or Lillias, the paper has only now made it into your hands."

The familiar hue of determination eclipsed the previous hurt in his wife's eyes. Ah, giving her a problem to solve proved a worthy distraction.

"Then—then we only have a bit more than a month to claim it?" She took the letter back and put it with the other paper, slipping them back into the envelope. "I don't fully understand this, Frederick, but I'm grateful for the gift and the heart behind it. We must do everything in our power to make that date."

"I agree, and it shouldn't be too difficult to accomplish if we leave as soon as your sister and her husband are informed." He offered her a firm nod. "I suggest we send a message to Mr. Barclay at the Clarion as soon as we reach your sister's house. We can notify him of our arrival and then make the subsequent travel plans."

"Of course. The sooner the better." She looked up from the paper. "And perhaps Lillias or Father will shed more light on all this?"

"The only way to know for sure is to ask them." He opened the car door for her, but she paused, looking up at him.

"The estate is called Mosslea," she said, as she took her seat beside Zahra. "What sort of estate do you think it could be? And what is Mosslea?"

He'd just returned to the front seat next to the driver, when Grace pushed forward. "Do you think it could be a castle? I've read that Scotland is filled with castles."

He'd never been so happy to see the curious and, at times, terrifying glint return to her sapphire eyes. "I've stopped guessing about our future adventures since I've been quite literally thrust into one after another since meeting you." He wiggled his brows to broaden her grin.

He gave the driver Mr. and Mrs. Dixon's address and turned in time to hear Miss Cox's quiet voice emerge. "Pardon me, but. . .what sorts of adventures do you mean?"

"It's one of the reasons we hired you on, Miss Cox." Grace answered, bestowing a bright smile. "Your references listed that you were not only excellent at fixing hair, but you were also very good with sutures, bandages, and medicines."

Grace didn't clarify, leaving Miss Cox, no doubt, to ponder the possibilities behind such an answer.

"Not that we expect you to need those skills for anything

other than usual bumps and bruises, mind you." Frederick added, praying his words were prophetic. "But our previous adventures tended toward mystery solving, which turned a bit dangerous at times, as you can imagine."

"D–dangerous?" Frederick caught sight of the young woman's rounded hazel eyes. Clearly, his matter-of-fact wording hadn't quieted any concerns.

"It is no worry, Miss Cox." Zahra joined in. "*Sayid* and Sayyida are very good at living. They escaped a tomb after it exploded."

"A tomb?" The young maid's pitch took an upswing. "Exploded?"

"After one man was poisoned and another stole a pharaoh's treasure," Grace clarified with another guileless smile.

"Poisoned?" Miss Cox's whisper barely made it to Frederick's ears.

This was not the best way to introduce the woman to becoming a lady's maid in their home.

"Please don't worry yourself, Miss Cox." Frederick sent Grace a look he hoped she would interpret as intervention. "Our visit this time is simply to see family."

"Yes. Purely to see family." Grace offered a look of understanding, and his body relaxed. "Before Lord Astley, I only dreamed of mysteries like murderous mistresses and haunted villas. I never expected to truly encounter them. And I certainly don't expect to meet thieves or ghosts at my sister's house."

His shoulders tensed again, along with Miss Cox's gasp.

"Ghosts?"

Grace's eyes widened at her mistake. "Oh, but not to worry, dear Miss Cox, neither Lillias nor my father have any interest in adventures, so I feel very good about us all being mystery free for a few weeks. In fact, you may very well become bored."

Grace's reassurance failed to bring color back into Miss Cox's cheeks. Frederick sighed. If the young lady was still with them by morning, he'd be surprised.

"Besides, my sister, Lillias Dixon, has only recently had a son, and I feel the adventures in motherhood will be the only real risk she's interested in taking for the foreseeable future."

"I am very good at taking care of babies." Zahra offered, her hands demurely clasped in her lap, though the twinkle in her eyes contradicted the pose. "At the orphanage, I was often tasked with taking care of them."

Already, Zahra had worked her way into his heart much too deeply, just like his daughter Lily had done. And Zahra's large, intelligent eyes took in everything, no doubt from her unpredictable early life. Frederick hoped she never knew such fear or uncertainty again. Not if he could help it.

His gaze shifted back to Grace. Of course, the girl may find a great deal of excitement in uncertainty and adventure. And perhaps that's the very reason God had brought her into their lives.

What other mother would share such similar interests and penchant for the unexpected?

His pulse ramped up just a little bit at the thought.

God, help him. Two of them?

"No doubt you are excellent." Grace took the little girl's hand. "And I'd imagine my sister will love your help, for neither she nor I have ever spent much time with babies."

The conversation turned to Zahra sharing a few of her young exploits, one including saving a baby from a thief and another where Zahra had to swim to save a little girl who'd dropped her doll into the Nile. At one point, Zahra had even evaded a crocodile.

Not to mention the fact that he'd actually witnessed Zahra shimmy up the side of a hotel to find them. For some reason, he could imagine his wife doing the very same thing as a child—or at least attempting it.

The small town of Harrington came into their view. Certainly larger than Astlynn Commons back home, but much smaller than he'd expected after passing through Richmond. A few brick townhomes lined the streets, along with varying shops. Most of the area looked well-tended, but as the driver steered their car farther away from the principal street, the buildings and neighborhoods became much less grand. After two more turns, the driver stopped their car in front of a neat but surprisingly small townhouse. Two stories of pale brick with what appeared to be a dormered attic space on top.

This was certainly a much less affluent neighborhood than he'd expected for his sister-in-law and her banker husband. Had Mr. Ferguson's reduced financial circumstances impacted Lillias too?

"I've never been on this side of Harrington." Grace's tone failed to hide her own surprise as he assisted her from the car. "But what a charming house. It's the perfect size for a little family, isn't it?"

When they'd first met, Frederick doubted Grace would have made such a quick assessment of the situation. Though quick witted and intelligent, her inexperience and youthfulness had shown through in so many of their interactions, but seven months had matured her. Perhaps, their particular experiences had sped the development of her already supple mind, but she'd changed. Held on to her light and imagination, but deepened in maturity and understanding.

And of course, her immense ability to love only appeared to grow broader and deeper, overshadowing his flaws and past.

But that may be because his parched heart had needed her vast depths of love so much when they'd met, and she'd only continued to lavish a ready acceptance and affection upon him that he'd never known.

His gaze dropped to the envelope in her hands, and his chest tightened afresh.

He'd do whatever necessary to protect her. His attention slid to Zahra. To protect everyone in his growing family.

"Perhaps Lady Astley and I should ensure this is the correct house before we all disembark." Frederick sent a look from Grace back to Miss Cox and Zahra. "We shall be back in a trice, ladies."

His statement brought out Zahra's smile but Miss Cox continued to wear a look of mild terror. When he'd taken her on, he'd thought that expression might lessen with familiarity, but for some reason, it only seemed more pronounced the longer she was with them.

"Lillias will be so wonderfully surprised, Frederick." Grace slipped her arm through his, giving it a little squeeze, her resident optimism rose to the occasion. "Even if things haven't turned out as planned about Father." Yet the tremor in her voice proved she still wasn't fully past the shock. "I know there has to be more to the story than we understand, but for now, I'm going to focus on meeting my new nephew and seeing if Lillias has found such bliss in married life as I have."

They'd only taken the first step up to the townhouse door when a scream split the afternoon air.

A woman's scream. And from the very house they meant to enter.

He and Grace exchanged a look, then his wife dashed up the stairs.

Dash it! He followed, bypassing her to reach the door first.

It stood slightly ajar. Frederick held out his arm to pause Grace's entry and, with a slow movement, pushed the door open with his foot.

Not even the ominous creak of the opening door could have prepared him for the sight in the entry hall.

His breath seized in his lungs.

A chill congealed to his bones.

In the middle of the foyer lay the unmoving body of Anthony Dixon.

And standing over him, knife in hand, was Dixon's wife and Grace's sister, Lillias, screaming.

Chapter 3

Icy cold pricked over Grace's skin and pierced all the way through her.

What was she seeing?

Lillias, knife in hand, over Tony's body? Grace gave her head a shake, wondering, not for the first time, if her fictional loves had somehow materialized into the real world. It would make sense, wouldn't it? As much as she consumed her beloved novels.

But perhaps she was dreaming. It felt very much like a scenario her errant brain might concoct when her imagination took a downward turn. Only two weeks ago, she'd awakened in tears from a dream where Frederick had turned into a ghost and disappeared through a wall, leaving her unable to follow.

How unthinkable of him, even in ghost form!

She'd almost been rude to him during the first few minutes after waking up because he'd been so thoughtless in her dream. Poor man.

But this? Lillias and Tony? This *had* to be a dream! Because these weren't strangers she'd just met in Egypt or Italy who'd been dabbling in stolen artifacts or paintings long before she ever met them. This was her family.

Her stomach knotted. Within the last hour her family had turned upside down with her father's deception, her mother's visit from the grave, and now this?

"Lillias?" Grace's whisper sliced the distance and drew Lillias' gaze up.

"Grace?" Lillias' voice broke. The knife fell from her hand with a sharp clang, and she staggered. Frederick rushed forward just in time to catch her before she crumpled beside her dearly departed husband.

Grace moved closer, her gaze landing on Tony's still form. She hadn't seen many dead bodies, but there was no mistaking his pallor or the gaping wound in his chest. The jeweled dagger lay nearby, its emerald-studded hilt smeared with blood.

Where had Lillias gotten such a weapon?

Frederick knelt, loosening the top button of Lillias' blouse. "Grace, can you find something for her to drink?"

Grace turned to comply, but he caught her arm. "Wait. We don't know if the house is safe."

Her attention shot to the hallways flanking the room. "You think the murderer might still be here?"

"I'm not certain." He glanced at the front door, still standing ajar. "From the color in his face, I don't think the deed was done long ago, so someone else could still be hiding nearby. "

A sudden realization quaked through Grace as she met her husband's gaze. "If there *was* someone else."

He gave an audible swallow, glancing down at Lillias' unconscious form before turning back to Grace. "Perhaps you should go send the driver for a policeman."

"And leave you here alone?"

His lips almost tipped, and he sighed. "Of course not, but I'm hesitant to leave your sister alone at the scene of the crime while it is fresh."

His one statement cleared Grace's mind into action. Her family or not, this was a mystery, and it could very well prove that any observation helped make more sense of the situation or cleared

Lillias' name, because at present it looked very much like her sister had murdered her own husband.

Grace had never even imagined such a thought, let alone truly suspected it to cross her mind! She shook away the shock and scanned the room. The dagger. The open door. Lillias' dainty hands, clean and unbloodied. Shouldn't there be blood if she'd wielded the knife?

"Look at this." Frederick gestured toward faint scrapes on the floor leading to a hallway.

Grace moved to join him, but before she could, the front door burst open. A man in a bowler hat and navy suit stood in the doorway, gun drawn.

"What's this?" he barked.

Frederick stepped in front of Grace, raising his hands. "We mean no harm."

"Keep those hands up. That's right." The man peered at them through a pair of rounded spectacles, his pale eyes shifting from Frederick to Grace and then back to the body on the floor.

His mustache was particularly unsatisfying. . .and crooked.

Very villain-like. An unrefined villain.

"Who are you?" Frederick asked, lowering his arms a little.

"I'll be the one asking questions," the man spat out. "I heard the screams during my circuit and came running."

What sort of accent did the stranger have? Certainly not Virginian. Was it northern?

"We just arrived," Frederick said calmly. "My wife's sister is in shock—"

"Just arrived in time to stab a man?" the stranger sneered.

"He was dead when we got here." Grace peeked around Frederick. "Honestly, must we converse with our hands in the air? We're not criminals."

"Your presence at the scene of a crime would suggest otherwise."

But he lowered his gun to his side, his beady little eyes taking inventory of the room. "Officer Clark. This is my jurisdiction. If you don't want trouble, tell me what happened."

Before Grace could answer, a scream pierced the room. All eyes turned to a doorway nearby where a maid stood with a baby in her arms, and unfortunately, her shriek inspired the baby's hearty response. Somehow, this cacophony roused Lillias from her faint.

Did most women scream at the sight of a dead body? Grace blinked a few times, trying to remember her fiction. Why hadn't she ever felt compelled to scream? She'd already seen a few dead bodies and, despite a deep sense of sadness and a little curiosity, she'd never felt the urge to scream. It just seemed to waste time, leave people's ears ringing, and give away one's position.

Officer Clark's eyes grew wide, and he lowered his gun even more as Lillias stood and stared down at Tony's body all over again. Her face paled anew.

"I'm not staying." The maid shook her head and, without hesitation, pushed the baby into Grace's arms. "I've put up with enough in this house with all the fighting." She looked back at the body in the middle of the room and backed away, shaking her head with such force her dark hair bounced in its bun. "Now you've gone and *killed* him?" With another gasp, the woman dashed down the hall, leaving Grace looking from the crying baby over to Frederick, then to Officer Clark, to finally land on Lillias.

"I—I didn't. . ." Lillias stammered and moved toward the maid's retreat only to nearly step on Tony. Her palm went to her chest. She swayed and dropped back to the couch, remaining seated and alert, at least.

That was progress.

Grace rushed to Lillias' side, taking a seat beside her and rubbing little Thomas' back. She wasn't certain if that is what one did with distraught babies, but it seemed to work. His little face burrowed into her neck, and she nearly forgot about the dead body in the middle of the room.

Baby Thomas was so small. Grace wasn't certain what she'd expected at four weeks old, but he snuggled nicely into the curve of her elbow.

"You killed your husband?" The officer returned his gun to the air. "How vile to be betrayed by his own wife."

In half a dozen steps, Frederick took his stance as barrier yet again between the weapon and Grace. Oh, he was just the most heroic of men, and she would have told him so if she didn't have a weeping sister to one side, a crying baby in her arms, and a dastardly looking officer pointing a pistol at them.

"That is a premature accusation, Mr. Clark." Frederick kept his tone measured. "There has been no investigation."

The officer narrowed his eyes and opened his mouth to respond when Lillias stood. "I—I didn't kill him. Of course not." Her voice wavered. "I found him. . .like this. The knife. . .was still in him."

"Likely story, Mrs. Dixon." Mr. Clark tipped his head, the slight warp of his glasses giving his pale eyes a sinister glint. He took a step back toward the door. "My colleagues will discover the truth."

With a tip of his hat, he turned to leave the room and nearly bumped into Miss Cox, with Zahra at her side. Grace stood, placing her body beside Frederick's to further block their view of the body, but Miss Cox had already caught sight of it. She stumbled back, nearly knocking over Zahra, who shot a narrow-eyed look to Mr. Clark as he bounded out the door. As if in line with the rest of the house, Miss Cox screamed.

Then fainted.

So much for keeping Miss Cox as a maidservant.

Frederick felt certain that as soon as the young woman awakened from her faint, she'd follow the path of Lillias' maid and retreat back across the ocean. He'd gladly pay her passage—poor woman.

This trip to visit Grace's family was meant to be scandal free. No drama, no murder. Yet here they were, mired in the most intimate tragedy of their young marriage. Frederick barely reached the maid in time to catch her before she collapsed, no thanks to Officer Clark. Then he carried the young woman to the settee across from Lillias and Grace, who had miraculously managed to quiet the baby.

Lillias, on the other hand, could not be quieted. Her sobs were as relentless as the accusations swirling around her. Murder. A contentious marriage?

"I didn't kill him," she wailed, pressing a trembling hand to her forehead. "You must believe me!"

"Of course you didn't," Grace soothed, sending Frederick a sharp look over Lillias' head. "That dagger is enormous, Frederick. Not a lady's weapon at all. And the force of the knife blow appears far too strong for a woman's hand."

Lillias' mouth fell open as she gaped at her sister, her face draining of color.

To prevent another fainting spell—and to distract Zahra, who seemed disturbingly unfazed by the dead body—Frederick shrugged off his coat and draped it over Tony's chest and face. "With Officer Clark fetching the police, the only thing to do now is wait."

"And sort out the story." Grace turned to her sister as Zahra took a seat next to Grace, the little girl's attention fixed on the baby.

"I've already told you." Lillias' voice trembled.

"It would be wise to tell it from the beginning once before they arrive, Lillias." Grace offered a gentle smile as Zahra coaxed the baby into her arms.

With his wife's focus on her sister, she didn't seem at all aware of Zahra's gentle manner with the babe. Frederick's new daughter kept revealing more and more aspects of her personality as she found her confidence and role in their little family.

Frederick couldn't resist the tiniest smile, despite the shadow of the moment, to see her bloom a little more.

Lillias' gaze flitted nervously between Grace and Frederick before darting toward the covered body. Her breath caught audibly, and she looked away.

"Start just before you came into this room," Frederick suggested, positioning himself near the door to keep a watchful eye. There didn't seem to be any hidden dangers within the house, but he refused to become too relaxed. Especially with a dead body still very evident before them. "What happened leading up to your return to the house?"

Lillias hesitated, her chin lifting defensively. Why did he get the feeling she was hiding something? Frederick braced himself. If things were about to grow worse—he glanced briefly at Tony's still form—he needed to be ready for Grace's sake.

He already knew she was strong, probably more than she realized, but even her tenacity had its limit, and he feared her greatest weakness likely came closest to heart.

"Eloise—the ungrateful maid who abandoned me—had taken Thomas for a walk," Lillias said, gesturing toward the doorway through which the maid had disappeared. "I accompanied them until they grew close to home." She looked away, fidgeting with her hands. "When Thomas started fussing, I told Eloise to take him through the back door to the nursery while I came through the front to check the post."

"Was Tony here when you left for your walk?" Grace asked.

"Yes." The word came quickly, but the hesitation that followed was telling. "But he slept in so I hadn't spoken to him yet."

"How long were you gone?" Frederick prompted, holding Grace's gaze as he did so.

"An hour? Maybe two?" Lillias shook her head and buried her face in her hands. "I don't know!"

"There's a great deal to process, I'm sure." Grace rested a palm on Lillias' back. "And I'm sorry to ask this, Lillias, . . .but do you recall if Tony was still alive when you came into the house?"

"What?" Lillias' head shot up, her body stiffening. "Of course he wasn't! I didn't kill him!"

"I only meant was he breathing? Did he say anything before he. . .breathed his last?" Grace clarified.

"No. He wasn't. . ." Lillias faltered, her shoulders slumping. "There were no words."

"Had you ever seen Officer Clark before?" Frederick interjected.

Grace sent him a look.

"He called your sister by name," he explained to Grace. "We never mentioned her name."

Lillias sent him a wearying look, clearly not following. "No, I—I don't think so."

Before anyone could respond, the front door burst open. Three policemen entered, the first with his pistol drawn. He froze mid-step, his gaze bouncing from one person to the next. His eyes lingered on Zahra cradling the baby before dropping to the shrouded figure on the floor.

It was the calmest murder scene Frederick had ever been a part of.

He paused on that thought for a moment, suddenly aware how very odd it sounded to his own mind.

"Which one of you is Mrs. Dixon?" The man barked the question, causing Zahra and Lillias to flinch.

Frederick spread his hands in a placating gesture. "Sir, there's no need for weapons. Everyone here wishes to cooperate fully."

The man lowered the gun reluctantly as a second officer, better dressed and more composed, stepped forward. His medium brown hair waved away from his face and matched the color of his close-shaven beard and mustache, his expression proving much more welcoming than the first man. "Detective Johnson," he introduced himself. "This is Officer Todd and Davis."

"Thank you for coming," Frederick said. "I'm Lord Astley, and this is my wife, Lady Astley. Mrs. Dixon, the lady of the house and my wife's sister." He gestured to Lillias, who gave a faint nod, her pallor concerning. "We're visiting my wife's family and wish to assist in any way we can." Frederick continued. "Officer Clark said he'd send you to investigate."

"Officer Clark?" The first man, presumably Todd, barked out the question. "Who the blazes is Officer Clark?" The one without the weapon raiseed his fist. "I'll not have any funny business, sir. I don't know what sort of law and order they keep over in jolly old England, but 'round here, we don't abide misleading the police."

"We're not." Grace came to Frederick's side. "He came shortly after my husband and I had arrived and said he was going to fetch more police. He left not half an hour ago."

Johnson raised a hand, silencing the room. "Wait. Are you saying a man calling himself Officer Clark was here, saw the scene, and left to find reinforcements?"

"Exactly." Grace nodded. "And he was rather rude about it too."

Frederick's stomach twisted. A man *calling himself* Officer Clark?

"He accused my sister of murdering her own husband without collecting any evidence or even examining the room." Grace continued, gesturing toward Todd. "I believe your policemen are in need of more thorough training."

"How did Officer Clark know to come to the house?" This from the detective.

Frederick held the man's gaze, a sickening awareness slowly beginning to dawn. "He said he heard the screams while on patrol and came to assist."

"What is it?" Grace's voice rose into Frederick's emerging thoughts. "What's wrong?"

Detective Johnson looked from Frederick to Officer Todd and then back, his lips pressing tight before he answered. "We will certainly begin an investigation on what happened to Mr. Dixon, but I believe there may be an unfortunate compounding factor."

The room grew silent in anticipation.

Johnson exchanged a grim look with Todd before addressing Frederick. "Our department doesn't have anyone by the name of Officer Clark."

Chapter 4

No wonder Officer Clark looked so suspicious.

He *was* suspicious.

In truth, Grace ought to have pieced it together herself. She was easily the most well-read on matters of detective work among everyone present—though Frederick had made remarkable strides in that genre since their marriage.

"Mr. Todd, could we have Officer Davis return to the station and gather men to remove the body, please?" Detective Johnson's voice cut through the room as he nodded toward Lillias. "I feel certain it would provide some small comfort to Mrs. Dixon."

Lillias released another whimper, and Grace moved back to her side, putting an arm around her shoulders. It was an odd thing as the younger daughter, to feel a sudden sense of protection over one's elder sibling, but this moment, not to mention the way things had changed between them since her wedding, shifted something inside Grace.

She hadn't much considered her role in the Ferguson family since marrying Frederick. Between their whirlwind romance, the adventures that followed, and the many attempts to keep themselves alive, personal reflection had hardly been a priority. And she hadn't even seen her sister in seven months to remind her of making any comparisons. Yet sitting here now, beside Lillias, Grace felt a curious blend of familiarity and estrangement settle over her. They were the same sisters as they'd always been.

Yet they weren't.

Officer Todd relayed Johnson's orders, and Officer Davis darted from the room.

"I'm sorry for the inconvenience, Mrs. Dixon," Detective Johnson continued, addressing Lillias with a measured tone. "But as you were the last to see your husband, we will need to ask you a few questions regarding his death."

Lillias nodded and sniffled, and Frederick, in perfect style, offered her his handkerchief.

"However, first things first," Detective Johnson declared, pacing the room with an assessing gaze. "If a person posing as an officer responded so quickly to your cries and then conveniently knew exactly where to find me and my colleagues, we must consider the possibility that he was involved in Mr. Dixon's demise."

Grace admired Detective Johnson's logical approach. From the wideness of his forehead, the sharpness in his pale eyes, his quick assertations, and his use of the word *demise*, Grace was already rather impressed by the man. Of course, experience had taught her that first impressions could be misleading, but Johnson certainly carried himself with an air of credibility.

That was a very good start.

"What—what do you mean?" Lillias eked out the question. "Someone had *planned* to kill Tony?"

The detective tipped his head and studied her. "Coincidences should always be suspect when crimes are involved, Mrs. Dixon. Our goal is to sort out why and who. This was no mere happenstance of a crime." He turned to the officer at his side. "Todd, would you make a sweep of the periphery and see if you note anything unusual?"

The older man, broad face pressed into a frown as if it didn't know another expression, gave the room an assessing look before he nodded and left out the front door.

"Now"—Detective Johnson approached the group, his attention back on Lillias—"did your husband have any enemies?"

Grace nearly smiled. An excellent question—and one she would have asked had the detective not claimed it first.

"Enemies?" Lillias echoed, aghast. "Tony? Enemies?"

Her sharp tone roused Miss Cox, who shifted on the fainting couch, sitting up slowly. Her dark eyes darted between the speakers before landing on Grace, who offered an encouraging smile.

The poor girl's frown only deepened.

"And who is this?" Detective Johnson nodded toward Miss Cox.

"Our maid," Frederick answered smoothly. "She accompanied us from Italy after our honeymoon."

Detective Johnson's brows rose, shifting his attention from Frederick to Grace. "So you've only *just* arrived?"

"Our ship arrived yesterday," Frederick explained. "We stayed overnight at an inn on our journey from the harbor. My wife hasn't seen her family since our marriage, and I thought this visit would be a fitting surprise before we returned to Havensbrooke."

"Quite the surprise," Detective Johnson responded dryly.

The man didn't seem to hold the same lightheartedness as their dear friend Detective Jack Miracle did. Johnson certainly carried himself with more gravity.

"But why would you suppose Tony had enemies?" Lillias asked.

"If he didn't have any enemies, Lillias"—Grace turned to her sister, the possibilities dancing through her mind—"Then someone planned to kill him for another reason. As Detective Johnson suggested, this was not a random act. Is there anything missing? Stolen?"

Lillias' eyes grew wide, and her face paled all over again. "I—I don't know. I've not had opportunity. . ."

Detective Johnson nodded thoughtfully and stepped closer to the body, lowering himself near the knife lying on the floor where Lillias had dropped it. "Is that the weapon?" His sharp gaze shifted to Lillias, who seemed to shrink under his scrutiny.

"Yes." Her voice trembled so much that Grace gave her shoulders another reassuring squeeze. "It—it was in his—his chest."

The detective studied her face. "I'll ask a few more immediate questions, Mrs. Dixon, then allow you time to process the situation before my return."

Well, at least if he was going to be more serious, he had a kind streak. That proved a very good characteristic for anyone, especially a detective, Grace thought.

The door opened, and Officer Todd reentered, looking a bit too red in the face for a casual walk about the premises, but he wasn't the smallest of men.

"Anything?" This from Detective Johnson.

Officer Todd gave his head a shake. "Nothing, sir, but the rain's put me off for a bit. I can send a man back to give a more thorough look later."

"A very good notion, Todd." Detective Johnson paused, as if in thought for a moment, and then lifted Frederick's jacket to peer at Tony's body beneath. "I'm concerned for Mrs. Dixon's safety, Todd. What do you think?"

"My safety?" Lillias nearly shrieked, standing so quickly she swayed.

Detective Johnson jumped to his feet to steady her, gently guiding her back to the couch. His frown deepened as he withdrew his hands, looking slightly perplexed by her distress. "Now, Mrs. Dixon, consider this: If the killer planned everything so meticulously to frame you for murder, it suggests you or this house may have been targeted. I'd feel better leaving an officer here to guard the premises. I strongly encourage you to remain at home for the next few days."

"Remain at the house?" Lillias' voice rose to a near panic. "Under guard?"

"Only until we gather more answers," the detective assured her. He exchanged a brief look with Frederick, who gave a slight nod.

Grace raised a brow. Did the detective already recognize Frederick's knack for solving mysteries? Surely a man trained to notice details would appreciate Frederick's skills.

"We don't know how long Mr. Dixon has been dead," Detective Johnson continued, glancing toward the body.

"It couldn't have been long," Grace offered. "His face was pale but not completely ashen, and his lips showed no signs of discoloration when we arrived."

Lillias gasped at her side, and Grace sent her a look. Her sister stared at her with wide eyes.

"And his skin was neither cold nor clammy—dulled, perhaps, but not lifeless," Frederick added, his brow furrowed in thought.

"I wouldn't guess more than half an hour at the time of our arrival, if that."

All eyes turned to Miss Cox, who blinked up to them as if she hadn't meant to speak aloud. She sat up straighter and cleared her throat, her cheeks flaming rouge.

Grace almost smiled. *Good heavens, they'd hired the perfect maid!*

Detective Johnson rounded the settee and lowered himself into the chair across from her. "How do you know this, Miss Cox?"

After a slight hesitation, the young woman raised those dark eyes. "My father was a coroner in Cornwall, sir. And just from the first look, well, I—I was raised around"—she shrugged a shoulder and grimaced—"dead people."

Detective Johnson's brows shot up. Frederick's followed suit, and Grace couldn't help but lean forward. "What a fascinating advantage you bring, Miss Cox. Far more useful than selecting hair clasps to match gowns, wouldn't you agree, Frederick?"

Her darling husband's brows creased, and he turned his attention back to Miss Cox.

"I'm sorry, sir," the young woman continued hurriedly. "I didn't mean to mislead you in Rome. Everything I told you—losing my mother on holiday and being robbed—was true. But I have more experience with"—she gestured toward Tony's body—"the dead and dying than with styling hair or hemming dresses."

Frederick exchanged a look with Grace before addressing Miss Cox. "We'll discuss this later."

Grace's chest warmed. From the look on his face, he'd already forgiven the girl. Dear man.

"Well, this situation grows more interesting by the minute." Detective Johnson braided his fingers together in front of him and turned back to Lillias. "Tell me everything you can remember from the time you entered the house, Mrs. Dixon."

Lillias' posture wilted further. Her voice faltered and tears overran her eyes as she described entering the house after a walk and finding her husband lifeless, in the middle of the room. Grace's heart gave a pang. No, of course her sister had nothing to do with Tony's death, even if—as the maid had said—they'd been fighting.

While the interrogation continued, Frederick and Officer Todd inspected the house at the detective's suggestion, returning to report that the cook and errand boy were out running errands, presumably leaving the home empty that morning except for Tony.

After having lived with a handful of servants in her father's home and then a dozen or more at Havensbrooke, Grace was struck by the dawning reality of the reduced state of Lillias' household with fresh clarity. Since their roles had reversed—Grace marrying an earl and Lillias settling with a banker—their lives had diverged in ways Grace hadn't fully appreciated until now. She held the esteem, title, and position Lillias had always craved. Without Father's financial assistance, Lillias had been forced to rely solely on Tony's income to sustain them.

Grace's mind worked as she glanced at Lillias. Her sister's reduced circumstances were glaringly apparent in the sparsely furnished room. What would that have done to her sister's heart? Her emotions?

"Do you know where your maid might have gone after leaving here?" Detective Johnson's voice cut through Grace's thoughts, the man evidently unfazed by the domestic contrast.

"Louisa?" Lillias blinked, her brow furrowing. "She mentioned family in Westwood."

"Excellent. And her full name?"

"Louisa Steen." Lillias rubbed at her forehead and Grace looked up at the detective.

"I'm sure my sister can provide more details tomorrow, Detective. She's clearly exhausted."

"Of course," Johnson said smoothly, though his expression tightened. "I'll return tomorrow after you've rested. In the meantime, I'll be questioning Miss Steen."

"Why would you need to visit her?" Lillias rose abruptly, tears welling in her eyes. "And—and I can tell you now that she wasn't happy in her job. We—well, we docked her pay recently, and she threatened to leave before this morning. No doubt she'll concoct some slander to make me and my poor husband seem villainous in your sight."

"Every testimony has its biases, Lillias." Grace interjected. "It's human nature." She sent the detective a pointed look. "Isn't that right?"

"Indeed, Lady Astley." His eyes narrowed, but he nodded curtly. "And we must strike while memories are fresh and evidence is within reach."

"Exactly," Grace agreed with a smile. "One never knows what clues might vanish after a day. Misdirection, accidental disposal—sometimes the very witnesses themselves disappear. Frederick and I have seen it all before in our mysteries, haven't we? Curses, ghosts, secret passageways."

Oh, what wonderful memories!

"Curses? Ghosts? Mysteries?" Lillias looked between them, bewildered. "How do you even know such things?"

"Books, mostly," Grace replied with a light shrug. "Though I did mention in my letters to you that Frederick and I have solved a few cases. Detective Jack Miracle himself asked for our assistance on his last one."

"Miracle?" Detective Johnson shot to alert. "The English detective who wrote a popular book about solving crimes?"

Grace's attention flashed to Detective Johnson. "The very same."

"I read his work. That last case of his was splashed all over the papers." Johnson's gaze sharpened, darting between Grace and Frederick. "How. . .convenient that you arrive just as a murder unfolds here."

A chill prickled Grace's skin at his sudden shift in tone. What was he insinuating?

"Are you suggesting we had some hand in it, Detective?" Frederick folded his arms across his chest in challenge.

"Everyone is a suspect." Johnson's smile was a crooked, humorless thing. "But I can rule out you and your entourage fairly quickly. A question or two with your driver or a look at your arrival tickets should suffice."

He reached for his hat and fixed it firmly on his head before gesturing toward Todd with his chin as a cue to exit. "However," he added, voice clipped and gaze settling on Frederick, "*I* don't intend to consult with you on this case. I'm more than capable of solving it without interference. Unlike Miracle,"—he spat the name as though it left a bad taste—"I don't need an audience."

Grace's brows shot high at the clear insult. Who would ever insult dear Jack?

"We would never impose, sir." Frederick remained unruffled by the accusation, his tone steady. "But should you require assistance, we would gladly help bring the killer to justice—for everyone's peace of mind."

Johnson dipped his chin in what might have been reluctant thanks before addressing Lillias. "Mrs. Dixon, expect me tomorrow afternoon."

He cast the room one last glance, then strode out, Officer Todd trailing after him.

Little Thomas took the silence that followed as permission to announce his discontent with an earsplitting wail.

"He's likely hungry." Lillias' voice sounded tired, and no wonder. With a deep sigh, she shifted toward Zahra and opened her arms. "I'll see to him and then, if your servant will keep watch over him"—she nodded toward Zahra—"I should like to rest in my room, undisturbed."

"Our servant?" Grace looked from Zahra to Lillias. "Oh Lillias, this is our adopted daughter, Zahra."

Lillias mouth dropped open and for half a second no sound emerged. "Your—your daughter?"

"Yes. I wrote about her in the last letter."

Lillias' brow creased as she took Thomas into her arms, studying Zahra. "But—but she's. . .Egyptian."

"She is." Grace took Zahra's hand, pulling her close for a hug. "And ours. Between me, Zahra, and Miss Cox, I'm sure we can manage little Thomas just fine, can't we, ladies?"

Zahra nodded solemnly. Miss Cox looked significantly less confident.

"I'm sorry to ask this, Mrs. Dixon." Frederick stepped forward.

"Should we find a hotel or would you like us to stay with you?"

Lillias glanced up, her expression dull. "We have two extra rooms, if Miss Cox and"—her gaze dipped briefly to Zahra—"the little girl don't mind sharing."

Grace gave Zahra and Miss Cox a quick look. When neither objected, she thanked her sister.

"I'll alert Mrs. James, the housekeeper, to ready the rooms for you once she arrives in an hour or so. She takes her half day on Tuesdays." Lillias took a few more steps toward the hallway, Thomas' discontent growing in volume. "And I do have a favor to ask of you, Grace."

Grace stepped forward instinctively. "Of course."

"Since you know the town better than Lord Astley, I'd like you to deliver a letter to Louisa's house this afternoon."

"Louisa?" Grace frowned and cast a quick look at Frederick before turning back to her sister. "Your maid?"

"Former maid." Lillias corrected, opening the door to a hallway just off the room. "I want to make sure she's prepared for Detective Johnson's visit tomorrow. It's a kindness I can show her that she doesn't deserve."

With that, Lillias slipped through the doorway and up a slender stairway.

Deliver a letter to her former maid?

Why did that seem. . .odd? Grace shook off the unsettled thought. Too many odd things had happened since they had first arrived at her father's house not even three hours ago. Why not this as well? After all, poor Lillias had been hit with one wound after another.

"Detective Johnson was not too keen on Miracle, was he?" Frederick stepped nearer the settee, his attention on the closed door behind Lillias.

Oh, what must he think of her family now? After all her

teasing about haunted manors and terrifying mothers-in-law, she'd brought him into a drama as tangled as his own. And this was only the beginning. The potential for further disaster was staggering.

"What do you suppose that was about?" Grace asked.

"I don't know." The words came slowly as he turned his attention back to Grace. "But it certainly changed the man's disposition toward us, and we could use as many allies at the moment as possible."

"Perhaps he'll warm up to us after a little while. We certainly aren't in competition with him. And why would that bother the man, anyway? Where murders were concerned, wouldn't the more help be the better?"

Frederick's expression darkened the slightest bit.

"What is it?" Grace asked.

He hesitated, his gaze flicking to Zahra and Miss Cox.

Zahra had been part of their adventures long enough to handle whatever they discussed, and Miss Cox's history certainly made her no stranger to darker subjects. Apparently, Frederick reached the same conclusion.

"One question Lillias never answered," he said.

Grace's mind whirred with her own list of unanswered questions: her father's bankruptcy, the elusive Scottish inheritance, Lillias' jittery demeanor about Miss Steen's interview. "Which one?"

"She never said whether her husband had enemies."

Grace blinked, her mind snapping to attention. That hadn't even occurred to her. "You think the killer had a grudge against Tony? Perhaps that impostor—Officer Clark?"

"He wore fake *sharib*."

All eyes turned to Zahra. She sat cross-legged on the edge of the settee, her solemn face framed by her dark hair.

Frederick crouched beside her. "What did you say, Zahra?"

"The false police." Zahra continued. "I saw him from the car before he came inside. He put on a"—she gestured to her upper lip—"*Sharib*?"

"A mustache?" Frederick touched the clean-shaven area above his own mouth. "Here?"

Zahra nodded earnestly. "And glasses."

Grace leaned forward, her pulse quickening. "So not only did he lie about being an officer, but he came in disguise. No wonder he looked so poorly put together. And that accent—honestly, it was dreadful."

Then she wondered for a moment if Edward Rochester's accent sounded anything like Fake Officer Clark's when he'd dressed up as a gypsy to trick the truth out of poor Jane Eyre.

"We'll need to mention this to Johnson tomorrow." Frederick nodded grimly. "Whether he likes our help or not."

Miss Cox, who had been hovering by the window, broke into the conversation. "Does this"—she hesitated, waving vaguely at the room, her face still pale—"happen to you often?"

"This?" Frederick asked, his lips twitching as though holding back a smile.

She gestured more emphatically. "Murder."

"Well, not very often." Grace smoothed a hand over Zahra's hair. "Sometimes, it's only theft. Or mannapping."

"*Mannapping*?" Miss Cox's voice shot up an octave.

"Kidnapping," Frederick corrected dryly.

Grace waved her hand dismissively. "But we've been fortunate—no children have ever been taken. Only adults. Frederick was kidnapped right off the front steps of our home in England. I was napped. . ." She paused on the word. *Napped* didn't fit *kidnapped* at all. "Taken during an antiquities heist in Egypt, which is where we found Zahra. Our dear friend, Detective Miracle, was nap—abducted from a boat in Venice, but thankfully, no children."

"I am good at hiding." Zahra sat up straighter, offering a rare smile. "And I can climb and run very fast."

"But we hope you won't have to hide, little one." Frederick took a seat beside Grace, his arm sliding in behind her to offer the slightest support. "You've already been through enough danger for a lifetime."

"I am not afraid," Zahra said, lifting her chin with a bravery that tugged at Grace's heart. "I am the right daughter for you, Sayid, because I am brave and I run fast."

Grace gave the little girl another hug. "You are very brave, and if we do stumble into trouble, Zahra, I'm glad you are fast."

"Indeed, and clever," Frederick added, tapping Zahra lightly under the chin. "Because it seems our quiet visit to America has taken a darker turn than I'd hoped." His gaze locked on Grace, his tone growing serious. "Whoever planned this didn't do so on a whim. They came here with purpose when everyone was out of the house—and it seems that purpose was to kill Tony Dixon."

A chill, equal parts fear and intrigue, threaded through Grace. She tightened her arms protectively around Zahra. "And if they're willing to make such a meticulous plan to kill Tony, who else might they wish to harm?"

Chapter 5

Frederick didn't like leaving Zahra behind, but he refused to let Grace travel to Louisa Steen's house alone—not with a murderer on the loose. At least with an officer stationed outside Lillias' house, he felt marginally better about Zahra's safety.

Marginally.

As Grace maneuvered the car through Harrington's streets, however, he began to wonder if Zahra, Lillias, and Miss Cox were actually safer than he was.

After securing their own car, Grace had *insisted* she drive to Miss Steen's, citing her greater familiarity with Harrington. It was true, of course—but familiarity hardly compensated for experience. She'd taken a grand total of three driving lessons before their honeymoon, and the results were. . . Well, they were currently testing his faith. After nearly mowing down a man on a bicycle, taking a corner at what felt like breakneck speed, and clipping a tree so closely the leaves brushed the side mirror, Frederick began to think he'd have had better odds fending off the counterfeit Officer Clark.

"I'm certain Miss Steen's neighborhood is just down this street." Grace grinned as she took another turn with alarming gusto. Frederick's fingers dug into the doorframe. "We used to visit a church member here when I was younger. She had the most glorious pink dogwoods—truly, they looked like something out of *The Secret Garden*."

He smiled. Despite it all.

How could he help it?

In the span of a single day, his wife had faced her father's deception, the loss of her childhood home, and her brother-in-law's violent death. And still her smile cut through the murky weight of it all, just as it had since the first day they'd met. He prayed that, even with tragedy closer to her heart this time, she'd cling to that inner sunshine. Over the months of their marriage, he'd come to realize he couldn't keep her safe—not entirely. So he'd learned to trust God for both their hearts.

Or at least, he'd gotten *better* at trusting God.

The houses on either side of the street formed two neat rows, each small and unassuming but tidy. Quaint, yes—and proving Miss Louisa Steen came from a working-class family.

Grace stopped the car on the street near a house with the number matching the address on the envelope Lillias had given her, but his bride didn't immediately exit the car. Instead, she looked over at him, brow creased.

"What's wrong?" Frederick asked.

Her lips pressed into a thoughtful line before she leaned toward him. "Do you think we should open the envelope first?"

Air burst from Frederick's throat. "What?"

"No, of course not. We shouldn't." She shook her head and reached for the door handle, then turned back to him. "But—"

"But?"

"But why would Lillias want us to deliver this letter to her former maid *before* the police interviewed her? That seems. . .odd, doesn't it?"

He couldn't deny it. The same thought had been nagging him since Lillias made the request, but between their brief conversations and Grace's rather spirited driving, there hadn't been an opportunity to bring it up.

"Grace."

"The letter isn't sealed, Frederick." Her wide eyes implored as her voice dropped to a whisper. "What if reading it could stop something worse from happening? Isn't it better to be prepared?"

Frederick exhaled a short laugh. "Darling, I admire the heart behind your reasoning, but I also know your keen sense of justice. You'd regret tampering with it later."

She studied him for a long moment, and then her shoulders drooped. "You're right. I would." She sighed, lips twitching faintly. "Mostly."

"Perhaps if we deliver it directly into Miss Steen's hands, we can observe her reaction and gather information without compromising Lillias' trust."

"You're right, as usual. My mystery-loving spirit got the better of me. I needed your good sense to rein me in."

He exited and rounded to her door to assist her. "I don't think it was the mystery-loving spirit as much as your protective heart," he said, offering her his arm and starting toward the front door of the house. "This is different from all our other. . .adventures. It's your family, Grace. But I hope it will be much more short-lived than our previous cases."

"*Cases*!" Her eyes flashed wide with her smile. "Oh, you called them cases. I love it when you refer to us as proper sleuths, Frederick. It's so exciting."

Her smile wavered—just the faintest flicker so subtle no one else would have noticed. But Frederick did. He knew those tiny shifts, those rare flakes of vulnerability in her bright optimism. The current situation hit her much more deeply than she let on.

"And," she added quietly, "with all the *factual* difficulties surrounding this particular situation, it helps to add a little fictional delight. Just enough to soften the ache of reality, don't you think?"

"One of the many benefits of fiction, darling." He placed a hand over hers on his arm, his voice dropping as he met her gaze. "But we're in this together, as we have been. Fiction or no." A playful wink accompanied his words. "But let's keep our detective minds sharp until we figure out what your sister has dragged us into, shall we?"

"Yes," she agreed, squeezing his arm with a conspiratorial smile. "Something feels more unsettled in that house than just the death of my brother-in-law."

Indeed.

Frederick reached the door first, keeping Grace just a step behind him in preparation for whatever they may find on the other side. His first knock brought no answer, but the second stirred movement. The door creaked open to reveal a much more composed Miss Steen.

"Can I help you?" she asked, her accent carrying the rounded tones of the nearby mountains.

Frederick nodded. "Miss Steen, isn't it?"

"It is." Her chin lifted, her eyes narrowing as she gave him a thorough once-over.

"Good afternoon. We've come regarding Mrs. Dixon."

Miss Steen's sharp gaze darted to Grace, then back to Frederick, and she cast a wary glance at the street. After a moment's hesitation, she opened the door wider. "He told me you'd be coming, but I didn't expect you till this evening or tomorrow morning."

Frederick's unease deepened. *He?* How did anyone know they were coming when they hadn't even known it themselves?

A silent exchange with Grace conveyed the same question. To her credit, her expression remained perfectly neutral save for a subtle quirk of her brow.

"Did he prepare you for our inquiry?" Frederick asked, keeping his question ambiguous.

"Said you'd want to know about the Dixons' house and all that was going on there." She chuckled and waved toward a pair of chairs poised around a simple table in the middle of the room. "With what he paid me, I'll tell you whatever you want to know."

Frederick's mind raced. *Paid her?* Who exactly did Miss Steen think they were? He gestured for Grace to take a seat, concealing his mounting tension with an obligatory smile. "Thank you for your cooperation. We're eager to get to the bottom of this matter."

"Ain't much guesswork to it." Miss Steen looked over at Grace. "Is that your secretary or is she one of them new female detectives I've heard tell about?"

"The latter, Miss Steen." Grace perked up at the mention, sending Frederick a saucy grin. "Detective Percy has been an excellent mentor in the process."

Detective Percy indeed. Frederick's brows lifted, his lips twitching, but he quickly masked the amusement, turning to Miss Steen with a polite nod.

"I've heard tell of female detectives but ain't never seen one with my own eyes." Miss Steen gave Grace a fresh look with an approving nod tagged on before she shrugged and looked back at Frederick. "I don't know how much help I'll be, but I'm glad to be rid of that house."

Grace flinched, just barely, at the blunt statement.

"And with what Mr. K gave me to share my thoughts?" Miss Steen added. "I'm planning to leave this town as soon as I can."

Mr. K. The name—or initial—landed like a stone in Frederick's gut. Whoever this Mr. K was, he had chosen a loose-lipped informant.

Air whooshed from his lungs.

Unless, of course, that was the point.

But if there was some Mr. K involved, it likely meant Lillias wasn't the murderer, didn't it? Yet, it seemed that *someone* wanted them to think so.

"How long had you worked for the Dixons?" Grace's question brought Frederick back to the conversation.

"Two months back." Miss Steen leaned back in her chair, folding her arms. "Started about a month before the babe was born, but I'd heard about them long before."

"Had you?" Grace continued.

"Reputations carry in small towns." Miss Steen answered. "And based on all I'd heard I should have known better than to take the position."

Frederick tilted his head. "Why is that?"

"Everyone knew about Mr. Dixon's gambling," Miss Steen said flatly. "Living with a man who can't control his vices is hard enough for a wife, let alone a child." She shook her head, her features dark with something that looked too personal to be feigned. "I grew up with a drunk. It's no life—always waiting for the next blow to fall."

Grace shifted beside him, her usual poise briefly disrupted. Frederick didn't need to look to know her thoughts were racing, no doubt rearranging the details into chapters and clues, the way she did with her favorite mysteries.

If the whole town knew not only about Tony Dixon's gambling but also any discord between him and Lillias, it didn't bode well for Lillias' reputation—or her defense.

"Are you saying"—Grace cleared her throat—"that Mr. Dixon was violent with his wife?"

"Violent?" The woman barked her laugh. "Not at all. He treated her as queenly as his funds would allow, letting her complain and shout to the top of her lungs about how poor they was. But he wasn't happy and neither was she is what I'm saying."

"So you found a household on edge when you arrived?" Grace leaned closer, her expression much too serious for his peace of mind. She felt it too. The hint of possibility that her sister may be in much more trouble than widowhood.

"Like you can't imagine." A ruthless grin erupted from the woman. "Those two were at each other's throats day and night—or at least during the little time he was home. And then the babe coming into the mix. . ." She shook her head, her voice dropping with weary finality. "The only peace anyone got was when Mr. Anthony was out gambling or Mrs. Lillias was asleep. That's the truth."

Frederick exchanged a look with Grace, a little apprehensive to voice the next question. With a deep breath, he turned to Miss Steen. "And do you know of anyone who would want to cause Mr. Dixon harm?"

Miss Steen snorted, a sharp, knowing sound. "You mean, besides his wife?"

Frederick shot a quick glance at Grace, whose face had gone pale. *Too pale.* He reached for her hand beneath the table, squeezing gently as he spoke. "It's a difficult accusation to make, Miss Steen."

"I'm just telling you what I saw," Miss Steen said, matter-of-factly. "Mr. Anthony wasn't exactly a saint and, truth be told, neither was she. But a woman can only take so much before something snaps." Miss Steen's eyes narrowed. "The fact is that house was a powder keg long before anyone lit the fuse."

Frederick's grip on Grace's hand tightened slightly. A powder keg, indeed—and they were standing squarely in its aftermath.

Besides Lillias?

Grace's thoughts froze, and a chill took up residence throughout her body.

Surely not.

Lillias wasn't capable of killing her own husband, or anyone else for that matter.

Was she?

After all, Grace had been the daughter in the family who'd indulged in all the gothic novels and mysteries, even staging her own investigations, which led to being trapped in a well in one instance and nearly arrested for trespassing on another.

But Lillias? She didn't even like to read!

Grace inhaled sharply, her mind racing. Perhaps *not* reading such stories had left her sister ill-equipped for life's darker troubles. Without a healthy dose of fictional woes, maybe Lillias' frustration had no proper outlet. A woman who never confronted imaginary perils might flounder in the face of real ones.

Truth be told, Grace had survived so many imaginary dangers, some of the real ones paled in comparison.

Thankfully, Miss Steen didn't seem to notice Grace's internal monologue, because she simply continued her answer, keeping her focus on Frederick.

"You can't really blame the woman," Miss Steen said, with a tone suggesting she could blame her quite easily. "Her husband was practically leaking money they didn't have. And she, being one of those high-and-mighty sorts, wanted to live in a certain way." She sent Grace a pointed look which only coiled the knot more tightly in Grace's stomach. "It was a mismatch from the start, I'd say. He didn't have the money to give her the life she wanted, and she didn't have the patience to manage life with less. Someone was going to break eventually."

Grace had read enough novels to steel herself against cavalier discussions of death—or so she thought. Her pulse betrayed her, racing ahead. Miss Steen's blunt assessment of Lillias and Tony's differences brought into sharp focus what Grace had been avoiding: the glaring plausibility of her sister's motive.

Grace hadn't considered—really considered—how deeply Lillias might have been affected by her circumstances. When they'd switched roles, Grace stepping into Lillias' place to marry Frederick, and Lillias marrying her child's father, Tony, the decision had seemed practical. The righting of a wrong.

But Lillias had been groomed for a world of gowns, servants, and soirées. Reduced circumstances might have felt like exile. And Father's financial ruin had made her position even more precarious.

But gowns and ballrooms don't lead to murder. Grace's breath hinged. Or did they?

She almost cringed.

And moral lapses weren't the same as murder, surely? Lillias' decision to deceive an earl and marry Tony hadn't been stellar, but Grace hadn't placed it in the same league as homicide. Then again, she and Frederick had encountered villains in their sleuthing—Celia Blackmore Percy had killed for status, Charles Smallwood for riches, and Daniel Laraby's treasure hunt had left bodies—including his own—in its wake.

The desire for money was terribly powerful.

And Grace's myriad fictional references only proved this all the more.

Determined to steer the conversation away from her sister, Grace leaned forward. "Were there any other possibilities? Someone who might have had a grudge against Mr. Dixon? Or perhaps Mrs. Dixon?"

Miss Steen tilted her head, unruffled. "Hard to say. Dixon was well-liked, far as I know. Though I wouldn't know much about his gambling crowd."

Frederick swept in with another question, likely noting Grace's befuddlement. "Is there a chance the murder was part of a robbery? Did the Dixons have anything worth stealing?"

Grace offered him a grateful smile. Yes. There was another possibility. Especially with the nasty false officer slinking around.

"I suppose there's always that chance." The woman offered a

nonchalant shrug. "The Dixons had more of the nicer things in their home than others in the neighborhood. Things that Mrs. Dixon brought from her father's house."

Oh, so perhaps her family hadn't lost all those wonderful heirlooms after all.

"What sorts of things?" Grace rushed ahead and quickly returned to a more "detective" character. "What would you have considered worth stealing, especially knowing the neighborhood as you do?"

Miss Steen puffed up a little at the comment, lifting her chin in thought. "Well, it's the usual things, except their home would have been prime pickings. What with the nice paintings and furniture. Even some of Mrs. Dixon's fine jewelry." Miss Steen nodded. "Some jealous or even clever neighbor or person within the social circles they frequented could have, I suppose, entered the house with that in mind."

The glint in Miss Steen's eyes as she mentioned Lillias' jewelry caught Grace's attention. Perhaps, Miss Steen wasn't as innocent as she appeared either. Or at least, Grace could focus on an option other than her sister.

"That information brings us to this morning." Frederick continued, looking all the more delightful with his tie just a little crooked. "Could you tell us your schedule before you arrived to find Mr. Dixon deceased?"

Miss Steen stiffened. "I ain't done nothing wrong."

"And I'm not implying you did," Frederick soothed. "We're simply trying to establish a timeline."

Miss Steen exhaled and nodded. "I got up early, had breakfast, then met Mrs. Dixon in her sitting room to collect the baby."

"And Mrs. Dixon seemed. . .well?" Grace pressed.

"As well as she ever was," Miss Steen replied, frowning. "She wasn't exactly cheerful. Always sad or angry about something—likely all the reasons I've already said."

"What happened next?" Frederick asked.

"I dressed the baby and took him for a walk in Carrollton Park."

"You returned directly after?" Frederick's tone remained neutral, though Grace detected the curiosity beneath it.

"Well. . ." Miss Steen hesitated, her face reddening. "I usually stop by the butcher's on the way back. Just to check sales for Cook."

Good heavens! Could the woman's face get any redder?

"Miss Steen." Frederick took his time, studying the woman, who looked away. "I feel as though there is more to your visit to the butcher's than you're confessing."

She swallowed audibly and looked away, pinching her lips closed. *What on earth?*

And then Grace understood. "Is there someone at the butcher's who you fancy, Miss Steen?"

The woman's face flushed a brilliant tomato hue. "Now that ain't none of your business. And I never let my visits interfere with my work."

Grace sent Frederick a look. Miss Steen's defensiveness confirmed it, though Grace decided to pivot gracefully, rescuing her from further embarrassment. "And Mrs. Dixon? What was she doing while you were out?"

"How should I know?" Miss Steen shrugged. "She didn't tell me her business."

A splash of cold unease slid over Grace's thoughts. For someone who fancied herself an amateur sleuth—her inspiration drawn liberally from the pages of Mary Roberts Rinehart—this wasn't her most brilliant moment. Her sister's life might depend on her wit, yet here she was, muddling through as if she were a dim-witted side character.

Frederick, far less prone to narrative despair, took the reins. "You mean to say she didn't accompany you?"

Then why would Lillias lie? Unless. . .

"Accompany me?" Miss Steen snorted. "The lady"—she laced the word with a sarcasm thick enough to spread on toast—"she wouldn't be caught dead walking with me. High-and-mighty types don't mingle with the help. Like I said, she put on airs. Once a grand dame, always a grand dame—until the bottom falls out. No wonder Mr. Dixon took to gambling."

Grace's mind raced. "Do you have any idea where Mrs. Dixon may have gone?" she asked, fighting the knot tightening in her throat. "Had she stayed at home?"

"Not a clue," Miss Steen said with another shrug. "She wasn't exactly confiding in me, now was she?"

Thankfully, Frederick intervened, because Grace was beginning to wonder if she knew her family at all. "One last question, Miss Steen. When was the last time you saw Mrs. Dixon before you left for your walk this morning?"

"Last I saw her was when I left the house with the baby." Miss Steen looked between the two of them. "She was dressed in her best and drove right past me in one of those cars, headed toward town."

But she was certainly back when Frederick and Grace had arrived.

Back and standing over Tony's dead body with a knife in her hand.

Grace pressed her eyes closed for a moment, attempting to process everything. Not to mention that her sister had lied about being on a walk with Miss Steen.

"Thank you for your time, Miss Steen." Frederick stood, offering his arm to Grace. "Please remain nearby in case you are needed. There is a good chance some officers may stop in tomorrow to engage in further investigation."

Miss Steen didn't answer, but walked with them to the door.

Frederick increased his pace to the car once the door closed behind them, leading Grace to the passenger side, before taking his own seat behind the wheel. No wonder he wanted to drive back. She was shaking like a leaf.

"I can't believe it," she whispered, looking back at the house.

"We've stumbled into something with claws, Grace." Frederick's tone was steady, but his grip on the steering wheel betrayed him. "And with this being your family, we'll need to stay especially sharp."

She nodded, drawing a deep breath, but it barely settled her nerves. Grace prided herself on her composure; now she felt like a trembling heroine in a Gothic novel. It wasn't her style. Her eyes fluttered closed for a moment, but as she rested her hands on her lap, the prick of something in her pocket drew her attention.

The letter. From Lillias to Miss Steen.

Grace pulled the note from her pocket as Frederick drove the car away from Miss Steen's house.

"I think we've earned the right to read this now," she said, unfolding it. "If nothing else, it might help us understand her state of mind."

Frederick glanced at her. "Or protect her from herself."

"What do you mean?"

"I'm not fully certain." He kept his attention on the road. "But I feel as if she's hiding something."

Which was a thought Grace had had during Detective Johnson's questioning. Her sister's reticence at times hinted to something more than just grief and shock over her husband's death. Something else wasn't quite right. Was it that Lillias didn't want to confess the difficulties in her marriage? Admit the financial fall?

Or was there something else she hid?

Grace opened the short letter, hoping to find Lillias begging Miss Steen to return to her duties, but she instead discovered Lillias' begging for something completely different.

I need you to tell the police I was with you on your walk this morning. I'll pay you a handsome sum if you do. You owe me for even giving you this job when you had no references. I'm counting on your cooperation, Louisa. Telling them otherwise would not bode well for either of us.

"She was bribing her for an alibi," she murmured, looking over at Frederick before reading the note aloud to him, her stomach knotting tighter with every word.

"Nothing is certain, Grace," he said, his voice softening. His gaze flicked to her, the tenderness there threatening to undo her entirely.

But Grace knew her fiction—and her facts. And in every genre she could think of, the clues pointed to the same devastating conclusion.

"No," she said, the words trembling on her lips. "But there's a very real possibility my sister murdered her husband."

Chapter 6

The Dixon house carried a strange sort of silence, as if the walls themselves mourned and shuddered at the events they had witnessed. Grace had recovered a sliver of composure on the ride back from Miss Steen's house, thanks to Frederick's steady reassurances and a good dose of silent prayer. But the very idea that her sister might hang for murder left her insides in an ongoing tremor.

"I don't envy the prospect of confronting Lillias about all this, Frederick," she admitted, pausing just inside the front entrance of the townhouse.

Frederick stopped beside her, his hand brushing her arm as his dark eyes searched hers. "Do you feel unsafe with her?"

Did she? Unsettled, perhaps. But unsafe? She shook her head slowly. "I can't believe she's capable of something so horrific. But the way the knife. . ." Her voice faltered.

He gave her arm a reassuring squeeze. "If you'd rather wait—"

"She needs to be prepared for the detective's questioning tomorrow, especially now that we have evidence she tried to buy an alibi from Miss Steen."

"Let's have a think first on our own. Then we'll speak to her. It will give you time to check on Zahra, and I can send a message to Mr. Barclay at the Clarion. Unless, of course, you'd rather draft it yourself?"

"Do you mind? I think it would be good to get some answers, don't you?"

"And perhaps a needed distraction?" he replied, a hint of a grin tugging at his lips.

"You know me too well." Her smile spread despite herself.

"Don't forget, darling." He straightened, adopting a mockingly serious expression and sending her a wink. "I *am* a detective, after all."

Grace nearly swooned. Words directly to her heart. Without another word, she rocked onto her toes and pressed a kiss to his lips. For all his cleverness, it was his calm strength that was the distraction she felt most at the moment.

He lengthened the embrace for a moment longer and then drew back. "Do you know where the kitchen might be?" He looked about the room with one brow playfully raised, continuing the needed levity of the moment. "I need to track down Lillias' errand boy, and I fear I'm terribly lost in this house."

"I think your detective skills will come in handy for that too."

His grin split wide before he turned and walked down the nearest hallway. Grace stood in the middle of the room, the presence of the police officer outside the front door only adding to the strangeness of the situation.

But was it strange? Truly.

She'd spent her entire marriage embarking on unexpected mysteries, and if something devastating could happen in Frederick's family, why not her own? It was a grim, equal-opportunity disaster.

Her shoulders tensed at the thought, but she drew in a deep breath and lifted her chin. If she'd learned anything through their adventures, it was that while she might have a knack for fictional mysteries, she wasn't too bad at solving the real ones, either.

And this mystery involved people she loved the most.

Clearly, God knew what He was doing by placing her right in the thick of it all.

She pushed aside her tangled emotions and set her mind on the mystery at hand. God had put *her* in this moment at such a time as this. She stood a little taller, like veritable Queen Esther.

The room appeared unchanged since her earlier visit. Even the bloodstain on the carpet between the two settees remained, a dark accusation in the otherwise genteel space. Most likely, with Lillias' reduced staff, no one had taken the stain in hand yet. Grace scanned the area with careful eyes. A crystal vase stood by the front door, untouched—an easy target for a thief, yet left behind. A beautiful watercolor painting, formerly of Rutledge House, hung prominently on a wall near the settees. Her father had once boasted about purchasing it for her mother at great expense. Not stolen.

She ventured farther, her eyes catching on other familiar objects. The front rooms were still lavishly appointed, the furnishings as elegant and ornate as those from the house she and Lillias had grown up in. But the illusion frayed the farther she walked.

The housekeeper had shown them to their rooms earlier, and the contrast had been startling. Frederick and Grace's room was sparse, with only a bed, a washstand, and a solitary landscape painting—another relic from their family home. The room meant for Miss Cox and Zahra was even barer, its walls devoid of any decoration.

For a woman who had adored extravagance her entire life, the barren spaces were completely out of character. Lillias had free rein of Rutledge House's treasures now. Why hadn't she taken more to decorate the other rooms?

She turned around in the main entry hall. And if a thief meant to steal something, they wouldn't have bypassed these easily accessible rooms or the treasures therein.

Some scuffs on the floor nearby drew her attention.

Small scratches could have been from anyone's shoes, but they were fresh, with a small trail of dirt. Could Tony have been killed somewhere else and then dragged into this room? And could Lillias have done that? Tony hadn't been a particularly large man, but it would have certainly taken a lot of work for Lillias to move him.

Grace's breath caught.

Unless, Lillias had an accomplice. Fake Officer Clark flashed to mind.

Grace gave her head a shake. It was quite probable that Lillias Ferguson Dixon did not kill her husband. Quite probable. Grace pushed through a hard swallow and took a few steps down the darkened hallway, following the dirt and minute scrapes on the floor.

The corridor wasn't long. A small study branched off on one side; a closet opened on the other. It ended at a door that led to the back garden. Unlike other townhouses in Harrington, this one backed onto a small, wooded park instead of another set of houses. The growing dusk blurred her view of the trees, and the scarcity of streetlamps in this quieter part of town cast long shadows over the ground.

It was the perfect spot for a clandestine meeting.

Or a murder.

But why would a murderer drag a body from outside into the house?

Her eyes widened as a sudden thought struck. Unless they wanted to frame Lillias. And if the murderer knew how to enter the house, they either had the time to work out an entrance, lived here already, or were intimately familiar with the property.

Which meant, he or she knew how to get inside again.

Or were already there.

A creak of the floor broke the silence behind her, and Grace was completely without her parasol. Usually, from what she'd read and even in Detective Miracle's book, a criminal returns to the scene of a crime because he'd left evidence behind and wished to retrieve it or because he hadn't finished the job. Grace scanned the space near her, but nothing proved a useable weapon, especially the rug, so she balled her hands into fists and spun around to find. . .empty space.

Until she looked a little lower than the possible culprit's height and stared into the face of Zahra. Air whooshed from Grace's body in a nervous laugh.

"Zahra." She bent to be closer to the little girl's level. "I love that you are excellent at being quiet, but maybe next time you could let me know you are close." Grace pressed a palm to her chest. "You surprised me."

"At the orphanage, we were all told to be quiet."

"Well, you're not in the orphanage anymore. You're with us," Grace said gently, taking the girl's hand. "And we want to hear from you."

Zahra tilted her head, studying Grace with an intensity that felt far too wise for a girl of ten—or however old she might be. No one seemed to know for certain.

"Miss Cox does not know about babies, Sayyidda." Zahra shook her head, her frown deepening, evidently taking Grace's words to heart and speaking her mind. "She is not smart with Thomas, but I have been teaching her while you were away."

"I'm so glad you are able, Zahra, however Miss Cox was hired to help you and me, not tend to babies." Grace squeezed the girl's hand and smiled.

Zahra looked unconvinced.

"But," Grace continued with a warm smile, "it's good you know about tending babies. I suspect I'll need your help one day when I have one of my own."

Zahra's gaze dropped to Grace's middle and her eyebrows rose.

"Do you have a baby growing inside you, Sayyida?"

Grace blinked at the directness of the question and then at the twinge of uncertainty swiveling up through her middle. Did she? From the talk she'd had with Frederick's Aunt Lavenia, she didn't feel any of the symptoms usually prescribed to a pregnancy. "I don't know."

"I will help you tend to the baby when it comes." Zahra nodded, her face as sober as usual. "Then you will want me to stay."

Grace sank to her knees, her heart tightening painfully. She clasped the little girl's hands in her own. "Zahra, we are your family now. That means we want you to stay whether you help or not. We've adopted you."

"Adopted?" Zahra echoed, frowning. "You say this word, but I do not know it."

Grace's heart ached. What a woeful mother she was turning out to be! She hadn't even considered that Zahra might not understand the depth of what *family* meant. To Zahra, "living" with Frederick and Grace likely felt no different than the transient stops she'd endured before: a mother's fleeting care, the streets, the orphanage. Merely existing under their roof, without any promise of belonging.

"Adopted means Frederick and I are your new parents," Grace said gently. "It means we'll care for you whether you're good or bad, whether you need us a little or a lot. It means you'll always have a home here, and more importantly"—she placed a hand over her heart—"you'll always have a place in here. Only you can fill it." She touched the little one's cheek. "We want to love you."

Zahra's brow creased as she studied Grace in silence and then, as if the conversation had never happened, she dipped her chin with a nod. "I will go help Miss Cox with the baby."

And back down the hallway she dashed.

Grace whispered a prayer heavenward for guidance and rose to her feet, brushing down her skirts. When she reached the main room, Frederick was striding toward her from the opposite hall.

"The message has been sent," he said. "But I doubt we'll hear from the Clarion until tomorrow."

Grace nodded and looked toward the stairway where Zahra had disappeared. "I do believe we need to talk more to Zahra about us being her parents. I don't think she fully understands that we're not sending her back to Egypt."

Frederick's expression softened as he followed her gaze. "Time and consistency will help. She's had little of either." He exhaled and turned back to her, his tone shifting. "But first, a more difficult conversation awaits. Do you want me to join you when you speak with your sister, or would you prefer to handle it alone? She and I have not really spoken since. . ."

Since he'd found out Lillias was trying to trick him into marrying her to cover up an unwed pregnancy and since learning of Father's actions to salvage a debt. A painful twinge pricked in Grace's chest, but she couldn't identify it, which always was worse than knowing what the feeling truly was. None of them had truly reconciled since Grace had taken her sister's place as Frederick's wife—Grace, the second choice. Second in beauty, second in charm.

And the marriage had not only meant to secure Frederick's estate's future with Grace's dowry, but hoped to move the family's dark reputation to more sure footing. With Father's debt and now Lillias as a possible murderess, Frederick had lost on both counts. And despite his sweetness toward her, the double sting had to hit so many things he valued. His home, his legacy, and his family's reputation.

"Would it be easier for you if I spoke to her on my own?"

The slight tension in Frederick's posture eased. Was he dreading the meeting as much as she was? Her heart twisted. He had so much to bear already, and here she was adding to it.

"I will go wherever you need me, darling." Yet the endearment held the same tenderness it always did. Could he continue to hold that sweet love for her after all these failures began to sink into reality?

Well, she certainly wouldn't add to his discomfort. She could face her elder sister alone. She'd done it before. Not often, though. And the last time had been to call her out on the entire marriage-pregnancy deception.

But she could do it alone.

"I think it's better if I face her alone," she said, more to steel herself than to reassure him. "Tomorrow will bring enough strain with the detective's interview after he speaks to Miss Steen."

"Very well." He held her gaze, nothing uncertain in those dark eyes. "But if you need me, I will be close."

She basked in his tenderness and drew in a breath. "Perhaps, you'd like to investigate the scratch marks we noticed on the floor from earlier while I meet with Lillias. They lead down a hallway to the outside." She gestured in the direction she'd come. "It seems that someone dragged Tony from there to place him quite obviously in the middle of the entry room."

Frederick's brows knit together, his gaze sharp. "An odd choice for your sister."

"I know. Which either means the murderer knew the house well enough to plant Tony's body in such a way as to frame Lillias or. . ." Grace hesitated, biting her lip.

"Lillias has an accomplice."

A thrill rose up through her at his choice of the word *accomplice.* He must have noticed her smile because he leaned forward and pressed a kiss to her forehead. "Detective talk and all that."

His tender whisper only twisted her guilt tighter. She caught his arm, her words spilling out. "Frederick, I'm so sorry for all the trouble this has brought to our door. So sorry for the deception and lies—and now scandal. I know I made light of our very first mystery together being about your family—"

"Grace."

"But now mine has caused an even darker situation! And we've lost funds for improvements to Havensbrooke, and—"

"Grace." His voice cradled her name, but the situation only kept getting worse.

"And now, to be dragged into this awful scandal with my sister after everything she did to you—"

"Darling."

The endearment worked like a charm, cutting through her momentary hysteria. She stilled, meeting his gaze.

"I don't have all the answers," he admitted, his voice softer. "But I've learned something from you." His lips tipped into a faint, knowing smile, and her own tugged upward in response despite herself. "To have the clearest head for this situation, we must focus our energy in the right place. Right now, what's important is finding answers for your sister. You needn't exhaust yourself worrying over future horrors conjured by your *very* creative mind."

His gentle teasing softened her frown further.

"I can't promise Lillias' situation isn't dire." He sobered, the weight of his words palpable. "But I *can* promise you this: My thoughts for *you* are secure. Havensbrooke may take time, but we'll manage it together. Do you understand?"

She nodded, desperate to hold fast to the security he offered. And yesterday, she would have done so without hesitation. But now—now, so many truths had surfaced in the past twenty-four hours, shifting the ground beneath her feet. Her sister's life hung in the balance, and Frederick's beloved estate teetered on the brink.

Grace prayed the next twenty-four hours wouldn't bring yet another revelation—a deception so great it could shatter Frederick's resolve beyond repair.

The cool evening air bit into Frederick's exposed face as he stepped out into the townhouse's back garden. A deep breath of night air filled his lungs, its chill seeping into his thoughts and dampening—just slightly—the rising tide of his concern.

He had told Grace the truth: His love for her was unshaken by the deceptions of her family or the financial blows to Havensbrooke. But Tony Dixon's murder and the unsettling revival of Lillias' lies had dredged up old insecurities. The ones that whispered he wasn't enough. That he was, and always had been, second best.

Initially, marrying Lillias had been a pragmatic decision—a dowry for a title. Yet that carefully laid plan had unraveled spectacularly, leaving Grace in its wake. Grace, with her irrepressible wit and warmth, had transformed his life. She'd made him believe in a future beyond obligation and legacy, loving him with a fierceness that refused to be diminished by his flaws. And without an ability to fight against such unfettered adoration, he'd grown to love her.

Fallen for her in turn, wholly and irrevocably.

More than Havensbrooke.

More than reputation.

If he'd learned nothing else, he thought with a grim twist of his lips, it was that God worked in situations in ways he could never understand, so worry about a future he had no ability to see only led to his own frustration and distraction.

And the last thing he needed right now was to be distracted.

He sighed and stepped forward, scanning the darkening area. Grace's earlier words echoed in his mind as his gaze trailed to a worn footpath leading from the house toward a forested park beyond. The scents of damp earth and hydrangeas mingled with the faint, acrid trace of coal smoke from the surrounding chimneys.

Crouching near the garden door, Frederick ran his fingers over scuffed boards and a faint trail of dirt. Subtle, but undeniable—a heel had dragged here, carving a groove through the grass. The image of Tony's bloodied body flared in his memory, and he frowned. The path extended farther toward the tree-covered park, where the trail grew faint but discernible.

Grace's voice echoed in his mind, her earlier question sharp and insistent: *Why move Tony's body into the house?*

He straightened, scanning the shadowed expanse ahead. The faint crunch of gravel underfoot—or was it just the rustle of leaves stirring in the evening breeze—pulled him toward the far side of the garden. His hand drifted to the pistol concealed beneath his jacket, a habit born of both his marriage to Grace and their propensity for falling into trouble.

Once their friend Detective Jack Miracle had succeeded in corralling them into a true criminal case, Frederick had accepted the presence of the weapon as a constant means of protection.

A distant bark broke the quiet, but nothing stirred nearby save for the trees swaying gently in the wind. He swept the area with another careful look and took a cautious step forward, his shoe catching on something hard and unyielding. Bending down, he brushed aside a scatter of leaves and twigs. A glint of polished silver met his gaze. He picked it up, holding it closer to catch some fresh hints of moon glow.

A cloak pin? The polished silver glinted in the dim light, its intricate design unmistakable to both his sight and feel.

A Celtic knot wove an intricate pattern around a gleaming emerald at its center.

What on earth was such a personal (and apparently expensive) item doing here? Turning the finely detailed pin over, he noted the faintest of inscriptions etched in Gaelic along the back. He didn't speak the language but knew a few words, none of which appeared on the inscription except one.

A Mhic.

My son.

This wasn't an ordinary piece of jewelry. It was deeply personal, its craftsmanship bespoke, its presence here profoundly out of place. Unease prickled at the back of his neck. Whoever had lost this pin wasn't likely to have done so casually. This pin was far too unique to belong to just anyone, and it was certainly out of place here in a modest townhouse garden in Harrington, Virginia.

He straightened, studying the path that led into the forested park. The smudges and drag marks continued faintly toward the tree line. He could follow them and risk exposure to danger or pocket the pin and retreat for the night.

A faint crunch of gravel drew his attention to the garden's far edge. Frederick froze, his fingers tightening around the pin. Another step forward, slow and cautious, revealed little beyond the faint play of shadows against the trees. He considered the drag marks leading farther into the park. Should he follow them now or retreat to plan his next steps by daylight?

He hesitated, the wind nudging him back toward the house as if urging caution. Decision made, he turned, but the relief was fleeting. A rush of footsteps shattered the quiet, and before he could fully pivot, a blinding pain exploded at the back of his head.

He stumbled, the world spinning, the ground rushing up to meet him. His arms faltered beneath him, and he tried to rise, but darkness clawed at the edges of his vision. Through the haze, a single thought burned clear: *I have to protect Grace.*

Pain crippled him back to the ground. His grip on the pin slackened, and as the world faded, he felt its weight lifted from his hand.

Then all went black.

Chapter 7

Grace smoothed her palms over the bodice of her dress, as if arranging armor, and knocked firmly on the door to her sister's room. From Miss Cox's report, when Grace had gone to check on the maid and Zahra, Lillias had only been out of her room once since entering it earlier, and that was to see little Thomas.

Not counting this morning, it had been seven months since Grace had last seen her sister, and their final exchange had not exactly been the kind one commits to sentimental recollection. Grace had cornered Lillias, demanding she confess her pregnancy to Frederick before the wedding. When Lillias refused, Grace had issued her ultimatum: "Tell him, or I will." Instead, Lillias had taken the third option—eloping with Tony under cover of night, leaving Grace to face both Frederick and their father's wrath alone.

Since then, the few letters Lillias had sent to Grace waxed stiff and eloquent about her provincial life as a banker's wife.

But now Grace understood why each letter felt shallow and weak.

Because they had been.

A gambling husband, a diminished household, and the ever-tightening squeeze of discontent: a threefold braid of discontent, all tracing back to that pivotal final conversation.

Guilt tempted a poisonous resurrection in her chest, but Grace shook her head. No, this wasn't her fault. Lillias had made her choice long before that confrontation—long enough, in fact, to create little Thomas.

Grace knocked again, more insistently this time. Lillias' voice, faint but audible, summoned her forward.

The room was a startling oasis of opulence, a stark contrast to the rest of the house. Paintings Grace recognized from Rutledge House adorned the walls, and a light oak bedstead with gilded edges dominated the room. The heavy curtains, fine wallpaper, and marble fireplace spoke to a life Lillias had clearly curated as compensation for everything else.

"I'm having Dorothy serve supper to you in your rooms," Lillias said from her place in a high-back chair positioned in the alcove of windows. "I haven't the inclination for socializing this evening."

Her sister's pale face and frown drew Grace farther into the room. "Of course not. No one would expect it, Lillias. And Frederick and I will tend to ourselves and the others, for the next few days, if that would relieve you."

Her sister looked up, her light blue eyes red-rimmed and tired. "I would appreciate that."

Grace's fight died a little and she continued her path into the room. "If there are other ways we can be of assistance, please let us know. Frederick and I both wish to help you."

One blond brow arched in response. "Can you find the person who killed my husband?"

Just having Lillias ask the question relieved some of Grace's concern. If Lillias wanted help to locate Tony's killer then it was less likely her sister was a part of his death, wasn't it?

"That's exactly what we mean to do." Grace took the question as invitation to sit across from her sister. "Which is why I've come to speak with you. I believe you have information that will help us try to figure this all out."

Lillias' eyes widened before her lips tipped crooked. "*You* mean to find the person who murdered Tony?"

Grace sat up straighter, offering her sister a reassuring smile. "I mean to try."

"You're serious." Lillias grin grew into a puff of a laugh, before her gaze trailed down Grace's body, leaving a strange sort of unease in Grace's stomach.

"Grace, this isn't one of your novels. This is real life." Lillias looked over at her as if speaking to a young child. "Though I appreciate your intentions, this task is not for you, little sister."

Grace blinked, her mind turning over the tone, the look—at once familiar and yet startlingly new. Had she misread it all these years? Had what she'd once dismissed as harmless endearment always been cloaked in condescension?

Her throat tightened, an unwelcome knot forming. Had she been so naive? So blind? What else in her past, taken for truth, was merely another lie wrapped in sibling civility?

"Lillias," Grace began, forcing her voice steady, "haven't you read my letters? I've been involved in much nastier business than this over the past few months, and none of it had anything to do with my imagination." She paused, reconsidering. Her imagination *had* gotten away from her a time or two, but still, it had all been undeniably real. "One involved almost being buried alive in a tomb, and the other—well, let's just call it a treasure hunt. Not that I was looking for treasure, but some very unpleasant people certainly were."

Lillias rolled her eyes. "There's no need to exaggerate. I'm sure your life as a countess is terribly exciting."

Words sputtered and died before Grace could push them out. Exaggerate? She rarely exaggerated. Life had proven itself more colorful and adventurous than any flourish she might add. Yet here she was, suddenly feeling absurd, as though caught playing dress-up. The sensation was achingly familiar, dredging up memories of their childhood relationship.

Grace's jaw tightened. "I'm not exaggerating."

"Of course not." Lillias' tone was smooth, infuriatingly placating. "I can see how inventing these little stories might help you adjust to such an unfamiliar role. After all, you were never raised for this kind of life, were you? Not as *I* was."

Grace studied her sister. Had Lillias always seen her as a simpleton? Yes, Grace adored stories—true, embellished, or entirely fictional—but her sister's words twisted that love into something trivial, laughable. Was that how she saw Grace? Truly? And though stepping into her role as Frederick's wife hadn't been without its awkward moments, Lillias made it sound as though Grace had stumbled through it like a village idiot.

To be honest, Frederick's staff had certainly suffered their share of shocks. And Frederick himself had as well.

But those looks of bewilderment had dwindled over the months—mostly.

Her shoulders dropped. Until today.

But that wasn't Grace's fault.

"I'm not making up stories, Lillias. And though being a countess certainly wasn't in my plans, I've adored getting to be Frederick's wife." And how had the conversation gone from Lillias as a possible murderer to Grace as a misplaced countess? Had Lillias excelled in this type of deflection in conversation all these years, turning fault and blame elsewhere?

Air shook from Grace in a shuddered sigh. Did she even know her own family? "Everything I wrote to you was true," she continued. "If you don't believe me, you can ask Frederick yourself. In fact, Detective Miracle asked Frederick and me to join him on his last case a—"

"Detective Miracle? His last *case*?" Lillias cut her off with a humorless laugh. "Do you hear yourself? Grace, you are not a detective, and you certainly shouldn't involve yourself in such dangerous nonsense. Poor Lord Astley. You've probably made him the laughingstock of all England."

Grace opened her mouth to respond, but no words came. Her thoughts scattered like a flock of startled birds. She didn't even know the woman before her.

It was only the crinkle of paper in her hand that brought her back to something solid. Something tangible. Something that mattered more than her sister's insults.

The scene cleared in her mind. She'd never expected her sister to be a Lady Catherine de Bourgh, but. . .here she was! Incarnate!

Which meant that Grace would have to shore up her inner Lizzie Bennet, wouldn't she?

She straightened, holding the letter aloft. "Please explain this."

Lillias froze, just for a moment, before her expression smoothed into practiced indifference. "I thought you were going to deliver that letter to my former maid," she said lightly, turning toward the window. "I see your need for adventure has led you to pry into private matters."

"Private matters?" Grace fisted the paper, a little uncertain what to do with the growing anger inside of her. "You told us this was a letter to ask Miss Steen back into service, but instead, you offered her money to lie about your whereabouts."

"And what if I was?" Lillias' tone was airy, dismissive. She stood and moved toward the window, her back to Grace. "I hardly see how it concerns you."

"It concerns me because you lied, Lillias," Grace snapped and stood, this moment too similar to one of the last conversations she'd had with her sister, calling her out on her deception of attempting to marry Frederick under false pretense. "Don't you see how that looks? It makes you suspicious."

Lillias turned, her expression hardening. "You don't understand anything, Grace. You never have. You're too busy playing detective, running about with your ridiculous notions, to grasp the reality."

Grace's breath hitched, but she refused to falter. "Then help me understand. Why would you need Miss Steen to lie? Where were you?"

"It doesn't matter." Lillias waved a hand, as if brushing away Grace's concerns. "I'm certain Miss Steen will see reason."

"Reason?" Grace barked out a laugh so sharp it even surprised her. "She's more than willing to give you up, Lillias. She told us of the fighting and the gambling, and she will happily tell the officers when they arrive tomorrow."

Lillias' composure faltered. "You think the officers will believe a gossiping maid over a lady of my standing?"

"They'll believe proof, and right now the only person with proof of her whereabouts is Miss Steen." Grace fisted her hand at her side, attempting to gain some composure. . .some understanding of what lay behind her sister's behavior. "You very well could be suspect in your own husband's death."

Grace hadn't meant to say things so plainly, but there it was.

And she didn't regret it.

Lillias' hand flew to her chest, but her chin remained high. "That's absurd. I would never kill my own husband."

"Would or wouldn't, the officers will decide. They'll examine the debts, the secrecy, the"—Grace hesitated, choosing her words carefully—"the disharmony in your home."

Lillias laughed, brittle and cold. "Disharmony? We hated each other by the end!" Her voice cracked, her pale blue eyes glistening as she turned back to the window. "Do you think I wanted this life? A shabby townhouse, no money, no respect? A husband who gambled away everything while you"—she whirled back, eyes blazing—"while you prance about as a countess, married to the man who should have been mine."

"You think I *wanted* to take your place?" Grace moved forward, her high-pitched voice foreign to her own ears. "I stepped in because you left me no choice, Lillias! You lied to all of us, and I won't be made to feel guilty because you are unhappy now. You made your choices, and I had to make mine for the good of our family."

And thanks be to God, He'd redeemed the choice and made it so much better than Grace had ever dreamed.

"And now you're reaping the rewards," Lillias sneered, words laced with sarcasm. "It's easy to play the noble savior from your lofty position as countess."

Grace's grip on the letter tightened. "I never tried to be anything but myself," she said, then paused. *Except, perhaps, when donning disguises for cases. But surely that didn't count.* "You were the one pretending, and it hurt everyone."

"You know I would've been a better match for Frederick than you," Lillias spat. "I know the rules. I could've upheld his title. But you—you've turned him into a joke with your wild escapades." She stepped closer, the fire in her eyes unlike anything Grace had ever seen before. "And you came along and took it all away, didn't you? Ruining all my plans."

Grace blinked, trying to piece together how her sister had managed to twist the narrative so tightly that Grace was somehow the villain in this story. True, she didn't exactly embody the grace and poise of the aristocracy. And it was true she'd left more than a few people shocked and perhaps offended by her lack of training in the art of high-class English living, but Frederick didn't regret it. And their adventures together had saved lives. Helped people.

Grace fought against the fear wiggling up through her middle, clawing at insecurities she thought she'd put to rest months ago.

"Your *plans* were going to ruin several people's lives all at once, and I couldn't stand by and let it happen. I only meant to help everyone we love."

"You've helped enough, *little* sister."

But the endearment had taken on a darker turn, meant to put Grace in her place.

She refused its power. "Please stop calling me that."

For a fleeting moment, Lillias looked startled. And then her lips curved into a smile so cutting, it could open letters. "Should I refer to you as your ladyship, then?" All attempt at cloaking any disdain vanished from her sister's tone.

Grace let out a breath she hadn't realized she was holding. Pieces of the past snapped together with the present, forming a grim mosaic of this newer, colder version of Lillias Ferguson Dixon. "I will not carry the weight of your jealousy, Lillias. A man is dead, and you are quite possibly in danger of being charged with his murder. And believe it or not, I've actually helped solve crimes like this. So instead of arguing over your petty ideas of who has gained what in life, you might try searching for answers—either within yourself or in the actions of others."

The words left her lips before she could second-guess them. But as they echoed in the room, Grace felt something shift. Not in Lillias—her sister's expression was as stony as ever—but in herself. A growing sense of clarity, of purpose.

Grace took a step back, her body trembling, her eyes burning with unshed tears she was determined not to release in front of her sister. "Tony's death wasn't just a 'mishap,' and you know it. You have a choice, just like you did when I found out about your pregnancy. You can choose to do what's right—or not. But when it comes to situations like this, there's only so much any of us can do to help you."

She turned toward the door, her hand on the knob, desperate

for an exit. For air. For a moment to think. But just as she began to pull it open, the door burst wide, slamming against the wall with a force that rattled the room.

A man stumbled through, his face pale, his hands stained with blood.

Lillias screamed.

But Grace took in the scene.

This wasn't just any man. No, the bloodied hands and wild-eyed panic belonged to none other than Grace's own Lord Astley.

The only thing on Frederick's mind was finding Grace.

He wasn't entirely sure how long he'd been unconscious. The moon hadn't seemed to have moved much in the sky, but with the pounding in his head, time felt like an unreliable companion. On the third attempt, he managed to rise, steadying himself with a hand against the house. The door hung ajar, a gaping invitation for trouble. His pulse quickened. Had his assailant left something else behind? Or worse, gone inside?

With the police officer on guard at the front of the house, anyone could have access from the back. Frederick pushed forward, up the steps into the hallway, stopping only when his dizziness forced him to steady himself against the wall.

It took what seemed forever to climb the stairs with him almost losing the contents of his stomach before making it to the top, but once his feet hit the solid ground of the upper level, his head began to clear a little. He reached up to touch the more bruised area at the back of his head only to bring his hand back covered in blood.

Lovely. That explained the throbbing, the nausea, and the nagging sense of déjà vu.

The memory flashed—Christmas, forcibly removed from his own home (he refused to use Grace's term of *man-napped*), only to be knocked unconscious when he attempted an ill-fated escape. At least this time, he hadn't been tied to a chair. Small blessings.

A raised voice echoed down the hall, clear and unmistakable. Grace. But angry? He stumbled, wondering if the hit to the head impacted his hearing. His wife rarely raised her voice except, perhaps, in joy. And angry? His body surged into motion. He busted through the door, ready to protect his wife from some villain who'd sneaked into the house, only to find her and her sister in the room.

Grace turned wide eyes on him.

Lillias screamed.

Frederick blinked at the pair of them, focusing on Grace as he waited for the room to stop spinning. "Are you all right?"

"Me?" Grace crossed the space between them in an instant, her gaze scanning his face. "Heavens, Frederick, what happened?" She took him by the arm and drew him toward a chair across the room.

Lillias backed farther away, her palm over her mouth.

"Attacked," he muttered, easing into the chair with a groan. "In the back garden. Thought he might've come inside."

Two warm palms rested against his cheeks, and he opened his eyes to find Grace examining his face. "Where does it hurt?"

His lips quirked despite the pain. "Back of the head. Knocked me out cold. But"—he hesitated, glancing at Lillias, who now looked like she might faint at any moment—"there were signs of a struggle. I think he came back to search for something he lost in the fight."

Her brows lifted. "You found something?"

"Yes, but he took it when he fled. Whatever it was, he wanted it badly enough to risk coming back."

Grace's gaze shifted toward the door, and Frederick followed it. Zahra hovered in the threshold, her small frame rigid and her face unnaturally pale.

He began to push himself out of the chair, but Grace's hand on his shoulder stopped him. In his current state, it didn't take much.

"He is going to be fine, Zahra." Grace cooed out the phrase as Zahra's attention switched from Grace back to Frederick. Her lost expression nearly pulled him from the chair. Had she seen similar things in her young life? Worse, probably. "But would you mind fetching Miss Cox? I think we could certainly use her assistance."

Zahra lingered for a heartbeat, then nodded and dashed from the room.

"Do—do you mean that the man who killed Tony was just outside the house?" Lillias stammered. She clung to the back of the chair as if it might save her from fainting.

"It seems so," Grace replied, though her attention stayed fixed on Frederick. She lowered herself to her knees beside him, taking his hand in hers. "We only parted less than half an hour ago. You couldn't have been unconscious long."

He closed his eyes, hoping to stave off the wave of nausea threatening to crest. "The pin was near the back garden wall."

"Pin?" Grace's voice came soft, but there was no denying the interest in it. "What sort of pin?"

He opened his eyes, holding her gaze. "Scottish."

"Scottish?" Grace breathed the word, and he could see her mind spinning faster than her driving. "Frederick. The inheritance? Do you think it could be a coincidence?"

He attempted a half-smile but felt it falter. "What does Detective Miracle say about coincidences?"

Her fingers squeezed his, and the familiar gleam returned to her eyes, brighter now than he'd seen all day. He'd always admired how quickly she could go from nurturing to razor-sharp sleuth.

"There is no such thing as a coincidence—only clues we haven't discovered yet."

Chapter 8

After witnessing her darling husband in such a state and knowing he could have died yet again—this time at the hands of some nefarious fiend—Grace decided it was time to set aside her sisterly frustrations and don her proverbial sleuthing hat. As any good detective knew, there was no time for pettiness when life and death were on the line.

Lillias, naturally, had nearly fainted at the sight of Frederick's wound, so Grace had sent her to fetch one of the servants in order to call a doctor and the police.

And here they were, an hour later, with Frederick stubbornly insisting on speaking to the police, despite the fact that it was well past midnight and he'd just been knocked unconscious.

The doctor seemed much more concerned about the way in which Frederick was wounded, than the actual injury, which simultaneously impressed and annoyed Grace. Her dear husband could have died.

Though, if Grace were honest, she'd had more than enough practice with the impending sense of Frederick's demise. Several times throughout their marriage, she'd thought him lost to her—dead or near enough to it—and a few more times, she'd even daydreamed about it, in a dark, maudlin sort of way. But tonight? Tonight felt different.

For some reason, it seemed darker, more dangerous. Perhaps because it was her family involved this time.

And the clearer view of her sister's mindset brought shadowy talons into the present.

Having been away from Lillias for all these months and having matured herself, Grace found herself reframing previous scenes with Lillias based on her sister's current actions and words. Other moments of similar condescension and dismissiveness. Other times when Lillias had been secretive or even laughed at Grace and her love of books and mysteries.

At the time, Grace had seen them as simple teasing, but had they been more? A jealousy underneath all along? Or had her feelings taken this turn once Lillias felt the sting of her reduced circumstances since marrying Tony?

And could those feelings have led her to murder?

For the first time, Grace wasn't too certain she wanted to solve a mystery. Not this one, anyway.

"Are you sure you want this conversation to happen now?" Grace asked, her arm tucked through Frederick's as they made their way downstairs to the study. It was more to steady him than anything else—he seemed to be holding himself together well enough, but his pallor prevented her from experiencing complete peace of mind.

"There are too many moving parts to delay." Frederick searched her face, his brow furrowing as he added, "What if you'd been the one out in the garden?"

She slowed them to a stop in front of the study door, where Detective Johnson and Officer Todd waited at Frederick's request. "We've had this discussion several times before, my dear Lord Astley. Only God has the power to protect us fully."

"But He gave us wits to use as well." He narrowed his eyes at her in an attempt at mock seriousness. He knew, as well as she did, that they had both teetered on the edge of something awful tonight. The teasing helped her heart stay steady, if only just.

"And we need more help than just ourselves in this situation, Grace," he added, his voice softer but no less resolute.

Her gaze swept over his face, noting that some pink had returned to his cheeks. "I know."

The tension around his eyes softened, and he squeezed her hand. "I will be all right."

She studied him a moment longer, a frown tugging at the corner of her mouth, then nodded before Frederick opened the door and led them into the study.

Detective Johnson stood from the nearby chair and Officer Todd turned at their entry. "Lord Astley, I am glad to see you upright considering your recent attack."

Frederick nodded to the man and led Grace to a nearby chair, taking the couch next to her for himself. "I am well enough, Detective, thank you."

"And Mrs. Dixon?" Officer Todd looked toward the doorway, expectantly.

"The doctor gave her something to help her sleep, as she was quite"—Grace tried to figure out which word would be best—"overrun with her nerves."

Yes. That seemed a perfect descriptor. Her sister appeared on the brink of some sort of breakdown. Hopefully, in a less homicidal direction.

"That doesn't seem to be your predilection, Lady Astley." Detective Johnson tipped his head, studying her with the faintest glint of amusement. "Not the swooning sort?"

"Not from dangers, sir," She shot back, a little pleased at her quick and somewhat subtle retort. She looked over at her husband. She wasn't a swooning sort of woman, but exceptions to that rule always came because of him, and she wasn't about to admit that to the detective.

"Clearly." Johnson turned his attention back to Frederick as Grace helped her husband adjust his position on the nearby couch. "And you felt this meeting necessary tonight, Lord Astley."

Frederick raised his gaze to the man. "Based on some information we've gathered today."

"Information you've gathered?" Officer Todd scoffed, his arms crossed in an unflattering stance. "And what exactly do you mean by that?"

Grace narrowed her eyes at the boorish man. Her husband was exceptionally impressive. Just wait until they saw him cane fighting. Or wielding a pistol. Or deciphering clues. Her cheeks grew hot at the loveliness of the memories. Officer Todd, no doubt, couldn't look nearly as dashing while embroiled in such villain-fighting moments.

The detective exchanged a look with the officer, and Todd frowned but said no more.

"Though we do have a history as sleuths, Detective, this time our involvement was much less intentional." Grace clarified. "And the information found us more than we found it."

The detective raised an eyebrow, clearly skeptical, but settled himself in the chair across from them. "What has happened?"

Frederick took a steadying breath and proceeded to recount their visit to Miss Steen's house as well as the attack in the back garden, his words as thorough as any detective could hope for. Grace couldn't help the proud smile that tugged at her lips. Clearly, the knock to the head hadn't hurt his memory at all. Nothing like what she'd read about in other mysteries. One man even forgot who he was and didn't remember for seven entire chapters!

How delightful to have a husband whose mind wasn't easily scrambled.

"Let me get this straight," Johnson began, his tone measured. "You, Lord and Lady Astley, ventured out to interview Miss Steen without notifying me—"

"As I mentioned before, Detective, our intention wasn't to interview her at all." Then Grace frowned at the unintended hint of a lie in her words. Of course, she was always trying to discover more information about a mystery. "Well, not entirely. We did mean to deliver the letter, but if Miss Steen offered us information, we were hardly about to refuse it, especially in the interest of finding Tony's murderer."

"But as I mentioned," Frederick continued, "we never delivered Mrs. Dixon's letter. Miss Steen, however, thought we were part of the investigation and provided us with information, as well as mentioning a man who had paid her for information—Mr. K."

"Rather inconspicuous, isn't it?" Johnson quirked an eyebrow, his tone dry.

"And Lillias' letter wasn't the heartfelt plea for reconciliation she'd told us that it was." Grace continued. "Instead, it was an attempt to coerce Miss Steen into providing a false alibi for Lillias—an entirely fabricated account of her whereabouts this morning."

The detective's gaze lingered on her for a long moment. "And you're certain of this?"

"Miss Steen was quite forthcoming," Frederick pressed his fingers into his forehead, still suffering from the effects of his attack. "She also mentioned she made contact with several people during her morning walk, all of whom could verify her whereabouts."

"Yet you still believe Mrs. Dixon is innocent?" Johnson asked, his tone even but probing.

Grace straightened. "Lillias may be hiding something—she *is* hiding something—but we don't believe she killed Tony. Or at least, if she was part of it, she didn't give the death blow."

Detective Johnson's brows flew upwards, but Grace couldn't

fathom why. The phrase "death blow" seemed perfectly accurate to her. Wasn't that the sort of thing detectives were supposed to get excited about?

"Then why lie about her whereabouts?" the detective pressed. "If she wasn't the main culprit, it's possible she was a party to it—especially given the unhappy marriage."

Grace couldn't help but bite her lip in thought. "I'm sure there are many unhappy marriages that don't end in murder," she suggested, but the words hung in the air uncertainly. Of course, in her extensive reading—fictional as it was—there was usually a fair balance. But perhaps, in this case, it was best to err on the side of optimism. *One can hope, at least.*

"Yet there are some that do." Detective Johnson's gaze sharpened.

"Well, yes," Grace conceded, refusing to relinquish her point in a grasp to save her sister. "But there are also plenty of mysteries where the murderer is someone entirely unexpected."

"And there is still the quandary of the suspicious man who paraded himself about as Officer Clark." This from Frederick. "It's possible he murdered Mr. Dixon, dragged him back into the house for Mrs. Dixon to find, and then waited outside for the discovery—*conveniently* in time to alert you and your officers. As you said earlier, it was all. . .very convenient."

"Convenience," Johnson mused, stroking his chin, "is the height of suspicion."

"That's what Detective Miracle says too." Grace couldn't resist the tiny grin that crept across her face. Their friend Jack seemed to have a habit of saying rather memorable things, most of them involving some obscure deduction about society or human nature. Johnson, however, did not seem to share her fondness for Jack's sayings. The detective's lips tightened, and a fleeting frown passed across his face.

"And where do you believe Mrs. Dixon was during the time of

her husband's murder?" This from Officer Todd, who'd remained poised against the wall during the entire conversation, his arms crossed in front of him, and eyes at a constant narrow.

Grace opened her mouth, paused, and then lifted her chin. "I don't know yet. But I fully intend to find out. I only need another conversation with her. Our last one was"—Grace's face grew hot at the memory of her sister's barbed words—"Uneventful, well, except for the part where Lord Astley showed up with a head wound. That was quite eventful."

A flicker of amusement crossed Johnson's face, though it vanished as quickly as it appeared. "I admire your determination, Lady Astley, but I must caution you—this isn't some sort of game. Real-life investigations require precision and restraint, not whimsy."

"Whimsy?" Grace repeated. What a strange word to use as a description for a very thoughtful sleuthing approach. "I assure you, Detective, my approach is entirely methodical, if, at times, accidental. And I wouldn't be surprised if whimsy didn't help matters along a little bit too. I'm certain you must use creativity in your cases as well as method."

Frederick pressed his fingers to the bridge of his nose his lips twitching at one corner.

"You know that I could have you both questioned for injecting yourself into this investigation or interfering with—"

"We don't mean to interfere, Detective." Grace rushed ahead. No need to have the man thinking the wrong idea when help was quite literally in front of him. "We are assisting. Like the Baker Street Irregulars, only—"

"Only married to a peer and decidedly not a street urchin," Frederick interrupted dryly.

"And with considerably more. . .propriety," Grace added, her smile spread full at her husband.

Frederick shot her a raised-brow look.

Well, swinging on ropes and swimming in rivers likely didn't meet the mark for *propriety*.

"In truth, Detective Johnson." Frederick continued. "We have no desire to interfere. Only assist, where we are able."

"And this is exactly how all of our other cases started." Grace added, hoping to help the bewildered-looking detective to understand. "We weren't *looking* for them. They just happened."

"Lady Astley," Johnson said slowly, his expression unreadable, "I'm not exactly sure why, but I feel as though you have a certain magnetism toward mishap."

Now, that wasn't very nice. As if she didn't have any sense to know her own mind. "That implies I'm drawn against my will, Detective, and I'm afraid to say that's simply not true."

A cough from Frederick drew Grace's attention. The slight twist of his lips revealed one of his covert laughs. But what had she said to amuse him? She shrugged off the curiosity. If laughter was medicine, then let him find it wherever he could. Heaven knew he certainly needed a strong dose after such an attack.

Detective Johnson's lips twitched, but he quickly smoothed his expression and pressed on. "And you believe the injury your husband sustained in the garden is connected to Miss Steen's confession?"

"Not directly," Frederick intervened. "However, it seems Mr. Dixon was dragged in from outside after a scuffle in the garden. The person who attacked him returned later to retrieve a missing pin."

"Exactly like in *The Mystery of Blackwood Hall!*" Grace offered, nodding toward Detective Johnson as if he might know the reference. "Although, in that case, it was the butler who—"

Frederick's pointed cough cut her off.

Grace clamped her mouth shut. Oh, right. Clearly, Detective Johnson wasn't the type to indulge in fictional whodunits. He probably read biographies. Or Melville.

"What appears to be of note here, Detective," Frederick continued, "is that I was attacked while Lady Astley was speaking with her sister, which would suggest Mrs. Dixon is not the one who attacked me."

"And Lillias faints at the sight of blood," Grace added helpfully. "It's rather unlikely she'd kill Tony, let alone stage his body so. . . theatrically. Could someone have moved him to implicate her?"

"Or," Johnson interjected, his gaze narrowing, "as you suggested earlier, she has an accomplice." He paused, studying them as if trying to gauge their trustworthiness. Beside him, Officer Todd lit a cigarette and exhaled a cloud of smoke with the air of a man deeply unimpressed.

"What can you tell me about Mr. Dixon?" Johnson asked finally, his focus shifting to Grace.

"Well," Grace began, straightening. "His father was a friend of ours. He served as the gardener at Rutledge House, our family estate. Tony lived in the gardener's cottage until about a year ago, when he transitioned to banking. As far as I knew, he was good-natured and kind, especially to me."

"And your sister chose to marry a banker?" The detective tipped his head a little, the glint in his eyes making Grace feel a little nervous. "After having lived in the affluence of your father's home?"

Grace glanced at Frederick for reassurance and found him nodding. Oh, how she loathed retelling this story. But the truth was unavoidable. She recounted overhearing Tony and Lillias' dalliance at Whitlock, Lillias' confession, Grace's confrontation, and the ultimate elopement.

As she spoke, Detective Johnson tilted his head so far to the right at one point that he resembled a curious owl. Officer Todd, who had taken exactly one drag from his cigarette, let it dangle forgotten in his hand.

After a pause much longer than expected, the detective

responded. "It seems," he began carefully, "both your sister and Mr. Dixon have a pattern of secrecy and reckless decisions. His gambling only reinforces that. Were you aware of it?"

"No more than you, Detective." Frederick shook his head. "We arrived in America yesterday and in Harrington this morning."

"And Lillias mentioned nothing about it in her letters," Grace added.

"Just this morning? Yes, I recall it now." Detective Johnson rose, and Grace and Frederick followed. Well, Grace followed; Frederick wavered before steadying himself with Grace giving a bit of support.

"I believe we've imposed on you long enough, Lord Astley. You're clearly in need of rest after today's events." Johnson moved to the study door but paused, turning with a heavy glance. "However, I must place your sister under house arrest. Her history and recent actions don't inspire confidence in her innocence."

Grace stiffened, holding her tongue from defending her sister. Of course Detective Johnson was right. Her sister did look guilty. In almost every way except physical ability. But in motive? Planning? Ingenuity?

Her heart sank. Yes.

They followed the detective and Todd to the front door, where Johnson paused to look back at them. "I have a few inquiries to make tomorrow and will visit Miss Steen, as planned, but I advise the two of you to stay alert." His gaze landed on Grace. "I'll double the patrols in case your assailant returns."

"Thank you, sir." Frederick closed the door behind them and turned to Grace, a weary smile half formed. "I have high hopes that the dramatics are at an end for the evening."

Grace stepped forward, wrapping her arms around Frederick's waist and pressing her head into the crook of his neck, as though sheer proximity could infuse him with the strength he'd expended that day. "I think we'd both benefit from a decent night's sleep after such a day."

His arms circled her, drawing her deeper into his embrace. He rested his chin against the crown of her head, exhaling heavily. "Indeed."

She tugged him toward the staircase, noting the slight drag in his step. His usually assured gait had given way to weariness, likely from a potent mix of exhaustion and the earlier attack. "Especially you."

Frederick paused mid-step, flashing her a sleepily amused grin. "Now whatever could you mean, my lady?"

How she loved him! And levity certainly seemed a better choice at the moment than more brain work.

"Oh, just that you've had a rather spectacular day of heroism and deserve some much-needed rest to protect that sharp wit of yours."

He chuckled, allowing her to guide him up another step. His weight leaned on her ever so slightly, a subtle reminder that he trusted her implicitly. That he believed in her.

All this while, she'd accepted his part as protecting her, of being the wiser and cleverer of the two of them. Perhaps for the first time, she realized he also relied on her. Not in some grand, sweeping way, but in the small things—her perspective, her thoughts, her steadiness.

But even today, Frederick had shown in small ways his belief in her abilities. In her being his equal. He considered her thoughts, allowed her to drive, looked to her for clarity.

It was a jarring thought, one at odds with how she'd been feeling since her conversation with Lillias. Her sister had always loomed large in her life, both as a source of admiration and insecurity. But in comparison to Frederick—his unwavering belief in her, the quiet way he invited her to be his equal—Lillias' endless criticisms and coldness felt brittle and irrelevant. How odd, to have lived an entire life with someone and only to realize how broken the relationship was when given a healthy comparison.

"Heroism, is it?" Frederick's voice drew her from her thoughts as they reached the first landing.

"Well," she said, tilting her head with exaggerated deliberation, "you've always been rather heroic. But today you not only survived an attack—you also endured my driving."

His laugh came easier this time, a low rumble that made her chest warm. "You do add a certain. . .unpredictability to my life, darling."

Darling. Exactly how he made her feel. Which seemed all the more poignant in light of everything happening now. He was her home, her future.

Her sister's influence was in the past.

"I do wonder how Tony's gambling may play into all this."

Grace shot him a look. "Yes. I've thought of that too. People do tend to wind up dead after cheating at cards, don't they?"

"Let's hope it's not as common as the novels suggest," Frederick said, as they finally crested the last step to the bedroom hallway. "But it's certainly possible."

Her brow furrowed as a new thought struck her. "And this fake Officer Clark? His timing was far too convenient, not to mention his disguise. Do you think he could be Mr. K?"

The name sent a shiver down her spine. It was just the sort of ominous alias one might find in *The Adventures of Sherlock Holmes.* She could almost hear Holmes' measured voice drawling about the "diabolical mind of Mr. K."

But this wasn't a novel. She couldn't simply close the book when things grew tense (not that she'd ever abandon a story mid-chapter).

This was personal—painfully so. Her sister's betrayal, her family's deceit, the danger they'd invited to Frederick's doorstep.

And the pointed attacks from her sister felt much less manageable than the possibility of a Scottish murderer lurking outside of the townhouse.

"I don't know," Frederick murmured, sitting heavily on the edge of the bed. "But do be careful, darling."

She moved to his side, deftly sliding his jacket off his shoulders. His wonderfully dark eyes lifted to hers, heavy with exhaustion "Ah, are you my valet now?"

Grace smirked as she brushed his hair back from his forehead. "I can be, though I doubt I'm as efficient as Mr. Elliott."

Frederick's hands found her hips, his grip light but grounding. His eyes closed as she began to undo his tie. "You're far better to look at than Elliott."

A soft laugh escaped her. "I'll keep that observation to myself. Wouldn't want to break poor Elliott's heart."

His responsive chuckle came weak, his eyes still closed.

She pressed a kiss to his temple before crouching to untie his shoes. He murmured in protest, but she shushed him. "You can barely sit up. Hush."

She focused on the laces, her thoughts spinning as she worked. She sighed, attempting to unknot the strings in one shoe. "Something doesn't make sense, Frederick?"

Ah, she finally detangled the string and slipped off both his shoes.

"Hmm?" came his hummed response.

She stood only to find her husband collapsed backward on the bed, eyes closed. Was he asleep?

A soft purr of a snore answered.

This only proved all the more how much he trusted her.

Or how exhausted he was.

But she preferred to think of it as a healthy combination of the two.

With a smile and a solid determination to pin this moment to memory, she maneuvered him fully onto the bed, tucking him in as best she could before turning to the mirror.

Love truly was such an enormous feeling. And if what she felt was the mere human side of it, how very incalculable God's love must be. It really should lead her to much less worry, shouldn't it? Even about all the current difficulties and hurts swirling around them.

Unpinning her hair, she worked her way out of her blouse with no small effort, missing Frederick's help and possibly straining a muscle in her side, to unfasten the back buttons.

Finally slipping into her nightgown, she crawled into bed beside him. His arm instinctively wrapped around her, pulling her close. And she nestled into the comfort and "aliveness" of him, resting her head on his shoulder.

But her mind didn't rest. There were too many questions. Too many puzzles to explore.

"If the murderer returned here after killing Tony, why didn't he kill you too, my dear Lord Astley?" she whispered into the quiet room.

Grace raised up to press a kiss to his cheek, interrupting another soft snore, but not waking Frederick. What a mess! She sent God a quiet offering of thanksgiving. . .and then a request for wisdom and safety.

This entire situation was looking more like Tony was specifically targeted, and hopefully they'd discover why before something worse happened.

Chapter 9

Frederick's head still ached, but his mind was clearer than it had been the night before. Waking to find Grace pressed against his side, her breathing deep and steady, anchored him in a way no tonic ever could.

She was safe.

He let out a slow breath, tension he hadn't realized he was carrying easing away. Grace often reminded him, with her cheerful certainty, that God held her life securely. Yet the gnawing concern for her well-being kept his senses perpetually on alert. It wasn't as if danger lurked around every corner of their married life—not every moment, anyway. There had been months of peace, tranquil interludes where he dared to imagine what a mystery-free existence might look like. But those interludes were fleeting, and he had to admit—if only to himself—that solving mysteries had begun to intrigue him almost as much as it did her.

Almost.

His gaze softened as it drifted back to her face. No one, not even the most dedicated enthusiast of serialized detective novels, could match his wife's insatiable appetite for intrigue. Yet he couldn't deny the pull he felt when a new case presented itself. It wasn't just the thrill of unraveling the puzzle—though he wasn't immune to the appeal of that—but the deeper sense of purpose that came with setting things right. After years of feeling like less than a hero, these mysteries—and the luminous woman who seemed to attract them like moths to a flame—gave him a reason to believe he could be something more.

Grace stirred beside him, her lips curving into a soft smile even before her eyes opened. The sight of it tugged a matching grin from him. It had been far too rare since their arrival, and no wonder. What he'd planned to be a sweet reunion of daughter with her sister and father had turned into a horrible sequence of lies, deceit, and now death.

How would this adventure, so near to her heart, impact her?

She stirred and blinked open those large sapphire eyes of hers, the soft smile on her face spreading as she looked over at him.

"Good morning, my dear Lord Astley," she murmured, her voice thick with sleep.

His finger reached out to spin a fiery red lock of her hair around its tip. "Good morning, darling."

She sighed and scooted closer, her head coming to rest on his shoulder, her palm on his chest. "How are you feeling this morning?"

"Currently, I am very well contented," he said, earning a pleased hum from her.

"Does your head feel clearer?"

"It does."

"That is wonderful news, for your brains are quite important to sleuthing."

His grin twitched. "I prefer them intact, most assuredly."

He almost felt her smile in response.

"I assume you took on the duties of valet for me last night?" he asked, his fingers absently twisting her loose hair.

"I did. And we both agreed not to tell Elliott you find me better to look at than him."

The memory surfaced in his still-foggy mind, and he let out a soundless laugh. "I fully stand by that observation."

Her delighted sigh warmed him to his core.

After a moment's silence, Grace stirred. "I think poor Miss Cox may not be with us for much longer, Frederick. After your impressive entrance to Lillias' room last evening and then Lillias' thorough tongue-lashing of the young woman when she didn't button Thomas' baby gown the right way, I'm afraid her salary may not fit our style of living."

He barely caught his chuckle. "I'm sorry for you and Zahra, but you managed fairly well without a lady's maid when in Egypt and Italy. Do you think you'll be fine until we return to England where you'll have Ellie at hand again?"

"Oh, I'm certain I'll be fine." She paused.

"You're worried about Zahra?"

She moved her head against his shoulder as if to shake it. "Zahra's lived on her own too many times for me to question her capability, though I do think she still needs our care for her as parents. I don't think she knows what love is like."

"And that," Frederick murmured, pressing a kiss to her hair, "makes you the best mother for her."

She gave him a gentle hug in appreciation of his praise. "I'm only feeling sorry for Lillias, as she won't have someone to help care for Thomas, though Zahra is willing, but she's such a little girl still and Lillias isn't too happy that Zahra is half-Egyptian."

Frederick's jaw tightened. Zahra was a little girl, for heaven's sake, and no child deserved such censure—especially not from someone whose own life choices hadn't exactly set her up as a model of virtue.

"If Lillias can't accept Zahra's help, she can hire someone else," he said, exhaling his frustration. "How did your conversation with your sister go last night?"

Grace's hesitation told him volumes. "It derailed before your grand entrance," she admitted at last.

"And?"

She sighed, her palm stilling against his chest. He gave her shoulder a reassuring squeeze, though the pause stretched a beat too long for his comfort.

"She confirmed Miss Steen's assessment of her marriage—and she's blaming me for her unhappiness."

"Blaming you?" Frederick frowned. "For what?"

Grace shifted enough to meet his gaze, her brow pinched in a way that made him want to throttle whoever put that shadow there—Lillias, in this case. "She said that if I hadn't confronted her about the baby, no one would have been the wiser, and the two of you would have been happily married parents by now."

Heat began a dangerous climb through his stomach into his neck. Lillias' complaint touched a nerve, stirring the buried ache of his own family's deceptions. His elder brother had been the result of a similar situation, a truth Frederick had only uncovered months ago with Grace's help. That lie had unraveled into a lifetime of Frederick being the family's black sheep—and worse, it had led to the tragic series of events culminating in his father and brother's deaths.

"Lillias made her choices," he said firmly, cradling Grace's chin. "She must live with the consequences. None of this is your fault."

Her brow puckered further. "But I've already broken so many rules about being a countess, my father's promised money is gone, and now you're related to a potential murderer."

Frederick bit back a grin at her tendency toward derailing into impending cataclysms. "Your sister did not murder her husband," he said, tapping her chin gently. "We'll figure out the matter of the lost money. And for the record, you are the perfect countess for me."

Grace didn't look convinced. "I hope you still feel that way when Lillias is charged with murder and Havensbrooke has to sell off land to keep the schoolchildren from starving."

"Grace!" He laughed despite himself. "I cannot predict whether your sister will be charged with murder, but we both know she's not the mastermind behind Tony's death. And the children of Astlynn Commons will not starve because of any financial setback. As you've reminded me, Havensbrooke has untapped resources. We just need to be inventive—something you excel at."

His reassurance did nothing to temper her frown. She needed a distraction and he had an idea of how to provide one. "I imagine we'll hear from Mr. Barclay this morning, and we can make arrangements to see him to get a better understanding about this inheritance of yours."

She popped up from her place at his side and stared down at him, all of her red hair falling around her pale shoulders. "That's right. And who is to know what all it will entail. Perhaps there will be some financial piece to it." Her smile grew and then she scooted away from him to the end of the bed. "We must speak with Lillias as soon as she is awake, Frederick."

He swung his legs over the side of the bed, a grin tugging at his lips. "Given what I know about your sister, I doubt she's awake yet, darling."

Grace froze mid-motion, narrowing her eyes at him as if calculating his logic. Then, with a sharp nod, she resumed dressing. "Very well. We'll check on Zahra and Miss Cox first, which should give Lillias time to rise. But we cannot delay. If we're to secure the inheritance, we'll need to travel to Scotland together—and we need to move quickly to clear my sister of suspicion."

A knock on the door pulled Frederick up from the bed and into more presentable attire. Grace stepped forward and opened the door enough for him to make out the look of an unfamiliar face.

"My lady?" The woman stuttered, looking confused and clearly in a bit of a fankle. Had her name been Mrs. James? The housekeeper they'd seen briefly yesterday? "I'm sorry to disturb you so early, but you and the earl have had mail arrive this morning."

Grace took the envelope and smiled. "Thank you, Mrs. James, isn't it?"

The housekeeper straightened, her cheeks coloring faintly. Frederick joined Grace at the door, buttoning his cuffs.

"Yes, my lady. Yesterday was my half day, so I wasn't here or. . ." She hesitated, visibly paling. "The horrible events."

"We're sorry our arrival has added to your distress."

The woman's entire body relaxed at Frederick's statement. "It's a shock, sir. . .my lord. A murder, and in this very house!" Her large blue eyes widened, her pale face stark against the dark bun pinned neatly at the nape of her neck. The striking contrast reminded Frederick of Snow White, a thought so absurd he nearly groaned. That was definitely something Grace would have thought.

The woman was much younger than any of the housekeepers Frederick had ever known, but considering the Dixons' finances, perhaps they had to choose a less experienced servant for smaller rates. And her accent hailed from across the pond.

"You find it as a shock?" Grace asked.

The woman's eyes widened. "Well, of course! No one would expect Mr. Dixon to be stabbed in his own parlor. If anything, I'd have thought one of those dreadful men he owed money to might have done him in elsewhere."

Frederick's eyebrows rose, but Grace was already leaning forward, her interest sharpening. "Dreadful men?"

Mrs. James paled further, stammering. "Oh, I shouldn't have said that—"

"It's quite all right," Grace reassured her, lowering her voice. "We're aware of Mr. Dixon's gambling troubles. Any information you have could help us uncover what happened."

"I–I'm sure I don't know much." But her expression didn't match her statement. "Mr. Dixon had a few men come by looking for money he owed them. I tried not to mention it to Mrs. Dixon because it always led to a row between the two of them."

"Were all the men from the gambling house nasty?"

The woman blinked over at Frederick, her hands wringing in front of her. "Well, not all. A few could be right dashing looking, but they wanted money all the same. Even asked for Mrs. Dixon." The woman's eyes widened. "But I tell them they won't find her at home in the mornings and she wouldn't have anything to do with them anyway."

Grace sent Frederick a look. So the strangers knew when people may have been absent from the house.

The woman's eyes widened as if she'd said something amiss, and she rushed ahead. "But I don't go telling Mr. and Mrs. Dixon's business to folks. You can't think that. Please don't tell Mrs. Dixon. Her temper is something frightful."

"Is it?" Frederick searched the woman's face.

"Has she ever hurt you?" This from Grace.

"Let's just say that I'm not too keen to get on her wrong side." Mrs. James stepped back, sending a furtive gaze along the hallway as if afraid Lillias would emerge at any moment.

"Not to worry, your secret is safe with us." Frederick offered.

"I'm much obliged." She nodded, taking another step back. "I'll have breakfast set up for you in the dining room within the next half hour, if that will be fine for you."

"Of course, thank you." Grace offered.

As the housekeeper turned to leave, Frederick stopped her. "Mrs. James, where are you from originally? I couldn't help noticing your accent."

Her smile faltered, and she answered vaguely, "North of

Yorkshire, sir. Until my family came to this side of the world."

"Well, I hope your adventure in America improves from what you've experienced so far," Grace said.

"So do I, my lady." She dipped her head and disappeared down the hallway.

Grace turned to him once the door closed behind them. "So that's an easy explanation for how the timing worked so well for no one to have witnessed Tony's death."

"And one of the likely culprits for any rumors spread throughout town." Frederick added. "She was much too free in giving personal information to strangers."

"There's no telling what else she's shared and with whom, especially with some of the men seeking Tony and his money."

"And"—Frederick held her gaze—"I wonder if any of those 'strangers' had accents that tended toward a more Highland direction."

Grace gasped. "Do you think? Like your assailant?"

"I wonder." His gaze dropped to the envelope in her hand. "I see the Clarion's emblem on the front of the envelope, so I imagine it's a response to my message from yesterday to Mr. Barclay."

Grace looked down at the note, as if remembering it was in her hand. "Yes, it must be." She slipped open the envelope and read over the brief comments. "He was happy to get our message and asks if he may come by the house to meet with us this afternoon." She nodded. "I'll send him a reply once we speak to Lillias." Grace looked back at him. "Frederick, if your assailant was Scottish and this inheritance is in Scotland, do you think Tony's death is tied to this entire situation in some way? It seems too much of a coincidence."

His thoughts exactly. "I don't know, but we'd best be on our guard for the very possibility."

Chapter 10

They'd kept the conversation light during breakfast for Zahra's sake, though Grace suspected the child could have handled more of the truth than poor Miss Cox. In fairness, Miss Cox already seemed discombobulated from sharing a room with Zahra. The little girl's nightmares were notorious—something Grace and Frederick only fully grasped after Zahra became a more permanent part of their lives.

And as Grace fully sympathized with such fits, especially after having occasional bouts of anxiety after almost dying in the sand trap of an undiscovered ancient Egyptian tomb, when she'd awakened to the little girl's cries, a sweet word here and there quickly put the dear one back to sleep.

Miss Cox clearly didn't have a gift for children, because, as Zahra explained after breakfast, Miss Cox began to cry too.

To be fair, some of Miss Cox's distress might be attributed to the chaotic events of the day prior and the unexpected responsibility of caring for a newborn. At one point in the night, Grace had entered the room to find all three—Zahra, Miss Cox, and the baby—crying in chorus. Grace quieted Zahra and took baby Thomas from Miss Cox, only for Lillias to appear moments later, her expression taut with exhaustion, to whisk the infant back to her own room.

It was quite possible that Lillias' anger stemmed from a mixture of not sleeping, the residual turmoil of her relationship with Tony, as well as the disappointments of life. And perhaps some jealousy brewed beneath too, only inciting an overall switch between unfriendly and despairing.

It hurt.

Not so much because of Lillias' accusations. No, Grace had lain in bed, praying through some of those hurts and came to understand them, in part. But the pain came more so for the realization that her sister had always sought happiness outside herself. The dresses were never modern enough. The furnishings needed to be updated. Grace was never proper enough.

She sighed. When her sister's affair with Anthony Dixon went against her own character as well as convention, Grace had thought it must be love, but had it been something else? Mere passion? Or rebellion? What else could explain the speed at which they fell out of each other's good opinions so quickly—for Tony to turn to gambling and Lillias to resentment?

After encouraging Zahra to remain in Frederick and Grace's room so that Miss Cox could attempt a nap after breakfast, Frederick and Grace asked to meet with Lillias in the study. She arrived resplendent in a dark blue gown adorned with their mother's jewels, her elegance marred only by red-rimmed eyes and a thin, brittle smile.

But Grace was beginning to understand that the sister and father she'd thought she'd known, were not the same in retrospect. The glossy-eyed view of an imaginative and naive child gave way to a little more clarity in hindsight. And she had to sort out where she fit within this new definition of her family.

"Bringing the reinforcements, are we, Grace?" Lillias glanced over at Frederick before she took a seat across from Grace. "Did

I not give sufficient answers to your little inquiry last evening?"

"We are here to *help* you." She kept her tone controlled, but unlike anyone else in the world, her sister had some sort of power over Grace's emotions that Grace didn't fully understand. "Not fight."

"Detective Johnson will be here this afternoon." Frederick moved to take a seat beside Grace. "And he already knows that you lied about accompanying Miss Steen on her walk yesterday morning, so it would be wise to share where you were so you can provide an alibi for the time of your husband's death."

Lillias' golden brows rose as she stared at Frederick, her bottom lip dropping ever so slightly from its frown. "She's tricked you into following along with her little fictional fantasies, I see."

Grace blinked as if struck, another blow of awareness rifling through her. She'd always known Lillias didn't appreciate reading the same way Grace did, but her words were laced with anger.

"I fail to comprehend, Mrs. Dixon."

Grace noted the formal address. Frederick hadn't called Lillias by her first name once since their arrival in Virginia. Was it deliberate? A protective boundary, perhaps? Why?

"As I see it, there is no fiction here," Frederick continued, his tone calm but unyielding. "Your husband has been murdered, and you are a suspect. If only it were a fantasy."

Grace straightened, a flicker of pride sparking through her frustration. Defending his wife while dismissing her supposed flights of fancy—a true hero, by any novel's measure.

"I'm sorry to repeat myself, Lillias, but before we can move on to other conversations, it's important that you share where you were yesterday morning when Tony died."

Lillias' gaze lingered on Frederick before shifting back to Grace, her expression wavering between defiance and resignation. Though her chin did not falter from its raised position. Grace suddenly became very aware of the position of her own chin. Did she raise hers with such stubbornness?

"I don't have to tell you." But something in her gaze weakened. "And perhaps I'd rather face the detective than admit anything to the two of you."

Though Lillias' gaze held both of them, Grace noted that Lillias' attention fell on Grace much more than Frederick.

"But we're the ones who care about you, Lillias. The detective and police won't." Grace sighed. "And if you won't tell us, I'll have no choice but to contact Father. He needs to know anywa—"

"No!" The word burst forth, quick and sharp. "He can't know—not yet."

"He'll find out eventually." Her sister's resistance didn't make sense.

"Not yet." The fight seemed to have left her. "I don't want him to know yet." She sighed and looked away. "It will break his heart."

Grace frowned. Their father had never been particularly fond of Tony. Why would his death—

"The reason I don't want him involved," Lillias began, her voice faltering. She looked away, her bottom lip trembling before she squared her shoulders. "I've sold so many of Mother and Father's heirlooms—to collectors in Harrington and Richmond. It couldn't be helped, you understand? Tony's debts, and my. . ." She swallowed, her voice steeling again. "I couldn't be seen in outdated clothes when our family is still of a certain standing."

Grace released her held breath. She'd entertained far worse scenarios: Lillias as the true gambler, an underground jewel thief, or—even more sensational—a murderess with a lover. But this? As tragic as it was, it seemed almost mundane.

"You were selling something yesterday morning? Is that where you were?" Frederick asked, his tone gentler now.

He'd heard it too—the fragility in Lillias' admission, the grief beneath her bravado.

It explained so much. The highly ornate rooms for guests' visibility, the barren ones hidden from sight. She'd been selling things for who knew how long, clinging to appearances.

Relief washed over Grace. At least Lillias wasn't a murderer.

"And you couldn't ask Father for help because of his financial troubles?" Grace asked.

Lillias' gaze snapped to hers. "How did you know that?"

A tiny pang of hurt renewed in Grace's chest—how many secrets had been kept from her?—but she pressed forward. "Frederick and I went to Rutledge House before coming here. Perkins told me. He also delivered some mail we should have received over a month ago."

"We?" Lillias gave her head a shake. "What do you mean, we?"

So her sister didn't know about the inheritance?

Grace looked over at Frederick, and with a smile of encouragement, she divulged what she knew so far about the inheritance, showing Lillias their mother's letter as well as informing her about the upcoming visit from Mr. Barclay.

Her sister's face shifted through myriad emotions from skepticism to shock. As Grace finished the tale, Lillias laughed. "This fixes everything, doesn't it?" She stood, pacing away from the chair. "Of course, Mother would fix things. Even from the grave."

Grace had read enough gothic novels to recognize the signs of a potential breakdown. Was her sister careening toward a wife-in-the-attic scenario? Surely not. Poor Thomas needed his mother intact.

"We don't know enough about it yet to say anything for certain," Grace cautioned.

"But don't you see? It's perfect." Lillias whirled toward her. "I can't keep living in Harrington after all that's happened. And I don't have the money to leave. But this—this could be a fresh start. A new place for me and Thomas. With an estate and funds and—"

"But we don't know what it entails yet, Lillias." Grace found herself playing the voice of reason, a role her sister had once claimed. It felt almost unsettling. "Mr. Barclay should make things clearer this afternoon, but there's no way we can claim the inheritance if you're under suspicion of murder."

Lillias sobered, her hands trembling as she gripped the back of a chair. "But I didn't kill him. And I can prove it." Her breaths came in short bursts. "I'll tell the police everything. Whatever they need. We—we can't let this opportunity slip away. It's the last piece of family land we can hold onto."

Family land. The phrase carried weight. Rutledge House might be gone, but the idea of securing something—anything—still mattered deeply, especially for women like them. And for Lillias, it seemed to mean even more.

"Oh, I wish I'd known about this before." Lillias pressed a fist to her chest. "If Tony had known, maybe. . ." Her voice faltered as she gazed out the window, visibly fighting for composure.

"I don't want the inheritance to slip away either, but there are very real dangers right now that we must address. And we'll know more about the inheritance this afternoon. Mr. Barclay is supposed to meet us at noon and go over more particulars."

"I've kept the very best things from Rutledge House, and they could certainly decorate a new estate. And Scotland? Tony had never traveled." Lillias' smile wavered but then brightened. "Mother would have loved knowing we would end up there, wouldn't she? Home of her grandfather and his family."

"We hope it all will work out in your favor, Mrs. Dixon, but you and Grace must both arrive together to claim the inheritance, and that will all depend on clearing your name." Frederick studied her before turning back to Grace. "The sooner we can have direct answers and clarity, the better."

Lillias sobered and returned to the chair, her body almost shaking. "What do you need to know? If I have a chance for this freedom, I'll tell you anything."

Grace and Frederick pressed for details: the collectors she'd dealt with, Tony's debts, his habits.

"Did he have any particular places he frequented for gambling?" Frederick asked, his chin tilted with a purpose that made him look like one of those detectives in Grace's mystery novels. All he needed was a fedora tipped just so and a notepad for his observations.

"The Lucky Coin was where he spent most of his time lately," Lillias admitted, her perfect brow creasing. "There was also mention of a place called the Captain."

"Are those in Harrington?" Grace asked.

"Yes, but on the far side of town." Lillias offered a weak smile. "At least, in that way he tried to remain more discreet."

"Did he ever try to harm you, Lillias?" Grace's question landed heavily.

Lillias turned sharply to meet her gaze, her pale blue eyes swimming with sudden tears. "No. Of course not. You knew him. He wasn't the sort."

Ah. There it was. Grace hadn't considered it—though she should have, as both a sister and a self-proclaimed sleuth: Lillias hadn't stopped loving Tony. For all her misplaced priorities and shallowness, her sister had genuinely cared for him. Not enough to alter her behavior or curb her desires, but love, in its flawed, messy way, had been there. And maybe that hurt more than not caring at all.

"Can you think of anyone who may have wanted to harm him?" Frederick's voice pulled Grace back to the moment. "Or someone who might claim his money?"

"I don't know," Lillias said, her sigh laced with exhaustion. "He owed several people but made an effort to pay them back, except. . ." She paused. "He mentioned an altercation at the Lucky

Coin a few nights ago." Her brows knitted. "Actually, now that I think of it, he hadn't been to a gambling house two nights in a row after that. Odd, since he'd been going almost every night for months."

"What did he say about the altercation?"

Lillias shook her head. "Not much. Just that he'd met a stranger he thought was dangerous and ended up in a fight. He was thrown out."

"But not the other man?" Frederick pressed.

"Apparently, the man had too much money for them to expel him."

"Did Tony mention anything else? What the man looked like or sounded like?" Grace asked.

Lillias' expression flickered. "Now that you mention it, he did say the man was a well-to-do foreigner. Parks? Clark? I can't recall."

Grace glanced at Frederick, but he gave nothing away. He was infuriatingly good at keeping his thoughts to himself when she most wanted a peek into his mind. They asked a few more questions before Miss Cox appeared, looking harried with a screaming Thomas in her arms. Lillias excused herself to tend to her son, leaving Miss Cox visibly relieved.

"If I may, my lord, may I take a walk down to the village?" Miss Cox asked, the poor girl in need of some respite, no doubt.

Frederick sent a questioning glance to Grace, who smiled up at Miss Cox. "Oh yes, please do. I believe a walk will be very refreshing for you."

The woman smiled as she left the room.

As soon as the door closed behind her, Grace joined Frederick at the window, keeping her voice low. "Do you think the man Tony fought with is our Mr. Clark?"

"It's possible," he said, turning back to her. "But this feels like too much for one man to manage."

"So we should probably consider that Mr. Clark is working along with someone else." Grace joined him at the window, her curiosity building alongside the bustle of the street below.

He looked down at her, the tension in his face softening, as he rested his palms against her hips to pull her nearer. "The sooner we can solve this case"—he raised a brow—"the sooner we can leave for Scotland and get away from all this."

She studied him back, a thrill spiraling through her at her dear husband's excellent mystery-inducing vocabulary choices. "What did you have in mind, my darling sleuth?"

"If you feel safe meeting Mr. Barclay alone with your sister," he said, "I thought I could visit the Lucky Coin."

Grace rested her palms on his arms, her lips curving upward. "An excellent idea. But you're no gambler, are you? Though at one point, I did wonder if you were a pirate."

"A pirate?" he echoed, his laugh low and warm.

"It was a silly girlish thought, although"—she rose on her toes and kissed the smile she so adored—"you are roguish in the very best of ways."

His palms tightened on her waist, the kiss deepening until a delightful warmth spilled through her. She hadn't realized how much she'd longed for his particular affection until he'd so delightfully bestowed it upon her welcome lips.

He pulled back slightly, his thumb brushing her cheek. "I've no mind for gambling, but I know how to ask questions."

"Indeed you—"

"I am very good at gambling." The small voice startled them both.

Grace turned to find Zahra emerging from beneath a tablecloth like a pint-sized spy. Her greenish-gray eyes were wide with conviction. "Father said I brought him good luck."

Oh, heavens. Not only had she been wandering the streets

of Cairo alone, but her father had taken her to gambling houses?

Frederick sent Grace a look before kneeling down to Zahra's height. "And what were you doing under the table, my little card shark?"

"I heard you tell Sayyida we must keep our ears open to stay safe," Zahra explained. "I keep my ears open to keep *you* safe."

Frederick chuckled softly, then offered his hand. Zahra studied him a moment before placing her small fingers in his. He led her to a settee and lifted her onto his lap. She didn't resist, instead leaning into him as though testing the fit of trust. Grace's chest tightened at the sight.

"I appreciate your vigilance," Frederick said, "but little girls are not allowed in gambling houses here."

"Then how are they to trick the dealers?"

Grace didn't know very much about gambling, but that question alone told her volumes about what Zahra's father had asked her to do for him.

"Perhaps they use their own wits or fates." Frederick answered, his voice so gentle. What a father he made! "But my goal is not to gamble, but to find answers so that you, me, and your"—he looked up at Grace—"your new mother, Grace, can return to Britain and introduce you to your little sister, Elizabeth, as well as your new home at Havensbrooke."

Grace almost smiled. Frederick had been resistant to publicly connect himself to his little illegitimate daughter in the past, but perhaps time and perspective had changed those concerns. Little Lily could certainly benefit from knowing her father loved her enough to claim her as his own for the whole world to see.

Grace joined them on the settee.

"Zahra, lamb, we appreciate your desire to keep us safe." Frederick's words tumbled forward in a gentle rumble. "And I'm certain you have a keen mind, but it's important for you to not put yourself into harm's way."

"Though it was very clever to hide beneath a table." Grace offered. "My usual hiding spot of choice was behind the doors."

"But right now, with dangerous things happening around us, it's important that you do as we ask. Do you understand?"

She studied Frederick without assenting.

"Unless it's an emergency," Grace added. "Like in Egypt, when you ran back to find Frederick while I was tied up in that burning house."

Frederick sent Grace a look she didn't fully interpret, but she had the strangest feeling she might not have been saying what he'd wanted her to say. In any event, Zahra could certainly benefit from the encouragement.

"And for now, it is best if you stay here with Grace while I make my way to the Lucky Coin alone, do you understand?"

She nodded this time. "But I will still keep my ears open."

Frederick sighed in the same way he'd done with Grace on several occasions. Grace really hoped she was able to give dear Frederick a son, because for some reason, she felt as though a boy might cause much less sighs than he seemed to experience surrounded by females.

"Very well. I feel certain Grace will appreciate your extra set of ears, especially when listening for a little baby in need." He set her on the ground and nudged her toward the door. "Now, will you run along to see how Miss Cox fares?"

"So you can speak to Sayyida alone?"

Grace grinned. The little girl really was too clever.

Much more clever about interpersonal situations than Grace had been at her age.

"I do." He gave her a mock-serious look and Zahra's lips almost tipped, until she dashed out of the room.

Frederick turned back to Grace. "If I'm to get back before

Detective Johnson returns, I'd better leave now." He touched her arm. "Be careful, darling."

"And you."

He'd just made it to the threshold of the door when Grace stopped him. "Frederick."

He turned back toward her. "Yes?"

"Why do you refer to my sister as Mrs. Dixon and not Lillias? She is your sister-in-law, after all."

He looked away and after a slight hesitation met her stare. "Don't know for certain. The way we began and the way in which she almost manipulated the situation into marriage with her, I just can't force myself into a more intimate level of acquaintance." His shoulders slumped as if the admission took some strength from him. "I don't trust her, Grace."

At the moment, Grace found it hard to trust her sister too. "You think she's lying?"

"Not about the facts, but about her motives. She's desperate, and desperation rarely leads to clear thinking. I hate to say this, especially about your sister, but keep your guard up, won't you? And use that clever mind of yours."

Her smile crooked a little at his benedictory tease. "I will."

Chapter 11

The Lucky Coin sat nestled between a well-worn tailor shop and a bustling bakery, the brass sign by its entrance gleaming in the midmorning sunlight and ushering welcome to passersby. Frederick stepped through the thick wooden door, the walls instantly muting outside sounds and dousing any sunlight.

Stale smoke lingered in the air, mixing with the aroma of beer and aged leather. The walls were paneled with dark mahogany, adorned with portraits of long-forgotten patrons who had once dominated these very halls, and now gathered dust. This place must have been quite exclusive in its better days.

The clink of glasses and clatter of dice blended in with murmurs of people making low-stakes wagers and high-stakes conversations. It was difficult to make out some of the figures in the room, as the lighting waxed and waned from shadow to light depending on location, but it appeared to be an eclectic lot of laymen, businessmen, and even one or two gentleman possibly slumming it for a thrill.

Behind the counter, a young attendant with slicked-back hair and a crisp, though worn waistcoat, gave Frederick a view from head to toe tip. . .and then stood a little taller. "Can I help you, sir?"

"Good afternoon. My name is Lord Astley, and I need a word with Mr. Hargrove, the owner of this fine establishment." Frederick hoped the information he'd learned outside the building proved true. "It concerns a mutual acquaintance."

"Lord?" The young man blinked, his professionalism flickering with faint curiosity. "Of course, sir. . .um. . .my lord. One moment."

Within minutes, an older man appeared. His hair swept back in a salt-and-pepper wave, and his sharp eyes assessed Frederick in one swift glance. He was as tall as Frederick but broader, with the kind of confidence that suggested he'd won more than a few high-stakes games himself.

"It's not every day we entertain such esteemed company," Hargrove said, a cautious smile lurking beneath a close-trimmed beard. He gestured to the room with a flourish, the tone of a practiced showman. "How can I assist, my lord?"

Frederick offered his hand in an attempt to breach any awkwardness from the man. "Thank you, sir. I appreciate any help you can give."

The man's brows rose as he took Frederick's hand. "You've come a far piece, haven't you?" His gaze moved down Frederick again, lips crooked into a knowing smile. "And I'd bet my cash purse, you're not here for gambling."

Astute man. Likely a requirement for his line of work.

"I'm visiting my wife's family in Harrington, and I've come to inquire about a frequent visitor of your establishment. Mr. Anthony Dixon?"

Hargrove's expression barely flickered, but Frederick noted the tightening of his mouth. "He's not been welcome here since his last visit due to his behavior."

"I'm aware," Frederick replied, inclining his head. "But I understand an unfortunate event occurred involving Mr. Dixon, and it's important I learn what transpired the night he was. . .asked to leave."

Hargrove's smile thinned as he folded his arms across his chest.

"How does a man like you know someone like Tony Dixon?"

"I'm his brother-in-law."

The man's brows shot up. "Is that so? Funny, he never acted as if he had family with means."

Frederick allowed himself a wry smile. "He doesn't."

Hargrove's laughter rumbled. "I'll wager you he has more than he thought."

"Had, Mr. Hargrove." Frederick corrected, holding the man's gaze.

Frederick's distinct switch to past tense wiped all humor from Mr. Hargrove's expression. The man hesitated, then inclined his head. "Let's discuss this in my office."

Hargrove led him to a tidy office tucked behind the main lounge. It smelled faintly of pipe smoke and polish, the desk perfectly aligned with a window that likely gave a discreet view of the front entrance. When Hargrove gestured to a decanter, Frederick shook his head.

"Thank you, no."

Pouring a drink for himself, Hargrove settled into his chair. "What happened?"

"I'm surprised the police haven't already visited you, Mr. Hargrove."

"In connection with Mr. Dixon?" He raised a brow. "No. Though I can't say the same for some of my other patrons."

Frederick waited for Mr. Hargrove to place his glass back on the desk and then continued the discussion. "Tony Dixon was found dead in his home yesterday morning." Frederick studied Hargrove, whose slight lift of his brows was his only response.

"And I'm assuming it wasn't from natural causes." Hargrove stated, taking a drink from his glass.

"Which is why any information about his altercation here would help us find answers."

Hargrove rubbed his jaw, then called out through the door. Moments later, a wiry young man with a shock of blond curls entered, looking as though he'd just been told he owed the house more than he had in his pocket.

"This is Caleb Rook," Hargrove said, nodding toward the boy. "He was working Dixon's table that night."

Frederick turned toward the young man, who stood, wringing his hands a little as he shifted his attention from Hargrove to Frederick.

The boy didn't look more than fifteen.

"Lord Astley has some questions for you, boy." Hargrove nodded. "About the fight between Tony Dixon and. . .um. . .what was the stranger's name again?"

"Mr. Clark, sir."

Mr. Clark? So, Lillias had heard correctly. Frederick attempted to keep his expression neutral. Could the entire case be as simple as a disgruntled gambler seeking revenge? But why set up the entire charade with a fake officer?

"Yes, some foreigner, as I recall." Hargrove gave a dismissive frown.

Frederick studied the lad, whose hands twisted nervously as his gaze darted between the two men.

"You've nothing to fear, Mr. Rook," Frederick assured him. "I'm simply looking for information."

Rook nodded, though his Adam's apple bobbed nervously.

"Sit down, boy." Hargrove barked, waving toward a nearby chair.

Rook obeyed immediately, his gaze darting back to Frederick, who eased back into the chair in hopes of helping the lad feel more comfortable.

"Was Mr. Dixon gambling heavily? Drinking?"

"He always gambled heavy." The young man laughed. "But no, sir. He wasn't one for drink."

"Left here more often depressed and sober than drunk," Hargrove added.

That information softened Frederick's opinion of the man slightly. One vice was plenty. "What led to the altercation with Mr. Clark?"

"Well, Mr. Dixon was at the baccarat table most of the night," Rook said, his fingers worrying the edge of his coat. "Lost a fair bit, I'd wager. Then Mr. Clark accused him of cheating."

Frederick leaned forward slightly. "And was Mr. Dixon prone to cheat, from your knowledge?"

"No, sir. That's probably why he lost so much," Rook replied with a grim sort of sincerity.

"That and bad luck," Hargrove chimed in, his tone bordering on philosophical.

Frederick nearly grunted at the sharp sting of that addition. Could Tony have been so desperate to gain favor in Lillias' eyes that he returned, over and over again, to gamble a losing game?

"What happened next?"

"They had words first, sharp ones, and then it turned physical. Mr. Dixon threw the first punch, but the other man was quicker. Mr. Dixon got the brunt of the hits before they were separated."

So Mr. Clark knew how to fight. An important detail, should Frederick find himself in a similar confrontation.

"Did this Mr. Clark say anything? Threaten Mr. Dixon?"

"I—I heard him say something about owing what's due. And then"—Caleb glanced at Hargrove, who gave a slight nod, apparently the arbiter of all things confidential—"I heard Mr. Clark say to Mr. Dixon. . ." Caleb straightened, evidently imagining himself as the Scotsman. "He said, 'You shouldn't have said that, lad. Things would have been different for you, if you didnae know that.'"

Didnae and *lad*? Those weren't typical American words.

"What did Mr. Dixon know?"

Rook shrugged, deflating like a punctured balloon. "I didn't hear that part, sir. But that's when Mr. Hargrove arrived and broke up the two men. Told Mr. Dixon to stay away."

"And Mr. Clark?" Frederick turned to Hargrove.

Hargrove shifted in his seat and offered a one-shoulder shrug. "He wasn't the sort you asked to leave."

Frederick raised an eyebrow. "What do you mean?"

Hargrove ran his thumb against his finger, his grin both sly and unapologetic. "He came with plenty of money to spend."

Ah, yes. The universal pass in establishments such as this. Money might not buy happiness, but it certainly bought tolerance. "And what did Mr. Clark look like? Could you place the accent at all? Scottish, perhaps?"

"Yeah," Rook's eyes brightened. "That's it. I thought I'd heard it before but couldn't place it. Old MacGregor, who used to come in here, sounded a lot like Mr. Clark."

"Would you happen to know where Mr. Clark is staying?"

"If the patrons don't tell, we don't ask." Hargrove answered. "But there are only a few places in town any man of his style would choose to stay."

Style, cleverness, a fighter, and Scottish. The profile of Mr. Clark was beginning to take shape, and it wasn't exactly a comforting silhouette. Frederick was no gambling man, but he'd wager the man who attacked him in the garden was the same as this Mr. Clark.

"Did he only come the one night?"

"No, sir." Rook shook his head. "That was his third night—the night of the fight."

"And has he been back?"

Rook glanced at Hargrove, whose brow crinkled like a well-worn map. "Not as I recall."

So Mr. Clark disappeared at the same time Tony Dixon stopped coming to the Lucky Coin? This sounded much less like a random brawl in a bar. No, it was much more strategic.

Frederick stood, mind spinning through this new information. What else should he ask? What would Grace ask? "Can you think of anyone else who would want to harm Mr. Dixon? Had you heard of any other threats against him?"

"None." Hargrove stood along with Rook. "Which is why the brawl came as such a surprise. Dixon was generally liked and never caused trouble."

"He'd even helped out a few other men who'd been down on their luck before," Rook interjected, his eyes widening as a new thought struck. "But I remember something else—the one thing that set Mr. Dixon off."

Frederick tensed. "What was that?"

"I'm not sure what Mr. Clark said, but Mr. Dixon responded with something like, 'We won't bring my wife into this' or 'I won't bring my wife into this.' I can't remember exactly."

So Mr. Clark had somehow threatened Lillias? How and why?

"Thank you, Mr. Rook," Frederick said, sending the boy a nod. "You've been very helpful."

As the young man left, Frederick turned to Hargrove.

"I'd appreciate your discretion about this," he said, rising to his feet.

"Of course, my lord," Hargrove replied, though his expression suggested he was already speculating.

Whatever Hargrove did with the information Frederick couldn't help. He'd gotten more than he expected in the conversation and hopefully enough to lead him to a discovery of who Mr. Clark really was.

And fast.

Grace spent some time with Zahra, Miss Cox, and baby Thomas after Frederick left, trying very hard not to keep looking at the clock or worrying about her dear husband. She'd never fully understand why God told His children not to worry, but then made worrying such an easy thing to do. Clearly, she needed a much better perspective on God's greatness and nearness than her current one.

At 11:45, Grace left Miss Cox and Zahra to their own luncheon and walked downstairs, to find Mrs. James speaking in quiet tones with Officer Todd at the front door. And Officer Todd's welcome grin didn't make him look as disinterested or sick as his usual expression. Oh no, he didn't seem disinterested at all. Neither did Mrs. James. Grace released a heavy sigh.

Mrs. James was certainly not the sort to be a confidante.

As she descended the stairs, Grace studied the housekeeper. Could the woman be dangerous? Or at the very least, bought for information? Grace barely held in a gasp. Of course, she could. She fit the role perfectly.

Officer Todd spotted Grace first and straightened, stepping back from Mrs. James as if caught pilfering biscuits. The motion alerted Mrs. James, who turned to meet Grace's gaze—and promptly flushed a guilty shade of red.

"Lady Astley," Mrs. James began, her voice flustered, "Officer Todd has come to replace Officer Penny as guard of the house."

"How good to have someone of your caliber keeping watch." Grace approached with what she hoped was a subdued smile, but she was never really certain. Other women seemed to look subdued so effortlessly.

The man tipped his hat. "I've volunteered, Lady Astley, since you have a guest coming to visit. Detective Johnson felt that a more experienced set of eyes would be required."

"That's very good thinking, Officer Todd." Grace studied him with polite curiosity, though she couldn't help but fixate on his near-unibrow. It loomed like an ominous cloud over his narrow eyes. "One can't be too careful with strangers in situations like this, can one?"

His prolonged stare set off an odd prickling at the back of her neck. Was it merely his unfortunate eyebrows, or something deeper? Grace decided it was safer to assume the worst. Any self-respecting heroine in one of her novels would.

And surely, the man couldn't keep a steady watch on the house if he was standing around flirting with Mrs. James.

"Mrs. James?" Grace turned to the housekeeper, whose complexion had returned to a regular hue. "Do you know if Mrs. Dixon has already ordered tea to be ready for our noon appointment?"

Grace smiled at her own sentence. She sounded very proper and countess-like when she'd spoken that sentence.

"She did, ma'am. And plans to serve it in the breakfast room," Mrs. James answered.

"Who should I be on the lookout for, my lady?"

The way Officer Todd said 'my lady' each time almost stole the very countess-like smile right off Grace's face. Or perhaps smiling even when one didn't feel very much like it was the very countess part. She hung on to her smile.

"A Mr. Barclay, thank you." Without another word, she stepped toward the breakfast room. She had just entered the sunlit space when the front bell rang. Curious, she paused in the doorway, keeping an ear tuned to the exchange at the front door.

The unique lilt of a Scottish accent carried down the hallway, weaving a sharp contrast to Mrs. James' rural English. How anyone could confuse the two was beyond her. After months of marriage to Frederick, Grace had come to appreciate such distinctions.

Frederick's tones were smooth, refined—like a first-edition novel bound in rich leather. This man's burr, on the other hand, was rugged and unpolished, more like a weathered folio discovered in a forgotten attic. Both held their charm, but there was something uniquely intriguing about the latter.

Perhaps it was the link to her mother's childhood in Scotland, a place Grace had only glimpsed through fragmented memories and wistful tales.

"You've come so far to visit us, Mr. Barclay," came Mrs. James' less refined voice. "What could bring a Scot all the way to Virginia?"

Small talk was certainly one thing, and something Grace failed at more than not, but Mrs. James only proved her immaturity by engaging in such intimate conversation with a guest.

"Personal business," was the Scot's clipped reply.

"Oh, I suppose you know Lord and Lady Astley from some visit to England?"

What was Mrs. James doing? No wonder Lillias fretted about rumors. Grace's mind ticked over the possibilities. Was Mrs. James simply indulging her penchant for tittle-tattle—a word Grace cherished for its sheer cheekiness—or was something more nefarious at play?

Nefarious. She almost shrugged. An equally exciting word.

People really didn't appreciate well-placed words as much as they ought.

"What has brought you to America, miss?"

The turn of the conversation from the clever Scot paused Mrs. James' response long enough for Grace to slip fully into the room for Mr. Barclay's entrance. Grace barely heard Mrs. James mention something about a need for change from her difficult home circumstances, but nothing more as they neared the room.

When it came to the housekeeper and the police officer, was it possible that Mrs. James proved the more dangerous of the two?

Had Officer Todd been gleaning information from Mrs. James, or had Mrs. James been deliberately distracting Officer Todd?

Grace's pulse quickened. Or, heaven help her, were they working together?

She barely had time to smooth her expression before Mr. Barclay stepped into view.

He was stout and broad-shouldered, his well-trimmed beard streaked with gray. He scanned the room, his stance tense, his expression leery, and then. . .his gaze fastened on her, and something softened around the edges of his pale eyes. He stopped in the doorway, almost in the exact place Grace had just vacated, and gave Grace a long look.

She folded her hands in front of her and offered him a smile. "Mr. Barclay? Welcome, I'm Grace Ferguson Percy." Then she paused, remembering how she was usually referred to socially. "Lady Astley."

The sound of her voice seemed to rouse him. He gave a quick shake of his head and stepped farther into the room. "You're the very image of your mother."

Of all the things she'd expected him to say, that was not on the list. "Oh." She pressed a palm to her chest. "I'm certain she wasn't as troublesome as me."

His smile spread slowly from one corner to the next, lighting his pale eyes, and Grace had the immediate urge to hug him. "I don't know as I'd make that claim, my lady."

"Truly?" Grace's laugh was light, though she stole a glance at the door. Mrs. James should have closed it once she'd deposited Mr. Barclay inside to retrieve Lillias.

Hmm. . .

"I knew her when she was no bigger than a sapling," Mr. Barclay said, his voice rich with nostalgia. "And she had a wee bit of mischief-making about her, to be sure."

Grace's throat tightened, her eyes stinging a little. Oh dear, she already adored the man!

"Having lost her so early in life, your words could not touch my heart any more than they do. And I rather like the idea of her engaging in a little wholesome mischief now and again. It makes me feel even more connected to her memory somehow." She gestured toward a small table near the large windows in the room. "Please, sit."

He obeyed, settling into the chair with a weathered satchel at his side. Satchels always seemed to carry secrets—or at least the potential for them.

A thrill rushed up through her. Oh, she liked him very much.

"I can already tell you're the sort she'd have been proud of." His eyes glinted with his growing smile.

And the way he rounded his vowels combined with his sentiment nearly had Grace wiping away a tear.

"I only received your information from Rutledge House yesterday, and here you are." She waved toward him. "Have you been in Harrington long?"

"When I didnae hear from you or your sister, I was concerned the inheritance may go unanswered, so I set out last week. I've only been in your wee town about four days, with my own visit to Rutledge two days past."

Ah, then he knew the transfer of ownership and likely the reasons behind the transfer even more than Grace did. "I imagine you sent word to my sister then?"

He nodded. "But I can see now why it went unanswered until your husband replied yesterday."

"Yesterday was certainly eventful," Grace kept her voice steady at the remembrance of such a day.

"My condolences." His face softened. "I regret adding urgency to your family's grief."

"Actually, I believe your timing is rather perfect." Grace offered him an encouraging smile. "It provided a welcome distraction to Lillias and, I believe, some much needed hope for her future."

He studied Grace a moment. "And for you?"

For her? "I'm much more interested in the fact that it is connected to our mother than anything else." Grace's top teeth skimmed over her smile as she leaned forward. "So as we wait for my sister to join us, I'd love to hear how you knew my mother. Was it only through the fact that you were her solicitor?"

The wariness he'd carried into the room seemed to dissolve. "We were cousins. She used to spend summers in Scotland before her marriage. She brought you and your sister once, when you were just wee bairns, but that was the last time I saw her."

"And was that when she. . .handled the matter of the inheritance?"

He nodded, his sigh heavy with memory. "Aye, it was the last time. She finalized everything then."

How sweet to know he cared about Mother, the tenderness in his voice undeniable. It made her want to rush across the Atlantic and claim this inheritance for dear Mr. Barclay as much as herself. "I barely remember her. A few songs she'd sing, her scent." The bridge of Grace's nose tingled a little. "And her laughter."

He chuckled. "Aye, she had a braw laugh."

His sentiments, accent and all these wonderful words! Grace's fingers curled tightly against her skirt to stop herself from crossing the table and hugging him outright. "And when you saw her last, did she seem happy?"

He tilted his head and narrowed his eyes for only a moment before his smile twitched a little. "Aye, she did. But she was also wise to your father's. . .ventures, as they were. I think that's why she secured this inheritance—for you and your sister. She was a good woman."

Grace leaned forward, with every intention of taking the man's hand into a gentle squeeze, but at that moment, the door burst wide and Lillias entered with Mrs. James on her heels, carrying the tea tray.

"Mr. Barclay, what a pleasure." She swept Grace a glance and approached the table, with Mrs. James stepping around her to place down the tray. "I'm sorry to have kept you, but I hope my sister offered you sufficient welcome."

"Indeed." He stood, offering his hand. "Mrs. Dixon."

Lillias' smile faltered ever so slightly. "You know my married name?" Her tone held just a hint of surprise, as though she were still trying to decide if that was a compliment or an intrusion.

"The town isn't large, and people were helpful in directing me to the daughters of Henry P. Ferguson."

Grace kept her shoulders from cringing a little, which was a huge feat in personal growth. If Mr. Barclay had heard anything from the locals, there was a good chance he knew exactly why a police officer guarded the house.

Lillias turned to Mrs. James and waved her away, following the woman to the door and closing it behind her. Then she turned. "What exactly did the *locals* have to say?"

He didn't answer right away. "A great deal, but I'd prefer to hear your story on things, Mrs. Dixon."

Lillias withered down into a chair and, after a deep breath, told Mr. Barclay of the events from the day before, including a brief mention of Tony's gambling difficulties and a jab at the fickleness of servants, before she remarked about the police's insistence that she not leave the house. "It's ridiculous to be a captive in my own home," she finished with an edge. "But there is still some concern for my safety, so I must comply."

Or concern for other people's safety from Lillias, but Grace decided that tidbit of information wouldn't have been very helpful to Mr. Barclay. He was a stocky fellow. He could probably take care of himself.

Mr. Barclay dipped his head, studying Lillias for a moment longer, before turning back to Grace. "Your mother spoke highly of both of you in her correspondence. She was quite pleased to be the mother of two daughters."

"It's so good to hear about her," Grace offered. "I often imagine what she would think of her daughters all grown up and hope she'd still think highly of us."

Grace met Lillias' pained expression and replayed her words. Oh dear, she hadn't meant that as a criticism of her sister. "And I'm certain she would have loved to know she had such a sweet little grandson."

"Yes, I had heard of your son's birth." Mr. Barclay turned to Lillias. "Despite the tragedy of your situation, Mrs. Dixon, I congratulate you on your son's safe arrival. I hope he will provide some comfort for ye during this difficult time."

"Thank you." Lillias said with less warmth than before, as she stood and placed a sandwich on a plate for Mr. Barclay. "I wasn't very old when she died, but I don't recall her mentioning your name."

"But she did mention Mosslea, did she not?" He took the plate with a nod. "In fact, I remember when you visited as a bairn."

Lillias poured him a cup of tea next, her porcelain brow creasing in thought. "I—I think I have vague memories of the place."

"Well, I hope you will have a future of many more," Mr. Barclay continued with a smile, a glint twinkling in his eyes. He turned to include Grace in the conversation. "Mosslea is not just any estate. It's a piece of your family's history. Your mother was deeply proud of it."

"I'm anxious to know more about it." Grace smiled, happy for the distraction from Lillias' current situation. "Is it near the mountains? Or a loch? I've heard lochs are a plenty in Scotland."

"As are mountains, my lady. And sheep. And heather and thistles." He chuckled, and Grace could almost picture wind-tossed hillsides, the sound of bagpipes drifting through the air. "Mosslea has been in your mother's family for five generations. When the previous owner, Alastair Blair, passed away unexpectedly, your mother became the next blood relative in line. Upon her death, the inheritance defaulted to the two of you. Your mother wished to ensure the estate remained in the family and hoped to provide any needed security, knowing how difficult financial freedom can be for women of the day."

"Her foresight does her immense credit." Lillias squeezed her hands together in her lap, but Grace's mind clung to a certain phrase Mr. Barclay had mentioned.

Unexpected passing?

"May I ask—how did Mr. Blair die?"

Lillias' humorless laugh interrupted Mr. Barclay's answer. "Grace, what a question! What does it matter how the former owner died? That isn't our business." She turned to Mr. Barclay. "Please forgive my younger sister, she has a tendency to dramatize situations." She lowered her voice, as if the next words were a confession. "She reads fiction."

Why on earth would she say that as if it were a *bad* thing?

"I do," Grace said, leaning forward with a touch of pride, "and I feel it's prepared me quite well for my life thus far."

Lillias rolled her eyes, but Mr. Barclay's lips twitched as though suppressing a smile. "I'm keen on a good piece of fiction now and again." His expression sobered. "But sadly, Laird Blair drowned in the loch by the castle after an evening picnic with his wife."

Lillias gasped. "Dear heavens, how horrid."

Drowned? After an evening picnic? Grace's whole body perked to attention. Not such a common death for men as more violent demises like being shot or stabbed. She cringed at the memory of Tony's lifeless blood and almost regretted her earlier quip about the massive number of lochs in Scotland.

Had Mr. Blair's death been a tragic accident like poor Ophelia's, or Hardy's Eustacia Vye? Grace's mind was suddenly spinning—why did fictional women so often choose drowning as their end? Or had he died a hero in rescuing another, like Dickens' James Steerforth? Or worse—had he been *forced* into that loch, his death a darker affair than mere misfortune?

The cool chill of an unanswered mystery swooped through Grace with familiar relish. Not that she *relished* anyone's death, but she adored the thrilling pursuit of finding answers. And there were a great many unanswered questions piling up right before her.

"Did you know Mr. Blair personally?" Grace asked, choosing a question nearer the one she really wished to ask: *Do you have any reason to believe Mr. Blair was murdered?*

"Indeed." Mr. Barclay took another drink of tea. "I oversaw his finances until recently when he transferred oversight to someone else at his wife's insistence. But the stewardship of the estate has long been in the Barclay family. We've always served in its legal matters, ensuring its rightful legacy and proper support for those who live within the village of Angloss. Laird Blair's tenure at Mosslea was not long, but he left a lucrative and positive legacy, which has benefited Angloss and the surrounding areas."

There was a deep-set passion in Mr. Barclay's words, a love for his people and land. A very good thing, unless turned in a not-so-good direction. "I can tell the estate means a great deal to you."

"It does. Generations of my family have lived in Angloss. 'Tis our family home and worthy of our protection from anyone who would see it harmed. I've seen what happens when places like Mosslea fall into the wrong hands. It's more than a piece of land. It's a home to those who live and work there—a part of their identity. Your mother understood that, and I believe you will too." He straightened, his gaze intensifying as he shifted focus from Grace to Lillias. "Which is why I must emphasize the urgency of acting quickly. The will's stipulations leave little room for delay. If the inheritance isn't claimed within the month, the estate will go to auction."

"Auction?" Lillias cried. "For someone else to buy?"

"Aye." The solicitor folded his hands, leaning forward slightly. "You can be sure the bidders won't be interested in preserving the castle's legacy. They'll see only its potential for profit—mines, timber, grazing land. And I can assure you, the vultures are already circling. Not two weeks after Laird Blair's passing, I had an offer made for the place." He shook his head. "It would be a travesty to see it mishandled and unappreciated."

Had he said castle? Grace blinked a few times, attempting to rework the image of Mosslea in her head from being similar to her dear Havensbrooke to something entirely different. So many mystery-loving clues were flying, Grace wished she'd brought her notepad and pen to the meeting. An unexpected death to the previous owner, a passionate steward desperate to protect his home, possible entrepreneur with a desire to own lucrative property, and a castle?

"A travesty, indeed." Lillias' voice pulled Grace from her mental image of fairytales and back to the very real mystery of this entire situation. "But even if we claim the inheritance together, how are we to manage such an estate? Are funds available for its upkeep?"

Oh, that was a very good question. One Grace should have considered.

"There are. More than enough, as Laird Blair's predecessor had secured monies for Mosslea's repairs before his death. The surplus, as well as the way you manage the resources of the land, are sure to keep you two in good financial stead for the foreseeable future."

"Well, we have every intention of claiming what is ours, do we not, Grace?" Lillias raised her chin to battle proportions. "What must we do? When can we leave? And—and how will we procure the expense?"

"Assuming your current situation allows for it, Mrs. Dixon, I'd be happy to leave no later than the first of next week."

"I am not at fault for my husband's death, Mr. Barclay, so we should have no difficulty on that score." The edge in Lillias voice brooked no argument, and Grace hoped the police proved as amenable to her sister's tone as Mr. Barclay.

"Very well." He dipped his head. "Your mother set up accounts for each of you in Harrington Bank to provide funds for travel and initial expenses."

"She thought of everything, didn't she?" Grace laughed. "How clever and well-planned."

"Aye." Mr. Barclay's gaze softened with his smile. "She was a clever one, ye ken?"

Grace's grin broadened at his warmth, and he continued. "The accounts have accrued some interest since they were established, so they should amply cover your travel expenses and any other immediate needs you may have." His gaze landed much-too-pointedly on Lillias, whose eyes gleamed like a child catching sight of presents on Christmas morning. Or at least, Grace imagined that's how a child's eyes might gleam. She hoped very much to find out firsthand one day, with Zahra and Elizabeth, and maybe four or five other little ones.

Oh! Christmas at Havensbrooke this year will be magnificent.

"Then let us proceed." Lillias slipped to the edge of the chair, nearer Mr. Barclay. "Where do we sign?"

Mr. Barclay cleared his throat, his expression turning serious as he leaned forward. "I dinnae bring the official forms with me today."

"What?" Lillias exclaimed, her brows furrowing. "I thought this was of the utmost urgency?"

"Aye," He continued, his tone deliberate. "But I needed to secure your intentions and interest before I brought the papers with me. There are only two copies of the will. One remains under lock and key in my possession at the hotel. The other is secured along with other important papers like blueprints, land surveys, and other personal items at Mosslea itself, in a safe location known only to the late Mr. Blair and myself. Now that I've met you and know of your intentions, we can secure another meeting for your signatures, and then I will escort you to Mosslea myself to give you a proper introduction."

It all sounded rather straightforward, if Lillias' possible charges as a murderess didn't complicate matters. Grace almost cringed. Certainly, a sentence she'd never imagined thinking. She shook off the thought, focusing on Mr. Barclay's satchel instead. "So what have you brought with you?"

"Why on earth would his satchel matter, Grace, when we have an inheritance to secure?" Lillias huffed.

"It matters a great deal, Mrs. Dixon." Mr. Barclay drew the satchel onto his lap and brought out a large envelope. "These are paintings and photographs of Mosslea and Angloss. There are a few of Laird Blair and the surrounding areas, and I located some photos taken of your mother." He turned his attention fully on Grace. "I feel you'll appreciate them."

"Most certainly." Grace took the offering into her arms as if the package was as fragile as baby Thomas. "Thank you."

"And when do you wish to meet for us to sign the documents?" Lillias interjected, doing nothing to hide the impatience in her voice.

Mr. Barclay turned toward her and drew his pocket watch from his jacket. "I will prepare everything tonight, so"—he glanced down at the watch—"would noon tomorrow suffice? In my hotel's private parlor."

"We will be there." Lillias stood, answering for the both of them, and Grace hoped she had more foresight into her personal freedom than Grace did.

"And my husband, Lord Astley, will join us as well."

Mr. Barclay stood, nodding toward Lillias with a courteous smile, before turning to Grace. His smile deepened, something warm and almost mischievous in his gaze. "I look forward to our meeting tomorrow."

And Grace had to curb the urge to hug him for the third time.

As he reached the door, Mr. Barclay paused, looking back at them with a hint of something unreadable in his expression. "One last note—should either of you have second thoughts or should complications arise, it is imperative you inform me immediately. Time is not on your side, and any delay could jeopardize the inheritance."

Lillias squared her shoulders. "There won't be any complications."

Grace hoped that to be true.

Mr. Barclay's lips twitched, a subtle expression that could have been approval or skepticism—or perhaps a mix of both. "Good day, ladies." He swept from the room.

The door had just closed behind him when Grace sent her sister a quick shrug of apology and rushed out of the room after the man. He'd not made it but a few steps down the hallway and turned at her approach.

"I'm so sorry, Mr. Barclay, and I'm certain you'll find this question impertinent, but what happened to Mr. Blair's wife?"

"His wife?" Mr. Barclay's brows shot skyward.

"You mentioned his death, but is she still living in Mosslea? Should we be considering her in our decisions?"

Mr. Barclay's confusion melted into a knowing smile, as if

some piece of the puzzle clicked into place. "Ah, I see. I didnae make that clear, did I?" He nodded once, then sobered. "It's a private matter, but since you'll be inheriting the rumors along with the estate, you ought to know, I s'pose." He sighed. "She drowned, along with him."

Grace's palm flew to her stomach. "Oh no."

"Aye, it was a sad discovery, make no mistake." He shook his head. "They'd gone out in a boat to visit the ruins on an island near the house—'twas a favorite picnic spot for the couple, so the house servants say. And on the return, the boat capsized."

"How awful," Grace murmured, struggling to process this new detail. "And they couldn't swim?"

Mr. Barclay hesitated before answering, his gaze growing distant. "I dinnae know if Lady Blair could swim, but the laird could, or so I'm told. They say he tried to save her, but. . ." He allowed the rest of the sentence to hang in the air like an unfinished thought.

So the heroic sort of drowning? "And the poor servants are the ones who recovered the bodies, I suspect?"

Mr. Barclay flinched at Grace's directness, or she supposed that was why, but after a moment, he answered. "Laird Blair's body was found by the servants, aye."

A wave of foreboding washed over her. "And his wife's?"

He sighed deeply, as though the weight of the story had followed him all this time. "They found her scarf and hat, as I recall." He pulled his hat from his head, adjusting it slowly. "Loch Ness takes its own, and they're none too easy to find beneath those depths."

With that, he dipped his head and walked down the hall, leaving Grace frozen in place. Loch Ness?

She'd heard of it. Read about it in a few obscure books in her family library about Scottish history, no doubt left there by her mother. But did Mr. Barclay's revelation mean that Mosslea was close to the mysterious loch and even more mysterious creature?

Grace looked back at the breakfast room door. She should talk to Lillias about everything, but after only a moment's hesitation, she dashed toward the stairs. First and foremost, she needed to write down every new clue she'd just uncovered and sort out a plan for the next adventure.

Chapter 12

"Lord Astley, I didn't take you for a gambling man."

Frederick had only made it a few steps outside The Lucky Coin before Detective Johnson materialized from the shadowy corner of the establishment. The man's tilted frown spoke volumes.

Frederick was trespassing in unwanted territory.

Johnson's dark overcoat and bowler hat silhouetted against the overcast sky gave him the look of a villain in one of Grace's cherished mystery novels.

"I'm not, sir." Frederick conceded with a smile. "Only visiting on a hunch."

"A hunch?" A derisive puff of air, like a snort, emerged from the man. "Taking up your wife's fictionalized mantle or stepping in your friend Miracle's footsteps by attempting more amateur sleuthing?"

"Amateur?" Frederick allowed the faintest smile. "I assure you, Detective, I leave the professional work to you. But wouldn't it be better to have more eyes on the lookout than fewer, especially considering the delicate nature of this situation?"

"Delicate? I've seen Mr. Dixon's wound. It was anything but delicate." One of Johnson's brows rose in challenge. "One might even consider it inflicted out of passion."

Frederick held Johnson's gaze, unflinching. "Do you genuinely suspect my sister-in-law?"

Johnson hesitated, his expression unreadable, before exhaling. "Less likely she wielded the blade herself. But as for her involvement? That remains to be seen."

The thought still hovered in Frederick's mind, but not with the same hold as it had yesterday. There was much more going on surrounding Tony's death than the disharmony of a marriage. "I have high doubts on that score, and I'm not one to play favorites as far as Mrs. Dixon is concerned."

Johnson's lips twitched. "Yes, from Lady Astley's detailed accounts, I understand why you're less than enchanted with your sister-in-law."

And seven months ago, the mere mention of Lillias had fueled his anger. Now it only reinforced his gratitude. Grace was a better match for him in every conceivable way—a divine intervention he had been too blind to see at the time.

"What do you say of moving this conversation inside, Lord Astley." Johnson waved toward a nearby restaurant with a much more appealing facade than the darker hues of the Lucky Coin.

Frederick inclined his head. As far as detectives went, Johnson was leagues apart from Miracle in demeanor. Where Jack had a knack for camaraderie and wit, Johnson wielded formality like a weapon. And it took very little brain work to deduce that the two men had crossed paths at some point in time.

Once seated in a quiet corner of the café, the scent of fresh bread mingling with the low murmur of patrons, Frederick decided to probe. "What's the story between you and Jack Miracle?"

A flicker of surprise lit the man's gaze, before his expression darkened.

Frederick fought back a grin. Perhaps he did gamble more than he admitted—though never with cards or dice. Curiosity was his vice, he supposed. One greatly encouraged by his wife. "Was it about some dueling cases between the two of you?"

Johnson released a heavy breath and took a drink from the glass the attendant just set on the table. The sudden heightening of color in Johnson's face flared an idea to life in Frederick's mind.

"A woman?"

Johnson froze, the rim of his glass halfway to his lips. When he finally spoke, his tone was grudging. "I may have underestimated your amateur skills, Lord Astley."

"A veiled compliment. I'll take it. But Jack's never mentioned any other woman," Frederick added, frowning. "Except his—" He stopped short, heat rising to his face. "His wife."

"Another sharp observation." Johnson traced the rim of his glass with his finger, his gaze distant. "We worked a case years ago. Edith was involved. She chose Miracle."

"And promptly left him for another man," Frederick finished, watching Johnson's head snap up in surprise. "Jack told me as much. Took some of his money, ran off, and filed for divorce within a year."

Johnson exhaled, leaning back in his chair as though the words had knocked the air out of him. "I didn't know."

"He's a good man and a good detective. Perhaps the lady wasn't the right one for either of you."

Johnson relented with a shadow of a nod, the topic mercifully left to fade. "So what did you discover from Hargrove?"

Frederick's lips twitched upward. Finally, back to business. Johnson's question, while gruffly delivered, was a subtle concession—accepting Frederick's assistance without outright admitting it. Baby steps. "Tony Dixon had a conflict with a stranger, a Scot it seems, who happened to go by the name of—"

"Let me guess." Johnson's brow arched with maddening smugness. "Clark?"

Frederick narrowed his eyes. How much did the man already know? "Indeed. And the altercation occurred two nights before Dixon's death."

"Did Hargrove mention anything about Dixon's regular temperament?"

Frederick took a measured sip from his glass, the burn in his throat barely masking the sting of recalling Tony's fate. A decent man undone by his own desperation. "By all accounts, he had a good reputation. Generous, even. But he was notoriously unlucky—cards, dice—a win from any form of gambling seemed to elude him."

"And banking didn't seem to suit him either," Johnson added. "Worked at the same firm for a year without a single promotion. Some miscalculated figures cost him his standing." He paused, looking up from his glass. "Evidently, he went into banking at his family's insistence. The man wanted to work with his hands."

"Farming?"

"Or building. A craftsman at heart."

Tony sacrificed his dreams for Lillias' ambitions? A banking position would have carried more prestige, after all. And did Lillias know? For some reason, that made the death of the man even worse. Despite the rumors of his and Lillias' marital conflict, some sort of affection had moved them. Both of them, if Frederick guessed.

"Speaking of strangers from across the pond," Johnson interrupted his thoughts, fixing him with a pointed gaze, "there's a Scot staying at the Clarion Hotel. Arrived recently. Keeps to himself. Ring any bells?"

Johnson already knew exactly why Frederick would be acquainted with such a man. Had Mrs. James alerted him of the note Frederick had sent to Mr. Barclay last evening? "Mr. Barclay is here on business concerning my wife and her sister."

“And what sort of business, may I ask?” Johnson’s right eyebrow raised.

Frederick mirrored the expression. “Barclay is handling an inheritance. Apparently a Scottish estate left by their mother. He should be meeting with Lady Astley and Mrs. Dixon even now to discuss the matter.”

“Oh, he’s already been there. Officer Todd informed me.” Johnson finished off his glass. “Curious timing, wouldn’t you say?”

The thought hadn’t strayed too far from Frederick’s mind, but he kept quiet.

“A Scottish pin found at the murder site. A foreign stranger who had an altercation with the victim before his death. The sudden arrival of a Scot to deliver an inheritance which conveniently resides in Scotland?” He stood and tossed a few bills on the table. “Curious.” He tipped his hat. “I’d keep a very wary eye out, Lord Astley.”

Grace walked to her room, envelope in hand, ready to delve into the photos Mr. Barclay had left, when a small shadowy figure down the hallway stopped her.

Zahra stood by the tall window, her long dark hair falling down the back of her pale pink dress, her body half hidden behind the curtain as she looked out. The same sweetness Grace always felt when she realized the little girl was theirs burgeoned through her, and she walked over the simple carpet toward her.

But just before Grace reached the window, Zahra turned and held out her palm to stop Grace’s forward movement. “Keep hidden, Sayyida. It is the false Clark.”

The warmth in Grace’s chest crashed into a chill, her pulse ratcheting up as she crouched and slid closer to the wall, keeping her body away from the window’s visibility.

Grace peered over the top of Zahra's head, which overlooked the back garden where the houses all stretched out around the large, wooded park area she'd seen yesterday. In daylight, it didn't look as foreboding, but the thickness of the trees not only offered shade from the sun but a cloak for more villainous options as well.

"He has no mustache," Zahra whispered, gesturing to her own upper lip with a gravity that would've been comical under any other circumstances.

Near the edge of the wood stood a very transformed Officer Clark, or what she could see of his profile at such a distance through a dirty window on an overcast day with a tree blocking part of his person. He gave off the same impression as the fake Officer Clark. He was tall, that much she could tell. With a sturdy body shape very similar to the man they'd seen rush into the house claiming to be the false officer. And his swath of brown hair matched her memory of the man too.

He stood apparently talking to someone, but the someone was shaded by trees. From where she stood, Grace couldn't quite make out his eye color or see if there were any facial scars, a very important tidbit of information for any sleuth to recognize, but his stature cut a memorable figure among the forested area. He wore a summer suit, well trimmed and, if she guessed right, rather stylish, but of course, her knowledge in such matters was always lacking refinement.

"Are you certain it's him?" Grace whispered.

Zahra shot her a look of withering offense.

"Well," Grace amended quickly, "I thought so too. But it's good to confirm. You are new to sleuthing, after all." She paused, softening. "But your instincts are remarkable."

Zahra's expression eased, and she nodded toward the window. "He is not as handsome as Sayid."

Grace nodded. "Very few are, you know." Common knowledge,

of course. She narrowed her eyes, trying to decipher the man's movements—or better yet, his lips. Was he talking about. . . elephants? Or chairs? Wind chimes? None of it aligned with villainous scheming—or logical conversation, for that matter—but Grace made a mental note to add lip-reading to her burgeoning detective training regimen. "Detective Miracle says a good detective looks beyond the typical," she murmured, leaning closer to the glass. "Can you see who he's talking to?"

Zahra shook her head, the motion releasing a faint trace of rosewater perfume. Grace's lips curved into a faint smile. Brushing Zahra's hair each night was a cherished ritual, a fragrant moment that reminded her of her own mother.

"Stay here and keep watch." Grace placed her palm on the girl's shoulder. "I'm going to the lower level to see if I can get a better view."

She moved quickly toward the stairs but nearly collided with Frederick halfway up. His smile—oh, that devastatingly charming smile—momentarily erased all thought. Zahra's earlier remark about his handsomeness floated back with new vigor. Handsome? No. The man was positively Byronic.

Even with a snore.

Grace rushed forward and his smile slowly faded.

"What is it?"

Grace grabbed his arm and tugged him down the stairs, her words a hurried whisper. "It's Officer Clark. Or rather, the false Officer Clark. Zahra spotted him in the back garden, skulking near the woods."

Frederick's expression sharpened instantly. "Where exactly?"

"Near the park. I couldn't make out the details of his face because of his hat, the dirty window, and the distance, but I feel certain it's the same man." She sent him a look as they rounded the doorway into the library. "How curious he would be here just after Mr. Barclay left." Her attention shot to him. "Do you think he knows about the inheritance?"

Without answering, Frederick took her and pulled her across the unlit room to the back window.

"Oh, Frederick," Grace breathed, spotting the man slipping deeper into the wooded park. "He's getting away."

Frederick's gaze flicked from the window to her face, then back again. Without a word, he turned and bolted from the room. A moment later, the back door slammed shut, and Grace watched through the window as her husband sprinted across the lawn after Tony Dixon's possible murderer.

It had to be him.

Frederick squinted against the hazy sunlight, the man's retreating form darting between trees just beyond the garden wall. The height, the build—they matched what he and Grace had seen the day before. Disguise or not, this was their man.

The warmth of the afternoon hit Frederick's face as he charged into the back garden, and the muggy feel of a needed rain, especially in this warmer climate, soaked the air. Shrugging off his jacket, he tossed it onto the rock wall before slipping through the gate into the forested park beyond. A soft breeze carried the faintest hint of something sweet, violets perhaps, though not quite. More like a perfume.

He cast a quick glance back toward the house and caught sight of Grace and Zahra peering down from the upstairs window.

Frederick managed a tight smile before plunging into the trees. The path ahead was well-tended, with tall oaks and elms planted in strategic intervals, their broad canopies shading more than they obstructed. He darted from tree to tree, keeping the man in sight but avoiding open exposure.

If anyone thought an earl's life was all leisure and opulence, they clearly hadn't married Grace. Life with her moved in a whirlwind of escapades, sleuthing, and occasional peril. Yet if Frederick was honest, the intrigue was beginning to take hold of him. His days as a reluctant accomplice to his wife's amateur detective efforts—Venice with Jack Miracle came to mind—had turned into something resembling resigned enthusiasm.

But this? Well, a month of leisure was beginning to sound rather nice. Didn't even the best detectives get a reprieve once in a while?

He conceded a sigh. If he could keep his wife safe, sleuthing did suit him.

The false Clark suddenly stopped up ahead and Frederick froze in place, the nearest tree too far for cover. As if sensing he was being watched, Clark shifted, his profile turning slightly toward Frederick. The angle gave a brief glimpse of a strong jawline and a shadowed cheekbone under the hat's brim—but little else.

Clark hesitated only a moment before vaulting a low hedge and sprinting into a denser stretch of trees.

With a grimace, Frederick broke cover and gave chase. His legs protested the uneven ground, his polished shoes ill-suited to the terrain. The man's tall frame weaved deftly through the trees, his pace unrelenting. Frederick dodged another tree, jumped a bush, and barely kept his footing over the uneven ground, all the while keeping his attention trained on Clark.

His breath came in sharp bursts as he pursued Clark, who navigated the terrain with an irritating level of ease. They burst from the woods onto cobblestone streets, the orderly buildings of the town looming ahead. Clark darted down a narrow alley, disappearing behind a parked Model T.

Frederick rounded the corner moments later, scanning the empty street. No hat, no man, no trace. He spun on his heel, searching frantically down alleys and behind crates. Nothing.

The man had vanished.

Frederick exhaled sharply and spun around once more before retracing his steps toward the house. He hadn't seen enough of the man's face to identify him later. The obscured features and the clever escape left him with more questions than answers. Whatever Tony's death had entangled them in, the impostor Clark was at the heart of it. And Grace's earlier question about the Scottish inheritance? Well, it was likely part of it all too.

As he retraced his steps, the back garden gate creaked open, revealing Grace with his jacket draped over her arm and Zahra at her side. His wife's vivid eyes sparkled, searching his face. "Are you all right?"

"Fine," he panted, brushing a leaf from his sleeve. "But he got away."

"Ah, but what a chase you gave." Her grin widened. "I had no idea you could run so fast. The way you disappeared into the trees—it was positively swashbuckling. Something straight out of *The Prisoner of Zenda,* though I don't recall Rudolf Rassendyll vaulting hedges with such flair."

Frederick arched a brow, his lips giving way to a reluctant smile. "Should I be flattered or insulted?"

"Flattered, of course." Her eyes rounded as if shocked by his question. "If nothing else, you've demonstrated that an earl can be both dashing and spry." A glint flared in those deep blue eyes. "Very reassuring for any future detective endeavors, my dear Lord Astley."

His lips twitched, a retort on his lips, when a voice behind them interrupted. "Does trouble usually precede or follow you, Lord Astley?"

Frederick turned to find Detective Johnson striding through the doorway, his expression equal parts curiosity and bemusement. He tipped his hat in Grace's direction. "Lady Astley."

"Your timing is impeccable," Frederick replied dryly.

Johnson's mouth quirked in a smirk. "Todd mentioned he saw you giving chase as he drove here for our meeting."

"And he didn't think to stop and lend a hand?" Frederick shot back, incredulous. "Not exactly the mark of chivalry."

"To be fair, by the time he saw you, the man was long gone." Johnson's smirk deepened. "Was it Clark?"

"Almost certainly," Frederick said, leading the way toward the house.

"Describe him," Johnson said, his tone sharpening.

As they walked inside, Frederick and Grace recounted the details, though Frederick's frustration grew with each step. He hadn't seen enough to be definitive. By the time they reached the parlor, Johnson's lips were pressed into a thin line.

"He matches the description of a foreigner staying at Gray's Hotel on the south side of town," Johnson finally said. "Registered under the name Roberts. Kept to himself, only arrived last week."

"So Clark is really Roberts?" Grace asked.

"Or both names are assumed," Johnson replied, shaking his head. "Todd and I plan to visit Gray's Hotel in the morning and see if Mr. Roberts has anything enlightening to say for himself."

A sudden crash sounded from down the hallway followed by a piercing scream. Johnson started toward the sound with Frederick on his heels. Good heavens, what now?

They met Mrs. James stumbling into the hall from the direction of the kitchen. Her face was ashen, and her hands trembled as she clutched at the doorframe.

"It's—it's Cook!" she gasped, her voice breaking. "Something's happened—she's on the floor, not moving."

"What?" Lillias appeared at the top of the stairs as they passed, her face pale. "I heard a crash!"

"Someone broke into the house." Mrs. James wiped at the tears on her face and waved them to follow her. "Cook is on the floor. I don't know if she's hurt, but she's not moving. You must help."

Chapter 13

After watching Frederick take off on such an adventurous run, Grace had hoped they'd have a moment to discuss their respective discoveries—his from the gambling house and hers from Mr. Barclay. But Mrs. James' declaration had flung everyone into a whirlwind of action, leaving no room for such luxuries as conversation.

Detective Johnson charged in the direction Mrs. James pointed, Frederick close on his heels, with Officer Todd trailing behind. Grace tightened her grip on Zahra's hand and cast a glance at Lillias as her sister descended the stairs. Poor Lillias looked as if she might very well be the next to collapse.

"What—what is happening to my family?" Lillias' voice trembled, her usual composure shattered.

For the first time since Grace's arrival, the real vulnerability of the situation showed on her sister's face. The lostness. And in that single moment, Grace *knew.* Lillias had nothing to do with any of it—not Tony's death, not the inheritance chaos, none of it.

But then why Tony and Lillias? Why now? And what on earth did this attack on poor Mrs. Lindsay—the cook, for heaven's sake—have to do with anything?

The same maddening thought kept circling in her mind. *The inheritance?*

But how did Tony factor into something that was Lillias' by right?

"I don't know, Lillias, but we're going to sort it out together."

To her surprise, Lillias didn't summon her usual derisive look. Instead, her expression softened, almost as if relief had found its way through the cracks of her fear.

"You stay here in the parlor and rest. I'll be back soon." Grace squeezed her sister's hand before hurrying after the others, Zahra's small hand still firmly in her own.

She wasn't entirely sure why she needed to keep hold of Zahra, but the whirlwind of Frederick's chase after the false Clark and the sudden attack on the cook left her uneasy.

And though Zahra had an excellent start at sleuthing, the little girl was still only about ten, and an introduction into any family shouldn't be this chaotic. Should it? Her thoughts spun back to her very unexpected introduction to Frederick's family upon marriage and she reevaluated her earlier idea. Perhaps dangers and mysteries were just a part of family introductions.

The kitchen greeted her with chaos: Detective Johnson and Frederick knelt beside Mrs. Lindsay, who lay sprawled on the tiled floor, bonnet askew, her face a ghostly white. Todd hovered by the open back door.

The breeze sent the curtains fluttering like restless ghosts.

A thrill traveled up Grace's arms at the very thought.

Ghosts seemed to be a part of family introductions too. At least where she was concerned.

Frederick knelt beside the cook, pressing two fingers to her neck. "She's alive," he said, relief evident in his voice.

"Alive?" The words burst from Mrs. James. Her eyes blinked wide and her shoulders slumped with a sigh. "Oh, thank heavens!"

"There's blood on the back of her head though," Johnson noted grimly, his sharp eyes turning to Mrs. James. "What happened? Did you see anyone?"

Mrs. James shook her head, her hands twisting in her apron. "No, sir. I was just coming back from the parlor after setting out the tea things when I heard the crash. Mrs. Lindsay has been known to take issue with the stove from time to time, so I thought nothing of it—until I came in and saw. . ." Her voice faltered, and she pressed a trembling hand to her mouth. "It was awful."

Grace looked down at the scene, trying to think despite Mrs. James' distractingly dramatic sobs. Grace was beginning to realize all the more how very few women are prepared for such scenes as unconscious cooks after a break-in and mysterious possible-murderers in one's back garden. However, Mrs. Lindsay could cook, which was much more than Grace could do. And Mrs. James could carry a tea tray without shaking it so much it threatened the teacups.

So why wouldn't it make sense that some women took dangerous situations with much more clarity than others. God *did* like variety.

And life was dangerous.

And people desperately needed good cooks and excellent tea.

So it made perfect sense.

"The intruder must have escaped out that way." Frederick gestured toward the open back door, his usual calm expression a shade grimmer. He turned to Mrs. James. "Is there a place we can lay Mrs. Lindsay where she'll be more comfortable?"

Mrs. James blinked and nodded. "Yes, of course. Her room." She stepped toward a small narrow hall next to the kitchen. "This way."

Lillias entered the room, her gaze flicking nervously to Mrs. Lindsay's unconscious form. "Lonnie, our kitchen boy, is up front at the door talking to one of his friends. Should I have him fetch the doctor?"

"Yes. Right away." Johnson motioned for Officer Todd to

help. Together, Frederick and Todd carefully lifted Mrs. Lindsay and carried her out of the kitchen, their hushed murmurs of conversation fading as they moved down the hall.

Grace's eyes roamed over the disarray: a spilled stew pot, an overturned stool, faint scuff marks near the back door. And then her gaze caught the garden wall outside, positioned perfectly to offer a view of Mr. Clark and the stranger's earlier rendezvous. Her breath shuddered out of her, as a new theory began to crystallize in her mind.

What if. . .what if Mr. Clark wasn't meeting a man? But a woman?

Grace's attention shot to the narrow hallway where Mrs. James led the men into another room with Mrs. Lindsay in tow. How ridiculous of her to overlook a very important possibility.

A fresh, unsettling thought bloomed in her mind, and for a moment, she stood frozen. How ridiculous not to have thought of it. Grace had read enough mysteries to know that the most unexpected culprits were often the most dangerous—especially if they were of the female persuasion. After all, hadn't the mastermind behind the Venice mystery been a woman? And the murderer of Frederick's father and brother had been a woman too.

A slow frown creased her brow. Women were terribly dangerous.

Grace began righting the room, Zahra moving to help. Meanwhile, the men murmured in conversation from the room next door, their voices rising and falling in such a way that Grace could almost make out their words. She longed to listen in, but her thoughts were quickly redirected when Lillias returned, scanning the room. Her face was still pale, and her eyes looked as though they'd borne the weight of a thousand sleepless nights.

"Lonnie's gone for the doctor."

"That was excellent thinking." Grace offered an encouraging smile.

Lillias pulled a shawl tighter around her shoulders, leaning her head against the doorframe. "This can't keep happening, Grace. My whole world is falling to pieces and I don't know what to do."

The weakness in her voice hinted that Lillias' strength may give out any moment.

"Well, sitting would probably be a good idea. Come, we'll sit while the others handle things." Grace motioned her toward the parlor, glancing back toward the kitchen hallway. Oh how she wanted to know what they were saying and observe Mrs. James' responses, but Lillias needed someone.

Grace straightened. She may very well be the only someone Lillias had. And what did typical women do when they were distressed? "We could have some tea."

But Lillias didn't move. Instead, her gaze trailed back toward the stairs. "I need to see to Thomas."

Grace's instincts told her that Lillias, in her current state, would likely do more harm than good attempting to navigate the stairs.

"I'm sure he's fine for the moment," Grace said gently. She turned to Zahra, lowering her voice to a near whisper. "Would you go check on Miss Cox with little Thomas, please?"

Zahra hesitated only a second, before disappearing down the hallway toward the stairway to the second level.

Lillias slid into the chair at the parlor table and pressed her fingers into her forehead. "You can't know what it's like. This life." The previous bitterness had quieted, replaced by a tone of resignation that Grace wasn't sure was any better. "It hasn't been all bad. Not at first." A weak smile flickered. "Tony wanted everything to be easy for me. Bought anything I asked for—or anything he thought would make my life more like what I'd been used to." She trailed off, her chin trembling. "He was happy too. We lived in this little world of ours and played house like we had money to spare."

Grace sat down next to her, questions ricocheting in her mind, but something paused her usual impulsivity toward answers. Grace had learned more about the value of listening during her last two mysteries. And in truth, sometimes people just needed to be heard. Perhaps, the carousel of emotions her sister had been through over the last two days, not to mention the previous few months, had started to settle into something gentler and more introspective than resentment.

"But it couldn't last." Her sister's weak laugh dissolved into a frown. "And I didn't want to let go of the beautiful things in my life. The status. The fashion."

"So Tony tried to work harder?"

Lillias nodded, but her eyes clouded over. "Especially with the knowledge of our baby coming soon, but. . .it wasn't enough to satisfy me." She wiped at her cheek, a tear slipping down. "Tony may have struggled with gambling, but I struggled with such a vile discontent that it led him to the gambling." A sob slipped from her. "No wonder I'm reaping the consequences now."

Grace reached for her sister's hand. "It's not all your fault, Lillias."

Lillias looked up, a frown crossing her features. "What do you mean?"

How to explain? "In many mysteries, what appears to be the main problem at first usually isn't the problem at all."

Lillias looked up at her, brow creased. "What?"

Oh, right. Lillias doesn't speak in fiction. Or mysteries. Grace tried to think of a nonfictional sort of analogy, which never came as quickly as the fictional ones, so to buy herself time, she smiled. "Would you like some tea?"

Lillias gave a small nod, and Grace reached for a cup.

"I wonder if it really is as simple as a conflict over a gambling debt." Lillias gave a small, weary nod, and Grace reached for the teapot with the utmost care. The pot still shook enough to make the lid rattle. She poured the tea quickly, her hand a bit too unsteady. A few droplets splashed onto her fingers, and she flinched, waiting for the burn.

But the tea was cold.

Grace glanced down at the cup, her brows knitting together.

"And why Mrs. Lindsay?" Lillias asked. "The poor woman had nothing to do with anything but the kitchen."

A very good question from her sister, which only proved that if given the right incentive, Lillias might think more clearly too. And currently they needed as many good brains at work as possible.

Grace pressed her fingers against the side of the teapot. It was barely warm. She glanced at the clock mantel. "Mrs. James said she'd just left this," Grace murmured, mostly to herself.

"What?" Lillias asked, before taking a sip from the cup Grace had set before her. "It's cold."

With a slight hesitation, Grace lowered herself into the chair next to her sister. Perhaps she should start with the least obvious concerns. "Lillias, how long has Mrs. Lindsay worked here?"

Lillias absentmindedly nibbled on a sandwich, eyes distant. "Tony hired her before we were ever married. She'd worked for his mother before her death."

Grace paused, taking a sandwich for herself, but the bite barely registered. She was more interested in what came next. "And what about Mrs. James?"

"Mrs. James?" Lillias took a sip of the cold tea and frowned as if remembering it was cold. "She's only been with me two weeks."

Two weeks? Grace tried not to raise an eyebrow, but she couldn't help it. "I see."

"I know she's immature and a gossip." Lillias sighed. "Heaven knows how many times I've already had to talk to the woman about sharing information to the newsboy or milkman, but what could I do? We needed help and her rate met my purse's approval."

Grace glanced toward the hallway, making sure they were still alone. An idea stopped her. As a housekeeper, Mrs. James had a great deal of access to information in the house. And as a gossip, what would she do with that information? "Where did she work before coming here?"

Lillias shook her head, half listening, half lost in some sort of thought Grace couldn't decipher. "I was an exhausted new mother with mounting debt and an absent husband. All I needed was someone to help me, and my last housekeeper had left without a word."

A sudden departure? Oh, Grace desperately needed to write all this information down. She always processed connections better when she looked at all the clues in writing.

The lostness on her sister's face curbed her immediate need to ask another question or to dash upstairs for her notebook. "That must have been a trying time."

"It was, along with Father's disaster," Lillias answered, her gaze returning to the nearby window, body stiffening. "Mrs. Dunn, my former housekeeper, had been with me since my first month married. To be treated in such a fashion when she knew very well how much I needed her—it was unforgivable." A humorless laugh erupted from her. "But what should I expect. Look at all that's gone wrong."

Lillias didn't need to know Grace's concerns about Mrs. James. Not yet. She'd share them with Frederick and perhaps Detective Johnson, but the last thing Lillias needed was another worry. So much had happened in such a short amount of time, and unlike Grace, Lillias hadn't experienced a great deal of drama or suspense through fiction to prepare her for it in real life, so information needed to be given in spoonfuls instead of ladles. She smiled at her own household references. Clearly, she'd been reading more of Lady Molly of Scotland Yard to use analogies from the kitchen.

"I can't understand the difficulties you've encountered." Grace squeezed Lillias' hand. "You must have felt so alone, but you're not alone now. We are here to help you, and maybe even start over."

Lillias' expression softened, just the slightest flicker of relief. "Starting over sounds like my only choice."

It wasn't much, but it was something. A start. Grace let out a small sigh, knowing how monumental that one flicker could be for someone like Lillias. "With that in mind. . ." She picked up the envelope Mr. Barclay had left with them, pushing aside her curiosity about the photos for now. There would be time for that later. "Mr. Barclay left information about the accounts Mother set up for us." She rifled through a few pages, deliberately avoiding the distraction of the photographs. "Here's an envelope with your name on it. Well, 'Lillias Ferguson' rather than 'Lillias Dixon,' but of course Mother wouldn't have known about your marriage."

Lillias took the envelope and glanced inside, a new sheen of tears filling her eyes. "It's the information for the bank account," Lillias murmured, her voice trembling. "Finally, something good in this disaster." She tapped the envelope against the table, her shoulders relaxing. "A way to start over."

Just then, Frederick, Officer Todd, and Detective Johnson reentered the parlor, and Grace felt a knot tighten in her chest at Frederick's grim expression. "Mrs. Lindsay is resting, but whoever did this is long gone," he said.

Johnson nodded. "Todd and I will search the grounds and then reconvene to discuss matters."

"Before you begin your search, Detective, these are the names of the collectors I visited yesterday morning." Lillias offered him a slip of paper and looked down. "Please keep this information private as long as you can. I don't want the socialites of Harrington to know what sort of circumstances my husband and I were in before. . .his death."

Johnson looked down at the paper and tucked it into his

jacket. "Thank you, Mrs. Dixon. Expect us to reconvene within the hour." He sent a look to Todd. "Gather a few more officers, and we can cover more ground."

The two men disappeared toward the front door, with Lillias trailing behind them, no doubt eager to see them out and return to the privacy she desperately needed.

Grace met Frederick's gaze. "Where is Mrs. James?"

Frederick's attention sharpened on Grace, and perhaps he was reading her thoughts as he'd done so well in the past. Without a word, he grabbed her hand and turned toward the kitchen, the sound of their footsteps muted by the carpets. They slipped down the narrow hallway toward Mrs. Lindsay's room and peered through the door. The sight before them almost made Grace stumble: Mrs. James, standing over the older woman's bed, holding a pillow.

Grace's breath caught, but it wasn't until her foot shifted on the creaky floor that Mrs. James spun around, eyes wide. A nervous laugh escaped her as she pressed her palm to her chest. "Oh, good heavens, I thought the assailant had returned." She dropped the pillow on the bed. "How may I be of service to you?"

"I believe Mrs. Dixon could use some refreshment, Mrs. James." Grace answered, stepping forward into the room. "As you can imagine, she's rather overwhelmed by all that's happened over the last two days."

Mrs. James' smile stiffened, and her gaze flicked back to the bed. "But Cook shouldn't be left alone in her state. I noticed her neck seemed crooked, and I fetched another pillow to make her comfortable."

"We'll stay with her until your return." Frederick answered without hesitation and then unleashed a smile so genuine Grace would have thought he meant it, but for the lack of change in his eyes. How did he do that? It was so clever. "I'm rather rubbish at anything like making tea or offering refreshments."

What a wonderful way to distract her! Oh, her dear husband was so clever. Grace pushed up her own smile. "And I'm not much better. I've already made a mess of the tea you brought into the parlor."

The smile on Mrs. James' face faltered. She sent a look from Frederick to Grace then down to Mrs. Lindsay, clearly hesitant.

"Don't worry. We'll keep a close eye on her." Frederick said. "No one ever wants to lose an excellent cook."

Oddly, his statement seemed to break whatever reserve Mrs. James had left. She relaxed, her face softening. "You're right." She rounded them toward the door. "I'll return as soon as I've seen to Mrs. Dixon."

She slipped down the small hallway. Frederick gestured for Grace to take the chair near the bed. "I'll stay by the door to keep watch."

"Very smart of you, Frederick. Because I think the walls have ears, but first things first. Just to be sure." Grace leaned toward Mrs. Lindsay's still frame and in a loud whisper said. "Someone is trying to steal your favorite cooking pot."

The woman didn't even flinch.

"What on earth are you doing, darling?" Frederick studied her as though she had sprouted feathers from her head.

Poor man. She thought her reasoning was quite obvious. "I had to make sure she was really unconscious, Frederick," Grace explained, "and couldn't hear us if we spoke about serious matters related to the case."

He squinted at her, the adorably confused look spreading across his face.

"Cooks always have a favorite pot. My grandfather used to say that a good cook would practically rise from the dead to save it."

Frederick's lips quirked. He folded his arms across his rather impressive chest and leaned against the door with a casual grace.

"Well then, it appears we are safe at the moment."

If they weren't in such a confined situation, Grace would be tempted to rush into Frederick's impressive chest and kiss him senseless until he whisked her away to their room. Her face grew warm at the very thought. He seemed to follow her thoughts because one of his brows tipped in response. Well, perhaps that wasn't so much his clairvoyance as her inability to maintain a neutral expression when it came to her admiration for him.

"You find the most unexpected times to divert my thoughts, Lady Astley," he said, his voice low and amused.

"You started it," she replied, a much needed smile playing on her lips.

One eyebrow arched in perfect synchronicity with the other. "Me?"

Her smile widened as her cheeks flushed. "You look rather dashing guarding the doorway in your linen suit."

His eyes darkened in that deliciously dangerous way of his, though his posture remained as calm as ever. "Perhaps we can discuss how dashing you think of me later, in our room?"

"I think that's an excellent proposal, my lord, worthy of extended conversation." She cleared her throat and folded her hands in her lap like the demure wife she knew she wasn't. "Now what did you discover from your visit to the Lucky Coin?"

He sent her a pointed look tagged on with a crooked smile that promised all sorts of things he didn't speak. It really was quite remarkable to blend so many exciting things together into what was becoming her life. Mystery, intrigue, tenderness, danger, motherhood, travel, romance. Marriage kept proving better than any work of fiction she'd ever read.

Well, she didn't like the *very* dangerous parts, except if it meant rescuing someone—or being rescued by her own personal hero.

And she didn't like the death parts for any reason.

Or the near-death parts, except when it involved the opportunity to cane-fight or watch Frederick wield a pistol.

But so many of the other parts proved positively delightful.

"Tony had an altercation with a man two nights ago. A foreigner," Frederick said.

"Scottish?"

He nodded. "Went by the name of Clark."

"Oh! Frederick." She leaned forward, her hands twisting in her lap.

"And if Clark proves to be this Roberts fellow, then Johnson and Todd will hopefully find out when they question him at his hotel."

Grace sighed back into her chair, trying to suppress a groan. "Then maybe we can end this entire situation before too many more horrible things happen." Her eyes flicked to Mrs. Lindsay and then back to Frederick. "I don't believe Lillias can manage much more."

"What are your thoughts about Mrs. James?" Frederick glanced back down the hallway before turning his attention back to Grace.

Before she could answer, her mind sparked, a memory flashing to mind. "Well, before I divulge that particular information, I just realized something. When we entered the kitchen, I noticed the windows into the back garden provide an excellent view of the area where Mr. Clark was meeting with our mysterious someone."

Frederick looked back toward the kitchen, then locked his gaze with hers. "And you think whoever Clark met with recognized that Mrs. Lindsay may have seen them?"

"I don't know for certain." Grace shrugged a shoulder. "But the information about Mrs. James does make me wonder all the more about her involvement in everything."

He tipped his head in anticipation of her elaboration, and she sent a quick look to poor Mrs. Lindsay. It felt a little strange to have such a vital conversation with someone unconscious in the room, but this was hardly the first time they'd done so.

"Lillias hired Mrs. James out of desperation after her former housekeeper left abruptly. Apparently, Mrs. James was referred by the previous housekeeper, according to her. Lillias needed someone to help with the baby and the house, and Mrs. James' inexperience was a bargain. She started working here two weeks ago."

Frederick's attention sharpened. "Not long after the inheritance became yours and your sister's."

"Exactly." Grace stood and began to pace, her mind whirring through what they knew so far. "Mrs. James' service hadn't been long, but enough to learn the workings of the house. She could easily allow people inside without garnering suspicion or anyone noticing. The murderer entered the house while everyone was out of it."

"Information an insider would know."

"Exactly." She rewarded her husband with a smile, then continued her pacing. "And she would have known when Lillias would return from her outing, allowing her to frame Lillias as a suspect."

Frederick's jaw tightened as realization set in. "Mr. Clark was there to cast doubt on your sister's innocence and to ensure the police were called quickly, leading to Lillias being placed under house arrest or, worse, convicted. Her potential guilt would strip her of the ability to travel at all." Frederick's gaze sharpened on her, as he came to the same realization flashing through her mind. "What happens to your inheritance if you and Lillias do not claim it?"

Grace swallowed. The weight of it all was beginning to settle on her chest. "It goes to auction."

Frederick's face darkened. "And who might want that land, Grace? Bad enough to kill for it?"

Her pulse quickened as the pieces began to fall into place. "There are resources on it. Coal, for one. But Mr. Barclay mentioned others." Her breath caught in her throat. "Frederick, Mr. Barclay brought the papers with him to his hotel for us to sign, in case we can't travel right away, so we can still claim the inheritance before the time is up."

The look Frederick sent her deepened the new chill running through her chest. "Mr. Barclay told you this just a few hours ago?"

She nodded. "And is it possible that Mrs. James overheard the conversation?"

Frederick's gaze hardened as he stepped back toward the hallway. "Grace, we need to find Detective Johnson. If Mrs. James is part of Mr. Clark's plot and she overheard your conversation. . ."

"Then there is a good chance the next victim in this growing list of victims will be dear Mr. Barclay."

Chapter 14

Mr. Barclay was in trouble.

Frederick could feel it in the pit of his stomach. Every piece of the puzzle Grace had revealed combined with the clues they'd already uncovered pointed to a single conclusion: Someone was after Grace's inheritance. And while the method was convoluted, each step—starting with Tony's murder—seemed deliberately aimed at that very goal.

Grace looked down at Mrs. Lindsay. "We can't leave her here alone."

"No." The vision of Mrs. James holding the pillow over Mrs. Lindsay's bed gave off unsettling hints of what may still be in Mrs. Lindsay's future. He held his wife's gaze, not for the first time relinquishing the power to protect her when the logical choice required them to part.

"Could we ask Miss Cox?"

Miss Cox? The poor woman had enough difficulty managing an infant, what would she do with a— He stopped. Hadn't she experience with the wounded and dying? "Excellent notion. Can we trust Zahra with Thomas?"

"I'm certain we can, especially with Lillias in the house." Grace moved toward him. "One of us should stay with Mrs. Lindsay, and the other can fetch Miss Cox, and then could we go to the Clarion?"

"Or first find Detective Johnson?"

His instinct screamed at him to prioritize warning Mr. Barclay. They could apologize to Johnson later.

"Perhaps we'll see Detective Johnson on the way to the hotel." Grace offered, searching his face. "But I think our first stop should be the Clarion."

"I hate leaving you here alone." He skimmed over her body. How would she defend herself? "Do you have your parasol?"

Realization dawned in those eyes. "Oh no, it's in our room." She nodded, her smile reassuring. "But I do have a knife hidden in my—"

"Very well." He cut off her sentence just in case someone neared, his grin tempting release. He didn't need anyone envisioning where his darling wife hid her assortment of various weaponry except himself. "Stay with Mrs. Lindsay. I'll bring Miss Cox back and discover Mrs. James' whereabouts."

"All right."

He dipped his head to give her a quick kiss. "Stay alert."

She nodded, and with one last lingering glance, he made his way through the kitchen and into the narrow passage leading to the mail rooms. He met no one until he reached the main stairs, where Lillias was descending.

Had she been so finely dressed when he'd seen her earlier? And why was she wearing a hat?

He didn't have time to contemplate his sister-in-law's fashion choices.

Her eyes widened the instant she saw him. A flicker of concern passed through her features, as though she was bracing herself for some new revelation. Considering the circumstances, it was no wonder.

"Have you seen Mrs. James?" He tried to keep his voice neutral, but patience was running thin.

Lillias sighed, her entire body sagging under an invisible weight. "Mrs. James? Oh, yes. She came by just a moment ago, asking if I needed anything."

"And where did she go?"

Lillias studied his face. "I sent her to the grocery because she desperately needed some fresh air. She was positively quaking from what had happened to Mrs. Lindsay, so I told her to go."

Before he could speak again, the front door opened, and in walked the doctor.

"Perfect," Frederick muttered under his breath, almost surprised at the relief that washed over him. It was fleeting, though. Lillias looked at him, brow furrowed, clearly confused by his reaction.

"Could you see the doctor to Mrs. Lindsay's room?" he asked, already turning away. "And send Grace upstairs? We need to leave for an important appointment without hesitation."

He didn't wait for Lillias' response, taking the stairs two at a time. Reaching Miss Cox and Zahra's room, he found Thomas sleeping soundly in his crib. Frederick quickly explained the situation, omitting the worst details about Mr. Barclay's safety but stressing the need for the women to remain in the room until they returned. "It's an unfortunate accident involving Mrs. Lindsay," he said, though the words tasted strange on his tongue.

Zahra watched him with the same intensity as always.

Miss Cox kept her usual scared expression.

He'd just left the bedroom when he met Grace in the hall.

"I retrieved my parasol, just in case." She smiled in her reassuring way, but the knowledge of her particular need for a parasol as her weapon of choice always came with a mixed feeling of reassurance and concern. "Do we search for Detective Johnson?"

Frederick took her by the arm and moved toward the stairs. "I'm afraid we don't have the luxury of time. We need to get to

Mr. Barclay as soon as possible."

She nodded, increasing her pace down the stairs just as the front door opened again to reveal the detective and Officer Todd.

Frederick leveled the detective a look, his body tensing in preparation at Frederick's approach. "We need to get to Barclay. There's not time to spare."

Johnson's brow quirked slightly, but he didn't say anything. He merely held the door open for them to pass.

"I'll explain on the way," Frederick tossed over his shoulder, his pace already quickening.

"And pray, Detective Johnson." Grace added. "Pray that we're not too late."

He couldn't breathe.

Something covered his face—something coarse and cold. Was it a cloth? A bandage? He had a vague memory of waking up the same way before, but last time, when he'd reached for his face, the pain in his shoulder and a sudden weakness had pulled him back into the darkness of unconsciousness.

A sudden panic swelled into his throat, squeezing at his consciousness. No, he couldn't go back into the dark again. He had to stay awake. He drew in a shallow breath, but it was enough to prove he could draw in another. Stay calm. Think.

After another breath, his mind cleared a little more, awakening awareness to other senses. The bone-deep cold seeping into his marrow. The strange scent combination of vinegar and smoke? And something else? An undercurrent of a sickening sort of aroma, but he couldn't place it. He shivered, the quake of a movement inciting an ache in his chest. His fingers prickled awake.

In the back of his mind, he seemed to know he'd been cold for a while. Asleep for a while too. But why? Where was he?

His eyelids fluttered open to darkness, a vacant kind, like being in a tunnel. Fatigue wooed him back into oblivion, but he forced his eyes to stay open, pushing beyond the gnawing ache somewhere on the right side of his chest. As his eyes adjusted to the blackness, a faint rim of light flickered at the top left corner of his view as if through some sort of net.

He settled his attention on the light and reached up for it, only to find something covering his arms and face. A sheet? Why was he covered in a sheet? Was he in his own bed at home?

With deliberate movements, he raised his left arm and pulled back the cloth from his face. The scents took on more potency and the light above spread to reveal a colorless ceiling with a pipe screwed into place up above, like something in a factory or cellar. With the cloth gone, he drew in a deeper breath, and although it pricked a pain in his chest, it also cleared his mind even more. He wiggled his fingers, and it was almost as if he could feel the warmth of his own blood traveling through each vessel in his body, awakening various areas of soreness or cold with renewed vigor.

He rested his palm against his chest to garner enough strength to move again and took inventory of the rest of his surroundings. He was lying on something hard and unyielding, nothing like his own mattress, and the faint sound of men's voices bled into his comprehension.

Another movement pulled at the ache in his chest, so he pushed back the sheet even more and reached a hand to touch his chest. Instead of brushing against the fabric of his shirt, his fingers slid along the familiar material of. . .a bandage? A memory flashed into his mind. He'd been in his home, barely awake, feeling the effects of a late night, and someone had rushed him.

Stabbed him.

His pulse took a faster pace in his ears, heating his chilled face, but he quieted the rising hysteria with another deep breath. *God, help me.* He clung to the phrase, though he neither deserved it nor prayed it nearly enough, but lying in utter weakness surrounded by darkness pushed him to a cognizance he'd long forsaken.

Need. At the life level.

He'd felt need in finances. In love.

Longing for things he didn't have and desperately wanted. Good things.

But this ache in his chest, this utter helplessness, reflected a need that struck much deeper.

Soul deep.

He drew in another calming breath and focused on the ceiling and the golden light flickering against it. This wasn't a hospital.

He focused in on the sounds of the men's voices, their conversation rough and casual-sounding, but he couldn't quite make out their words. They were close on his left. Friend or foe, he didn't know, but he couldn't stay here.

Bracing his mind for the movement, he gathered his strength and pushed up on elbows, the ache in his chest increasing to a sting. He sat up with a groan, the world spinning for a moment before settling into focus.

The room was filled with shadows and long box-like shapes suspended on what looked like various tables. He blinked and followed the glow away from the shadows toward the table in the center of the room where a single oil lamp stood. Two men sat across from each other, their clothes careworn. One was older, grizzled with a face that spoke of years of hard work, while the other was young, barely out of his teens by the look of him.

"Three aces," the older one said with a chuckle, laying down his cards. "You've got the luck of the devil tonight, Sam."

Sam, the younger man, opened his mouth to respond when his eyes focused forward. His jaw dropped and his face paled to an ashen hue.

Why was he looking at me with such fear? After all, I was the one in need of medical attention.

"J–J–Jim," the young man stuttered, his voice a whisper of terror. He raised a shaking finger. "It's—it's a ghost."

A ghost? Where? For some reason, the idea of a ghost might make sense in these circumstances and in this desolate and dark place.

"Now don't you go being a spoilsport about losin', boy." The older man laughed. "You ain't gonna—"

"He's there," Sam repeated, growing whiter, if that was at all possible.

The older man, Jim, turned and his annoyance transformed into shock.

What was wrong with these men? "Could you help me?" His voice cracked, hoarse from disuse, his throat sore.

The younger man's eyes widened in shock before his body gave way, collapsing in a faint beside the table.

After giving a look at Sam and taking a deep breath, the older man stood. "Well, they got you wrong, didn't they?" He grabbed the lantern off the table, his yellow smile spreading in welcome amidst the eerie half-shadows.

"I—I don't understand."

"I'd 'spect not." Jim lumbered forward, stepping over his unconscious partner with a dismissive glance, his wrinkled grin half in shadow, half in lantern light. "And you'll have to forgive Sam."

Jim's movements sent the lantern light swaying the shadows in the room to an almost dizzying amount. The boxes on all sides shook a little. What were they? "Forgive him? Why?"

Jim shrugged a shoulder, grin crooking. "It's the first time he's ever seen somebody rise from the dead."

"What?" That didn't make any sense. "What are you talking about?"

"I'd say you've either been sick or hurt badly to be in this place."

He lifted his lantern as he grew nearer. "What's your name?"

"Name?" His head felt strange, the room a contrast of blurry and odd, but something began to dawn in the back of his mind. An inexplicable type of dread to add to the cold. He sifted through his foggy thoughts for the answer. "My name's Anthony Dixon."

"Well, Anthony Dixon, you're not the first I've seen wake up in this place. Not often, thank God, but more than anyone should know." He chuckled, the light growing brighter as he came to stand directly in front of Tony. "At least we found out before you went in the ground."

"What?" Tony gave his head a shake, his shoulder aching so deeply, he looked down to assess the problem only to himself shirtless except for the bandages twisted across his chest. His gaze rose, vision clearing on the nearest box.

Wait a moment. That wasn't a box.

And this place wasn't a hospital. The chill in his bones intensified. "Where am I?"

Jim shrugged a shoulder, his expression partly consolatory and partly amused. "Prepare for a shock, mister."

A shock. Tony was already trembling from the cold and the weakness that seemed to seep within every part of his body.

Maybe he didn't want an answer, because he already knew, and voicing the truth would only make the nightmare real.

"You, Mr. Dixon, are sitting inside your own coffin in the morgue cellar."

As the words hit slow comprehension, the weakness overtook Tony all over again and with one last look at the older man, all went dark.

Chapter 15

Every facet of time fought against their trek to the Clarion Hotel, almost as if it knew the outcome as much as Frederick. Evening shadows stretched long and sharp against the gas-lit streets, lending an air of foreboding that seemed to seep into his bones.

If something had happened to Mr. Barclay, it would confirm the worst—that someone was indeed after Grace and Lillias' inheritance. But if they reached him in time, perhaps they could secure not only the inheritance but also catch Tony's killer and Mrs. Lindsay's assailant in the process.

If. . .

As he took the steps up to the main entrance of the ornate building, he tugged Grace's hand a little more tightly through his arm. Johnson had advised Grace to stay behind at the house, a very reasonable request for any other woman.

But his wife was no stranger to the consequences fraught with the darker side of human nature, and having her be a part of any investigation fit their relationship, especially after all the practice they'd had.

Despite the desire to keep her safe always gnawing at the back of his mind, Frederick couldn't imagine engaging in these situations without her.

The air in the lobby of the Clarion smelled faintly of cigar smoke, rich perfume, and fresh varnish, securing its reputation as the most prestigious hotel in Harrington. The leather furnishings and hand-carved moldings underscored the point. Johnson led the way to a large mahogany front desk, Todd on his heels. The soft murmur of patrons and tinkling glasses in the nearby dining room set a hopeful precedent that all was well.

Mr. Barclay was fine.

And Detective Johnson could set up a watch to ensure safety for a transfer of the inheritance of its rightful owners.

"We're here to see Mr. Barclay," Johnson announced, flashing his credentials to the young clerk at the desk.

The clerk blinked, his hand halting mid-flip through the guest ledger. "Is he in trouble, Detective?"

"We hope not." Johnson answered.

"Do you know if Mr. Barclay has had any visitors this evening?" Grace asked, stepping forward. "Any guests?"

"Not that I've seen, ma'am." The clerk ran a finger down the page. "He's kept mostly to himself since he arrived. Takes his meals in his room. I just figured. . ." He trailed off with a shrug. "Well, him being a foreigner and all."

"The room number?" Johnson pressed.

"Mr. Barclay is in room twelve, just up the stairs."

"Todd." Johnson gestured with his chin for the officer to lead the way with him directly behind, and Frederick and Grace pulling up the rear.

Frederick exchanged a glance with Grace. A flicker of concern passed over her features, and if he wasn't mistaken, her grip on the parasol tightened. He stifled a groan. The very last thing he wanted was to envision his wife battling a murderer again. The fact that she'd successfully done so—more than once—was no consolation. If anything, it was downright terrifying.

Todd approached the door to room twelve cautiously, his pistol drawn as he scanned the hallway. He gave a nod to Johnson, who knocked firmly.

"Mr. Barclay? It's Detective Johnson."

Silence.

Johnson knocked again, louder this time. "Mr. Barclay, I'm here with Lord and Lady Astley. They need to see you."

Nothing.

The sinking feeling in Frederick's chest plummeted further. Grace's hold on his arm became almost bruising. He glanced at her. She felt it too—the gnawing dread of the worst possible outcome.

Johnson tested the handle. It turned easily, the door creaking open into a room steeped in shadow. A chill spilled out, heavy with an unnatural stillness.

"Wait." Johnson's whisper was sharp, halting Frederick midstep. "Todd." Johnson gestured with his chin for the man to enter first.

Officer Todd slipped around the doorframe and within a moment light blinked awake in the room.

Frederick's chest squeezed at the sight. Grace gasped at his side.

The room was chaos. Papers were scattered like fallen leaves across the rug. A chair lay overturned. The curtains billowed faintly, stirred by a draft from the open window. But it was the figure slumped over the desk that held Frederick's gaze.

"No," he murmured, stepping forward.

Grace clung to his arm, her face pale. "Oh, poor Mr. Barclay." A sudden sheen filled her eyes. "All of this. . .just because he was connected to our inheritance."

"It does seem to be the common thread," Johnson said grimly as he approached the desk. Then he stiffened, leaning closer. "Wait—he's breathing."

"What?" Frederick rushed forward with Grace just behind him.

Johnson checked Barclay's wrist, nodding. "There's a pulse."

"Was he attacked?" Frederick leaned in, noticing the swelling at the back of Barclay's head.

Johnson tilted the man upright, revealing a pale, slack face. "Looks that way."

"Oh, thank God." Grace exhaled, some tension melting from her shoulders. "What is it about this case? Everyone's getting hit on the head and then run off on. It's becoming a theme."

Johnson's lips twitched. "Do you expect assailants to wait politely for apprehension, Lady Astley?"

"It would be considerate, wouldn't it?" Grace arched a brow, a light flickering in her eyes. "It's just that there seems to be an awfully lot of head hitting of poor, unsuspecting people who've done very little to deserve such attacks." She sighed. "Though I suppose I'll settle for not having another funeral on our hands."

"Whoever was here is gone now," Todd said, reentering the room from the closet.

Frederick approached the fireplace, where a faint warmth still radiated. A small flame flickered among charred debris. "And they didn't leave long ago. The fire's fresh—someone's been burning. . ." His voice trailed off.

"Paper," Grace said sharply, already at his side. She dropped to her knees with a swish of skirts, her parasol clattering to the floor. "Oh no, Frederick."

Her exclamation tugged him down beside her. The faintly acrid smell of burned parchment filled the air as Grace began sifting through the remains. The fragments were small, curling at the edges as if they were trying to retreat from discovery. A blackened scrap revealed the word *testament,* and Frederick's stomach knotted.

Pulling out his handkerchief, he carefully fished through the debris. Among the ashes, he unearthed a corner of parchment bearing the words *inheritance* and *legal transfer,* their meaning unmistakable even beneath their charred edges. Another piece bore the faint remains of a signature ending in *Ferguson.*

"Those were the copies Barclay brought for Lillias and me to sign tomorrow," Grace whispered. Her finger traced the singed edge of what remained of her mother's signature.

Johnson loomed closer, his shadow dark against the flickering light. "Someone destroyed them," he said grimly, scanning the room as though the culprit might suddenly materialize. "Judging by the state of things, they didn't want to leave anything behind."

"Whoever it is must be after the estate." Grace stood abruptly, her gaze sweeping the chaotic room. "If Lillias and I don't claim it in less than a month, it will go to auction. Mr. Barclay said that there were already buyers waiting in the wings to purchase it."

"And your sister knew about the inheritance as well?" Johnson's tone sharpened.

"She only found out about it from us yesterday afternoon and learned specifics from Mr. Barclay today."

"With the alibi Officer Todd confirmed, your sister is cleared of further suspicion." Johnson shrugged a shoulder. "And without documents to confirm your inheritance, the risk to you, your sister, and anyone associated with you should be reduced."

"Not necessarily, Detective." Frederick's response brought all eyes back to him, even Grace's.

"What do you mean?" Johnson asked, his gaze snapping to him.

Frederick turned to Grace, his palm moving to her arm. "These were just copies, weren't they?"

Grace blinked. "Yes, of course."

"Then there's another copy of the will and the legal documents linking you and your sister to the inheritance," Frederick's gaze steadied on her.

Johnson tensed, suddenly on alert again. "And where are these papers?"

Grace met his eyes. "Scotland," she said. "Inside Mosslea Castle."

"The will was destroyed? No." Lillias surged from her chair, pacing toward the window like a wind-up toy on its last frantic rotation. "Everything hinged on that inheritance! Thomas and I were finally going to be free—free of Harrington, free of its shadows. A new start, a new home, a life unburdened."

Grace pressed her lips together so tightly they might have sealed shut. It took a Herculean effort not to retort with the obvious—that Mr. Barclay, now unconscious thanks to an assailant, had rather larger problems than the postponement of her sister's plans. But after all Lillias had endured—her husband murdered, finances obliterated, their cook comatose—it hardly seemed the moment to provoke a fit.

And when Lillias had a fit, if they were anything like the ones she used to have when they were younger, the entire house knew about it.

Father had called them "episodes," as if labeling them lent sophistication to what were, in truth, well-timed performances that ended whenever Lillias got her way. Grace had often escaped into a book, letting the tirade dissolve into the background.

"Things are not lost, Lillias." Grace looked over at Frederick. They'd discussed options on their drive from the hotel, where they'd left Detective Johnson, Officer Todd, and a few other officials combing through Mr. Barclay's hotel room and interviewing various other people regarding the poor man's attacks. "We both have some money laid aside from Mother which, if the figures that Mr. Barclay gave us are still accurate, should help you create a fresh start wherever you go."

"Yes, I made certain to withdraw mine this afternoon while you two were off playacting as detectives." She added a derisive sniff for good measure. "Why you can't leave this ugly business to professionals is beyond me. Meanwhile, I've had to manage the stress of this wretched situation alone."

Alone? Grace frowned, agitated heat climbing her neck. Lillias had a much bigger flare for dramatics than Grace did, and that was impressive. Miss Cox, Zahra, and the doctor had been here all afternoon. Of course Thomas couldn't be counted—he was hardly useful as an infant. Mrs. Lindsay was unconscious, and Mrs. James might well be a suspect, but alone? Hardly.

And playacting as detectives? Grace sat a little straighter at the offense. Jack Miracle had praised their work, even inducted them as detectives in their own right. How did Lillias always manage to make her feel so insignificant? It seemed deeply unsisterly.

"Our playacting, as you so charmingly call it, likely kept you alive." Frederick's sharp tone cut through the air, pulling Lillias', and even Grace's, attention. "Had it not been for our help, I sincerely doubt you'd have gotten those funds or the information about the inheritance as quickly as you have."

The words landed like a hammer, and for once, Lillias faltered. Her gaze dropped. Grace blinked at Frederick in astonishment. No one had ever come to her defense where Lillias was concerned, let alone stood up to her sister with such measured ferocity.

Frederick, all affronted dignity, was an even more magnificent sight than usual. Grace realized that, although the elder sister, Lillias Dixon may not very well be the stronger, cleverer, or more resilient of the two of them.

And that thought was completely new to Grace.

It somehow made her want to smile a little.

Which would have been inappropriate considering the circumstances, but it still didn't stop her from wanting to.

"So much good your detective work has done us," Lillias muttered, breaking the spell. "The will is destroyed. And even the funds Mother left will run out eventually. I'll need to find someone."

The murmured words barely made it to Grace's ears, and she wasn't fully certain she comprehended them. Find someone else? Grace shot Frederick a look, and even his brows rose in surprise.

"Find someone?" Grace echoed, brow furrowing. "What do you mean?"

"To marry," Lillias snapped. "What else can I do?" She turned back to them and marched to the tea table, pouring herself a cup with a hand shaking as badly as Grace's ever did. "Father has no money, Tony is. . .gone"—her voice wavered on the word—"and I have a child to provide for. I must find a husband willing to take us in."

"I don't know how long Mr. Barclay may remain unfit to travel or when all your affairs will be in order so we can do so." Grace stood, almost as much in surprise at her sister's statements as in the need to solve this dilemma. "But the inheritance isn't lost to us yet, Lillias."

Lillias froze, teacup halfway to her lips. "What?"

"There's another copy of the will at Mosslea," Grace explained. "Mr. Barclay mentioned it. If we get there within three weeks, and if he's well enough to travel, he can help us find it. "That is, if we want to continue with seeking to claim the inheritance at all."

Frederick raised a brow, the corner of his mouth twitching upward in a way that seemed to question her very use of the word *if.* Grace nearly smiled back. It was true—wasting Tony's sacrifice, the faint chance of another will, and the excitement of another mystery seemed downright reckless.

The teacup clattered onto its saucer as Lillias stared. "Another copy?"

"Don't you remember? Mr. Barclay told us this afternoon." Grace nodded. "He said there was a safeguard—a second copy—hidden somewhere in the castle. And he seemed to know exactly where."

"And if Mr. Barclay isn't fit to travel," Frederick added, his gaze meeting Grace's with an approving glint before shifting to Lillias, "will you allow us to playact a little longer to help find it?"

"There's clearly no time to waste." Lillias sent him a glare and placed her cup on the table with a decided clink. "I say we leave for Scotland in the morning."

"In the morning?" Not that the idea didn't sound thrilling, but how on earth could they do it? Grace frowned. It seemed rather strange to be the one advocating for reasonable thinking. "Lillias, we're hardly in a position to set out immediately. Mr. Barclay isn't conscious, your cook is wounded, and there's Tony's. . .arrangements to consider." Grace softened her tone. "We need at least a few days."

"If Mr. Barclay cannot accompany us, we will need all the time we can to search for the hidden will," Lillias shot back. "So not only must we travel across the ocean and find Mosslea in Scotland, but we'll also have to search a castle for a will hidden somewhere in its walls." Lillias pressed a hand to her forehead and dissolved into the nearest chair. "Oh, heavens. I sound like I'm quoting the plot of one of your ridiculous novels."

It really was sad how unappreciated good novels were in her family.

Frederick, however, took up the mantle with a grin. "Precisely why you should be reassured. Grace has an uncanny knack for using fiction to solve real-world problems." He stepped to Grace's side, the playful glint in his eyes softening as he addressed Lillias. "We'll do everything in our power to secure the inheritance—and to keep you safe. But this only works if we cooperate, Lillias."

The use of her Christian name landed stiffly from his lips, but Grace saw the effort. He didn't trust her sister—Grace couldn't blame him—but he was trying, and that was something.

A knock at the door interrupted the moment, and Grace turned to see the last person she expected. Mrs. James. The sight of the housekeeper threw Grace's assumptions into a whirl. If the will was destroyed and with that any possibility of Grace and Lillias signing it on this side of the Atlantic, then why would Mrs. James still need to serve as housekeeper while working for Clark?

The young woman looked from one person to the next and dipped her head. "I'm sorry to interrupt, Mrs. Dixon, but the doctor is on his way out and refused to leave without speaking with one of you."

Lillias sighed as if exhausted by the request, so Grace moved to the door. "I'll see to him, and perhaps you could help Lillias with the necessary arrangements in the meantime?" She paused, her expression softening as she addressed Frederick. "I have no idea how to plan a funeral, but I'm afraid you've had an unhealthy amount of experience with them."

Lillias sent a look to Frederick, and Mrs. James' brows rose before Grace followed her out, plucking up her parasol on the way out of the room.

"She has the very best heart, I am sure, but I can't imagine having to live with her and not become exasperated every day." Lillias sighed, studying Frederick with those pale blue eyes of hers.

He'd once contemplated those eyes would belong to his future wife.

Once hoped a real romance would grow between them, even if they'd been resigned to an arranged marriage.

But God had chosen better for him. He'd never have contemplated marrying Grace. She'd been too much outside the realm of what he thought he'd needed for Havensbrooke and his legacy.

But she'd been everything God had known Frederick had needed for his heart, soul, and future. And he was profoundly grateful.

"I'll be happy to assist you in any of your funeral plans, if I can," he said, curbing the sudden edge in his voice. "I'm sure you must be feeling overwhelmed."

His distaste for her previous statement didn't go unnoticed. One of Lillias' golden brows arched. She didn't speak, but her silence was heavy as she walked back to the tea table, warming her cup with another pour of the amber liquid.

"It seems neither of us got what we wanted for our futures," she remarked. "I settled for a poor banker and ended up a widow, cast out from polite society." Her voice wavered slightly, betraying emotions she clearly wanted to suppress. "And you're stuck with my silly sister—her fictional whims and her lack of refinement, which I'm sure, have already blighted your social standing."

"Refinement?" Frederick choked out a laugh. "Is that truly the greatest concern you have about my marriage to your sister?"

"Oh, I cannot even imagine what you've had to endure with her disposition." Lillias shook her head and offered a look of mock sympathy. "An earl of all things! She may have a sweet heart and, at times, engage in interesting conversation, but as a meaningful life partner for aristocracy?" Lillias waved her hand toward Frederick and scoffed. "She's a disaster. A child. No wonder you regret what's happened."

"Regret?" Frederick face went hot. "I've never regretted anything less in my entire life."

His statement brought Lillias' gaze up and put her body to a stop.

"If that's the sum of your thoughts on my wife," Frederick continued, deliberately lingering on the word *my* to emphasize his connection and acceptance, "then you never really knew her at all." A fire smoldered in his chest, deepening his voice. "Grace may be unconventional and naive at times, but she is far from silly. Her lack of refinement is the least of my concerns because she is not only a willing student to learn new things, but her kindness has overcome many of the social obstacles placed before her. You not only dismiss her advice but underestimate her intelligence and strength of character—qualities I value deeply."

Lillias' eyes widened, a sudden sheen filling them despite the curl of her lips into a frown. "You—you *love* her." She shook her golden head and pointed toward the door where Grace had just exited. "Her, with her ridiculousness and nonsense talk of books and solving mysteries." Her voice shook. "And no doubt, she's been an embarrassment among your acquaintances, a laughingstock to your mother, and fumbled who knows what else." Her gaze hardened as she stepped forward. "Things *I* had been trained for. The life *I* could have lived with you."

"Do you hear yourself?" A derisive laugh burst from his lips. "Grace's small idiosyncrasies are nothing compared to the real embarrassment you nearly brought on your family by attempting to deceive me into marriage. And now? Not only are you behaving with jealousy toward your own sister, but the scandal around your husband's death, his notorious gambling, and the gossip surrounding your marriage has brought much more disgrace to your family than any of Grace's decisions. Your past ingratitude for a husband who buried himself in debt to please your whims, and your current ingratitude for a sister who would risk her life to save you from your own mess—those are the only shocking things I see here."

Frederick took a deep breath, his voice lowering. "Grace Percy has one of the purest hearts in the world, and I would be a fool to not cherish such a love. I know exactly what I've been given, and I will not take it for granted again. Let her have her adventures and mysteries, for I'm more than happy to embrace them with her."

He took a final, deliberate step back, then gave a formal bow of his head. "Excuse me."

He'd barely made it out of the room when he met Grace coming toward him, her smile slowly sinking as she examined his face. "Are you all right?"

Frederick forced himself to unclench his fists and release a slow, controlled breath. If Grace had endured such veiled criticism her whole life, no wonder she thought she was always causing trouble for him in one way or another. He gave his head a shake at the pain in the thought and without hesitation—without caring who might be lurking in the hall—he slipped his arms around her waist and pulled her toward him, catching her gasp with his lips. Her smile spread beneath his assault, and she wrapped her arms around his neck with her delightful abandon, lengthening the embrace.

As he drew back, her smile bloomed.

"In the hallway, Lord Astley?" Grace's beautiful eyes sparkled as she looked up at him, and she wiggled her brows. "How scandalous."

He hadn't been the only one with a past that shaped his opinion of himself. But he'd not continue the deplorable pattern set out by Lillias. Oh no! He was learning a great deal about love and gratitude, and it began when Grace entered his life.

He slid a thumb over her cheek, wrangling his emotions into a steady control. "Scandal is vastly overrated."

"Very unaristocratic of you, my lord." She teased, searching his face, her smile gentling a little. Had she borne the brunt of her sister's ire in silence? Carried her subtle barbs without complaint?

Oh, how very different his life could have been if their marriage agreement hadn't been turned on its head.

"How did you find Mrs. Lindsay?"

Grace blinked at his question. "Oh, she still hasn't gained consciousness, but she's alive." She turned and slipped her arm through his. "And improving. Miss Cox is with her now for a little while, but I mean to take a watch." She lowered her voice as they neared the stairs. "Wounded sleeping people with too much information are quite vulnerable to unexpected attacks that keep them from waking up and sharing that information, as we know all too well from poor Mr. Graham in Egypt. So I asked Detective Johnson to provide a watch over Mrs. Lindsay's room through the night."

"That's an excellent idea, darling."

She smiled her gratitude and then her expression fell. "Did you have any luck offering some insight to my sister?"

Frederick swallowed, his mind briefly flicking to the prickly exchange with Lillias. "Yes," he said carefully, turning his focus back to Grace. "I was able to share a great deal of hard truths that she needed to hear."

Grace's gaze softened as they continued up the stairs, her voice dropping to a whisper. "Did you notice Mrs. James is still here?" Her brow furrowed. "That's unexpected."

"Unless she's gathering further information."

"Or trying to finish the job with Mrs. Lindsay," Grace added and then frowned. "If Mrs. James is a culprit at all. I suppose she *could* be innocent. We've been wrong before, but she's certainly suspicious."

"Then it's a very good thing an officer will stay the night," he added, turning to start down their hallway when Miss Cox topped the stairs behind them.

"Thank you for sending the officer to take my place. Despite my father's occupation, I'm not very comfortable with wounded people."

Frederick offered a sympathetic smile, but couldn't resist a little jest to lighten the mood. "Was spending time with Mrs. Lindsay better or worse than taking care of Thomas?"

Miss Cox's cheeks reddened a little, and she offered a reluctant smile. "The babe is growing on me, my lord, so I'd prefer him."

"Well, it's a good thing you do." Grace offered. "Because I

believe my sister is ready to hire you as the new nanny."

Miss Cox's shoulders sagged slightly, but there was a softness in her expression that hadn't been there before. "With that in mind, Mrs. Dixon is afraid to stay by herself tonight, what with the possibility of another attack still lingering." She looked between them. "She's asked if she can share the room with me, if you two don't mind keeping Zahra with you for the night."

Frederick fought the sigh that nearly escaped his lips. His carefully planned evening alone with Grace, one in which he intended to express just how much he appreciated her, was rapidly slipping through his fingers. "Of course. Make whatever arrangements you need to ensure Mrs. Dixon's comfort. We have a settee in our room which will suit Zahra quite well."

Miss Cox curtsied, a faint blush lingering on her cheeks as she made her way down the hallway toward her room.

He paused just inside the doorway of their bedroom, brushing a lingering kiss across her lips. Without hesitation, she responded with welcome enthusiasm. Perhaps there was still a chance for a little quality time with his wife?

Her smile was all warmth, and she held on to his jacket, looking up at him with a glint in her eyes. "I suppose we'll need to make plans to travel to Scotland once the funeral is over."

Frederick nodded, pulling her deeper into the room, his fingers tightening at her waist. "If we have any chance of finding the will before the time is up."

"At least we'll be much closer to Havensbrooke again."

His smile split wide. He loved how she'd not only fallen in love with him but also with his home.

And being the budding detective she was, she seemed to deduce the direction of his thoughts, because she turned toward the bedchamber.

"Closer," he said, backing her gently until her legs bumped

the end of the bed. "But still hours away. I mean to wire Elliott and Blake to have one of them meet us at the dock. Another trustworthy soul would be good to have in this case."

Her smile flashed wide, and she rocked on tiptoe to kiss him. "I love it when you talk sleuth."

He chuckled and buried his face into her neck. "If that's the case, my dear Lady Astley, let me regale you with a very thorough investigation of the many ways I can take your breath away."

Chapter 16

Frederick stood by the window, his waistcoat half-buttoned as he gazed at the darkening sky outside. The air seemed to press in, thick with the promise of a storm, and he couldn't help but feel that the weather's temper mirrored his own. The time was slipping by far too quickly, what with packing for Scotland, helping Lillias with the last of the estate matters in Harrington, and finishing up whatever investigation they could with Detective Johnson.

The small inconveniences of having to order breakfast out and Lillias' penchant for sleeping late into the morning didn't help with efficiency, but at least the police officer had remained on watch the whole night and alerted Frederick that morning that Mrs. Lindsay had begun to make some murmurings toward wakefulness.

A good sign for the investigation, especially if she could identify her assailant and the person with whom Mr. Clark had been in conversation—perhaps the same person.

And an officer had stopped in to share that Mr. Barclay had awakened during the night. Not for long and somewhat confused, but he had stayed awake long enough to take a few drinks of water. The nurse reported it as a good sign that he would heal.

So perhaps they could truly leave for Scotland within the week. Frederick would feel much better with Elliott or Blake at hand.

In fact, he planned to contact Jack Miracle too, just to see if he could gain any counsel in the matter. There was a good chance that Detective Johnson's jurisdiction didn't include Scotland.

"Did Detective Johnson take the dagger?"

Frederick turned toward his wife, who'd been sitting at the desk for a good half hour writing in her notebook. Zahra, curled up on the settee with her own pages, barely looked up from her scribbling.

"The dagger?"

"Yes, the one Lillias found in Tony's chest," she said matter-of-factly, her eyes not leaving her notes.

Grace's directness always caught him off guard, just as it did now. He hesitated, glancing at Zahra, who gave him a slight shrug before returning to her work.

Frederick then answered, "Yes, as I recall."

"Well, that's one less loose thread in all this." She tapped her pen against the notebook and looked up at him, her teeth biting into her bottom lip. He could practically see the gears turning in her mind. "So far, I have these clues:

1. Lillias and Tony were in debt and unhappily married. Lillias was selling family heirlooms for money, and Tony was gambling badly, in a vain hope of resurrecting the romance they had seemed to lose in their near-poverty.

Frederick stepped from the window, his lips crooking at her mixture of facts and creative narrative.

2. Fake Officer Clark is a gentleman with a network of spies—or at least one who's managed to insinuate herself into the house to gather information for Mr. Clark's dastardly deeds.

Grace raised her pen toward him. "My bet's on Mrs. James, but her continued presence here, long after the will's been destroyed, leaves me. . .uncertain."

"She has an angry face, and she does not like the baby," Zahra said, not looking up from her page.

"That alone raises enough red flags," Grace muttered, tapping the pen again. "What kind of person doesn't like babies?" She raised an eyebrow at Frederick. "What do you think?"

Before he could answer, Grace moved on:

3. Whoever hit you on the head, presumably Mr. Clark, has ties to Scotland. And I'm afraid his disguise—specifically the fake mustache—was as poor as his American accent.

Frederick couldn't help chuckling. "Indeed. A man who fails both at facial hair and accents is hardly a criminal mastermind."

His comment paused her response for a moment, just long enough for her to reward him with a grin.

"4. Mr. Barclay wasn't attacked until yesterday, so our murderer didn't know about the will—or who the solicitor handling it was—until then. They must have come to Virginia to stop us from getting to Scotland, and when they found out about the will, they decided to destroy it, hoping to end the matter once and for all."

Frederick stepped closer, a thought forming. "Unless," he interjected, "they—or their spy—overheard something that suggested there was another copy of the will hidden at Mosslea."

"Which should then send him directly across the pond, shouldn't it?"

"Unless they feel there is other information to clarify where the will is or—" He stopped, a sudden and unwelcome thought coming to mind.

"What?" Grace lowered her pen.

"They plan to eliminate any chance of you or Lillias getting to Scotland at all." He held her gaze, hoping his vague explanation would convey the gravity of the threat.

Grace was quiet for a moment before she leaned back in her chair, tapping her pen thoughtfully. "That's curious, Frederick. Detective Johnson mentioned Tony's wound wasn't made by a skilled hand. But it doesn't take a great deal of practice to come up behind someone and clonk them on the head."

"Do you have experience on that score?"

Her lips tipped at his teasing. "No, but I've imagined it, and I feel with the proper incentive, my aim could prove very accurate." She frowned. "Though I'd hate the idea of hearing someone's skull crack."

"It is not a loud sound," Zahra added. "Like a melon getting hit by a stick."

Grace's eyes widened as she glanced at Frederick. The casualness with which Zahra described that sound hit him with a pang. The very idea she even knew what it sounded like. . .

"Thank you for the clarification, Zahra." Frederick offered a tight smile, and the little girl looked up at him with a whisper of a smile on her face.

"So we need to make sure the murderer—Clark, or whoever it is—doesn't find out about the other will," Grace continued, writing a few more notes before standing. "I should speak to Lillias. I don't think she fully grasps the danger we're in, and I need her to be on guard, especially around Mrs. James."

"I'll go and see about Mrs. Lindsay." Frederick said, gesturing toward Zahra. "Would you like to come along, lamb?"

Without hesitation, Zahra placed her paper and crayons aside and skipped to Frederick's side, taking his outstretched hand. He drew in a deep breath, embracing the moment. It was a sweet feeling. One he'd known with his daughter, Elizabeth, but he'd not allowed himself to embrace until now. Until Grace.

As they walked from the room, he cast a glance over at Grace, his heart swelling with a strange mixture of hope and determination. Once they were back in Havensbrooke, things would change.

And hopefully, he'd have a chance to make it right.

Grace's mind swirled with questions about the entire case.

Too many things.

Why did Clark seek out Tony instead of Lillias if he truly wanted to stop them from claiming the inheritance? Why incapacitate Mr. Barclay but not kill him outright? Did he have another motive—or was he simply bad at murder?

She rapped on Miss Cox's door first, assuming Lillias may very well be in there since she'd chosen to sleep there for the night. When no one answered, Grace pushed the door open. With the darkness of the sky, only the faintest afternoon light shone through the lace curtains to reveal an empty room. Grace turned the switch on the wall and illuminated the room with electric lights.

The beds had been made already.

By whom? Mrs. James?

Come to think of it, Grace hadn't seen Mrs. James all morning. Her pulse shifted up a little. The crib stood in the corner, as usual. The dressers waited on each side of the two beds in the room, so why did her scalp tingle with warning.

She hadn't seen Miss Cox at breakfast and had assumed she was taking care of Thomas. With a quick turn, Grace left the room and continued down the hallway to Lillias' room. After a few unanswered knocks, she entered—and found the room just as empty as the first.

Bed made. As if not slept in.

Her pulse took an upswing. *As if not slept in.*

Grace rushed to the wardrobe, pulled open the door, and sucked in a breath. Empty.

No, no, no.

Lillias hadn't done what Grace had feared.

Certainly not.

But as Grace took in the room, a single slip of paper waited on the desk by the farthest window. An envelope with Grace's name on the front.

Grace didn't need to open it. Her heart already knew.

But the lines penned in her sister's hand confirmed her fears:

I left money with Mr. Broom at the funeral home yesterday to cover anything needed for Tony's burial. I've given Mr. Arbor notice to end the lease we have on the house by the end of the month with significant payment and detailed directions to box up and ship all my belongings to me at Mosslea.

I loved Tony and, God help him, he loved me.

Don't you see? It's all my fault. His gambling, our estrangement, his death.

And with whatever I have left in me, I'm determined not to have Thomas grow up in a place where the only thing anyone will remember about their father is the shadows surrounding his death. We both need to start over, and this inheritance is my lifeline.

I will find the will if I have to tear the castle apart stone by stone.

I mean to take what's been offered to us, a rescue Mother provided, even if I must frustrate you, Frederick, and Detective Johnson to do so.

My life in Harrington is over.

Forgive me, but I didn't see any other way.

Lillias

PS Miss Cox is with me, and we mean to take the first ship out of port in the morning.

Anger proved an unfamiliar feeling for Grace.

She knew it, of course. Had experienced it, yes—but not often.

Right now, though?

All she wanted to do was tear this letter into a thousand pieces and scream into a pillow.

How selfish! How childish!

Did her sister have any consideration for anyone else in the world besides herself?

Could grief and desperation lead someone to complete and utter lunacy?

Grace spun away from the desk, crumpling the paper in her fist. Her eyes stung with an uninvited burn, the precursor to tears that always accompanied her fury.

No wonder sibling conflict was such a frequent plot device in fiction. *King Lear*, *The Taming of the Shrew*, the Greek gods—oh, and the very nonfiction rivalries in the Bible.

Her pace quickened as she stalked down the hallway, her fury propelling her forward.

Well, she certainly wasn't going to kill her sister like Cain, but giving her a solid shake? That sounded like an excellent idea. Grace had never seriously entertained the notion of shaking her sister before, but it was oddly appealing now. The thought almost brought a smile to her face, which to her surprise, eased the tension building in her chest.

Of course logic returned just in time to remind her that she had far more pressing matters than shaking her sister like a marionette.

Just as Grace rounded the corner, she spotted Frederick and Zahra approaching. Frederick's expression tightened the moment he saw her, a worried frown creasing his brow. Before she even reached them, he shook his head.

"She's gone."

Evidently, Frederick had also developed a form of clairvoyance where Lillias was concerned.

"They must have left in the night." She gave him the letter.

He read it over, giving his head another slow shake.

A roll of thunder rumbled in the silence, and Grace's body tensed. No! A storm at this moment? She couldn't think clearly when thunder was involved. "How could she do this?" Grace's voice squeaked as she tried to raise her volume over other incoming thunder. "We can't keep her safe if she's not with us."

Frederick folded the letter, his expression hardening. "Because she knows we'll follow her." He held her gaze. "And we *must* follow her if you're to claim the inheritance together."

"Could she not have waited a few days?" Another rumble tumbled into the conversation.

"She's desperate," he said softly, his hand brushing Grace's shoulder in a gesture of comfort. "And when people are desperate, they convince themselves they're doing the right thing, even if it's reckless and selfish."

Grace stiffened as another growl of thunder rumbled overhead. She tried to distract herself with the mystery at hand. "And what of Mrs. Lindsay?"

"Awake." Frederick glanced toward the kitchen. "The officer said she's already named Mrs. James as the person speaking with Mr. Clark in the back garden. So now we know they're connected."

Grace edged a step closer to Frederick at the sound of the next thunderstrike. *Christmas. Think of Christmas. It's a beautiful, happy, joyful time with lights, greenery, presents, and mistletoe.*

Her gaze slid to Frederick's lips. *Mistletoe was a very good thought.*

"And—and has Mrs. James been kissed or, er, seen this morning?"

Frederick tilted his head, examining her. One eyebrow arched slowly. "No. When the officer went to check her room at six o'clock this morning, it was empty. The window was open."

Waking up in Frederick's arms. Now, *that* was a good thought.

Nice and distracting. And in the past, when they'd been alone, Frederick's excellent cuddling and kissing skills had served as the perfect storm distraction. But Grace glanced at Zahra.

No, that wouldn't be the best option right now. They were solving a mystery. And they had a daughter to consider.

Grace forced a whimper under control. "Then she's gone after Lillias."

Was that her voice? So high pitched?

Frederick's brow shot up.

Zahra looked between them, her gaze narrowing on Frederick. "Are we going after Mrs. Dixon, Sayid?"

Frederick glanced out the nearest window as the rain pelted the glass. "Of course we are. She'll not get much done alone, and I'm afraid she's not prepared for the people who may be pursuing her."

The thunder crept in again, and Grace moved another step closer to Frederick. "Daisies are very beautiful."

Frederick turned his attention back to her, his gaze searching her face. *Where was his clairvoyance now? Had he used it all up on Lillias for the moment?*

"And I love strawberries. . .and bunnies. . .and those Italian sunsets are nice too."

His eyes widened as another rumble shook the house, sending Grace directly into his chest. His strong arms wrapped around her, and he lowered his chin to her head. She could have sworn she felt him smiling.

"Zahra, do you think you could go to your room and start packing?"

The little girl nodded and dashed down the hallway, leaving the adults in silence.

"And snowflakes," Grace muttered into his shoulder, burying herself as deeply into him as her body allowed. "Snowflakes are just lovely. I'm sure Zahra will love seeing snow."

Thunder rumbled again, but Grace could only focus on the comforting weight of Frederick's arms around her. She hated thunderstorms. She'd gotten better over the years—she didn't hide in small, enclosed spaces during them anymore—but the irrational terror still had a way of creeping in. How could she help it? It had started during a storm the night her mother had died, giving birth to her baby brother. Her mother's screams had been drowned out by the storm, until those screams stopped forever.

She tried to take a deep breath to regain some sense of control, but it got caught in her throat, lodged there like a sob.

Silly. Weak. Detectives were not afraid of storms. And mothers certainly shouldn't be.

"It's just a storm, darling," Frederick murmured against her hair. "But I know you could use a little distraction. And I'm never hesitant to provide one."

She nodded, tightening her grip on him as she searched for a semblance of reason, but sometimes fear was far more persuasive than reason.

"Run along to our room, and I'll let the policeman know we will be packing our things for the next hour, so that he will keep watch over Mrs. Lindsay."

Grace looked up at him and sniffled. "I'm not a coward, Frederick." Just to reassure him.

"I know." He smiled in the dashing way she felt all the way to her toes. "But being afraid does not make one a coward. I'll not be far behind."

With that promise from his very kissable lips, she turned and started toward the main stairway, covering her ears as she went. But before she could escape to the relative safety of their room, a sharp knock came from the front door.

She froze mid-step, her hand instinctively covering her ears against the growl of thunder. Who would be knocking at the door in the middle of a storm like this? Another knock came—this time harder, more insistent. Grace glanced down the hallway. With the servants absent and the house eerily quiet, she had little choice but to investigate herself. Could it be Detective Johnson? Perhaps he had more information about Mr. Barclay—some piece of the puzzle they'd missed. Her gaze flicked to the stairs again, lingering on the safety of her room. . .and Frederick's promise to distract her.

Maybe she wouldn't answer after all.

The knock came again, followed by a muffled voice. "Please, open the door. Lillias!"

Grace's blood ran cold. The voice was familiar—impossibly so.

Every concern about the thunder fled her mind completely. She may pretend to believe in ghosts, but she didn't really believe in them, though she'd been on an alarming number of ghost hunts in her life. This voice was not the mumbled, distant sound of a phantom. It was unmistakably *alive.*

She took a step toward the door.

"Lillias," the voice called again, followed by a desperate series of knocks that only made Grace's pulse race faster.

Could it be? Could her mind really be playing such a cruel trick on her? Was this a hallucination brought on by the storm, or—she straightened, her fear pushing aside some of the dread clouding her thoughts. Well, there was only one way to find out.

With a quick turn of the lock and a pull of the door, Grace swung it open.

But instead of proving herself wrong and sane.

She proved ghosts were real.

Because standing in front of her, drenched from head to toe, his face pale and body trembling, stood Anthony Dixon staring right back at her.

"Grace?"

Her breath caught, as though her lungs had decided to skip a beat in protest. The ghost knew her name. Of course, it knew her name—every legendary spectre knew its victim's name. Dickens' ghosts all knew Scrooge's name. King Hamlet called his son by name. Did the headless horseman know Ichabod's name? She couldn't remember.

"What are you doing here?" Tony's ghost asked her as he leaned a palm against the outside doorframe, as if to steady himself. "Are you going to let me in?"

Let him in? Oh no! Every legend where someone let a spectre in the house ended very badly for the living people.

So she did what any rational person afraid of storms who was talking to their dead brother-in-law should do.

She shut the door in his face.

Chapter 17

Frederick rounded the hallway to see Grace as she stared out into the storm with the front door wide open, her face much too pale to be normal. He hurried his pace.

He was almost at her side when he caught sight of someone standing just beyond the threshold. But before he could do anything, Grace slammed the door shut, narrowly missing the poor soul outside.

"What are you doing?"

She spun toward him, her eyes impossibly wide. "That was Tony Dixon," she said, pointing a shaky finger toward the door. "At the door. The ghost of Tony Dixon knocked and I opened it. And there he was."

A knock came, almost as if to underscore her words. "Grace, let me in."

Grace's eyes grew wider. If that were possible. "See?"

"Tony Dixon?" Frederick repeated, as if the name might suddenly make sense if he said it out loud.

She nodded solemnly. "His ghost."

He narrowed his eyes at his wife. There had to be a rational explanation for this. "Grace, ghosts don't knock." Had he truly said that out loud?

"How do you know?" she shot back, her voice high pitched and panicked. "I think Jacob Marley knocked before visiting Ebenezer Scrooge."

Another knock interrupted her, this one more impatient. "For heaven's sake, I'm not dead!"

"A villainous ghost would say that, Frederick," she squeaked and then met his gaze. Whatever she saw there seemed to calm her. "You're right. If he were truly a villainous ghost, he'd just walk through the door."

Frederick stared at her a moment longer and then opened the door, revealing a shivering Tony Dixon who, in Grace's defense, looked as if he had crawled out of a graveyard somewhere and was barely clinging to life.

With a nod of gratitude, Tony stepped across the threshold and would have collapsed to the floor if Frederick hadn't caught him. He felt very much flesh and blood. Drenched, shivering, and cold, but alive.

"Grace, call for Zahra. We'll need her help. Have her bring a blanket from the bed and meet me in the library. The smaller room will be much warmer than this open space."

Grace sent another look to Tony, then Frederick, and ran up the stairs, calling for Zahra as she went.

Frederick adjusted his grip, shifting Tony's weight onto his shoulder, and half-dragged, half-led the man into the library. Tony let out a groan as he settled into the high-back chair by the fire, his movements sluggish but intentional.

Was this really happening? Tony Dixon wasn't dead?

Frederick crouched beside him, studying the man who, by all logic, should still be in the morgue. "I imagine you have quite the story to tell."

Tony's breath shuddered as he forced himself upright against the cushions, his face pale and hollowed out like old parchment.

He ushered up a weak smile, his brown hair plastered over his pale forehead. "Certainly not a fun one and a little impossible to believe."

"I'm fairly good at believing the impossible." Frederick raised an eyebrow. "Allow me to fetch tea and sandwiches for you, and then I'll be back to hear it. I know Grace would want to as well."

Tony caught Frederick's arm as he stood. "Where's Lillias?"

Frederick's shoulders slumped a little, and he nodded. "I'll explain everything when I return. For now, rest and get warm." He shrugged a shoulder, tagging on a grin. "And try not to do anything ghostly, especially when my wife enters the room."

Tony coughed out a laugh, and Frederick made a clipped pace to the kitchen. He hadn't seen Tony since learning the man had tried to maim him during a horseback ride due to jealousy over Lillias. Had that only been seven or eight months ago? It felt like a lifetime, and certainly their situations had changed dramatically since then.

To his surprise, Mrs. Lindsay sat in the kitchen, sipping some tea, and tried to stand as he entered the room. He waved her back to her seat. "Thank you, Mrs. Lindsay, but I'll see to things myself while you recover."

The last thing he needed was to try and catch someone else from hitting the ground.

"I'll not have an earl poking around in my kitchen like a scullery maid."

He dipped his head in reference to her words and offered a smile he hoped she'd accept. "You've had quite the time of it the past day, and I'm capable, perhaps not as much as a scullery maid, of finding something to eat."

Mrs. Lindsay's chin lifted in quiet approval, though her eyes were still narrowed. "I've already made some sandwiches, knowing you all would be needing them after my layin' up," she said with a huff. "Doesn't do well for a cook to leave her kitchen unattended."

"I'm certain no one can use this kitchen quite as well as you." Frederick scanned the space. "And I'm in awe that you've already been up enough to make sandwiches."

"And tea." She gestured toward the side table. "Tea's steeping on the stove there, under the cozy, and the sandwiches are in the icebox." She pointed. "There."

He followed her directions, chuckling quietly to himself. "You are a wonder, Mrs. Lindsay."

In all his adult life, Frederick would never have imagined himself in a modest townhouse kitchen, preparing sandwiches for his mistakenly deceased brother-in-law after his sister-in-law went missing on a quest to find a will in a castle she wasn't even supposed to be in.

He shook his head as he balanced the tray carefully.

And this was his life.

He met Grace and Zahra just outside the door to the library. Grace held a large blanket in her arms and sent him a look of relief. "Oh good. You're going in too. I just wanted to make sure we all saw the same thing at the same time."

Frederick paused, balancing the tray in one hand, and raised an eyebrow. "I assure you, Tony is quite solid—and alive. Though he may not feel like it at the moment."

Grace peeked past him at the door, biting her lip. "I must admit, I've never read where a ghost chose to stand outside in the rain when he could very well materialize through a door. So at least that's in his favor as proof."

"I do not think ghosts are usually polite," Zahra added, and Frederick's grin slipped wide.

"Ah, Grace. More proof." He gestured toward Zahra. "Ghosts are not usually polite." Frederick gave a faint chuckle as he nudged the door open with his foot.

Grace rolled her eyes, though her smile almost made an

appearance, until the door creaked open and Tony, still slumped in the chair, came back into view. "He still looks ghostly," she whispered, following him into the room with Zahra at her heels.

Zahra tilted her head, her little face scrunched up in concentration. "He does not look very dead, only very wet."

Tony let out a raspy laugh from the settee, accepting the blanket Grace handed him and wrapping it around himself. His teeth chattered, but he managed a weak grin. "I am that."

"This is Zahra." Frederick set the tray nearby. "She's our daughter we adopted from Egypt."

"Adopted?" Tony took a longer look of Zahra and pressed his head back against the chair. "What an introduction to the world outside of Egypt."

"She's probably seen worse." Grace stepped to the tea and poured a cup, offering it to Tony, her expression still wary.

He shot Zahra a look before taking the teacup from Grace. His hands shook the cup all the way to his mouth, but after a few sips he offered a relieved sigh. "Thank you. It feels like I haven't been warm in weeks. Definitely not since I woke up."

There was a quietness about Tony Dixon, maybe even humility? Had that been a trait of his before his financial troubles, or was it something learned from hardship?

Frederick understood that type of life learning all too well.

"Where exactly did you wake up?" Grace slid down on the settee nearby, her attention fully fixed on Tony. Frederick guessed his wife was still trying to convince herself Tony wasn't going to evaporate before her eyes.

Tony's head lolled back against the settee, his body seeming less tense than it had been. "The morgue."

Grace gasped.

"Good night, Dixon," Frederick muttered, crossing the room to sit beside Grace. "The *morgue*?"

"Nearly terrified one of the watchmen to death." Tony's eyes opened slowly, and he gave a weak shrug. "Once he called the doctor and consulted the coroner, they determined I wasn't actually dead."

"My faith in the medical community has just grown exponentially." Frederick's tone was dry, inspiring a tired grin from Tony.

Tony's mouth twitched in a weak grin. "The doctor said the wound was shallow, but the blood on my shirt made it look worse. Someone must've assumed I'd bled out. The watchman told me they'd had several accidents that day, so I was sent to the cellar until the coroner could 'process' me for the police." He shivered, and Frederick was certain those chills had more to do with the memory than the cold.

"Shallow wound?" Frederick clarified.

Tony nodded. "The doctor thought I'd been stabbed by someone untrained or interrupted in the process. The coroner believed that the cold in the cellar slowed my bleeding, my pulse, my breathing—it made everything look like I was. . ."

"Dead?" Grace finished for him, her eyes wide. "Tony, if you hadn't awakened when you did. . ."

"Don't mention it, Grace." He raised a palm to stop her. "I can't think about it, especially after waking up in a room full of coffins."

"You must have felt like you'd stepped straight into *Dracula*," Grace whispered.

"Or a nightmare." Tony took another sip of tea, his hand steadier.

"And they just. . .released you from the morgue?" Frederick couldn't quite grasp the idea of it. "Shouldn't they have sent you to a hospital?"

"They were going to," Tony admitted. "But I escaped."

"Escaped?" Grace repeated, her initial shock giving way to the unmistakable gleam of fascination.

Frederick could just imagine the images she was creating in her head.

His shoulders tightened. None of those imaginings could equal what it must have been like for Tony. Nightmare, indeed.

"I couldn't stay. They wanted to call the police, get me to a hospital, but all I could think about was Lillias and the baby. How afraid she must be." He raked a hand through his damp hair. "I've made mistakes—plenty of them—but I wasn't about to let them think I was dead and unable to protect them." His voice broke, and his head dropped back against the chair. "So I walked out when they weren't looking. Found my way home."

"You realize we have to alert the police," Frederick said, breaking the silence. "They're searching for your murderer." He paused and reevaluated his sentence. "Your presumed murderer since you're clearly alive."

"Or mostly alive." Grace added helpfully.

Both men turned to her.

"Well, look at him," she said, waving toward him. "He's far too pale to be fully alive. Tony, you need sustenance if you're to make a proper recovery."

Tony smirked faintly. "If it's any comfort, Grace, I *feel* mostly alive." He reached for a sandwich, though his hand still shook.

"Did you see who attacked you?" Frederick asked, steering them back to the matter at hand.

Tony pulled his attention from Grace back to Frederick. "I did. At least a blurry memory of him, but I'd met him before."

"Mr. Clark?"

Tony froze mid-bite. "You know him?"

"There's much to explain," Frederick said carefully. "But first, how much did *you* know him? Do you have any idea why he'd target you?"

Tony took another bite, clearly savoring the food. Had it been almost three days since he'd had a proper meal? Not that Frederick would consider a sandwich a "proper" meal, but more than he imagined waited in a morgue.

"I met him just this week." Tony squinted. "Is it still this week? My days are all muddled." He shook his head, clearing it. "At first, he seemed pleasant enough—a bit too friendly, perhaps—but I've dealt with his type before at the Lucky Coin." He looked between them. "I—I assume you know of my. . .difficulties there."

Frederick nodded, silently urging Tony to continue.

"He was overly interested in Lillias. Even asked about you, Grace. That put me on edge. Then he kept trying to get me drunk, plying me with whisky. When I refused to talk, he grew agitated. I noticed his accent slip—Scottish—and called him out. I told him I'd go to the police in the morning to find out who he really was." Tony set the cup down as if he'd used up too much energy holding it. "He threatened me. I threatened back." His eyes withered closed. "I suppose he acted on his threats."

Frederick met Grace's gaze again. Unlike their previous mysteries, where the perpetrator's identity was shrouded in secrecy, this one offered a peculiar twist. They knew the players and motives—but not the next move.

That was the real mystery.

An unsettling one.

"But. . .I've spent all this time explaining and haven't seen Lillias." Tony sat straighter in the chair with a sudden rush of energy. "Would you get her? Thomas too?"

The room fell silent. Grace looked at Frederick and, with a deep breath, leaned forward, touching Tony's hand as if to brace him. "Tony, Lillias isn't here."

"Not here?" His expression tightened, and he looked from Grace to Frederick. "Where did she go?"

Frederick found himself preparing for impact. Grace took a deep breath, glancing at him briefly before pressing on.

"Actually, she's gone to Scotland."

"Scotland?" He shot upright, his exhaustion momentarily forgotten. "Why? And with the baby?"

"She went to claim an inheritance—a castle our mother left us in her will. We didn't know about it until the day you. . ." Grace trailed off, glancing helplessly at Frederick.

"Died," Frederick supplied.

"Her mother? But she's been gone for years." Tony frowned, confusion giving way to frustration. "She never told me about any will. And what castle? Lillias doesn't even *like* Scotland."

"Well," Frederick interjected, reclining slightly as though preparing for a long evening, "there's a lot to explain, so I'd suggest you prepare yourself. Because there are far more surprises to this story than your rather theatrical return from the dead."

It had taken the rest of the day and part of the next morning to finalize everything for travel. Of course they could have left sooner if not for the hours spent with Detective Johnson confirming that Tony Dixon was, indeed, among the living and reviewing every tangled thread of this increasingly bizarre case.

They'd hoped Mr. Barclay might recover in time to join them—after all, the man held the secret of where to find the will inside Mosslea. But poor Mr. Barclay had only stirred once from his coma, babbling incoherently about horses and whisky before slipping back into unconsciousness. Evidently, the kind man had been hit much harder on the head than either Frederick or Mrs. Lindsay. The doctor was optimistic he'd recover his senses. . .eventually.

Unfortunately, "eventually" wasn't a schedule they could afford.

Grace sighed as she pinned her hair. Mr. Barclay's absence would truly put a damper on finding the will in a prompt and direct manner. Her lips spread into a smile. But Mr. Barclay's delay did provide one tiny opportunity if viewed from the right perspective.

It would give her and Frederick a chance to engage in another treasure hunt, except this time, it wasn't for actual gold treasure or in an island cave, it was for an inheritance. . .and in a castle.

Already, Tony seemed to be gathering strength, even as he spouted his dislike of ocean travel. They'd only been aboard ship two days, when he'd shown much more color in his face than any ghost should have, and his sleeping had improved a little. Well, apart from his nightmares.

But Grace understood those.

Hers had grown much less frequent, but she knew the irrational fear of reliving the moment. All the more for dear Tony, who had almost been buried alive. And from Grace's preliminary research, the possibility of something like that happening wasn't as remote as she'd imagined.

Was that where Poe got his ideas? She paused mid-pin. Contemplating being buried alive? Or another story where he actually writes about a man burying his arrogant enemy alive. She shuddered and went back to finalizing the packing of her trunk so it would be ready when the ship reached Glasgow and they began to disembark. Perhaps deep thoughts about mortality also led Poe to write his detective stories. Now wasn't that a clever segue? Perhaps she should renew her Poe reading to assist in sleuthing knowledge, especially if she came upon a murder that happened in a room without an entrance or escape.

She glanced out the porthole at the roiling sea.

Where was her sister?

They were already two days behind her. Who could know for certain how she and Miss Cox had managed their trip across or if Mr. Clark had already caught up with her, held her at knifepoint, and forced her to walk the plank. Perhaps Mr. Clark and Lillias weren't even on the same ship. That would make her feel so much better.

Grace frowned. Passenger ships didn't have planks, did they?

"It's almost time for dinner," Frederick entered the room, buttoning his shirtsleeves as he approached, his bowtie dangling around his neck. "You look deep in thought. Planning our next move?"

"Not exactly." Grace turned toward him. "I was contemplating Poe. And murder mysteries. And planks on passenger ships, which I realize now is quite ridiculous."

Frederick arched a brow, his lips twitching. "A thoroughly practical train of thought. And here I assumed you'd be pondering wills in hidden compartments or how to convince the captain to shave a day off the voyage."

Grace brushed a stray hair she'd obviously missed away from her face. There was a weariness in Frederick's posture. Was something wrong? "Well, I wouldn't mind knowing where and how Lillias is right now, but there's nothing I can do about it at the moment except pray."

"And contemplate possibilities, no doubt." His smile softened, but his gaze held a weight that set her nerves humming. "We will find her, darling."

"What is it, Frederick?" She stepped closer, searching his face.

He rubbed a thumb over her cheek and released a heavy sigh before taking her hand and leading her to a nearby chaise. Oh, he was settling her in. This couldn't be good. Hadn't he just said they would find Lillias?

He sat next to her, his hand never releasing hers. "While you were busy with Poe and planks, I was catching up on the papers. We've been so distracted with your sister's situation and our honeymoon, I hadn't paid much attention to news."

"That sounds harmless enough," she said lightly, hoping to ease whatever burden had him so grim.

He nodded and gave her hand another squeeze as he held her gaze. "Evidently, there's been an assassination."

Grace blinked. Well that certainly wasn't remotely among the list of things she'd expected him to say. "An assassination? Where? Who?"

"Bosnia," he answered, grimly. "Archduke Franz Ferdinand of Austria. *And* his wife."

Grace pressed her palm to her chest. "And his wife?"

"They were shot last week, on the 28th of June. It's being framed as a nationalist act of defiance, but it's far more than that." His jaw tightened. "This could unravel everything."

"Everything?" Grace echoed, her imagination spinning in a dozen directions. "Do you mean war?"

Frederick's silence was answer enough.

Grace's pulse quickened. "And Britain? Could we be drawn in?"

He ran a thumb over her knuckles, his gaze steady but somber. "The alliances across Europe are a tangled web. If one nation falls, others may follow. I hope cooler heads prevail, but we must prepare for the possibility that they won't."

Grace stared at him, the enormity of what he was saying sinking in. "And Britain too?"

"I don't know. Hopefully it will all be sorted in a peaceful and mutually respectful way." His voice remained calm, maybe even hopeful, but it held an undercurrent of uncertainty. "Regardless, it's my duty as a peer of the realm and a former military man to be ready for whatever lies ahead. My position means I can't ignore what's happening. But I admit. . .it feels like the world is shifting beneath our feet."

She refused to comment on the fact that they currently rode on a ship across the ocean so the world was quite literally shifting beneath their feet; instead, she leaned close to him, placing a kiss on his cheek. "If the world is shifting beneath our feet, dear

Frederick, then we must trust in the one who holds the whole world all the more."

His gaze found hers and he smiled, pulling her hands to his lips in an act of love and solidarity. "Indeed, darling. Indeed."

Chapter 18

Frederick gave his head a sharp shake as Glasgow's harbor loomed into view, its steel-gray waters rippling beneath a muted July sky. War? Surely not. Yet with the unrest creeping across Europe and alliances shifting like sand underfoot, he couldn't ignore the nagging sense that something far darker than a mysterious castle or a makeshift murderer hovered just beyond the horizon.

To his right, Grace held Zahra's hand, her expression more subdued than usual. It wasn't often his wife allowed shadows to settle across her face; she was far too skilled at inviting sunshine into any gloom. Even now, despite her quiet demeanor, he could see her mind working, likely forming some quip to draw him out of his thoughts.

And he would let her.

Whatever lay in the future, his focus had to remain on the tangible dangers of the present.

Tony, leaning against the railing to his left, seemed a man transformed after their six-day voyage. Rest and enjoying some distance from recent events had restored his color and given him a renewed sense of purpose.

To start over.

To set things right.

To redeem his family.

Frederick understood that kind of resolve. It was the kind that burned through doubt and left behind something sharper, something unyielding.

"It reminds me of Liverpool when I arrived in England with you for the first time." Grace pressed a hand to her hat, a necessary precaution given her uncanny ability to lose them.

Frederick's lips twitched. Her knack for misplacing hats was, in its own way, impressive.

"Did Liverpool look as dark and smoky as this?" Tony asked, wrinkling his nose at the sooty skyline.

Grace leaned forward, craning her neck to look around Frederick. "Not to worry, Tony. As Lord Astley once assured me upon my arrival, the landscape improves dramatically the farther one ventures from the city. For country-hearted folk like you and me, the change will be a welcome relief." She turned toward Frederick. "How long should it take us to get to Angloss from here?"

"I can't say with certainty," he admitted, his gaze fixed on the ship easing into its berth at the Queen's Dock. "Travel in Scotland is unfamiliar territory for me, particularly the Highlands. Remote areas tend to keep their own schedules."

Tony groaned, throwing up his hands. "So we're fumbling our way through Scotland in search of some obscure little village? This is madness. Grace, I know from your letters that you thrive on this kind of harebrained adventure, but I'm a banker. I don't have the constitution for being stabbed, nearly buried alive, or employing housekeepers who moonlight as murderers."

"And I'm an earl," Frederick interjected with a grin. "Adventures are often thrust upon us, whether we seek them or not. But occasionally, they lead to something remarkable." He tipped his head toward Grace, his eyes warm. "I wouldn't trade the adventure that brought me to Lady Astley—not even your part in it, Tony."

Tony responded with a resigned smile, though his muttering suggested he remained unconvinced.

The ship docked with a jarring clang, and the sounds of Glasgow surged around them—a cacophony of shouting dockworkers, screeching gulls, and the rhythmic groan of cranes lifting cargo from the bellies of steamships. The air was thick with the mingling scents of coal smoke, brine, and the earthy tang of the Clyde.

Frederick leaned on the railing, taking in the scene below. The dock stretched out in a chaotic tangle of warehouses and cranes, with merchant vessels and passenger liners moored in uneven rows. Overhead, smoke from the towering funnels wove itself into the low-hanging clouds, blurring the line between industry and gloom.

The crowd on the dock was a kaleidoscope of movement and color. Families clung to one another in tearful reunions, businessmen exchanged brisk handshakes, and dazed newcomers hesitated at the edges, wide-eyed at the industrial sprawl. Near the customs office, a brass band struck up a jaunty Scottish tune, its cheerful strains stubbornly defying the grime of their surroundings.

Grace nudged his arm, her expression brightening as she pointed toward the band. "If nothing else, Frederick, at least Glasgow welcomes us with music."

"And soot," Tony added with a grimace, brushing at his sleeve, following them toward the gangplank.

"It's about time."

Frederick's head jerked in the direction of the familiar voice.

Waiting at the bottom of the gangplank, in a linen suit as light and pristine as the environment behind him was dark and dingy, stood Frederick's cousin and friend, Stephen Blake. The man wore casual as effortlessly as his smile, tossing a hand up as Frederick's gaze met his.

A sudden wash of relief spilled from Frederick's head to his feet. Blake. A capable and trusted friend. Frederick desperately needed another set of eyes and ears, and possibly fists, in this situation.

"Mr. Blake!" Grace's joy was so effusive it even teased a small grin from Tony. "What a delightful surprise!" She descended the gangplank with Zahra at her side, Frederick just behind her. "I was so hopeful you'd come."

"It's rather bad manners to miss such a glorious welcome as that, my dear Lady Astley." Blake stepped up to greet them. "And I try my very best not to have bad manners."

As poised and prepared as Blake remained, the look on the man's face when Grace pulled him into a hug even shook his cousin's composure a little. Perhaps Grace felt the relief too. They could certainly use his help and, if history informed the present, Blake could use a little family time.

Blake cleared his throat, crouching slightly to address Zahra. "Ah, the famous Zahra." He extended a hand. "*Céad míle fáilte*."

The girl tilted her head, frowning. "That is not Egyptian or Arabic."

"You're absolutely right," Blake laughed. "It's Gaelic. Some people here in Scotland speak it. It means 'a hundred thousand welcomes.'" He gestured broadly to the surroundings, as if to encompass the entire country.

"That is a great many welcomes for such a dirty place," Zahra said, one brow arching in challenge.

"Ah, you are clever," Blake replied, winking. "What if I said *ahlan wa sahlan*?"

Frederick blinked, his attention snapping to his cousin. Had Blake just spoken to Zahra in Arabic? When had his cousin learned Arabic?

Zahra's smile flared wide, and she responded in kind, her pronunciation far superior to his cousin's attempt.

"Freddie, old chap!" Blake straightened, clasping Frederick's hand with a grin that gleamed as brightly as his suit. "Some aristocrats collect fine works of art, but it seems you collect people."

Frederick pulled Blake into a hug. "Thank you for being here," he whispered in his cousin's ear before stepping back and saying, "Only the best people."

"Well, if you're going to go about collecting people, only the best will do." Blake turned to Tony, extending a hand. "Last we met, you were stealing brides and trying to kill earls. I trust your hobbies have improved?"

Tony's jaw dropped before he found his footing, shaking Blake's hand with a wry smile. "I've since married the bride and befriended the earl. Improvement enough?"

Blake gave a mock-serious nod. "Excellent progress. Keep it up."

"However, he is recently back from the dead, Mr. Blake," Grace added, joining in the teasing she'd begun to embrace between her, Frederick, and Blake.

Blake's brows rose to his golden hairline. "Is that so? Well, I hear that's all the rage. Resurrectionists and whatnot—mostly for the wealthy and eccentric, of course. Thought of trying it myself once, but the planning seemed rather tedious." He shuddered dramatically. "Too many late nights and missed meals."

Tony coughed out a laugh. Frederick caught himself smiling, his tension ebbing. Blake's ability to ease a room—or a fraught situation—was unmatched.

As they started walking, Frederick took Zahra's hand while Grace slipped her arm through Blake's.

"You have been sorely missed, Mr. Blake," she said warmly. "I'm sure we'd have solved everything much faster with you around."

Blake grinned, tossing a glance over his shoulder at Frederick. "That was my wedding gift to you, Lady Astley—allowing you the full honeymoon experience, life-threatening moments and all. Wouldn't dream of denying you that."

Grace's laugh rang out into the crowd, garnering a few looks, and Frederick's entire body eased some more. He had a great deal of confidence being able to manage these cases with only Grace's help, but the addition of a clever and capable friend made everything better—for his peace of mind, if not for the future lives of the people he loved.

"Have you heard anything from Elliott?" Frederick fell in step beside Blake, keeping Zahra between them, a small but instinctive act of protection.

"Indeed. I stopped by both Havensbrooke and Kerth Hall to make proper assessments before arriving here." He offered a pointed look to Frederick. "Keep in mind I am only industrious when it involves saving family members or living luxuriously at other people's expense."

Grace's laugh trilled again, a sound which had sounded less frequently over the past few days. And no wonder with all they'd had to handle since arriving in America. Perhaps Frederick should never have taken her there.

But then, she may not have had the opportunity to learn about her inheritance at all. Why did the good so often have to braid with bad things in life?

"So what did you discover about our very favorite valet?" Grace asked, sending Frederick a brilliant smile, her eyes alight and beautiful.

Thank God Blake came.

Blake winced, as if the news was too scandalous to share in broad daylight. "Well, I'm sorry to say it aloud, my dear Lady Astley, but there is definite talk of"—he paused for effect, his voice dropping to a stage whisper—"matrimony."

"Oh Frederick. Did you hear that?" Grace sent a look across Blake. "So when did he ask her? How?"

Blake raised a finger in mock warning. "Ah, but you misunderstand. He didn't propose—she did. A rather bold move, though appropriate considering their. . .adjusted status."

Frederick shook his head, a smile tugging at his lips. Clearly, he needed Blake and Grace in his life on a regular basis. "So she swept Elliott off his feet, then?"

Blake turned toward him. "It would seem so, which, if you think about it isn't all bad. Men are constantly expected to foot the proposal-bill, so to speak, where feet-sweeping is concerned, so it's nice to hear that turnabout is fair play every once in a while. Let men know the exhilarating terror of being on the receiving end of a proposal."

"What a wonderful story for our dear Elliott." Grace sighed, embracing Frederick's motley crew of friends, servants, and family as her own as only she would. "I'm so happy for them and the fact they'll live close enough to visit us often."

"Indeed." Blake nodded sagely. "I'm quite keen on maintaining relationships with wealthy friends. They always provide the best accommodations. And I'd say this relationship is off to an excellent start. As they're both former thieves, a mutual stealing of hearts seems an appropriate final crime."

Frederick barked out a laugh just as Blake stopped in front of a magnificent Rolls Royce Silver Ghost Tourer, painted a striking blue. Of course Blake would be driving a car like this—effortlessly opulent, impeccably maintained. Even in Scotland, he managed to find the pinnacle of luxury.

"Thank you for admiring my beautiful Evangeline." Blake patted the side of the car with affection. "And though the old girl"—who looked anything but old—"is large enough to carry us all, she's not large enough to hold all of your luggage, so I've already made arrangements with the porters for the rest of your things to be delivered later." Blake opened the car's rear door with a dramatic flourish, bowing slightly. "Now, shall we head north before the weather turns sour? We are in Scotland, after all. The skies here are as unpredictable as the locals."

As the engine purred to life, Blake glanced back at them with a gleam in his eye. "We've a long ride ahead, so do indulge me. I want to hear every detail: the mysterious inheritance, the resurrected Tony, and—oh, I can only hope—a possible damsel in distress?"

Frederick exchanged a look with Grace, who was already laughing at the prospect. For the first time in days, he felt the weight of their recent troubles lift, if only slightly. Whatever awaited them in the north, at least they had a quite capable friend on their side.

As the motorcar crested the final rise, Grace leaned forward eagerly, the wind tugging at her hat despite the car's modest speed. It had been a long drive. So long, the day had waned into sunset, which meant they wouldn't have any time to investigate the village or the castle today, but at least they could start afresh in the morning.

Below, nestled like a forgotten jewel among the verdant hills and pine-speckled slopes, lay Angloss. The village spilled toward the shimmering expanse of Loch Ness, which stretched out under the twilight like liquid silver, serene and otherworldly.

It was impossibly romantic.

She couldn't help but smile at it. Just the view sent a sense of home through her in the strangest sort of way. She didn't remember visiting Scotland, but it somehow felt like a memory borrowed from the stories her mother used to tell. The rolling hills and the smell of pine mingled with the faintest hint of peat smoke sent a wave of homesickness for the Blue Ridge Mountains she hadn't felt in years.

The contrasting hues of sunset cast a golden glow across the landscape, enchanting every stone building and cobbled street with a halo, especially the two steeples bookending each side of the village. As if on cue, a church bell tolled faintly ahead, welcoming them—or perhaps warning them of what lay ahead.

A quaint cluster of stone cottages with slate roofs lined the road as they entered, reminding her so much of Astlynn Commons at Havensbrooke.

Blake's voice pulled her from her reverie. "Lovely little place, isn't it? These villages always remind me of something out of a storybook. You half expect a talking fox to greet you at the pub."

Grace laughed. "Or a huntsman offering directions to the nearest poisoned apple."

As they rolled through the village, her eyes wandered over the modest shops and the cozy pub with its swinging sign: *The Loch's Rest.* Flower boxes spilled over with blooms so bright they defied the somber stone facades. But her gaze was irresistibly drawn to the castle.

Mosslea Castle stood sentinel on a rocky promontory above the loch, its silhouette both regal and forbidding. The turrets reached skyward, their crenellated edges jagged against the dusk, while ivy climbed the weathered walls, as though nature was determined to rcclaim its own.

Grace's pulse quickened as they drew nearer, the details sharpening.

This was her ancestral home. Powerful lairds roamed those halls. Elegant ladies danced and made merry. Knights guarded the gates, and battles brimmed close enough to threaten the ancient structure.

She supposed. She didn't really know for certain about the battles or knights, but one couldn't think of a castle not featuring at least one battle or two. The faintest of lights appeared to flicker past one of the blackened windows and disappear.

Her breath caught. What was that? A night watchman?

A housekeeper?

"It truly is like something out of a novel," Grace murmured, hardly aware she'd spoken aloud.

Frederick glanced over his shoulder from his place in the front seat, his lips crooked at a playful tilt. "Let me guess—*Jane Eyre*?"

She shook her head, her eyes still fixed on the castle. "No, this is more gothic than Thornfield Hall. It's. . .wilder. I can almost feel the stories pressing against its walls. Secrets and curses and—"

"Drafty halls and an appalling need for maintenance," Blake interjected from the front seat, his eyes twinkling in the rearview mirror.

She shot him a look. "And romance. Mystery. Can't you feel it? The air practically vibrates with it."

"I think the air feels cold." Zahra muttered, burrowing deeper into Grace's side. "My bones feel it."

In early July? Grace wrapped her arm around the little girl's shoulders. There was certainly a dampness to the air that Zahra had probably never known. "I'm afraid this climate will take a bit of adjusting to, Zahra. It's very different than Egypt, even in summer."

"I do hope we can leave the drama and danger to a minimum at this point and just have a practical solution to the entire thing." Tony voiced from beside her. "I've had my fill for a lifetime."

"I'm afraid, Tony, you've signed on for it until we have sorted out Mr. Clark's nefarious plan, secured our inheritance, and safely returned you to your wife," Grace said, trying not to sound snippy at his gloomy tone. After all, the man had just started living again over the past few days. She patted his hand. "I know it can be a bit overwhelming, but you're not alone in the adventure now. Neither is Lillias. You have us."

His smile didn't seem to spread as quickly as it ought for such a declaration.

"I see a hotel up ahead." Blake announced. "Since I assume you all will not be staying the night in the castle for this evening?"

"Not until we have more information, I think." Frederick

answered, peering through the car window in the direction Blake gestured. "Yes, that should do. Rowan's Roost, is it?"

"Indeed, and a quite encouraging name for our temporary abode, I might add." Blake shot back. "Especially considering our current adventure."

"What do you mean?" Grace leaned forward in the car, trying to look ahead too.

The wooden sign for the inn not only held its name but a symbol of a tree with what looked to be red berries. Two birds alighted on the tree.

"If my Scottish lore is on point, the rowan tree is said to ward off evil and protect heroes," Blake explained, shooting a grin at Grace through the mirror. "Or heroines, as the case may be."

"I like the sound of that." Tony said. "I may just stay inside the hotel for the rest of the time we're here once I find Lillias."

Grace opened her mouth to respond, but her attention snagged on a pair of figures across the street from the hotel. A woman in a black mourning dress pushed a stroller, her blond hair catching the dim light.

"Stop the car." Grace gasped. "Blake, stop! It's Lillias."

Blake brought the car to an abrupt halt as Grace craned her neck, her pulse racing. It *was* Lillias—there could be no doubt. But the man beside her—

Tony's growl shattered the quiet. "No. It can't be. *No.*"

Frederick twisted in his seat, his brow furrowing. "What is it?"

But Grace already knew. Her heart sank even before Tony voiced the terrible truth.

"That's him." Tony's voice was guttural, raw. "That's the man who stabbed me. That's Clark."

Chapter 19

Frederick sent Blake a look as if for clarification.

Mr. Clark was walking with Lillias? Here in Angloss? Out in the open?

All the pieces began to converge in his mind.

Of course. If Mr. Clark wanted Mosslea and the wealth associated with its natural resources, and he'd learned of a new will, why wouldn't he rush forward at the first availability in order to find it.

And in Scotland he wasn't likely known for going around stabbing people. At least, from his appearance nonchalantly walking down the street of Angloss. So he could parade around as a typical Scot charming ladies and doing business.

Though, come to think of it, Frederick had known a few Scots who could stab someone before breakfast, then charm a roomful of ladies and down a pint by supper. That might actually be the very definition of a Scot.

Tony shifted toward the car door, his posture taut with purpose, but Blake was faster. The man leapt from the vehicle with a fluidity that suggested he was part foxhound. Tony barely had time to reach for the handle before Blake was leaning in, all business, his hand resting lightly against the car frame to block Tony's view.

"Stay calm, Mr. Dixon. This is not the time for mindless heroics."

"I won't sit here and do nothing!" Tony's voice cracked, and he shifted toward the door. "Lillias is out there with *him*. He's dangerous."

"He likely is." Blake straightened slightly, his body shielding Tony's movements from the pair now passing on the opposite side of the street. Lillias laughed at something Clark said, a sound that sent Tony lurching forward like a wound spring.

"She doesn't know who he really is," Tony ground out. "She's walking into a trap."

"And charging out there would only snap it," Blake's calm voice edged with steel. "If you reveal yourself now, he'll bolt—or worse, he'll use Lillias as a shield. You've already seen what he's capable of, and I doubt we've met the limits of his cunning."

"But arrogance is his weakness." Frederick leaned forward, joining the fray. "Parading about the village like a peacock shows he thinks he's untouchable."

"Precisely." Blake nodded in agreement. "That's how we'll beat him. But not if you turn this into a melodramatic reunion in the middle of Angloss. Right now, you're our best card, and he doesn't know you're in the deck."

Tony's jaw tightened, but Frederick pressed on. "Clark doesn't suspect you're alive. That gives us a distinct advantage. He won't act rashly while he believes he's in control."

"And if he's befriending Lillias, it's a very good sign," Grace offered, her smile too bright for the fury on Tony's brow. "It means he's not found the will yet. He'd hardly waste time charming her if he'd already destroyed the evidence."

Tony gaped at her. "Befriending my wife?"

Grace's expression didn't waver. "Yes. Frustrating as it may be, it's a good sign."

Tony's gaze flicked toward the street again. Lillias tilted her head toward Clark, her laugh catching the breeze. Tony's entire body tensed as if ready to spring from the car, but Grace's hand on his arm held him in place.

"What would happen if you charged up there?" Grace's voice softened, but her words landed with precision. "Besides nearly stopping Lillias' heart when she sees her dead husband walking toward her?"

Grace's unique phrasing of the scenario seemed to do the trick. Tony's jaw slacked.

Grace continued. "Besides, we don't have proof to secure Mr. Clark's villainy."

"Especially here in the Highlands," Blake said, lowering his voice to a conspiratorial whisper, as though someone from the village might be pressed against the car door with a glass to their ear. "Clark could be the local favorite son. Accusing him of attempted murder and destruction of property might be about as well-received as marching into a ceilidh wrapped in an English flag."

Frederick smothered a laugh behind his hand before turning to Tony. "You said it yourself—Clark doesn't know you're alive. That's a rare advantage we can't afford to waste. The moment he learns the truth, the game changes, and not in our favor."

Tony raked his hands through his hair, leaving it sticking up like the aftermath of a windstorm. "So what am I supposed to do?" he snapped, his frustration spilling over. "Sit here like some ghost while he plays games with my wife? Courts her?" His palm shot toward the direction Lillias and Clark had walked, his voice rising as he continued. "Probably feeding her lies about how he's a decent human being and not some conniving, murderous—"

"I know it has to be hard, old bean, but for now we need to bide our time and outsmart him." Blake leaned against the doorframe, his arms crossed. "If Clark's playing a game, we need to play smarter."

"And he's focused on the will," Frederick added. "If we find it first, we take away his leverage. That's the priority. Once we have it, we can deal with him on our terms."

Tony hesitated, his eyes flicking from Blake to Frederick. Finally, he gave a reluctant nod. "Fine. But if I even *think* she's in danger—"

"You'll be the first one we send in, mate," Blake interrupted, his grin returning with full force. He reached over and gave Tony's shoulder a reassuring pat. "For now, though, patience. Clark's arrogance is our greatest asset. We'll let him think he's ahead until we pull the rug out from under him." Straightening, he nodded toward the road ahead. "Let's get to the castle and start searching. If this all goes to plan, you'll be the hero Lillias deserves."

Tony muttered something unintelligible as Blake closed the car door.

"So, we'll keep Tony hidden, gather clues, and hunt for a long-lost will in a centuries-old castle." Grace's grin spread enough to light her eyes as she met Frederick's gaze. "Oh, that does sound like an absolutely marvelous adventure."

Tony groaned and sank lower into his seat, his arms crossed in defiance of the world at large. Blake's grin widened, as if he'd just won a particularly enjoyable round of cards. Zahra, their quiet observer, gave Grace her usual curious once-over, as though she were still trying to puzzle out how the woman's mind worked. And Frederick simultaneously thanked God for his wife. . .and prayed for the safety of everyone when her fictional prowess somehow became much more real than it ought to be.

The little bell above the hotel door jingled as the group entered, the cozy interior of Rowan's Rest wrapping them in a curious smoky scent. Grace tilted her head, trying to place it—peat, perhaps? She could identify the delicious aroma of baked bread well enough, and the combination created a homely charm. The intimacy of the surroundings wrapped around Grace like a hug.

A Scottish hug.

She liked it.

Zahra lingered close to Frederick's side as they entered, her wide, grayish green eyes catching the lantern light. Grace wondered what the girl made of all this—a world of rugged hills and whispered legends, so far removed from the sunlit streets and sand of her homeland.

"Not very big, is it?" Tony grumbled, falling in behind them.

"It's clean and tidy," Blake replied, nodding appreciatively toward the room. "Both top marks on my list. And judging by the smell, the food promises to be excellent." He stepped ahead, tossing a grin over his shoulder. "I sent a message ahead to reserve rooms, so they're expecting us."

"Blake is incredibly convenient to have around," Grace whispered to Frederick, noting the way her husband was watching his cousin with that perpetual mix of admiration and skepticism.

"No argument here," Frederick murmured, though his brows knit as if Blake were a particularly intriguing puzzle. "I've always known him to be efficient, but I'm starting to suspect he's uncannily so."

"Well, I'd rather have uncanny efficiency on our side than on Mr. Clark's."

"He has good eyes." Since Zahra spoke so infrequently, her words always seemed to matter more.

"Good eyes?" Grace leaned down to listen. "Hazel?"

Zahra stared back, her expression unchanging. "Safe."

The word pricked at something in Grace's chest that she couldn't quite define, but she placed her palm on Zahra's head, pushing up a smile. Being a mother really entailed controlling ones emotions at so many levels. "Yes, I think he is very safe."

A cheerful innkeeper bustled from behind the counter, her ruddy cheeks and bright smile suggesting that gossip was as much her currency as coin.

"Welcome to Angloss," she said, clasping her hands together, her accent as warm and calming as Mr. Barclay's. Grace already felt a kinship to her. "I'm Mrs. MacIntosh. Would you happen to be the party with a Mr. Blake?"

"Indeed, we are. And I am Mr. Blake," he declared, stepping forward and wielding his charm like a sword. Mrs. MacIntosh's smile deepened, practically glowing under its influence. Grace envied how easily Blake put people at ease. Her own smiles, though heartfelt, often seemed to elicit puzzled looks or polite chuckles—particularly when she veered into topics like unraveling fictional murders.

Perhaps it was a matter of practice.

The only person she'd been really practicing her smiles on had been Frederick, but from all she could tell, her practice had been working very well.

"Do you have a fine room for Lord and Lady Astley here and their daughter Zahra?"

"Lord and lady?" Mrs. MacIntosh preened a little and sent them a rosy-cheeked smile. "Oh aye, we do. The finest in the inn with a view of the loch and Castle Mosslea."

"Excellent." Blake continued, waving toward Tony whose flat cap was pulled low and scarf wrapped high despite the summer heat. The disguise was hardly convincing, but in a small village where no one expected to see a supposedly dead man, it might just do the trick.

"And I feel that the two of us can share as long as the room is fitted with two beds?" Blake didn't wait for Tony's response before turning back to Mrs. MacIntosh. "Is that possible?"

How very clever of Blake! Grace felt almost certain he wanted to share a room with Tony to keep an eye on the man. If not for health reasons as he recovered from being mostly dead, then to keep Tony from losing all self-control and revealing himself to Lillias.

Mrs. MacIntosh's gaze flickered toward Tony before settling back on Blake. "Aye, a nice big room."

Her voice held a melodic lilt that seemed to settle into the very air. Grace found herself drawn forward. "We hope to visit the castle in the morning. Would you happen to know who we might speak to about gaining access?"

The innkeeper's expression shifted, her brow creasing. "The castle?" She hesitated. "I wouldnae wish to visit it, if I were you, my lady."

"And why not?" Frederick stepped to her side, softening his question with a smile of his own. Yes, her darling husband had a wonderfully charming smile too. "Is it not open for tours like other Highland castles?"

"Aye, Mr. Locke, the gardener will give anyone a tour for a fee. Lives in the gatehouse at the end of the village," Mrs. MacIntosh replied. But then she leaned in, her pale eyes sparkling with the promise of a tale worth hearing. "That said, not many visit since Laird Blair passed. No one wants to risk it."

"Risk?" Blake asked, leaning casually on the counter as if they were discussing the weather. "And whatever should we know about this risky castle, Mrs. MacIntosh?"

Mrs. MacIntosh's gaze darted over her shoulder before she answered, as if fearing someone might overhear. "It's haunted."

"Haunted?" Grace nearly gasped. Could this adventure get any more fantastical?

Blake tilted his head in mock gravity. "A ghost in general, or are we dealing with a very specific kind of ghost, Mrs. MacIntosh?"

"Aye, very specific," she answered with relish. "The Grey Lady. But we all know who she really is."

Mrs. MacIntosh's storytelling instincts were impeccable, pausing long enough to ensure someone asked the question. Frederick obliged with perfect timing. "Not all of us, I'm afraid. I believe you have five thoroughly uninformed visitors as far as this Grey Lady is concerned."

The innkeeper's grin widened, her triumph evident as she delivered her answer. "She's said to be the wife of the former laird, Alistair Blair."

"The man who drowned in Loch Ness?" Grace clarified.

"Aye," Mrs. MacIntosh confirmed, lowering her voice. "Her shawl and hat were found floating beside his body, but she herself was never recovered. Some say the kelpies took her. Others believe it was the monster."

The monster? The Loch Ness monster? Grace's breath caught. Ghosts and kelpies and sea monsters all in one case. It was almost as if Christmas had come five months early just for her.

"Have you seen this Grey Lady, Mrs. MacIntosh?" Blake asked. "Because I feel as though you are quite the trustworthy sort in all this business."

"I've seen her light at night passing by the windows of the castle when naught a person is within the walls." The woman nodded to her audience as if to add credibility to her claim. "Most say she's looking for her husband among the halls because she misses him so."

"I'm surprised they don't see her walking the edge of the loch in search of him—or at the very least for her hat and shawl," Blake murmured, smoothing a hand over his mouth. Was he hiding a smile? "Remarkable how predictable the supernatural can be. Always returning to the scene of their death, as if they've read the script."

Frederick cleared his throat and, if Grace wasn't mistaken, his lips almost tipped into a smile too. "So this ghost only began her haunts after the death of Laird Blair?"

"Aye," the woman replied. "On full moons some claim to hear

her weeping from the battlements. Her hair's dark and wild about her shoulders, like the wraith she's become."

"No wonder she's searching for her shawl," Blake whispered at Grace's side, earning himself a pointed look.

Grace stifled an eye roll and turned to Zahra, who gazed up at her with unwavering seriousness. Thank heavens someone understood the gravity of the situation.

"But she gave us a reprieve for a month." The woman continued. "So we thought, she'd found her peace, until two nights ago when she was spotted again."

A month of silence from the ghost?

And then her sudden return two days ago? *Two days?*

What did Detective Miracle say about coincidences? "Mrs. MacIntosh, did you ever meet Lady Blair?"

The woman's gaze sharpened on Grace. "Aye, my lady. Not often, mind you. She wasn't one to mingle among the common folk once she married the laird, but I'd met her before they married and saw her on occasion after."

"What did she look like? I mean when she was alive."

At her periphery, she caught Frederick and Blake watching her. Tony had started taking some of the scones from the countertop.

"Like her brother. Dark hair, blue eyes, and face as pale as if death already had a claim on her."

Grace's mind snagged on a detail or a thought. Something lingered among this information she couldn't quite pin down. "You mentioned knowing her before she married. Were she and her brother from the village?"

"No, but they moved here with their parents years ago when they were but children. Their parents passed on from a horrible carriage accident ten years ago, and the village pitched in to help the pair. But Malcolm Kane left not long after, taking his sister with him. He's become a well-to-do businessman in Edinburgh."

And that's when both Frederick and Blake jerked to attention.

There was the pin.

"Malcolm Kane?" Blake repeated. "And his sister?"

"Moira Kane, God rest her."

"And has Mr. Kane been back to the village since his sister's unfortunate demise?" Frederick asked, his very good brain making the connections Grace's was beginning to form as well.

"Aye, arrived back two days ago from a lengthy business trip." She gestured toward the door. Again, two days ago? "He stays in his parents' old home on the edge of the village. A regular at the Loch's Rest, if you have a mind to try and meet him."

"I'm always keen to talk business with fellow entrepreneurs," Blake said, pushing back from the counter. "Especially if it's about purchasing land."

"Then he's the one to talk to. He's been buying properties near here for six months—places I didn't imagine folks would ever sell. He seems to be very persuasive."

"Perfect." Blake patted the counter, his charming grin firmly in place. "And if you don't mind, I'd like you to keep my interest in meeting him to yourself, Mrs. MacIntosh. You know how businessmen can be—if they know they have an edge, they'll take it."

She sobered and nodded in commiseration with Blake's statement. "I'll do just that, Mr. Blake. Now, I can imagine you're all tired and likely a wee bit peckish. I have some soup and bread I can have sent up to your rooms, if you'd like."

"That would be lovely, thank you," Frederick said.

"And we only have a few pieces of luggage for tonight," Blake added, "but more's on the way from the dock. It should arrive tomorrow, assuming the men keep to schedule."

"Very good, sir." Mrs. MacIntosh tapped her temple with a knowing smile. "Me and my husband and our sons, Charlie and Rory, will keep a keek out for them."

The narrow stairway creaked under their weight as they ascended to the rooms above. Tony disappeared into his shared room with little more than a grunt of acknowledgment, leaving Blake lingering in the hallway. He gestured toward Frederick and Grace's door, then followed them and Zahra inside.

"I think we may have our culprits," he said, once the door closed behind them.

"Malcolm and Moira Kane?" Frederick placed his and Grace's bags on the bed.

"Indeed," Blake answered.

The firelight cast a low glow across the room, where a large bed stood on one side near a wardrobe and washstand, and a couch and desk waited on the other beneath a long row of windows. Grace crossed the room, drawn to the view of Mosslea Castle perched on the rocky outcropping. The moon painted the loch in silver, its reflection shimmering like a second world below. She'd never been inside a castle. She'd imagined them aplenty—what reader wouldn't? But the reality was both breathtaking and eerie. Especially at night. Especially haunted.

"Any signs of life?" Blake coughed. "Or death, as the case may be?"

Grace threw him an exasperated grin. "You're incorrigible."

"And yet, not wrong," he quipped, grinning.

She returned her gaze to the castle. "Wouldn't it be helpful if the ghost joined the search for the will? I'm sure that would speed things along."

Frederick stepped up beside her. "I wouldn't be surprised if she already has."

Her husband's comment sparked a connection. "Do you think she's like the protagonist of *Lady Audley's Secret*? That woman would do almost anything to gain or keep her social standing and money."

"Or perhaps a variation," he mused.

"Or perhaps," Grace mused, "our naive Mrs. James, the 'inexperienced' housekeeper, is actually Moira Kane. And since Laird Blair's death didn't transfer the estate to her brother, they've concocted an elaborate scheme to claim the land another way."

"Watson"—Blake moved to her other side and tapped his temple with a grin—"I believe you've cracked it."

"You used the Sherlock reference for my benefit, didn't you, dear Mr. Blake?" Grace teased.

"If the reference fits, my lady." He tipped an imaginary hat to both Grace and Frederick before sobering. "All the same, I hope you'll keep those sharp eyes and clever heads on high alert. If our deductions are correct, even if both Kanes do not appear to prefer choosing rather nasty ends to people in order to get what they want, they're not against it. Finding the will may be one piece of the mystery." He tipped his head toward the castle. "Staying alive may very well be the other."

Chapter 20

Having traveled a great deal in various places over the last several months, Frederick had become accustomed to different accommodations to fit the culture and atmosphere of the places they'd visited, but nothing had hemmed him close as this Scottish village surrounded by mountains.

The room fit the same description. Close quarters, low ceiling beams, and mismatched furniture gave it an air of peculiar charm. For privacy, the room offered a small adjoining space with a single bed and dresser, which Zahra happily accepted as her own. Still, she'd joined them at the small table by the window, savoring the simple Scotch soup and freshly baked bread.

For a moment, Frederick imagined a simpler life, free from the grand halls and the expectations of titled gentry. He realized how drastically his perspective had shifted over the last seven months. His heart had found its home, not in the cold, calculated world his parents had tried to carve out for him with their harsh words and callous actions, but in this small, unassuming moment—here, with his family. And despite the looming uncertainty of Havensbrooke's financial future or the weight of the Astley legacy, he knew his family would be enough.

"Do you ever feel like we're living in the middle of a penny dreadful?" Grace asked, offering Zahra another piece of bread as though her words weren't at all jarring. Not so much because of the statement, but because of how accurate it felt. She spoke with an ease that made the fantastical sound entirely plausible. "Grandfather used to collect them and kept them for ages. I read and reread many of them as a child, and now it feels as though we've landed right in the middle of one."

"What is penny dreadful?" Zahra asked, looking up from her soup.

"Stories in magazines." Grace answered, sending the little girl a smile filled with such love it gave him another glimpse into the mother Grace would become, even if he had to curb a little of her adventurous nature until their children were old enough to manage the excitement. Fortunately, Zahra's history proved a well-suited match for Grace's imagination and their current circumstances. "Usually about pirates, scoundrels, or highwaymen—and always with a bit of mystery and romance thrown in."

"And *shabah*?" Zahra looked over at Frederick, who, despite his still-roaming grasp of her native tongue, was often better at sorting it out than Grace.

"Ghosts?" he clarified, not missing the way Grace's lips curled into the slightest smile at his response.

Zahra nodded, taking another sip of her soup.

"Oh yes. Sometimes even worse things than ghosts." Grace glanced toward the window, where the silhouette of the looming castle, Mosslea, stood tall against the darkening sky—an almost *too* perfect visual example of a penny dreadful in reality. "However, Zahra, what we have here, as in many penny dreadfuls, is a person who isn't really a ghost but wants us to believe she is."

"So she can sneak," Zahra added, her eyes narrowing a little as she said the word.

"Exactly." Grace sent a proud look to Frederick, clearly happy their daughter had already caught onto the sleuthing role.

"And as the wife of the previous owner, she knows the castle much better than we do, which means she is at the advantage." Frederick added, joining into what he supposed was bound to be family discussions for the majority of his married life.

"I do wonder if Mrs. James. . .um. . .Kane. . .I mean Lady Blair." Grace sighed. "Why do we always seem to meet people who can't keep a single identity? I thought it was just something about the air in Venice."

"Because we're sleuths, darling." The moment the word left his lips, Grace's smile bloomed. And if Zahra hadn't been sitting with them, he had a feeling his wife would have breached the distance to reward his usage. "It *is* part of the job."

"True." Her large blue eyes danced, telling him of her appreciation much more than words. "But if Lady Blair did marry Lord Blair only for the money and land, it is likely she's the one who killed him, or at least helped with the planning."

"Which means she's quite serious about finding the will, Grace," he warned.

"You mean dangerous," Zahra interpreted, her bluntness making the gravity of the situation hit a little harder than expected. So much for trying to guard Zahra from the darker side of this investigation.

"Yes, very dangerous," Grace reiterated, her voice gentle yet firm as she glanced at Zahra, then took another spoonful of soup. "But I'm certain we can find out more by just asking the locals. People in small villages always know something important."

"I can sneak," Zahra offered with a smile, a glint of mischief in her eyes. Frederick's chest tightened. The warmth that had been there a moment ago evaporated. "I'm very good at sneaking."

"Oh, you are, are you?" Grace grinned as if this were the most natural thing in the world. "And you're small, so you can fit into places we can't. That could come in very handy, don't you think, Frederick?"

"Indeed, Zahra," he replied, his voice strained by the effort to keep his composure. "But if you're to sneak, you must only do so when we know exactly where you are."

He shot a prayer heavenward. *God, help me.* He had two of them to protect from themselves and the world. He sighed. And only God could help him as far as that was concerned.

Frederick looked out toward the window again, the moon's glow casting ghostly hues down upon the black silhouette of Mosslea, inciting the hairs on the back of his neck to rise ever so slightly. He hoped any "ghost" proved as simple a solution as the last two, because Frederick wanted nothing more than to sort out this entire affair quickly and without someone he loved getting hurt. . .or worse.

"I'm glad we were able to slip from the hotel without meeting up with your sister this morning, Lady Astley," Blake said from behind the steering mechanism of his car. "Normally I would have had us complete the short walk to the castle, but this way, we can keep Tony hidden in the car and still look the part of the eager castle hunters the villagers believe us to be."

"We'll have to talk to Lillias at some point, Mr. Blake," Grace replied from the back seat, wedged between Tony and Zahra, as she had been the day before. "She's very much a part of all this, whether she likes it or not. And she's expecting us."

"True enough," Blake acknowledged, gesturing ahead. "But don't you think a good understanding of the landscape will help us plan before we drag the little puzzle of your sister and Mr. Kane into it?"

Tony tensed at her side at the mention of Mr. Kane.

"Most certainly," Grace said, flashing Blake a playful smile in the rearview mirror. "How convenient it is that you're so adept at sleuthing, Mr. Blake. It's almost as if this isn't your first case, given how much you know about everything."

Blake grinned. "I've dabbled on occasion."

"Boredom leads to mischief where Blake is concerned," Frederick chimed in, casting his cousin a pointed look. Blake's laughter rang out.

"It's my way of making boredom work for me."

Blake brought the car to a stop in front of a stone gatehouse, with a path leading to the castle looming on the horizon, its gray stone walls merging with the overcast sky. The faint scent of rain in the air seemed only fitting for their situation. After all, a sunny day spent searching for a will guarded by a ghost just didn't seem right.

"Tony and I are going to take a look around the castle while the three of you go on the tour." Blake announced once they'd exited the car. "We can cover more ground that way and keep Tony out of sight of Lady Blair, in case she is Mrs. James."

"Or mistake me for one of her own ghostly acquaintances," Tony quipped, his humor returning—albeit faintly—after his, well, death.

Grace let out a laugh. "Imagine that! Dueling ghosts."

Tony's humor failed to rise to her teasing, and with a nod to them, he followed Blake around the loch side of the castle grounds.

Before Frederick, Grace, and Zahra had reached the entrance of the gatehouse, the door swung open to reveal a rather spindly man. He huddled slightly, his thin white hair sticking out in various directions, much like Baby Thomas'. His pale blue eyes, framed by a weathered face, scanned them before a welcoming smile spread across it.

Grace fell in love with him on the spot. Partly because she had a weakness for older people. . .and smiles. But something about the man also tugged at a distant memory—one she couldn't quite place. Had she met him before?

He dipped his head to Frederick. "Come to see the castle, aye?"

"Indeed, we have, Mr. Locke, is it?"

"Aye." Mr. Locke's voice creaked like the hinges of an old door. "Been the gardener here for nigh on fifty years." He turned his rheumy eyes to Zahra, then back to Grace, his smile dropping into open-mouthed wonder. "You—you look just like her."

Warmth spilled through Grace's chest and rose into her eyes before she fully comprehended why. "Her?"

"Must be Elspeth Blair's daughter, then. Wee Grace?"

The heat in her eyes took on liquid form. There it was. The name. Elspeth. Grace hadn't heard it in so long. Her father always referred to her as "your mother," or rarely, "Ellie," but the way Mr. Locke said it—his accent curling the name—made it feel like a long-lost memory rising to the surface.

"Yes, I am," Grace said, reaching out and taking his bony hand in both of hers. "I only have faint memories of her, of you, and this place, but what a delight to finally return and find such a fixture here who knew my mother."

"Aye. A grand lass, she was. As good a heart as ever there was." His fingers squeezed hers in return. "And it's in you too. In your eyes." He waved his hand toward her face. "You don't last as long as I have without seeing certain things."

Grace caught a glance at Frederick, who had stepped closer, his palm gently pressing to her back. Something about Mr. Locke reminded her of ancient trees or wise elves from fairy stories—mysterious, yet reassuring. She wanted to know more. Ask more. The loss of Rutledge House still felt fresh, but standing here in a place connected to her mother, with someone who had known her, made it feel a little less like so much had been lost. "I'd love to hear more about her if you'd be willing to share. Perhaps over tea?"

His brow rose in surprise. "Aye, I'd gladly do so. 'Twould be good for the both of us, I'd say. Me to recall better days, and you to know from where you've come." He gave his head a shake. "Your sister came yesterday to tour the castle, but she didnae seem as keen to talk of your mother or the past. I'm glad to hear you're willing."

"Not only willing, happy to." Grace gave his hands another squeeze before releasing them. "Would you be available tomorrow?"

Mr. Locke studied Grace's face, his smile softening. "Aye, I've nothin' but time, lass." He chuckled, then looked toward the castle. "And if you want, I'll have ye join me here at the gatehouse tomorrow. We'll take another keek of the castle—if you're keen."

"I'll certainly be. . .keen." Grace's grin grew so wide it pinched her cheeks. "And this is my darling husband, Lord Astley, and our daughter, Zahra."

"Lord?" The man's gaze swung to Frederick. "Beggin' your pardon, sir. I hadnae idea."

"It's no matter here, Mr. Locke," Frederick interrupted, waving away the man's concern. "I'll happily disappear as the husband of Elspeth Blair Ferguson's daughter in this—and many other—respects, so you needn't worry about ceremony."

Mr. Locke looked between them, his eyes calculating, as if weighing them in some ancient balance. Those eyes seemed to hold more than any pair she'd ever encountered—even more than the ones she'd seen in Egypt. "Aye, ye'll do nicely here." He nodded, then gestured toward the castle path. "You're lookin' for Laird Blair's will, I wager?"

The warmth in Grace's face instantly froze. She exchanged a glance with Frederick, the chill spreading. Oh no. Had Lillias told him everything already?

"Did my sister tell you?" Grace asked, keeping her voice as steady as she could manage.

Mr. Locke nodded as he turned back toward the gatehouse to

fetch a ring of old keys and a walking stick. "Aye. When she came with Mr. Kane." His smile vanished completely at the mention of Mr. Kane.

"And you're not too keen on Mr. Kane?" Frederick asked.

Mr. Locke closed the door of the gatehouse with a quiet thud and gestured toward the castle path ahead, clearly avoiding an answer. "Let me show you Mosslea."

As they walked a few steps, Mr. Locke pointed to the left, where the loch shimmered in the distance. "She'd sit out there by the loch with her sketchbook, drawing the water and the hills."

Grace moved a little closer to him, captivated. "My mother?"

"Aye. She and the previous laird were thick as thieves when they were weans." Mr. Locke's walking stick made a rhythmic thump against the stone path as they climbed the incline. "Only children of only children, they were. Loved the same things."

"Like what?" Grace sent a grin over her shoulder to Frederick, and he smiled back.

Yes, she should be thinking very sleuthy thoughts right now, but certainly her dashing detective would keep his investigative hat on while she learned a little more about the woman whose laugh she barely remembered.

Who gave her this brilliant and noticeable hair color.

Who read stories to her at night which incited her own love of story.

Mr. Locke's eyes twinkled afresh, and he gestured with his stick toward the castle. "I'll show ye."

Ah, Frederick knew well the grandeur and shadow of an old family home.

Despite its description as a castle, its exterior and many aspects of its interior reminded him of his home, Havensbrooke, even down to the frayed rugs and dusty tapestries. But the beauty was there too, seasoned with time in some ways. High ceilings arched overhead, supported by darkened wooden beams whose sturdiness mocked their weathered appearance. Beveled windows flung patterns of light across dining rooms, ballrooms, and sitting rooms far too large to heat properly. The mingled scents of beeswax polish and damp stone lingered in the air like a memory.

He drew a deep breath. Of all the places he'd traveled to, this echo of home settled him most—though it was hard to fully appreciate when it came bundled with a ghost hunt, a missing will, and the lurking possibility of a murderer.

"Those were favorites of Laird Blair and your mother." Mr. Locke's voice interrupted his reverie, drawing Frederick's attention to a massive fireplace adorned with carved wooden figures on either end of the marble mantel.

Frederick narrowed his eyes. He'd seen them before. Something from Scottish folklore. Sleek, horse-like creatures with wild manes and eyes gleaming with an unsettling intelligence.

"Kelpies," Grace murmured, stepping closer, her tone laced with a sense of wonder.

Mr. Locke grinned, his expression crinkling with approval. "Ah, so ye know a bit of lore, do ye?"

Her gaze lit as she looked at the old man, and if Frederick guessed, Mr. Locke was deciding on whether to adopt Grace as a granddaughter or not. Very good. A charmed Mr. Locke was a helpful Mr. Locke, especially if it led to learning more about Grace's mother—or uncovering useful leads for their investigation.

Investigation. The word still snagged in his thoughts like a boot heel on a loose floorboard. How had this become his life?

"Mother read Scottish tales to me as a child," Grace explained, brushing her fingers over the carvings. "I've done some research since." She recited softly, "'Beware the kelpie,' the old folks say.

'He will lure you into a watery grave.'"

The words seemed to shiver in the air, bouncing off stone walls and sending a faint chill through the room.

Zahra slid her hand into his, and he gave it a squeeze.

"Are they real?" Zahra asked, her young voice adding brightness to the room.

The gardener chuckled. "Real enough, lass, if you've a mind to believe. And dangerous enough if ye've the foolhardiness to defy them."

The tour continued, revealing carvings of other mythical creatures: selkies, fairies, wulvers, even a Loch Ness Monster. Mr. Locke patted the latter fondly. "Cannae live here without one." He patted the creature one last time and continued, keeping them on the main level.

At one point, Grace gestured toward the stairs. "Will we tour the upper levels?"

"No, my lady." Mr. Locke sent a look in the direction she pointed. "Those are private chambers for whoever takes the castle next. I've no permission to lead people there."

Her brow furrowed slightly. "Would my mother have stayed there during her visits?"

Mr. Locke hesitated, his expression tightening before he spoke. "Aye. The family rooms. In fact, the chamber at the end of the hall was Laird Blair's favorite."

Was it Frederick's imagination, or had the man emphasized that detail as if daring them to investigate? "His study, perhaps?" Frederick prompted, adopting an air of casual curiosity.

"No, my lord." Mr. Locke's grin returned, sly as a fox. "He had his study for peace and quiet from a bothersome wife, but the Laird preferred a more. . .expansive retreat." He glanced at Grace, his eyes twinkling with mischief. "Much like a selkie slipping away to the sea."

Grace exchanged a look with Frederick, and he knew she'd also caught the implication. But Mr. Locke, apparently satisfied with his cryptic hint, offered no further elaboration.

They stayed a little longer, but Mr. Locke didn't offer any further clues or hints, and when they made their way back to the car, they found Blake and Tony waiting inside.

"Nothing much to report except for a little skiff docked among the underbrush at the edge of the loch," Tony explained once they'd all settled into the car, and he'd tugged off his hat.

"And the two of you?" Blake asked.

Without further encouragement, Grace shared their conversation with Mr. Locke, interspersing information about her mother in between more significant details for the investigation like the lay of the castle, Mr. Locke's dislike of Lady Blair and possibly Mr. Kane, and the hint of something important about Lord Blair's rooms upstairs.

"Well, it certainly sounds as if we have a plan for tonight." Blake drew the car to a stop in front of their hotel.

Frederick drew in a deep breath for strength as Blake's grin took a mischievous upturn and Grace's eyes lit with mystery-loving fire. "And that is?"

"Anyone up for a late-night treasure hunt in a haunted castle?" He wiggled his brows. "Nothing brings a family closer, I've heard?"

Chapter 21

"Why didn't you tell me you was Elspeth Blair's daughter?" Mrs. MacIntosh announced the moment Grace and her party stepped into the inn. They had just returned from a walk on the outskirts of the village so Blake could, as he'd put it, "gather information about the lay of the land."

Grace wasn't entirely sure what that meant, but since Blake said everything with such confidence, she had decided it must be a very smart choice.

"I didn't think it would be important," Grace replied with a polite smile. She sent a glance around the dining area, now bustling with villagers. The place had been empty when they'd first arrived, but it seemed Mrs. MacIntosh's proclamation was drawing quite the crowd.

"You're a Blair! That's always important in Angloss. Has been for centuries. We thought the Blair line ended with Laird Alastair, but here ye are." She gestured toward Grace as though presenting a long-lost heirloom.

"And her sister's here too," came a voice from among the patrons.

Grace spun toward the crowd, locating the author of the voice. As soon as her eyes met his, she knew. She was staring into the face of Fake Officer Clark, otherwise known as Mr. Malcolm Kane.

Following his subtle gesture, her gaze landed on Lillias, seated beside him at the table.

Frederick stepped to Grace's side, Blake a step behind him. Zahra had been sent up to their room, and thankfully, Tony had remained behind from their walk, likely to avoid the temptation of confronting Lillias if he'd seen her.

Praise God for small favors.

The crowd returned to their conversations as Grace reached the table and got a clearer view of Mr. Malcolm Kane. Why did dastardly men have to be handsome? She knew meanness didn't change ones looks, but it ought to give fair warning to the unsuspecting public at large.

"Grace." Lillias gestured toward the others. "Lord Astley."

Her attention hinged on Blake, clearly trying to recall his name. "Mr.—Mr. Blake, is it?"

"Mrs. Dixon." He gave a subtle dip to his head, his eyes remaining as sharp as her husband's. Of course, that was the only giveaway to their otherwise affable appearance, but Grace assumed that's because she knew both of them so well.

"It's good to see you're safe and sound, Mrs. Dixon." Frederick gave Lillias a meaningful look that Grace hoped Lillias actually felt. Her choice to jaunt off from Harrington had made everything more difficult for the rest of them and possibly more dangerous for herself.

"Please, join us," Lillias said, motioning toward Mr. Kane, who rose with infuriating grace. "May I introduce Mr. Malcolm Kane, an associate of my dear Tony's."

Grace froze, her composure slipping entirely.

"It's no wonder you're surprised, my lady," Kane said smoothly. "What would a Scot be doing for business in Virginia?"

"It is. . .a curiosity," Grace managed to say, pinching the napkin in her lap to keep herself grounded. The Scottish accent shouldn't be paired with such a sneaky man. It just seemed wrong. A disgrace to all the sweet Scottish men like Mr. Barclay and Mr. Locke.

"Mrs. Dixon may have exaggerated a touch, referring to me as an associate," Kane continued, sending Lillias a warm look that made her blush furiously. Oh goodness! Her sister was a much easier victim than Grace had thought possible. Charmed by a murderer!

And then Grace realized that, for the first time in this entire case, she and Frederick were seeing Mr. Kane up close. This was the man who had stabbed Tony, wounded Mr. Barclay, and cavorted with Mrs. James to wound poor Mrs. Lindsay.

Scoundrel.

Grace raised the napkin to cover her sneer even though she'd not been served anything to drink or eat just yet.

Gratefully, Mr. Kane continued without any apparent notice of her dislike of him. "I have a house here in Angloss, though I travel frequently for business." His grin creased at the corners of his eyes in a very un-scoundrel-like way. "My business tends to take me all over the world, but I usually work out of Edinburgh. However, Mrs. Dixon's late husband was an acquaintance of mine through the bank as I interacted with him on several international transactions. I'm currently assessing property in this part of Scotland for a few clients, and when I unexpectedly met Mrs. Dixon aboard ship and heard of her tragic loss, how could I not offer to escort her to the very place I call home." He glanced at Lillias, his expression softening. "It was the least I could do."

"How generous of you." Frederick's calm behavior spilled added calm through her.

Grace unclenched her fingers from the napkin she'd been wringing to shreds and took a deep breath.

"And fortuitous!" Blake chimed in, signaling to the server with a flick of his wrist, as though they were all merely discussing the weather. "Travel in Scotland is notoriously treacherous. Imagine a bereaved American widow navigating alone. Heroic of you, Kane. Positively heroic."

The ease with which Blake disarmed the table was nothing short of miraculous. Even Kane seemed charmed, raising his glass in a toast. "To chivalry, aye?"

Truly, how Frederick and Blake managed to ooze such charm while navigating lies, half-truths, and thinly veiled threats mesmerized her. Perhaps she ought to study their technique. Charm could be a useful weapon for a detective, after all.

She summoned a polite smile. "How fortunate we are to have such gallant company. Still, you must have business to attend to, Mr. Kane."

"Actually, I plan to stay a few more days," Kane said lightly. "The country air agrees with me. Besides, I've offered my assistance in sorting out the matter of the missing will."

All her life, Grace had always thought she was the snitch of the family! But offer her sister a charming man with a mesmerizing accent, and she was ready to forget all about the danger surrounding Tony's death—er. . .almost death—and Mr. Barclay's attack.

But Grace couldn't show her concern. Lillias' safety relied on Grace's composure, so she decided to win at the man's game. Or at least try.

And keep drumming up her own charm. . .hopefully.

Blake and Frederick proved excellent models.

"You must be the perfect person for such an assignment," she said sweetly, glancing at Frederick for reinforcement. The flicker of shock in his eyes might have distracted her if Blake's amused grin hadn't fueled her further. "Especially as someone with ties to the community. We're strangers here and quite at a loss as to where to look."

As if by magic, Kane's smile widened. Grace straightened in her chair, feeling a sudden surge of confidence. What had Blake said about Kane's weakness? Arrogance? And what hero didn't appreciate a damsel in distress?

Her grin stretched farther. Yes, she could play that role—keep Kane distracted and hopefully ignorant of the fact she didn't like the man.

"I'm more than happy to help," Kane said smoothly. "In fact, my sister was married to the previous laird, so I'm well acquainted with the castle."

"I'm sorry for your loss," Frederick offered, his tone impeccably sincere. "This must all be very difficult for you."

"Which makes him all the more understanding of my position," Lillias interjected, her gaze softening as it settled on Kane. "He knows what it's like to lose someone and is determined to help me secure my future."

Grace's stomach twisted. Her sister actually believed this man was a hero. Romantically, even.

It was either a testament to Lillias' desperation or Kane's acting skills—or perhaps the incredible power of a Scottish brogue. Grace wasn't certain which one, but she didn't feel any draw toward Mr. Kane romantically at all, so his Scottish persona couldn't be the complete reason.

"It's rather late for a search today," Kane continued, "but I'd be happy to escort you to the castle tomorrow. I have business in the morning but could meet you here around four."

Blake exchanged a quick glance with Frederick and Grace before answering for the group. "Indeed. Four it is."

Kane stood. "Well, I must be off, but I look forward to seeing you then."

"Thank you so much, Mr. Kane." Lillias said, her smile too bright. "For everything."

Mr. Kane doffed an invisible hat and excused himself.

As soon as Kane was out of earshot, Grace turned to her sister, trying to desperately keep up her charm offensive, even with Lillias. "It seems you've gained a friend in Mr. Kane quite quickly."

"You can't understand how perfect he's been," Lillias replied, lifting her glass. "When I met him aboard the ship, I was utterly lost. He arranged everything—travel, lodging, everything. It was as if he'd been sent just for me."

Sending himself, rather. Grace quelled a frown. "Of course, but to confide in him about the will?"

Lillias stiffened, her chin lifting. "Trust doesn't take years, Grace. Sometimes you just know when someone has good intentions."

"And incredibly convenient timing," Blake interjected smoothly, his words laced with irony. "An acquaintance of your late husband on a transatlantic voyage, of all things, ready to swoop in at just the right moment. Remarkable coincidence."

"It's no coincidence," Lillias snapped, her eyes flashing. "It's fate. Heaven knows I needed help, and Mr. Kane stepped in when no one else would."

Frederick cleared his throat, leaning forward with a calm that offset Lillias' rising defensiveness. "Fate often wears a convincing mask."

Her eyes flashed as she looked between them. "You think I'm being naive. That I can't tell when someone's genuinely trying to help."

"Not at all." Grace took her sister's hand. "It's just that there are clearly some dangerous people invested in learning about this inheritance, and it's wise to be careful."

"I think I'll retire for the evening." Lillias stood abruptly, her movements stiff. "I need to get back to Thomas, and I'm certain Miss Cox would like some reprieve. Thank you all for your. . .concern."

"May I walk you back, Mrs. Dixon?" Blake rose. "It would be

my pleasure to uphold the noble and heroic behavior of Mr. Kane."

Lillias hesitated, her frown softening. "Thank you."

Grace stood. "We will meet you here tomorrow?"

Lillias nodded and then paused. "The more brains we have to help us locate this will, the better, Grace. Not everyone has to take up the mantle of a would-be detective to make accurate decisions."

With that particularly misguided barb hanging in the air, Lillias and Blake exited the hotel. Grace resisted the urge to make a face at the door, settling instead for a resigned sigh.

"How will we search the castle with Mr. Kane among us?" she asked, turning to Frederick. "And what if we find it while he's there? Is he likely to attack one of us to retrieve it?"

"Perhaps," Frederick admitted, resting his elbows on the table, his steady gaze meeting hers. "But perhaps having Mr. Kane close is precisely where we need him to be. It's easier to keep an eye on someone when they're in your midst rather than scheming in the shadows."

"Unless he's already several steps ahead of us," she countered. "He does have a ghostly sister stationed inside the castle. We could be walking into a trap."

"Perhaps, but we have several things in our arsenal Mr. Kane does not." He took Grace's hand.

Grace arched an eyebrow. "And those are?"

"Your clever head and newfound friendship with Mr. Locke."

Grace's grin twitched. "Mr. Locke was very kind."

"And I daresay from our brief acquaintance with him, he is not only amenable to you but also knowledgeable." He raised a brow. "And we have a very alive Mr. Dixon."

She grinned, her tension easing even more. "That is true."

"And Blake."

Grace's laugh loosed. "Indeed, he is quite the charming addition to our arsenal, but you've forgotten one key addition."

Frederick raised an eyebrow, his lips curving slightly. "And what's that?"

"You, my dear Lord Astley," Grace answered, watching his smile broaden. "You're the calm to my—"

"Dizzying inventiveness?"

She laughed. "Which I'm sure you mean in the best way."

"Without a doubt." He spoke the words so gently, she felt certain he meant them in a way she didn't fully understand but liked a great deal.

They moved toward the stairs to their room, but before they alighted, Grace turned to him. "You know, Frederick, I was thinking that for our search of the castle tonight, we really ought to take a rope."

"And how are you certain this is a secret way into the castle?" Grace asked as she kept close to Blake on the path through the trees.

Frederick followed a few paces behind, his lantern swaying with his movements, while Tony brought up the rear, muttering occasional complaints about roots and brambles.

Frederick sighed. What a ragtag troupe they made: his fiercely determined wife, his infuriatingly clever cousin, and Tony—whose sole contribution thus far appeared to be an impressive inventory of complaints. If someone had told him a year ago that married life would involve midnight excursions in pursuit of a potentially murderous businessman and his questionably spectral sister, Frederick might have called them mad. Yet here they were.

Blake turned slightly, his lantern casting a mischievous gleam across his face. "You question my ability to commune with the local fae and extract their secrets?"

Grace's quiet laugh filtered through the darkness, the sound pulling a grin from Frederick. If they were bound to die in a trap set by a deviant businessman and his pseudo-dead sister, he might as well do so with some of the people he loved best.

Well, except Tony. He barely knew the man and hadn't been particularly impressed thus far. But will-hunting in a haunted castle beside his beloved wife and his best friend? That wasn't the worst way to go.

"I'm so glad to hear that the local fae were so obliging," Grace said, shaking her head with silent laughter.

"I may have followed our enigmatic Mr. Kane after escorting Mrs. Dixon to her hotel," Blake admitted with an exaggerated tip of his chin. "He led me straight here."

Frederick's brows rose. "Remarkably convenient, isn't he?"

"Suspiciously so," Blake agreed, his grin ruthless. "Though Mrs. Dixon seems convinced he's the very paragon of helpfulness."

The castle wall loomed ahead, its jagged silhouette rising through the trees.

"How can the two of you speak so casually when we're quite literally walking through the forest at night toward a castle where the man who tried to murder me could be in wait?" Tony's voice pitched higher than usual, the tremor betraying his unease.

"Would it help to speak more formally, sir?" Blake quipped, sparing a glance over his shoulder as they stepped into the castle's clearing.

"Never mind," Tony muttered, deflated.

Grace, brushing a stray leaf from her sleeve, interjected with an air of pragmatism, "If Mr. Kane came this way after meeting us earlier, it's a clear sign he knows he's not supposed to be here without an official escort."

"And," Frederick added, "he's either searching for the will or—"

"Preparing his sister to frighten us tomorrow," Grace finished, her gaze lingering on the looming stone walls.

"I usually avoid performances before the curtain officially rises,"

Blake said, striding toward a small door at the base of one turret. "But in this case, I think an early viewing might be worthwhile."

The door creaked open with a groan that reverberated like an ominous note on a church organ, revealing a spiral staircase winding into the castle's depths. Blake raised his lantern, the flickering light licking at the cold stone.

"Now, Lady Astley, where did Mr. Locke suggest we begin our search?"

"Upstairs," Grace said, her voice hushed as her gaze darted toward the narrowing staircase. She placed a hand lightly on Blake's arm. "And Blake, just so you know—I wouldn't advise splitting up."

"Oh?" Blake arched a brow, his tone the picture of polite curiosity.

"Novels," Frederick cut in, deadpan. "Bad things happen when parties split up. Ghosts, murderers, malevolent housemaids—it's always worse alone."

Blake's grin was wicked. "Good advice. Since we are possibly making contact with a fictional ghost in the land of myths and legends, we ought to stick to the rules of fiction, indeed."

"Laugh all you like," Grace's voice lilted with her own good humor as she followed close behind him up the stairs, her fingers brushing the cold stone wall for balance. "But just wait and see. My fictional knowledge has been proven true more often than not."

"I've no doubt of it," Blake replied, casting a glance over his shoulder. The lantern light deepened the mischief in his eyes. "Fiction usually comes from somewhere very nonfictional."

Frederick smiled at their whispered banter, a pleasant distraction in the deepening darkness of the stairwell. The air felt damp, thick with the scent of earth and stone, and much cooler than an early July evening. It creeped into his bones, nearly inciting a chill.

When they reached the first landing, a hallway stretched out before them to the right, the passage dark except for the faint moon glow casting pale light through the windows.

"Douse your lantern," Blake whispered, extinguishing his own. "Too easy to spot."

Frederick obeyed, leading the group through the shadowed hall. The massive windows they'd admired earlier that day now seemed eerie, their pale light giving shape to the wide, yawning darkness on either side. However, the windows' placement above the stairs offered a clear view of their next move.

Frederick turned to address the group when a strange sound filtered in from somewhere above them. It sounded like something scraping against stone as if stone-upon-stone or metal-upon-stone. Frederick stopped in his tracks, his ears straining.

"Well," Blake muttered, his voice low but still managing to sound irreverent. "If I were a spectral horse trying to lure someone to their doom, I'd definitely start with that noise. It's the right mix of creepy and obnoxious."

Grace shot him one of the most confused looks. "We're not near enough to water for kelpies, dear Mr. Blake."

"Ah," Blake had the decency to look utterly flummoxed. "So what's the proper culprit, then?"

Grace caught on to his teasing. "Perhaps a brownie. They're shy creatures, but famously helpful. They might tidy up while we search."

"Convenient," Blake said with a wink at Frederick. "Imagine waking up to a cleaned castle after all this nonsense."

The banter dissolved as they reached the grand staircase. Grace pointed toward the upper floor. "Locke mentioned the laird's favorite room—at the end of the hall."

Frederick's gaze caught on the mantel nearby, where two kelpie carvings loomed, their wild eyes gleaming in the moonlight like warnings.

They climbed the stairs, their footsteps a slow, groaning rhythm on the ancient wood. Each creak seemed louder than the last, as if the castle itself whispered for them to turn back.

At the top, the air grew sharper, colder, the fine hairs on Frederick's arms standing to attention. The corridor stretched out before them, lined with closed doors on either side. At the very end, a set of double doors waited with anything but welcome.

"Stay close." Frederick's voice breathed near Grace's ear bringing her a step nearer, and that is when he noticed something that sent a chill through his body.

The scraping had stopped.

Chapter 22

"Sounds as though the brownies have finished their work," Blake whispered as Frederick led the way down the hall. "Efficient fellows, aren't they. Not even two o'clock."

Grace studied his face. The words were light, but the tension beneath them wasn't lost on her. Blake was on edge, just like Frederick. Whatever had been making the noise had stopped, and the silence now hung heavy like the moment before a thunderstorm.

"That's the room, I'd wager." Frederick gestured with his doused lantern. "The one at the end of the hall."

"Lovely," Tony muttered. "Because there's nothing ominous about approaching a dead man's favorite haunt in the middle of the night."

"Glad to see your humor's resurrecting, Dixon." Blake's choice of words and deadpan expression nearly loosened Grace's grin altogether. The man seemed determined to keep levity very much alive no matter the circumstances.

Unfortunately, the levity was short-lived when a faint creak echoed somewhere to their left. They froze. Tony may have whimpered, but Grace couldn't be sure whether it was him or a door.

"Did anyone else hear that?" Tony's whisper cracked.

Grace nodded, her fingers brushing the cold, uneven stone

wall, as though it might provide some tangible barrier against the unknown. "It sounded like a door—"

Another swish followed by a high-pitched groan reverberated through the hall. One of the double doors up ahead swung open of its own accord. Grace swallowed through her tightening throat. It only seemed to open by its own accord. Flashes of memory of her ghost hunt in Havensbrooke came to mind.

That ghost hadn't been real. It had *felt* real, though.

She drew in a steadying breath. And neither was this one.

The room beyond the door was drenched in pale moonlight. Tall, arched windows cast shadows that stretched long and sharp across the stone floor, like claws reaching into the void.

"This feels like a very bad idea," Tony muttered, sidling closer to Grace than he had been a moment ago.

"Stay together," Frederick said firmly, reaching for her hand. His grip was reassuringly warm against the icy air.

On her periphery, Grace caught sight of Blake pulling his gun from somewhere inside his jacket. A gun. Very good idea. Not helpful with ghosts or kelpies or probably even brownies, but with a flesh-and-blood murderer, a helpful addition to their arsenal. She'd always found having a man with a gun in these sorts of situations very helpful.

Blake took the lead, as any man with a gun ought to do, and approached the open door as if he trained to do something very similar. It was rather fascinating to watch and incited all sorts of questions she'd have to reserve for later.

Just before they reached Blake at the door, a strange whisper filtered across the cold air. What was it? Grace looked up at Frederick, who had an ever-tightening grip on hand.

"Oh, absolutely not," Tony hissed, backing up a step. "I draw the line at ghostly whispers in the dark."

The whisper came again from the left where the hall turned

down into darkness. Every hair on Grace's head answered the call of fear, very much like she'd felt the first time she'd read Poe's "The Raven." Naturally, she'd followed it up with every other story of his she could find, thus ensuring an entire week of sleepless nights haunted by beating hearts, madmen, and the occasional black cat.

She forced logic to the forefront. What had the whisper said? It sounded like, "Alastair?"

Frederick frowned but said nothing, his jaw tightening as they stepped into the room after Blake. Grace felt the tension evaporate almost instantly. She'd never felt quite so attune with a dead person before in her whole life. Laird Blair's favorite room was a library.

"I believe this particular ghost hunt was tailor-made for you, darling." Frederick sent her a smile, his gaze still alert.

"It only proves all the more how much he and my mother had in common." She took in the heady, familiar scent of old leather and ink mingled with just enough dust to threaten a sneeze.

Floor-to-ceiling bookshelves lined the walls, their contents a delightful chaos of ancient tomes and newer, well-worn volumes. Interspersed among them were intricately carved wooden creatures—Scottish selkies, kelpies, and even a particularly regal faerie queen mid-flight.

"Well, Laird Blair was nothing if not committed to the theme," Blake muttered, his voice low as he surveyed the room. The pistol in his hand was held so naturally that, had Grace not watched him draw it, she might not have noticed it at all.

She shouldn't be surprised he had a pistol. After all, he was the one who'd taught her how to use one.

"Do you think he commissioned these?" Grace released Frederick's hand and walked to the nearest shelf, running her fingers over a carving of a stoic-looking brownie clutching a broom. "They're all so unique."

"We're not here to catalog a dead man's mythical menagerie,"

Tony grumbled. "We're here to find a will and save Lillias."

Grace pulled back, rolling her eyes, but didn't argue. The others had already dispersed, each taking a different section of the room. She began methodically pulling books from her shelf, more out of curiosity than necessity. The moonlight spilling through the windows created jagged patterns on the floor and gave enough light to read titles on the spines, if the words were large enough, but not see the words on the pages.

Not that Grace was trying.

Much.

And you never knew—any one of these might trigger a secret passage. She'd seen it happen before.

"Is anyone going to tell me what we're actually looking for?" Tony's whisper broke the quiet.

"A place to hide a will," Frederick answered from a bookshelf on the opposite wall.

"Or a clue to where a will might be hidden," Blake added from across the room.

Were Frederick and Blake on their third bookshelves while she was still on the first one? She bit down on her bottom lip. Perhaps she'd been looking at each book a little too thoroughly. But a pale spine caught her attention: *A Blair's Account of Scottish Myths and Legends.* The words gleamed faintly in the moonlight. Blair. Her Blair's?

The book felt oddly light in her hands as she flipped it over to see the front. At the bottom of the cover in embossed letters was her cousin's name, Alistair Blair.

"I think I found something," Tony crouched near the empty fireplace, where two large bookshelves framed the mantel in on both sides.

Grace tucked the book under her arm and turned toward him. "What is it?"

Tony looked up, his eyes wide and his face as pale as the moonlight filtering through the windows. "I know this bracelet." He held up the item, turning it over in his hands as if trying to convince himself it was real. "The stones, the initials. What—what is it doing here?"

"What do you mean?" Blake asked, leaning over Tony's shoulder to inspect the bracelet. "You can't make out the inscription in this light."

Tony's hands shook, his grip tightening on the jewelry. "I don't need light. I know what it says." He looked up, meeting Grace's gaze. "This is the bracelet I gave to Lillias on our wedding day. What is it doing here?"

Before Grace could formulate an answer—or at least something comforting—a loud creak shattered the stillness. The bookshelf beside Tony tipped forward with agonizing slowness, books cascading like an avalanche.

"Tony!" Blake barked at the same time Frederick shouted, "Grace!"

The moment erupted into chaos. Blake moved toward Tony, and Frederick grabbed Grace's arm, pulling her into him and out of the way, just as the massive structure crashed to the ground, sending a deafening echo through the room.

Books and dust exploded in all directions, and Grace had two corresponding thoughts: First, someone possibly had just tried to kill them with falling books, and second, why would anyone ever choose to damage an entire bookshelf of books that way?

As the dust settled, Blake stepped forward, coughing and waving a hand in front of his face. "Is everyone all right?"

Grace glanced up at Frederick, who still had her firmly cocooned against him. His brow was furrowed, his gaze raking over her for any sign of injury. She gave him a small, grateful smile, and he let out a breath that seemed to have been stuck in his chest for hours.

"Define *all right,*" Tony groaned from somewhere beneath a mountain of books.

Grace exchanged a look with Frederick before they rushed toward Tony, Blake already clearing a path. Tony lay sprawled on the floor, one leg pinned beneath a fallen chair that had been buried in books.

They all began removing the books to clear a path to him.

"Is it broken?" Frederick asked.

"I don't think so." Tony answered, pushing himself up to a sitting position and sending Blake a rather impressive glare. "But I'd like it noted that this was one of the most ridiculous ideas of all time—searching a castle at night with a murderer on the loose?"

Blake snorted as he grabbed one end of the chair. "If pessimism were a form of strength, Mr. Dixon, you'd have lifted this chair—and the bookshelf—by now."

Tony's frown deepened as Frederick and Blake hoisted the chair away and Grace helped him stand.

"Can you walk?" she asked, steadying him.

"I think it's a sprain," Tony answered.

Frederick slipped an arm under Tony's shoulders, taking his weight and freeing Grace to clear a path through the books.

"This bookshelf didn't fall on its own," Blake said, inspecting the area where it once had stood. "It was pushed—conveniently, I might add." He tilted his head up toward the balcony that wrapped around the room, its shadowed shelves looming like sentries. "Our ghost likely staged this little accident from up there." Blake cast the room a look, his steely gaze defying the humorous tilt to his lips. "I suppose this is the part where we reconsider our evening plans?"

"For once, Mr. Blake, I actually agree with you." Tony groaned as they started toward the library door.

They made their way out of the room, the oppressive silence following them like a shadow. Grace cast a look back the way they'd come. Why was Lillias' intimate bracelet in the castle library? And why would someone try to hurt them over it?

As they descended the stairs, the faint prickle of being watched raised the hairs on Grace's neck. She couldn't shake the sensation, and the implications churned in her mind like a storm. If the clues added up, only two people could be behind this—and both were willing to kill to get what they wanted.

The room was dimly lit by the soft glow of a single oil lamp, its wick turned low to keep the light from spilling under the door to Zahra's adjoining room. After helping Tony to his bed to convalesce, Blake had claimed an armchair in their room and lounged with his head tipped back, looking every bit like a man who had earned a moment's respite after narrowly avoiding being flattened by airborne furniture.

The fire crackled softly in the bedroom hearth, its warm glow painting flickering shadows on the walls and giving the welcome sense of safety they'd lacked only half an hour before. Frederick sat on the small couch nearest the window, one leg stretched out and an arm draped casually over the armrest. His gaze, however, was fixed on the dark silhouette of the castle in the distance.

The room was quiet save for the occasional pop of a log in the fire, the three of them lost in their own thoughts, he supposed. Though Blake looked like he might be asleep. He stole a glance at Grace, who was removing her jacket after checking on Zahra. Despite her composed exterior, Frederick knew her well enough to recognize the slight tension in her shoulders. She had been too close to that falling bookshelf. His stomach tightened at the memory of the chaos—the crash, the dust, the instant terror of imagining her crushed beneath it.

She hadn't been, though. Thank God. His Grace always ended up right where she should be in moments like that—safe, with him. The knot in his chest loosened just slightly at the thought. If their marriage had taught him anything, it was that his strength had limits. And he had to trust the people he loved most to the one who loved them more.

Blake broke the silence, his eyes still closed. "If tonight has taught us anything, it's that libraries are far more dangerous than I previously gave them credit for. And I gave them plenty of credit."

Grace flashed Blake a grin as she settled next to Frederick on the couch, tucking herself into his side. He instinctively shifted to wrap his arm around her shoulders, drawing her closer, the warmth of her body a welcome contrast to the lingering chill of the events of the evening.

"Very dangerous and wonderfully intriguing, all at the same time," Grace added, teasing.

"Ah, yes," Blake murmured from his chair. "Like women."

Grace let out a quiet chuckle, and Frederick gave her shoulder a gentle squeeze, glad to have her safely at his side.

"Do you think Lady Blair knew who we were?" Grace asked. "Or recognized Tony?"

"I can't say," Blake replied. "But from the distance and the moonlight, I'd wager she wouldn't have recognized Tony. However, I'm certain she and her brother knew exactly who we were."

Grace leaned her head back against Frederick's shoulder, the scent of rosemary and mint from her hair filling his lungs with another reminder of her safe place beside him. He brushed a kiss against her hair and noticed the book she held on her lap.

"What have you there?'

"It's a book I found in the library authored by Alistair Blair," she said, turning the cover so he could see it. "But I don't believe it is exactly what it appears to be."

"That's not ominous at all, darling," Frederick said with a wry grin.

Her smile widened, and she leaned in to brush a quick kiss against his lips—nothing more than a fleeting brush, but enough to send warmth through him. He was just about to make a remark when Blake's voice interrupted.

"Fair warning," Blake said, not bothering to open his eyes. "I am *not* asleep."

Grace opened the cover of the book, and her fingers paused over the hollowed-out center. A secret compartment? Frederick's gaze sharpened as she slowly revealed a folded letter tucked inside.

"Frederick, do you think it's the will?" she whispered, unfolding the page with delicate fingers only to reveal a short missive in some calligraphic hand.

> *If you're reading this, I am likely dead.*

"Well," Blake squinted over at them, sitting up straighter in the chair. "That's quite the opening gambit." He waved toward her. "Do continue."

> *I have long suspected my wife of marrying me for my wealth and nothing more. But she's developed an unhealthy curiosity about the estate, the coal mines, and any other resources of Mosslea. I've grown to mistrust her and am suspicious that she's taking some of the family jewels I've kept protected along with generations before me. If I am gone, I pray the next Blair can make Mosslea more secure than I was able to, but perhaps there is still time for me to change the course of the estate's future. I hope it is not too late.*

Frederick took the letter from Grace and examined it, then handed it to Blake. "His signature is here, with a date from four months ago," he said. "Not long before the man was found drowned."

"Our first real proof, I believe." Blake said, waving the letter in his hand. "But not enough. As far as the village knows, Lady Blair drowned along with her husband, so we have to catch her to prove this."

"It's a breadcrumb, at least." Frederick offered. "And if there's this, there has to be more."

"But what about Lillias' bracelet?" Grace turned to Frederick. "She toured the castle with Mr. Kane yesterday, but it doesn't seem accurate that she would have dropped her bracelet there and left it without notice. Not that one."

Blake stretched, his chair creaking slightly as he settled more comfortably. "Didn't you mention that Lady Blair played at being the Dixons' housekeeper?"

Frederick and Grace exchanged a quick look, and Blake continued, "If she had a penchant for jewelry, it wouldn't be a stretch to think she took it."

Frederick raised a brow, his mind already chasing down the implications. "And then left it for us to find? A message? A warning, perhaps? Someone carefully positioned it in just the right spot to be flattened by a bookshelf?"

Blake shrugged casually, stretching his arms above his head. "Possibly. Or it could be something as simple as an accident. With all the chatter about a second will, it seems the Kanes might be rattling their cages a bit. And we all know how mistakes tend to slip through when the cage gets rattled." He paused, eyes twinkling. "Though, I'd rather our next clue not come with a side of airborne furniture."

Frederick tossed a look back to his cousin. "I'll make sure to inspect every shelf before you're near one again then."

Blake grinned mischievously, dipping his head in an exaggerated bow. "I'll take that as a promise, old man." He backed toward the bedroom door, adding over his shoulder, "By the by, I've got a bit of news. A friend of mine has some further information on Mr. Kane. I plan to meet with him tomorrow—hopefully he'll shed some light on things."

"A friend?" Frederick tilted his head, narrowing his gaze as he looked at Blake more closely. "What sort of friend?"

Blake's grin widened, and he theatrically doffed an imaginary hat. "Ah, you know. One of those sorts who seems to know everything about everything. Don't worry, I'll bring him around for tea—if we survive the next few days."

With a wink, Blake slipped out the door, leaving Frederick and Grace alone once more.

"We're running out of time, Frederick." Grace looked up at him, searching his face. "Not so much days, but time itself. It's like a feeling, creeping in the air, as though if we don't find that will soon, something worse will happen. Something that will make sure neither Lillias nor I can ever claim our inheritance."

He pulled her back against him, her words reigniting his previous concern. "Let's get some rest, darling," he said quietly, pressing a kiss to her forehead. "Tomorrow, we'll have answers. We must."

Blake left after breakfast, declaring with great pomp that he had "urgent business" in a nearby town, which Grace strongly suspected translated to checking on their luggage and rendezvousing with his so-called friend. She could only hope this mysterious acquaintance could provide them with further proof of Mr. Kane's nefariousness.

Meanwhile, Frederick volunteered to take Zahra on a leisurely walk by the loch, which conveniently kept him near the gatehouse while Grace paid a visit to Mr. Locke. Sleep had evaded her the night before, her mind stitching and unstitching the fraying threads of their mystery. But despite all the uncertainty, one thing was sure: Mr. Locke knew far more than he'd let on about Lord and Lady Blair.

So with Frederick's clever suggestion in mind, she needed to make wise use of her time with him.

Mr. Locke welcomed Grace inside his gatehouse apartment with a grin. He'd donned a frayed suit and plaid bowtie to "dress up" the tea a bit, and he led Grace to a small table and chairs by a large window overlooking the back gardens of the castle.

The dear man, his weathered face etched with a lifetime of sun and soil, offered Grace a plate of sandwiches, fruit, and shortbread. His calloused hands trembled slightly as he poured her a cup of tea, but nothing as bad as the way she poured tea.

Their conversation meandered through lighthearted tales of her mother and Alastair Blair as children. Mr. Locke painted vivid pictures of them darting among the gardens, setting up sanctuaries for fairies (strictly no toads allowed), and fishing for the mythical loch monster with sticks and string. Grace found herself laughing, drawn in by the warmth of his stories and the pictures it put in her mind of her own dear mother.

Grace couldn't help but smile at the warmth in Mr. Locke's words, the love for his work and the people he'd come to see as part of his own family. It wasn't just the gardens he'd nurtured over the years—it was the lives within them. That realization only deepened her respect for the man, though it also made her wonder just how far he'd go to protect the place and its secrets.

After a second sandwich and a piece of shortbread, Mr. Locke leaned back in his chair, studying her with a look so gentle it nearly made her tear up.

"You have much of your mother's eyes, her expressions and intelligence. I see it." His crackly voice warmed his words, and his smile only made them sweeter. "The kindness too. I see it."

Grace's chest tightened at the words. "I'm so glad you see

those things," she replied softly. "It makes me feel like part of her is close by."

"Aye, you do. She was a curious one, your mother—always asking questions, always wanting to know the stories behind the flowers, the land, the people." He nodded toward her chair. "She used to sit right there, pestering me about the names of every plant in the garden."

Grace smiled. "She adored gardens. She created one at our house in Virginia—it was spectacular. Father said she designed it to look like the one from her childhood, so it must have been this one."

Mr. Locke straightened a little, his pride shining through. "She loved this land. Proper love, ye ken? She and Laird Blair—both of them understood the value of the old ways. They respected the past and its stories."

"Yes, I noticed the wood carvings around the castle," Grace said, leaning forward. "They're beautiful—so intricate."

His face lit up. "Ah, those. Aye, I made them for him."

"All of them?" Grace asked, laughing as she picked up a strawberry from her plate.

"Every last one," Mr. Locke said with a satisfied nod. "The laird would tell me the stories he loved, and I'd bring them to life in the wood."

Grace shivered slightly as the memory of the large carved wolves in the library surfaced. The gleaming eyes and snarling mouths had felt unnervingly real. "Some of them looked *very* lifelike," she said with a half-smile.

"Aye," Mr. Locke said with a chuckle, leaning in as though sharing a secret topped off with a wink. "They're my eyes in the castle, ye ken?"

Grace snorted into her tea, quickly covering her mouth. "Well, if those eyes could tell you where the will is, Mr. Locke, it'd save us all a great deal of trouble."

His expression turned sly, his hand lifting his cup in an almost toast-like gesture. "Ah, lass, but where's the fun in that? Even if I did know. Besides," he added, his voice dipping low, "I think you've already been pokin' about in places you ought not."

Grace felt her cheeks flush. "Your eyes at work again, I see."

He sipped his tea without answering, though his smirk did all the talking. Well, even if he didn't know where the will was, Grace imagined he had his suspicions. Especially with the connection he had to the estate and Laird Blair.

"Forgive me for being so direct," Grace said, setting her cup down. "But what happened between Lord and Lady Blair? I have the distinct impression theirs wasn't a—happy marriage."

The humor drained from Mr. Locke's face. "No. Not happy. But not because of the laird. He married her for love. She"—he shook his head, his lips pressing into a tight line—"she married him for the coin. Anything that glittered or could be spent, that's all she cared for. Not him."

"And he knew?"

"Aye, he knew," Locke said, his voice thick with regret. "Told me so himself. He loved her anyway. Foolish man. But I caught her once, ye ken, stealing from him—taking the family jewels. Confronted her, I did, but she—she had a way of making a man feel smaller than a blade of grass." He paused, his jaw tightening. "Cold as ice, that one. But she got her due."

A shiver slid up Grace's spine at the sudden chill in his tone. "Did she?"

"Aye." His eyes steadied on hers. "She killed him. I saw them that night—her walking him down to the loch. He was in no state to be walking, looked like he'd been drinking, but now I wonder if she didnae do something to him. They went out on the boat, just like they used to when they first married. And the next morn I found his body on the shore."

Grace's breath caught. "I'm so sorry," she whispered. "And her? You didn't find her body?"

"No." His gaze darkened. "The kelpies got her."

"The kelpies?" Grace blinked, unsure if she'd heard correctly.

"Aye." Mr. Locke nodded solemnly. "Even the demons of the loch couldn't abide her villainy. They dragged her down to the depths for what she did. That's why her spirit haunts the castle now. It's her penance."

Grace thought it wise not to challenge the man's tale, though the corner of her mouth twitched at the fantastical turn. She could certainly appreciate a little fiction thrown into a story. "Mr. Locke, I'd like to make things right for my cousin Alastair. The only way to do that is to find the will. If we don't, Mosslea will be auctioned off." She hesitated before adding, "I believe Mr. Kane wants it."

"Her brother?" Mr. Locke's eyes narrowed to slits.

"Yes." She almost said *aye* just to see what it felt like. "If anyone knows where Laird Blair might have kept a second copy of the will, it would be you. The only way my sister and I can continue the Blair legacy is to find it."

"And your sister?" he asked, his gaze sharp. "She'll honor it?"

Grace hesitated, then smiled faintly. "The will leaves the estate to both of us equally. Neither of us can make a change without the other's agreement. My sister's looking for a fresh start, and I think Mosslea is that place."

The silence stretched like a taut string between them until Mr. Locke cleared his throat. "Toward the end, the laird asked me to carve new pieces. Creatures with secret compartments in them. He never told me why. Just said it was important."

Secret compartments? Grace's heart quickened. Like the book she'd found. "Are they still in the castle?"

"As far as I know." Mr. Locke's voice softened. "He kept them close. Treasured them. They'd be in a place special to him."

"His favorite room?" Grace asked, sitting up straighter.

"Aye." Mr. Locke's eyes glimmered anew as he raised his teacup. "If ye can find it."

Chapter 23

Lillias arrived before Mr. Kane, and Grace knew immediately something was wrong. Her usually poised and polished sister looked pale, her eyes sunken with fatigue and haunted by something she wasn't ready to name. A stark contrast to the Lillias of the previous evening, who had dazzled over dinner.

"I'll take Zahra to keep an eye out for Mr. Kane," Frederick said, a quick glance at Grace confirming he'd also noticed Lillias' state. He ushered their daughter toward the window seat, leaving the sisters in a semi-private corner of the drawing room.

Once they'd settled, Grace leaned forward. "What's wrong? Is it Thomas?"

Lillias blinked rapidly, shaking her head as her breath hitched. "No, Thomas is fine. Miss Cox has proven surprisingly capable once we worked through her difficulties with diapers."

Grace was pretty certain everyone had an initial discomfort with diapers. "She seems to be a much better fit for you than me."

Lillias' gaze flickered to Grace, a ghost of a smile on her lips. "I couldn't have managed without her." Her shoulders drooped. "But I shouldn't have taken her from you."

Something was certainly wrong with her sister! Grace opened her mouth to ask what was wrong, when Lillias leaned closer. "Do

I seem like I'm going mad?"

Not the question Grace had been expecting. However, as someone who had occasionally wondered the same about herself, she felt uniquely qualified to respond. She tilted her head, studying her sister. "No. Why would you ask that?"

Lillias pressed a fist to her chest and leaned back, her eyes darting to the floor. "It's all this talk about the ghost in the castle. It's gotten into my head."

There was talk about that.

"And the stress of finding the will."

"Understandable." Grace nodded.

"And then, Tony."

Grace froze, her sister's hand grabbing hers before she could form a response.

"That's the problem, Grace. It's Tony."

"What do you mean?"

Lillias swallowed again, her voice dropping to a whisper. "Yesterday, I thought I saw him. I was walking down the street, and there he was, staring at me from a window. I was sure of it. But when I looked again, he was gone."

"That could have been anyone," Grace said, attempting a smile that felt as fake as the assurances coming out of her mouth.

"I thought the same." She lowered her voice even more and glanced around as if someone was listening. "But then last night I woke up feeling like I was being watched. When I opened my eyes, Grace, I swear I saw him standing over Thomas' cradle near the window." Her voice cracked. "When I turned on the lantern, he was gone."

Grace tried her best to keep a steady expression, even as her heart plummeted to her toes. They had to find that will before Tony unraveled everything—or worse, before Kane or his sister grew desperate.

"You've been grieving." Grace covered her sister's hand. "Perhaps rushing into a connection with another man isn't the best for your heart right now."

"I miss him, Grace," she admitted, her voice quivering. "I don't want to, but I do. We were both selfish creatures—me more than him—but I can't hate him for it. I want to. It would be easier. But I can't. He was a good man."

The moral dilemma ricocheting through Grace at the moment required Herculean strength to control. And then, as if to prove his idiocy, from behind a nearby curtain peeked the very man of whom they spoke. His gaze held Grace's, pleading.

She gave her head a sharp shake, which Lillias interpreted as disapproval. "What? You don't think he was a good man?"

"Of course, I do. He loved you." Grace struggled to keep her voice even, glaring pointedly at Tony until he finally ducked back behind the curtain. "I wonder, if you could see him right now, what would you say to him?"

Lillias stared, her fingers working nervously in her lap. "I'd tell him I'm sorry. That I was wrong. And I'd ask if we could start over." She pinched her eyes closed, tears slipping down her cheeks. "I'd promise to be better." She looked back to Grace. "Frederick was right. I took it all for granted."

Grace didn't have time to further the discussion because Frederick and Zahra reentered with Mr. Kane beside them. Mr. Kane's suit was so fine it practically screamed his wealth, a jarring mismatch for the modest surroundings.

"Are we ready?" he asked, offering his hand to Lillias.

With an idea of where the will might really be, Grace tried to sort out how to sneak upstairs in the castle, locate the right carving with a secret compartment, and keep Tony from putting them all in danger.

Secret compartment?

That's what they were looking for? Hidden caches in the wooden sculptures scattered throughout Mosslea. Frederick pinched the bridge of his nose as he walked between his wife and Zahra, trailing behind Mr. Kane and Lillias on their way to the gatehouse.

To his quiet exasperation, Grace had even enlisted Zahra in the search.

And Zahra brightened at the very idea of such a scavenger hunt. They may not be related by blood, but Grace and Zahra certainly shared a love and stamina for adventure.

And the entire choice to include Zahra could prove a good one, as Kane seemed to completely ignore Zahra's existence. Oh no, he only had eyes for Lillias, which proved rather unnerving. Lillias seemed markedly less starry-eyed today.

Had the conversation between her and Grace led to such a transformation?

When they reached the gatehouse, Mr. Locke didn't respond to their knock, but he had left the gate unlocked and open, as if to confirm Grace's suspicions that he wanted them to have free rein to search the castle.

"I suppose the old man's hoping we'll find the will too, dear Mrs. Dixon," Kane remarked, offering his arm to Lillias with a practiced charm. "He's not even going to censure our search anymore."

He swept forward with the confidence of a man accustomed to getting his way. But Frederick felt a prickle of unease.

Something about this was too easy. Too simple.

Perhaps he'd become overly suspicious since being dragged—enticed—into Grace's sleuthing escapades, but Locke didn't seem the sort to abandon his post so conveniently.

Frederick touched the spot where his revolver was concealed

beneath his coat. Where was Blake? He leaned close to Grace, threading her arm through his. "Keep your guard up," he murmured near her ear. "Something about this doesn't sit right."

He gestured for Zahra to keep to his side.

The search began uneventfully enough, with cobwebs disturbed and long-forgotten sculptures unearthed from rooms that seemed untouched by human hands—or cleaning rags—for decades.

The first hidden compartment of note was discovered in a selkie sculpture in the dining room. Zahra, with admirable discretion, brought an emerald ring to Frederick while Kane and Lillias busied themselves on the far side of the room.

"Where did you find this?" Frederick sent a glance to Kane, keeping his voice low.

Zahra nodded toward the sculpture. "Hidden compartment, as Sayyida said."

The next prize came from a large kelpie sculpture, where Frederick unearthed a pearl necklace neatly concealed in its stand. He slipped it into his pocket, his expression neutral. There was no knowing how many treasures Grace had uncovered, but the glow on her face as they entered each new room was evidence enough that she was thoroughly enjoying the hunt. Of course, they "looked" in other places, to keep Kane from suspecting anything, but between him and Zahra, they'd already found a ruby with the Blair crest on it, a set of diamond earrings, two jeweled pins, and a ring.

The Blair family treasures.

When they entered the library, Kane froze in the doorway, his gaze sweeping the scene before him. The bookshelves lay toppled, books strewn across the floor like the aftermath of a literary tempest.

To Grace's credit, she kept her expression from giving anything away. She even managed a pleasant half-smile, though the way Malcolm Kane's eyes lingered on them suggested he knew they knew.

Frederick didn't like that look. It had the flavor of a fox watching hens from the shadow of the coop. Had Kane finally reached his limit of patience? Was this the moment he planned to eliminate anyone who could claim the inheritance? And where was Kane's elusive sister?

"Do you think things like this happen often in old castles?" Lillias ventured, stepping gingerly around the sea of books. She nudged a heavy tome with her toe as if it might bite. "Didn't we see a fallen portrait in one of the other rooms?"

"Indeed," Malcolm replied smoothly, though his gaze flicked toward Frederick, a glint of something sharper than politeness in his eye. "Old houses are certainly. . .unpredictable."

Suppressing the urge to check his revolver, Frederick gave a curt nod and turned to right one of the suits of armor near the fireplace. There were four of them, one stationed in each corner of the room. The one he adjusted, holding a broad sword, wobbled slightly before settling, its empty visor staring out at the mess. At least someone was keeping watch.

"Frederick, look."

Grace's voice drew his attention. She stood near the fireplace, her focus on something jutting out from beneath the mantel.

A lever—and one cleverly disguised in the woodwork.

It was almost hidden—*would have been hidden*—had the bookshelf still stood upright like last night.

She met his gaze with a knowing look, her lips twitching in the barest suggestion of triumph. "Alistair Blair's favorite room?" she murmured before shrugging and pulling the lever.

A grinding, creaking sound filled the air as the floor near the mantel shifted, splitting open to reveal a narrow doorway. The movement sent a cascade of dust into the air. Frederick coughed. Kane, on the other hand, seemed to lose his composure entirely.

"What?" Kane exclaimed, stepping forward, his voice tight. "How did you—?"

"Secret compartments aren't as uncommon as you might think," Grace answered, as if it was commonplace then peered into the narrow opening.

"I suppose not." Kane gave his head a shake, visibly regaining control. "My sister lived here for almost a year and never found this place. She always assumed her husband took solace in his library. Not in an entirely separate room." He chuckled hollowly. "How clever."

The space split the mantel from the wall, offering a small doorway only slightly taller than Zahra, but passable for taller individuals if they ducked. Frederick stepped forward, peering into the space. "I'll go first."

The space beyond was dimly lit by three narrow windows on the east side of the stone walls with a view of Angloss and Loch Ness and the east gardens a hundred fifty feet or more below. More shelves lined the walls with additional books, mostly further exploration of Scotland, history, or lore, complete with further carvings to explore.

Several small slits carved into the other walls in the room, offered views into other rooms in the castle. "This isn't just a hidden room," Frederick murmured, his unease solidifying. "It's a surveillance chamber."

"Possibly how Alistair discovered the sneaky habits of his wife?" Grace whispered, as Zahra slipped passed them to one of the nearby bookshelves covered in sculptures.

Once the little girl set her mind to a task, she proved as focused as his wife.

"What a spot." Kane emerged behind them, his earlier irritation replaced with admiration. "And the room is larger than I expected. At least half the size of the library."

Grace ran her fingers along the wall, finding one of the peepholes and leaning in to look. Her breath caught. "I can see the dining room from here."

Frederick followed suit, finding a peephole that granted a view of the great hall. His stomach twisted. "Whoever used this room could keep watch over the entire house."

"And that's the entry hall," Kane muttered from another peephole. "Old Blair had more up his sleeve than I realized."

Lillias lingered near the entrance, her eyes darting nervously around the space. "I always thought Grace exaggerated in her letters, but. . ." She swallowed hard. "This is real."

Grace turned to her sister with raised brows. "I told you, I don't exaggerate half as much as you think I do."

"I imagine no one's been in here since Blair died." Kane's grin spread too wide for his statement. "This has to be it!"

Frederick's sentiments exactly, especially after Grace told him the hint Mr. Locke had given her.

Kane took the dusty oil lantern on the desk in the center of the room and, tugging a match case from his pocket, brought additional light into the room.

They all moved amongst the space, Kane and Lillias scouring the drawers and shelves, and Frederick, Grace, and Zahra pretending to look at the books, but attempting to locate more hidden items in the carvings.

It was Grace's soft gasp that drew Frederick's attention. She was standing before the largest carving: a delicate fairy whose features bore an uncanny resemblance to her.

"That can't be you, can it?" he asked, stepping closer.

She smiled, tracing the fairy's face. "It looks more like my mother." Then her expression shifted, her eyes snapping to his. "Frederick."

Her tone was all he needed. Moving to block Kane's line of

sight, he pretended to admire the carving while Grace's hand moved with deliberate precision. She ran her fingers over the sculpture until, with a faint click, the fairy's head shifted, revealing a long cylindrical compartment hidden within.

It wasn't empty.

Inside was a folded piece of parchment. Frederick couldn't fully make it out from its position, but there was a very good chance from its style of paper and hidden position that they'd found the will.

Of course! From all Grace had said about Laird Blair's love for his cousin, Grace's mother, and with the knowledge Grace and Lillias were next to inherit, why wouldn't the man hide it here for them to find?

"Finally," he murmured under his breath. This was what they needed. Proof. Something solid to tie this infernal mystery together. Now if they could just locate Kane's sister, the entire facade could unravel.

Grace glanced over her shoulder, her movements smooth and practiced as she slipped the parchment up the right sleeve of her day suit.

"You did that as if you've done it before," Frederick whispered, leaning closer.

Her lips parted in mock offense before curving into a sly smile. "It's where magicians hide things. Grandfather taught me."

"Of course he did." He shook his head, fighting a smirk. "Your enigmatic grandfather—full of useful tricks—"

A sharp intake of breath interrupted him.

He and Grace turned to find Lillias holding what appeared to be a photograph. Her face pale.

"What is it?" Grace asked.

"I don't understand." Lillias blinked down at the photo and then back to Grace's face, before turning to Kane. "This—this is Mrs. James," she stammered. "Why is my housekeeper in a photograph with you, Malcolm?"

Frederick's attention snapped to Kane. The man had stepped back toward the narrow passage, one hand in his pocket. The other held a revolver.

"I'm sorry, my dear," Kane said, his tone almost regretful. "I really didn't want to have to kill you, after all, I have a great distaste for leaving children without parents." He sighed, shaking his head as if deeply upset. "But you've left me no choice."

Chapter 24

Grace took a step back, instinctively placing herself in front of Zahra. The little girl, ever resourceful, had somehow managed to vanish beneath the nearby table, a feat Grace couldn't help but admire. Being small did have its advantages—though Grace doubted she'd fit under there without upending the entire thing in the process.

"What are you talking about?" Lillias stammered, her eyes darting between Kane's face and the revolver in his hand. Her voice quavered, barely above a whisper. "Kill me?"

Malcolm Kane shrugged with the kind of casual indifference better suited to discussing the weather than plotting murder. "I had hoped to make this transfer of Mosslea simple. Legal, even. Romance the bereaved widow, gain the castle, live happily ever after—or at least comfortably." He gestured toward the photograph in Lillias' trembling hand. "My sister had made it look so easy with the laird. Everything was going along smoothly until you lot showed up."

Frederick shifted subtly, angling himself between Kane and the others. His hand moved toward the hidden revolver in his own jacket, and Grace hoped very much her dashing hero knew what he was doing.

"I wouldn't have involved you at all, Lillias dear, if things had gone as Moira and I wanted from the beginning." He leaned back against the wall, evidently content to listen to his own voice. "We had no idea about you and your sister's claim to the estate until Moira had already ended things with Alastair." He shrugged. "Or rather ended Alastair." Malcolm tsked in mock consolation. "We wouldn't have known at all, if my very clever sister hadn't seen Mr. Barclay visit Mosslea one day to discuss things with Mr. Locke, and he mentioned some American sisters who were to inherit. That propelled the plan into motion."

"That's where I came in." As if on cue, the hidden door creaked open farther, revealing Mrs. James—or rather, Lady Moira Blair—in an impeccably tailored blue day dress. Gone was the understated housekeeper. In her place stood a woman whose posture screamed self-assured villainy.

Oh, she'd played her part as a silly housekeeper so well. So convincingly. It boggled the mind.

And though Lady Blair stood a few inches shorter and didn't wear the dress quite as well, her arrogance and steely look reminded Grace of Celia Blackmore Percy, the woman who had killed Frederick's father and brother to gain her riches.

But the cold look in her eyes was the same.

Devious women were clearly meant for the stage.

"Mrs. James?" Lillias' palm went to her throat. "You weren't a housekeeper at all?"

"Clever one, aren't you?" Lady Blair's lips curved into a serpentine smile. "No wonder my brother liked you so much. Easy to manipulate." Her gaze swept the room, lingering on Grace for a beat longer than necessary. "How else did you think everything fell into place, Lillias." She cooed Lillias' name with such mockery, the sound trilled a chill up Grace's arms.

Oooh, Lady Blair was very good at being bad.

Despite her real-life observations, fiction clearly warned about underestimating a smart woman with a thirst for power. Celia had killed at least three people, if not four, by the time she was caught. How many had Lady Blair killed in her tenure as a villainess? Not to mention the ones she'd conked on the head.

"Malcolm wanted to find a cleaner way to take the inheritance instead of just killing one of you." Her smile twitched as she looked over at her brother. "He's always had such a weak stomach for bloodshed. Promised him I'd try to keep things civil." Her smile sharpened. "But civility only gets you so far, doesn't it?"

"You don't need to do this." Frederick stepped nearer Grace, his voice calm. "If it's the inheritance you want, I feel certain these ladies would give it up to save their lives."

Grace shot her husband a look. Would she? And then realized the ridiculousness of the very question. First off, she loved her family much more than any castle. And secondly, how could she claim an inheritance if she was dead, anyway?

"Well, we can't just let everyone walk away and tell tales." Lady Blair scanned the room, her smile still in perfect placement. "Blackmail may be my brother's preference and much tidier, but sometimes, one must adapt to the situation with a more decisive hand."

She extended her hand toward Mr. Kane.

Grace's breath caught as he handed the revolver over with an apologetic shrug, as though conceding to a minor inconvenience. But before Lady Blair could raise the weapon, something small and glittering arced through the air, catching the light as it flew.

The sound that followed—a sharp *thunk*—was decidedly unladylike.

Lady Blair yelped, clutching her head as she stumbled back against the wall. The revolver slipped from her grasp, clattering to the floor.

Grace turned in the direction the projectile had come, to see Zahra's arm raised as if she had thrown something. Had Zahra just hit Lady Blair with a ruby?

Frederick didn't waste a second. He lunged for Mr. Kane, tackling him, their struggle carrying them toward the open doorway of the hidden room. Kane managed to land a solid punch to Frederick's jaw, sending him back a step, but Frederick seized the man's jacket and drove him against the wall.

A sharp metallic scrape echoed and the doorway slid closed, separating Frederick and Mr. Kane in the library from the ladies in the secret room.

For a moment, the four women stood frozen, the shock of the sudden separation rendering them speechless. The faint sounds of the struggle outside filtered through the walls—grunts, the scrape of furniture, a crash, and the dull thud of bodies colliding. In their struggle against the mantel, someone must have hit the other side of the secret door's lever, causing the men to be separated from them.

"What is happening?" Lillias' voice broke the silence, rising in pitch with every word. "I can't die, Grace. I can't!"

"Be quiet, Lillias." Grace's gaze darted to Lady Blair, who was regaining her footing. "There's a door at the bottom of the stairs. Zahra, take Lillias and move toward it."

"What? Without you?" Lillias' voice quavered.

Lady Blair managed to regain a standing position, the red welt where Zahra hit her bright on her pale forehead.

A large ruby ring lay nearby, presumably the projectile Zahra had thrown with exceptional aim. Perhaps Frederick could enroll Zahra in cricket. Or baseball. Did girls even have teams for those sports?

Lady Blair wiped a palm over her forehead, her attention landing on Grace. Something in the look seemed to communicate that Lady Blair saw Grace as a threat or at least a challenge.

Her attention flicked to the revolver lying on the floor, then back to Grace.

What to do? Grace slid a hand into the left sleeve of her day dress, her fingers touching the handle of her favorite throwing knife. The knife? Or race for the revolver?

"Lillias, move toward the door," Grace repeated, her sister still frozen in place.

At that moment, Lady Blair lurched forward, Grace with her. But instead of going for the gun, the woman grabbed the lantern from the desk in the center of the room.

The lantern? Before Grace could fully comprehend her next move, Lady Blair sent her an eerie smile and threw the lantern to the floor. Flames erupted, ravenous and bright, leaping to devour the scattered papers lying about.

"Grace!" Lillias shrieked, shrinking back against the wall as smoke began to curl upward.

Zahra darted to Grace's side, and Grace grabbed her hand, yanking her away from the rising flames now licking at the rug. Through the haze, Grace spotted Lady Blair slipping through a side door, her exit punctuated by the ominous click of a lock.

"Grace," Lillias wailed, her voice trembling. "How will we escape? We're trapped!"

Grace inhaled sharply, sliding her knife back into its sheath. The gesture did not go unnoticed.

"Were you going to *throw* a knife at her?" Lillias squeaked, her face a ghastly shade of white.

The last thing Grace needed was her sister swooning into the fire. "Zahra, check the door Lady Blair used. Quickly!" She held the little girl's gaze. "And mind the flame. It's only going to grow the more books and old furniture it reaches."

Not to mention the faded curtains or the wall of dusty tapestries on the opposite side of the room from the windows, but Grace didn't want to contemplate that.

Zahra nodded and darted around the smoke away from the flame.

Grace turned to Lillias, grabbing her by the shoulders. "Lillias, listen to me. I need you to stay alert. We've not much time before this room is in flames and we need to sort a way out."

A whimper rose from her sister's throat.

"It's locked, Sayyida." Zahra announced, coming back to her side as the flames took hold of the nearest bookcase to the door Lady Blair had just exited.

Lillias' eyes began to roll back but Grace gave her cheeks a little smack, bringing Lillias' eyes wide open. "I'm sorry, Lillias, but you cannot faint. For Thomas' sake, you have to keep your head. Do you understand?"

Lillias blinked, tears welling in her eyes, but nodded. Her chin quivered, but at least, she didn't faint.

Grace turned to survey the room. One door was locked, but. . . Her gaze landed on the secret door in the wall. She rushed over, pushing against the panel with all her strength. Nothing. Not even a budge.

"Here!" Zahra pointed out the lever, half-hidden in the shadows. Grace yanked it down with all her might, but the mechanism refused to budge. The men must have damaged it in their fight.

Flames licked up one wall, consuming the bookshelf now and getting ready to light the next one. Smoke rose, dark and thick, from the rug nearby. They didn't have long.

"We're going to die," Lillias screamed, backing away from the flames toward the wall of windows.

"No, we are *not,*" Grace snapped, her attention darting to the windows above her sister's head. The space was narrow, but just wide enough for a body.

Grabbing a nearby chair, she spun around and, with all her

might, flung the chair toward the window. The glass shattered with a satisfying crash, the opening immediately pulling some of the smoke out of the room.

"We're going to have to try and escape out the window." Grace slid a second chair underneath the window she'd just broken and climbed up, peering out of the fractured frame. To the left was a sheer drop, but to the right, about twelve to fifteen feet below them, was a balcony. All they had to do was make it there.

The flames lit one corner of the tapestry, the old cloth peeling back like paper, demonstrating the tapestries were not an option. And then she caught sight of the one set of curtains, floor-to-ceiling, probably ten feet from top to bottom.

Lillias cried out, pressing herself against the wall near Grace.

She needed something to do or her sister was going to continue to be an unhelpful distraction. "Lillias, help me get these curtains down."

Lillias blinked over to Grace and then looked up at the curtains, her brow crinkling with confusion, but that was much better than terror.

"Why? What are you going to do?"

Grace gestured toward the window. "We're going to jump out the window."

Kane's knee jabbed into Frederick's ribs, loosening his hold on the man as they tumbled into the library. The sound of the secret door sealing shut behind them echoed with finality in Frederick's chest.

"No," he muttered, already moving toward the door, his heart hammering with the fear of Grace and Zahra being trapped on the other side, facing whatever danger Kane had in store. Before he could make it, Kane shoved him hard, sending him crashing to the floor. His shoulder struck stone, hurling a burst of pain through his body, but he gritted his teeth, refusing to let it slow him down.

With a twist, Frederick freed an arm and slammed his fist into Kane's face. The satisfying crunch on impact sent Kane stumbling back, giving Frederick just enough space to scramble to his feet, his breath coming in ragged gasps.

"Grace!" he called, his voice hoarse as his fingers scraped around the edges of the stone, searching for any latch or lever that might release the door.

Lady Moira Blair presented every bit the malevolent mastermind of this entire scheme, her brother a willing pawn. He knew her kind. Had fancied himself in love with her kind once, before he knew any better.

Kane was back in an instant, crashing into Frederick's side and sending him careening into a nearby bookshelf. The structure groaned under their combined weight, threatening to topple and crush them both. Frederick jabbed his elbow into Kane's stomach, knocking the wind out of him and sending the man stumbling back just as a crash of glass shattered from behind the sealed door.

Glass? A chill raced up Frederick's spine. He had to get to her—had to get to them.

He darted for the wall, his hands skimming the stone, searching for a way to reopen the door. "Grace," he grunted, slamming his fist against the unyielding stone in frustration.

The scrape of metal on metal cut through the air behind him. Frederick whipped around to find Kane grinning, holding one of the swords from the suit of armor. The blade gleamed, wickedly glinting in the afternoon light.

Fire ignited in Frederick's chest. He didn't have time for this. He had to get to Grace and Zahra.

Frederick twisted, narrowly avoiding the slash that would've split his chest open. His pulse thundered in his ears as he dodged again, jumping to the right. Another suit of armor loomed just ahead.

Perfect.

He dashed for it as Kane closed in, the glinting blade swinging wildly.

Frederick yanked free the sword just in time to meet Kane's blade with his own. The force reverberated through his arm.

"I can't let you and your little entourage live, Astley," Kane growled, pushing all his weight into the strike, the edge of his blade grinding against Frederick's. "Even without the inheritance, you know too much."

Frederick gritted his teeth and shoved Kane back, planting his feet to block another brutal strike. The clang of their swords echoed like a warning. He parried another savage chop, deflecting the next lunge and sending Kane stumbling. The man quickly righted himself, his breaths coming hard.

They circled each other in a deadly dance, dodging the fallen books and broken furniture. Smoke was beginning to fill the air. Something was on fire?

"You're wasting your time," Kane growled, swinging with renewed force. "The women are as good as lost. And I'll soon send you to join them."

"You underestimate them." *God, help them.* Frederick tightened his grip on his sword. *"And me."*

Before Kane could retort, a shrill scream echoed from the other side of the wall. Frederick's blood ran cold, his stomach dropping to his knees. What was happening to them?

His head whipped toward the sound, and Kane took full advantage of the distraction, slamming his blade down with terrifying force. Frederick twisted just in time to block the strike, but the impact jolted up his arm. Kane's next move caught Frederick off guard, slicing across his sleeve and grazing his skin. He winced but tightened his grip on the hilt, meeting Kane's furious gaze.

This had to end. His family needed him.

Summoning every ounce of strength, Frederick brought his sword down in a hard chop, knocking Kane off-balance. With that precious moment of advantage, Frederick lunged, driving the blade into Kane's side.

Kane staggered, a strangled cry escaping his lips. But he wasn't done yet—he lashed out wildly, his desperate strikes more about fury than skill.

Then, just as Frederick prepared for another strike, a door creaked open behind him. He braced himself to turn when Kane's expression stilled him.

"Malcolm Kane?"

Ah, Frederick knew that voice and understood Kane's look of shock perfectly.

Kane's sword lowered slightly, his eyes wide in disbelief. "You–you're supposed to be dead," he stammered, the words coming out as little more than a breathless whisper.

Frederick kept his stance, waiting for Kane's next move, as Tony stepped to Frederick's side. "I have too much to live for."

The distraction was exactly what Frederick needed. With a sharp twist of his wrist, he shifted his grip on the sword and swung the pommel up in a swift, decisive arc. The blow landed squarely on Kane's temple, the sound of impact sharp and final.

Kane crumpled to the floor, the sword slipping from his grasp with a dull, metallic thud.

Frederick didn't even glance at the unconscious man. His focus was already on Tony. "The women are in trouble," he said, running toward the door. "We have to get to them."

Chapter 25

Grace tugged down the velvet curtains with all her might, her heels scraping against the floor for leverage. The heavy fabric gave way with a groan, the rod surrendering in a dramatic crash that sent dust and a spattering of soot into her face.

Lillias erupted into a coughing fit behind her, waving one hand dramatically while the other clutched her chest. Her usually pristine complexion was now smeared with an ashy hue. A laugh tickled Grace's throat, but she swallowed through it. She suspected she looked no better, and with her red hair flying in all direction, she might very well be mistaken for one of the weepers of Scottish legend. The caoineag.

Ignoring her sister's theatrics, Grace snapped the curtain fabric free and draped one length carefully through the jagged window to shield against the remaining shards. She knelt in front of Zahra, brushing a stray curl from the girl's face and clasping her small shoulders.

Grace drew a steadying breath, the acrid smoke stinging her throat. If Zahra could scale a wall in Cairo, she could manage this. *Oh Lord, please let her manage this.* "The balcony's to the right, not directly below us," she said, forcing a calmness into her voice she did not feel. "I'm going to swing you toward it, and you'll have to jump. Can you do that?"

Zahra fixed her with a solemn nod, her light eyes steady and unflinching.

"You can't just drop her out a window." Lillias followed behind Grace as she led Zahra up to the only exit from the room. "She's a child."

"She's a very smart child." And this was their only option. Grace looked down at Zahra. "And more than capable." Grace lifted Zahra onto the sill, placing the girl at the same eye-level as herself. "Don't let go until you are sure, all right?"

Zahra gave another one of her nods and without warning, wrapped her arms around Grace's neck. The sweetest sense of overwhelming joy pooled through Grace as she enclosed the little girl in her arms for a quick embrace. More than heat from the fire stung her eyes. This was part of being a mother.

Swallowing hard, Grace pulled back and cupped Zahra's cheeks. "Ready?"

Zahra turned toward the window in response.

Grace secured one end of the curtain rope to the iron bracket used to hold back the curtains, just to give her some additional leverage. The other end dangled down toward the balcony below. Zahra tested the makeshift rope with a firm tug, her small hands displaying a confidence that spoke of her past life on the streets.

Yes, her little one had done this before.

"Careful," Grace whispered, catching Zahra's eyes once more before the girl disappeared over the edge.

She moved with practiced ease, swift and fluid, quickly reaching the end of the cloth and. . .a twenty foot drop to the ground below. Now came the tricky part. Giving her enough of a swing to get her to the balcony on the right. Grace gripped the curtain, swinging it back and forth to build momentum. Zahra moved in tandem, her small frame swaying like a pendulum. On the third swing,

Zahra released her grip and landed on the balcony with the grace of a cat. She turned, flashing Grace a broad, triumphant smile.

"Remarkable," Grace muttered, her lips twitching despite herself.

There was one.

Grace turned to her sister. The air had grown thicker with smoke, the tapestry on the opposite wall a bright square of fire. "Now you, Lillias."

Lillias shook her head, her face paling all over again. "I can't."

"You *must*." Grace's tone left no room for argument. "There's no other way."

"But what if I fall?"

Grace drew in a deep breath. "You *may* die if you fall." Grace steadied her attention on her sister. "You *will* die if you stay."

Lillias audibly swallowed, blanched, and steeling herself, approached the window. With much less finesse, Lillias slipped her legs over the edge, wrangling with her skirts to push through the space. Her entire body shook, but she took hold of the rope and dipped over the lip of the window, climbing down the same trek Zahra had just taken. Her descent was slower, her movements jarring, but with skirt billowing around her, she managed.

As she neared the bottom, Grace began swinging the curtain again, attempting to get Lillias as close to the balcony as possible. Her arms burned from the effort, and her throat felt raw from smoke, but she didn't stop. Not until she heard the sound that froze her from head to foot.

A sharp *rip*.

Her breath caught. "No! No, no, no." She leaned out the window, panic rising like the flames below. "Jump, Lillias! The curtain won't hold!"

"I can't—"

The fabric gave way with a gut-twisting *rip*. Lillias shrieked as she tumbled, her body smacking against the stone railing of the balcony with a sickening thud.

Grace's heart plummeted.

But then—praise heaven—Lillias hooked her arm over the edge of the railing like Robinson Crusoe's hold on the chest as he drifted at sea. Good. Halfway there.

Zahra bolted to the edge, clutching the back of Lillias' gown in an attempt to pull the woman the rest of the way over the railing onto the balcony. Lillias' feet flailed in the air, skirt flying.

Grace was certain her sister would never have imagined looking so undignified.

Out of nowhere, a figure rushed onto the balcony. Grace's breath hitched. *Mr. Kane? What on earth—*

Her tension shattered as Lillias' voice, shrill but unmistakable, echoed upward. "Tony?"

Oh. Grace sagged against the window frame, her relief spilling out in a shaky laugh.

Tony wrapped his arms around Lillias, hauling her to the safety of the balcony. But as he crushed Lillias to his chest, murmuring something she couldn't make out, the two of them melted into an embrace long overdue.

Grace averted her gaze as their reunion transitioned into a lip-on-lip reconciliation.

But she had little time to dwell on the reunion as another figure appeared below.

Frederick.

Her favorite face in the world.

He wrapped an arm around Zahra, his gaze lifting to meet Grace's. He moved to the edge of the balcony, his gaze locked onto hers, and Grace felt as if the entire inferno paused, holding its breath. The weight of his worry, the raw desperation on his face—it was as though he were willing her to survive through sheer force of will.

Well, if her last sight was Frederick's face and her next would be Jesus, it wasn't the worst way to go.

But the pained expression on her dear husband's face, the worry lining Zahra's brow, and the smoke stinging her throat sent her into motion.

Her gaze darted around the room, searching for a solution. The tattered curtain hung useless below, fluttering in the fiery draft. But—her eyes landed on the heavy ropes used to tie back the drapes.

Ropes. Of course! She almost laughed. They hadn't failed her yet.

She rushed to untangle them from the remaining curtain, dousing a spark from the fabric as she did. The ropes were thick, meant to hold the weight of the drapes, and she tied them together with knots she prayed would hold. Securing one end to the iron bracket, she tossed the rope out the window, tested the strength with a quick tug, and climbed onto the sill.

"Grace!" Frederick's call grew over the sound of the fire.

She sent him a look, hoping it conveyed a little of how much she loved him, before she drew in a deep breath, gripped the rope with both hands, and slipped over the edge. Her fingers burned against the coarse threads in the rope, but little by little she slid closer to her goal and farther away from the fire.

The balcony was so close, but the angle was wrong. She needed to swing closer.

Twisting her body, she pressed one foot against the castle wall and shoved off. The rope arced, and she hurtled toward Frederick. He reached for her, but his fingers fell short.

She swung back, pushed off again.

This time, his hand grazed the rope.

A jolt sent her heart slamming against her ribs. The rope slipped a few inches. Either the knots were unraveling, or the fire was claiming her anchor.

With one last propulsion off the wall, she leaned forward toward her husband and he caught her by her forearms. He pulled her over the railing and into his arms, holding her as though he'd never let go. His face pressed into her hair, and she felt the trembling in his chest, the quick rise and fall of his breaths. She breathed in this safety, his home.

A second later, another pair of arms wrapped around her middle.

Grace looked down to find Zahra hugging them both, her face pressed against Frederick's side.

Frederick's smile bloomed as he looked into Grace's face, and with a shift of movement, he placed a palm against Zahra's head.

They were safe.

Together.

Malcolm Kane was not in the library.

Frederick's chest tightened as he shot a glance from Grace to Tony. "Where's Kane?"

Tony blinked, his mouth opening uselessly for a moment, before spinning on his heel and rushing down the hallway toward the grand staircase. Frederick followed, their boots pounding against the wood until they came to an abrupt halt at the top of the stairs.

At the bottom stood Stephen Blake, looking for all the world like the Cheshire Cat after a banquet. He leaned casually against the newel post, a cigarette dangling between his fingers, his smirk a declaration of triumph.

And there was the tableau to his left.

Lady Blair, tied up so tightly she resembled a poorly wrapped Christmas roast, glared daggers at anyone foolish enough to meet her eye. Beside her, sprawled on the floor, lay Malcolm Kane, unconscious and similarly trussed up. Standing guard over him was none other than Mr. Locke, a shovel in one hand and his boot planted squarely on Kane's back as though the man were freshly tilled soil.

Frederick barked out a laugh, equal parts relief and disbelief. "What a vision," he muttered under his breath as Grace and Zahra caught up with him.

"Now you show up?" he called down to Blake, his voice carrying across the vast room.

"Better late than never, old boy." Blake took one last drag of his cigarette before extinguishing it in a tray with the nonchalance of a man who'd just completed his afternoon tea. His grin softened into something more serious as Frederick descended the stairs with Grace firmly in tow. "Mr. Kane, it seems, did a bit of tampering with my car." He gestured with his chin toward the gardener. "And ironically enough, locked Mr. Locke in his own cellar, so we were a bit late to the party."

Ah, the party. Frederick glanced sideways at Grace, his grip on her hand tightening as if anchoring himself to her. Her hair was a wild tangle of red, her cheeks streaked with soot, and her dress bore unmistakable evidence of their earlier peril. Yet somehow, she looked radiant—untamed and indomitable. His Grace.

"No matter," Frederick said, waving a hand toward the stairs. "The dancing wouldn't have suited you, Blake. Far too refined. And I know you prefer your smoke confined to cigarettes and salmon."

Blake's grin tipped even wider, his gaze flipping from Frederick to Grace. His gaze rose to the stair landing, where Tony and Lillias stood, arm-in-arm. "And what about those two?"

"I do believe they've turned a new leaf," Frederick said.

Blake's lips curled into a frown his eyes didn't match. "Perhaps I'll remain here with the scoundrels, then, Freddie. All this near-death sentimentality is a bit too much."

"Mosslea needs the Blairs among its walls," Mr. Locke declared, a leathery grin creasing his face as he ground his boot into Kane's back. The bound man let out a muffled grunt of protest. "It's not right without a Blair in these walls."

"But the fire?" Lillias asked as she and Tony descended, her arm still looped protectively through his.

"Clever design, that," Blake interjected with his signature insouciance, throwing Locke a knowing wink. "The damage is contained. The rest of Mosslea is as solid as ever."

"You mean, we can still live here?" Lillias asked, looking from Blake to Locke and back again.

"Mosslea's stood through centuries, Mrs. Dixon," Locke declared, puffing out his chest.

"And have you seen the size of this place?" Blake gestured expansively. "If one room burns, you've still got at least two dozen more to choose from. Truly, the height of luxury."

Lillias turned to Tony, her smile luminous despite the soot-streaked tear trailing down her cheek. "I think this is a very good place to start over, don't you?"

Even Tony, the eternal curmudgeon, managed a smile that softened his weathered features. "As long as I have you and Thomas with me, I'll start over wherever you want, Lillias." He gave her hand a firm squeeze, his voice low but steady. "The right way this time?"

She nodded, her expression resolute. "The right way."

Hopefully that resolution would prove true. Staring at one's own heart and seeing the brokenness within has a tendency to turn a willing man or woman in the right direction. Frederick grinned. And the right kind of love too.

"Well, I'm clearly the odd man out in this parade of sentiment," Blake drawled, raising a brow as he surveyed the group. His gaze flicked from Lillias and Tony to Frederick and Grace. "All this romance is downright suffocating. Your bride alone, Freddie, has enough adoration pouring from her eyes to wilt a man where he stands." Blake waved toward Lady Blair, who sent him an impressive glare. "And here I am, always catching the wrong ladies."

Grace laughed, leaning her head over on Frederick's shoulder. He squeezed her in a little closer. "Oh, don't worry, dear Mr. Blake. The right woman will certainly come your way when you least expect her. Just think of how Frederick and I met."

Blake folded his arms across his chest and gave a dramatic sigh. "I try not to, Lady Astley. My heart can't take the strain." He placed a hand over his chest, feigning anguish. "One can only endure so much."

Frederick smirked, resisting the urge to point out that Blake's heart was likely the most resilient part of him, considering the number of times it had apparently been shattered by society's finest. Grace gave a knowing chuckle, and Frederick thought, not for the first time, that Blake had a particular knack for diffusing tension with his sharp wit. The right woman would appreciate that in him.

Along with so many other fine traits.

The sound of heavy boots on stone drew everyone's attention to the open front doors as a pair of police officers marched in, their uniforms crisp against the backdrop of Mosslea's lingering smoke. They moved with purpose toward the "villains," as Grace liked to call them, prepared to take Lady Blair and Kane into custody.

Blake exhaled, an exaggerated puff of relief. "Ah, saved from any further romance talk by some of my favorite types of people."

Frederick caught the subtle flicker of something in Blake's expression as he turned to address the police. It was so brief it could have been missed by anyone else, but Frederick knew his cousin too well. Beneath the easy bravado, there was a flicker of longing, a rare crack in the armor. It struck Frederick then, a quiet hope blooming in the back of his mind. Perhaps the right lady for Blake wasn't so far off, after all.

Mr. Barclay arrived only a few days later, bruised, occasionally forgetful, but still sharp enough to finalize the legal transfer of Mosslea and Angloss into Lillias and Grace's capable hands.

Grace settled onto the settee in their modest room at Rowan's Rest, her gaze drifting to the castle silhouetted beyond the window. Lights winked from the right wing of Mosslea, a declaration of Tony and Lillias' first evening as its new stewards. Watching them over the past few days, as Mr. Barclay painstakingly guided both couples through the intricacies of inheritance, was unexpectedly heartening—like reading a last chapter of a beautiful story when one thought all was lost.

Perhaps the two of them were truly starting over.

With their priorities in the proper places.

And Miss Cox? Well, she agreed to an official position as a nanny to little Thomas, delighted to care for a baby rather than sort out fashions, hair styles, and the latest shoe styles.

Grace could relate to the preference with her whole heart.

Now, if only Father could be lured to this side of the Atlantic. . . Her thoughts trailed wistfully. To have everyone she loved most within a drive or train ride seemed a dream worth chasing.

Frederick's quiet presence pulled her from her musings. He closed the door to Zahra's adjoining room with the softest click, having just read to the little girl. His footfalls were unhurried as he crossed the room to join her, the firelight gilding the edges of his frame in hues of amber and gold. He settled beside her, the couch dipping under his weight, and without a word, she leaned her head onto his shoulder.

She would never tire of his strength. His nearness.

And each adventure only deepened her appreciation of finding safety and comfort in those magnificent arms of his.

He took her hand, their fingers tangling with an intimacy born of their love and gratitude. She sighed with her smile.

"Are you certain you're ready to return to Havensbrooke by the end of the week?" His voice was low, a warmth brushing over her hair.

She squeezed his fingers and nodded against his shoulder. "I think we've been gone long enough, don't you?"

He pressed a kiss to her head, and she could envision his smile. His heart longed for his grand estate and the walls he'd promised to secure. "I don't want you to feel rushed, darling. Or think that I value your claim to Mosslea any less than mine to Havensbrooke."

She tilted her face up to him, one brow raised in a teasing tip. "I won't deny I'll probably find an excuse to visit Mosslea whenever I can."

Frederick met her silent request and kissed her.

She sat up, turning toward him, her palm resting against his chest, her gaze roaming over his face. "But Mosslea is not home." She pressed another kiss to his smile. "And my dear Lord Astley, I do believe it's time for us to go home."

Acknowledgements

There is no way I can express my gratitude for all the readers who have fallen in love with Lord and Lady Astley through this series. *The Mistletoe Countess* had originally been a stand-alone, then two books. . .and now four! Thank you to all you readers who have loved, celebrated, and encouraged this series. It has been a delight to write, and I hope we can get at least one more story out of our amateur sleuthing couple.

It's an amazing feat that this story came to be at all. Hurricane Helene hit my part of the world and pushed every deadline back and disrupted so much. I'm so grateful for the team at Barbour, particularly Becky Germany and Becky Fish, for their hard work to bring this story to you.

I'll forever sing the praises of my dear friend, Jennifer Boice, and her tireless efforts to help me brainstorm this story into existence. I love how invested she gets in the stories of my imaginary friends, and I'm so grateful she's willing to be that listening ear that every writer needs.

As *always*, thanks to the early readers and encouragers who try to keep me sane and on track while I write these stories. In particular, Beth Erin, Joy Tiffany, Anne Herron, and Tiffany Wade.

I'm ever thankful for my agent, Rachel McMillan, who is a

tireless supporter of me and my imaginary friends and allows me to regularly bother her with questions, comments, or celebrations.

I'm so thankful for my family. Not only do they love me, but being the creatives they are, they celebrate this piece of my life with such sweetness.

And thank you to my heavenly Father who allows me to spread joy and hope through writing these stories. It truly is an honor and a joy to me to get to do it.

Pepper Basham is an award-winning author who writes romance peppered with grace and humor. She is a native of the Blue Ridge Mountains where her family have lived for generations. She's the mom of five kids, speech-pathologist to about fifty more, lover of chocolate, jazz, and Jesus, and proud AlleyCat over at the award-winning Writer's Alley blog. Her debut historical romance novel, The Thorn Bearer, released in April 2015, and the second in February 2016. Her first contemporary romance debuted in April 2016.

You can connect with Pepper on her website
at www.pepperdbasham.com,
Facebook at https://www.facebook.com/pepperdbasham,
or Twitter at https://twitter.com/pepperbasham

FREDDIE AND GRACE MYSTERIES

The Mistletoe Countess

He was never supposed to become an earl. She was never supposed to marry him. But when the nevers become reality Christmas of 1913, Frederick and Gracelynn team up in love, life, and a little bit of amateur sleuthing to solve a Christmas murder mystery.

Paperback / 978-1-64352-986-8

The Cairo Curse

Get swept away to Egypt as a long overdue honeymoon becomes a murder mystery adventure. Newlyweds Frederick and Grace Percy join their strengths to save a possibly wrongly accused widow and not join the victims of *The Cairo Curse* in this delightful sequel to *The Mistletoe Countess.*

Paperback / 978-1-63609-472-4

The Juliet Code

Join newlyweds Freddie and Grace on their long-awaited honeymoon in 1914 in Venice where once again they are caught up in adventure and mystery with Detective Jack Miracle. Drawn into a world of the rich and unusual, they try to break the code to missing artwork allegedly hidden in Renaissance paintings of Shakespeare's tragic heroine Juliet.

Paperback / 978-1-63609-694-0